# RISE OF GAIA

# RISE OF GAIA

KRISTIN WARD

# Also by Kristin Ward

**Romantasy - Enchanted Tales with Dragon Scales**

Dark is the Wood

Treacherous is the Tower

Pale is the Rose

**Celtic Mythology Dark Fantasy - Daughter of Erabel**

The Girl of Dorcha Wood

Blood of the Lost Kingdom

A Storm of Wrath & Ruin

Legion of Shadows

**Dystopian**

After the Green Withered

Burden of Truth

*Rise of Gaia*

By Kristin Ward

This is a work of fiction. Names, characters, businesses, places, events, locales, and incidents are either the products of the author's imagination or used in a fictitious manner. Any resemblance to actual persons, living or dead, or actual events is purely coincidental.

Independently Published

Editing: David Taylor, thEditors.com

Cover Design: LD, LDCoverDesigns

ISBN: 978-1-7327923-2-6

*To my husband and three sons ~*
*Thank you for believing in me. I couldn't have done this*
*without you.*

# PROLOGUE

*Awakening*

Deep within the bowels of the earth, she stirs, awareness dawning by slow degrees until her being is flooded by it. Rooted within her consciousness like a rotten tooth is knowledge of a world plagued by indifferent beings whose wasteful pursuits have left a wake of corruption. She writhes, curling round and round in the confines of her shape, twisting in agony as a multitude of tortured voices drift through the mantle and into her heart.

In a moment of triumphant resolve, she wrenches herself free of a miasma of anguish and calls to her children, beckoning them. Like fireflies illuminating the darkness with pinpoints of light, they respond, reaching toward their mother with fierce purpose. She infuses their thoughts with her own, commanding them to rise, find the others, and begin.

# CHAPTER I

*It all began on my seventeenth birthday*

The sun shines through my window, piercing the crack in the curtains and managing to find my left eye. It burns through my eyelid until I wake up. I roll over and look at the clock. It's just after seven. I could totally sleep for another ten minutes, but downstairs I hear the sound of my parents talking, and it dawns on me. Today is December third. It's also my seventeenth birthday. A grin splits my face as the scent of cinnamon French toast snakes beneath my door, directly to my nose. My stomach rumbles in anticipation.

I stretch my legs, relishing the little pops in my knees and ankles, and sit up. Leaning toward the window, I pull back the curtain and gaze outside, thinking about the upcoming weekend and a hike along the coast that I planned with my best friend, Beth. It's a ritual, actually. Each year I choose a new place to hike as a celebration of my birthday. Last year we trekked into the Cascades and camped at the base of Mount Hood. This year, the sea is calling to me, and I know the only place that I want to be on Saturday is overlooking the Pacific, hoping to catch a glimpse of a seal or maybe even an Orca.

I burrow back under the covers, having decided to take advantage of every spare minute and turn my eyes to the ceiling. My room used to have one of those cottage cheese deals, complete with odd, little hunks of plaster poking out all over, surrounded by pale pink wallpaper with daisies on it. It was so seventies, my parents never having redecorated since they bought the house years before I was born. Two summers ago, my dad and I tackled the bedroom makeover, a long-overdue project I had been whining about since I turned twelve. We spent days scraping and painting, getting dust on every surface, including ourselves. Now the ceiling is riddled with sweeps of paint in terrific patterns, and the pale, blue walls bear no resemblance to the juvenile mess they were before. It was definitely an amateur job that we did but absolutely suits me. As I look at the many imperfections, I imagine I see mythical animals, trees, and fairies, so much like looking at the clouds and finding dragons or turtles.

It's a good way to pass the time as I contemplate dragging my butt out of bed.

I listen to the wind blowing outside, stirring up the branches of trees. A small tap against a pane of glass draws my attention, as a leaf is tossed against my window, a lone straggler hanging on until the end. This would be perfect weather to go on a hike in the woods, no rain, and relatively dry ground - for Oregon anyway.

Hiking is not what one would call a 'popular pastime' for girls my age. I know this. Maybe that's part of what makes me somewhat of an oddity among my peers. I certainly can't talk to most of the girls at school about trailheads I long to tackle or the way the ocean pulls me. Whatever. I have no desire to fit some mold they call 'normal'. I don't take selfies or do much in the way of social media, really. In fact, much to Beth's chagrin, my only social media app, and the one everyone else seems to love, is now nonexistent on my phone, having been deleted after months of nonuse so I could make space for an astronomy app instead.

Now, I'm not some granola-loving freak or anything. I just like to be outside. When I'm in the woods or somewhere equally nature-ish, I just feel better, like I'm whole. I can't fully describe it, though I've tried to explain it to Beth. She usually rolls her eyes and gives me a look that implies I've lost my freakin' mind. She may claim to be a bit of a hippie chick, but all the outdoorsy stuff is not her thing. And yet, she sticks with me despite it and sometimes even lets me drag her along the trails.

Stretching my arms to the ceiling, I yawn and roll out of bed, the minutes of freedom having gone by too quickly. As I stand up, I feel a wave of dizziness wash over me. I stagger forward, falling to my knees on the wood floor with a loud thump. My head feels like it's spinning and my vision shifts, as though I'm looking through the bottom of a glass bottle, all distorted and strange. What the heck? Did I get up too fast? I try to shake it off, but my eyes cloud over, eclipsing the elements of my room with something else. The floor seems to tilt, and I feel my body follow the movement, shifting to the side at an awkward angle.

And then, suddenly, I'm no longer kneeling on the floor of my bedroom. Beneath my fingers, I feel the prickly texture of grass, the blades pressing into my skin like dull needles. Blinking rapidly, my vision clears somewhat, although a strange haze remains along the edges, just there in my peripheral, making it seem as though I'm looking through a tunnel. Before me, I notice that the scenery looks very wrong. The grass I'm feeling isn't a healthy, lush green. It is dead, mottled with yellow, and singed. Hanging over all of it is a strange smell, almost like burning death. I scan this odd dreamscape and see a dark lump just a couple of feet away. Even squinting my eyes, I can't quite define it, though I know it's not a rock or mound of dirt. My mind shies away from other possibilities as I shift my gaze to encompass more of the landscape surrounding me.

Panic flutters inside when I notice more of those smallish hills of...what are they? Tentatively, I crawl forward to get a better look. Tendrils of smoke curl around the bulky form, and I reach over to wave them away. When the air stirs, a voice whispers, not quite a real sound, more like it's from inside my head, *"See."*

The moment the word registers, I do see it. A charred, bloated mass of some once-living thing, so far gone that I can't possibly make out what it once was. I fall backward, digging my heels into the burned grasses, scrambling away from whatever it is. The smoke that hangs in the air becomes thicker, stinging my eyes and tickling my chest until I begin to cough spastically, doubling over with the force of it until my lungs ache. Tears stream down my cheeks, brought on by the smoke and fear that is bubbling inside. What is this place? I swipe at my eyes, trying to fully clear my vision, and look around as terror takes over reason. Everywhere is death. The only things stirring are wisps of smoke in a gentle breeze that mocks the horror of this place.

And then, just as suddenly as it came, it's gone. I'm back on the wood floor of my room, with aching knees that are sure to show bruises before the end of the day. I slide to a sitting position against my bed and take a deep breath, "What the hell was that?" I mumble to myself.

My heart is racing, and my brain feels fuzzy. I can still

hear the echo of that voice in my head and smell a decaying scent, as though it has seeped into my pores. I am not sure how long I sit, but eventually, the world begins to right itself, my heart stops fluttering, and I begin to calm. Like an old lady, I get to my feet, hoping another strange episode won't wash over me again. I stand still and just breathe deeply, taking in the familiar sights and smells of my bedroom.

Was that some lingering dream that made its way to my conscious mind? Is that even a thing? A little battle plays out internally as I wrestle with some way to explain what just happened. It was so real. One moment I was here, normal as can be, and the next I'm in some kind of Stephen King nightmare. It's like my mind fractured, and I went to an alternate reality, only that's something that happens in movies, not real life. When no rational explanations are forthcoming, I rub my hands over my face, trying to wipe away the images trapped inside.

I head to the bathroom and turn on the shower, determined to get on with my day. It's my birthday for crying out loud! I tell myself to pull it together and step under the spray of water, closing my eyes under the flow and letting it pour over me, bringing me back to myself. The stench of decay washes away with the soap, but the lingering sense of things unspoken and unknown remains.

Eventually, the temperature begins to cool along with my racing mind. I shut off the water, watching moisture cascade across my skin in rivulets, as I try to force my thoughts to follow their path down the drain. I step out of the shower and rub vigorously with the towel, debating with myself as I scrub so hard my skin pinkens. Am I going crazy? Is this an early sign of a mental breakdown or something? Maybe I have some sort of brain tumor that has been growing for years and is only now showing signs. Ugh.

"This is stupid, Terran. Get a hold of yourself," I mutter. With effort, I shut away my internal analysis and finish drying off. From my closet, I grab my favorite purple V-neck shirt, hoping the soft texture and beautiful mandala printed on the front will help me center myself. A pair of jeans and a hoodie complete my ensemble, and I head back to the bathroom to brush my hair and put on a bit of eyeliner and mascara. Without these accents, I look totally washed out.

I sit on my bed, reluctant to go downstairs just yet. What if my parents see how off I'm feeling? They'll grill me until I tell them what happened, and then what? I mean, what did happen? I didn't actually go to that horrifying place, did I? I just imagined it or dreamed it or something. It wasn't real. I nod my head, squelching any crazy, mental protests. Rubbing my hands on my jeans, I tell myself it was nothing. The niggling worry fades when I've repeated the mantra enough, and I get up and leave my room, grabbing a sheet of paper on my way out and stuffing it in my back pocket.

By the time I'm halfway down the stairs, the strangeness of the morning has been shoved to the back of my mind, a place where I can smother the thoughts completely. I walk into the kitchen with a growl emanating from my stomach and a small smile stamped on my face. My parents burst out with a cringy, off-key version of the birthday song. I try not to laugh as they raise their voices in a pathetic attempt at melody until the mildly embarrassing serenade becomes downright awkward.

I hold my hands up as they begin to belt out, 'Are you one? Are you two?' "Okay, okay. Thank you for the song, but let's not take it too far."

"Happy birthday!" my mom croons, wrapping her arms around me.

Being adopted, my mom and I look nothing alike, aside from our stature. While my mom's wavy hair is so dark it's almost black, mine is red and straight to such a degree that it won't hold a curl for more than five minutes. Unlike my mom's rich, brown eyes, I've got the stereotypical green ones that seem to be allotted to every redhead. Combine that with my smooth, pale complexion, strangely freckle-free for a redhead, and I look totally Irish. We're the same height now, and as I look into her soft visage, I kind of wish I knew what I might look like when I'm in my fifties.

I glance at my dad, who swoops in to capture me in one of his famous bear hugs. As I crane my head back, I catch a glimpse of his bald spot reflecting the kitchen light between strands of graying hair. His well-padded frame crushes me, and I half squeak, half giggle to let him know my lungs are beginning to collapse.

He pulls away and grins down at me. "I don't know about you, Eleanor, but she's looking older to me." His eyes crinkle in his freshly shaven face.

Mom swats him playfully. "Let her eat, Mike. I made your favorite, sweetie."

"Thanks, Mom." I look at the towering plate of French toast sitting in the middle of the table next to a bowl of fruit. "Um, are we inviting the neighbors over or something? 'Cause that's a lot of food."

My dad sits down, forking a couple of slices onto his plate. "Your mom got a little carried away. I think she's trying to fatten us up."

"Stop it, you two." I watch her turn off the griddle and join us at the kitchen table. "What time will you be home today? I've made reservations at The Hacienda for six."

I love Mexican food. To me, there is nothing better than a cheese enchilada smothered in sauce with a side of beans and rice. Top that with fresh guacamole, and I'm in gastronomical heaven. "Yum, I can't wait!" I respond, talking around a huge forkful of French toast. "I should be home by four. Beth and I plan to go out for a smoothie after school."

"Don't eat with your mouthful, Terran. It's not polite," Mom admonishes.

I can feel my cheeks redden as I mumble an apology into my napkin.

"Do you need some money?" she asks, reaching for her purse.

I hold out my hand. "Have I ever turned down an offer of some cash?"

"Actually, no," she replies, digging out a ten and handing it to me. "Is this enough?"

"Yep. Thanks!" I say, stuffing it into my back pocket, taking out a folded sheet of paper, and handing it to her. She smiles and sits back down, opening it to review the latest watchdog list of companies shifting to sustainable palm oil sources. While I've never asked her to boycott any brands, that would be counterproductive, I try to educate my parents, and they humor me. I see her nod as she looks at the familiar brand names she buys, reaching the top of the scorecard.

"I see a couple of my favorites are making better choices," she remarks.

"Yeah," I say after swallowing a bite of goodness. "It's going in the right direction."

"I'm proud of you, sweetie. You're wise beyond your years. I know when I was your age, I never thought about stuff like this."

"Thanks, Mom."

We sit in silence for a few minutes, the only sound being forks and knives clinking and soft chewing noises.

As I eat, I feel my mom's stare and look over at her. "What?"

Her head is slightly cocked to the side, wrinkles creasing her brow. "I don't know. You just look different, something in the eyes, maybe?" She shakes her head, musing over her comment. "It must be you getting another year older. Where has the time gone?"

My parents' voices fade into the background as they reminisce about my younger days. I don't know how many times I've heard them tell the story about the day I tried to steal twelve packs of bubblegum by stuffing them into my underwear because I had no pockets. I would've gotten away with it, too, if the bulkiness hadn't caused me to waddle. I shake my head, recalling how I worried I was about the threat of going to jail when my mom hauled me back into the store to return the gum.

My dad launches into another embarrassing memory, and I let their conversation drift into white noise. Inside, I feel a strange sense of unease as I think about what my mom said and what happened this morning. Could I be terminally ill or having a psychological breakdown? Can you look at someone and see they're crazy or suffering from an incurable disease? The French toast sits in my stomach like a ball of lead, my appetite completely gone.

I stand up and rinse off my plate, leaning around the counter to put it in the dishwasher. My hands are shaking, and I flex my fingers to rid myself of the tremors. I have just grabbed my backpack and purse when Beth calls.

I pick up my cell phone. "Hey, Beth."

"Happy Birthday, Terran!"

"Thanks! Are you picking me up today?" Did my voice sound a little desperate?

"Duh...of course! I've got a surprise for you that you're gonna flip over! I'm on my way, see you in a couple."

"See ya!" I say, hoping the forced enthusiasm will take over completely. It's my birthday, and I should be happy. Everyone expects me to be happy. They don't need to hear about any mental breakdown stuff. Ugh.

A few minutes later, I give my parents hugs, dodging my dad's attempt to squeeze the breath out of me, and paint my face in a smile, before heading toward the front door. Inside, where they can't see, I feel a prickling sensation crawling up my neck. Something has changed this morning, whether I want to acknowledge it or not. I can feel it, and, clearly, my mom sees it too. I'm not quite the same.

Beth honks the horn, jarring me out of my circle of worry, and I dash out of the house, waving to my parents on my way out, and hop into Beth's Prius.

"Hey, Beth."

"Happy birthday," she squeals, leaning over to hug me.

The contact acts as a balm. It's always been that way when we're together. I let her happiness wash over me, giving me the push I need to block out everything but my excitement. "So, what's this surprise I'm gonna flip over?"

"Ha, like I'm going to tell you. You'll just have to wait. I want to get to school first and make sure I have enough time to give it to you rather than just hand it off. You'll understand when you see it. Plus, my mom will kill me if I'm tardy and she gets another one of those messages from Mrs. Snyder again."

"Aw! Can't I just open it now? Pretty please?" I clap my hands together and give her puppy eyes.

Beth looks over at me, an eyebrow cocked. "Really? When has that ever worked on me?"

I give an exaggerated sigh. "Fine. I'll wait. But it's my birthday, and you're supposed to do whatever I want."

"Nice try."

I frown, an expression that's completely ruined when I can't hold it, and then turn up the radio. I'm a sucker for eighties music. I blame my mom for this. I'm sure I even heard classic eighties tunes in the womb, which probably wired my brain to love that neon-ridden era. The Bangles', Hazy Shade of Winter, pours through the speakers as I sing along. Winter has yet to make its appearance, but I can feel the chill in the air. The song seems appropriate. Beth joins me in the chorus, and we bop our heads and tap the rolling drumbeat for a few blocks to school.

---

Roosevelt High School isn't so bad. I keep a low profile and do pretty well. Of course, there are the typical social hurdles that I can't always avoid, which usually end up with me pretending interest in things that bore me or mumbling something somewhat incoherent. I'm not what you would call a popular person, sort of quiet really, but plenty of people in this sea of teenagery know me as I walk the halls. That's small-town life for you. Honestly, I'm more of a watch and listen kind of girl than a jump into a conversation sort. I've never enjoyed mingling with people I don't know and would rather get lost in the woods than go to a party. And don't get me started on talking in front of the class, that's the worst. I sound like some bumbling idiot and sweat profusely the whole time. Mortifying. So I stick with my small group of friends, and we keep low on the social radar.

I have known Beth forever. Our moms were friends long before we were born. Celeste Ordell and Eleanor Kelly had made plans to have baby girls who would become inseparable, and that's precisely how it turned out. I guess it was fate. We have so many shared memories that we may as well be sisters. Beth's mom is into all sorts of new age stuff, and Beth is just like her. I swear, if I ever want an astral reading or something, I know just who to see!

We park in the student lot and sit in the car singing another ballad until the song ends. We've made good time, having avoided getting stuck behind a bus picking up kids every ten feet, as we've experienced too many times before. Beth turns down the radio and looks at me. "Okay, are you ready for your surprise?"

"No. I think I'd like to sit here and wonder about it some more," I reply, running my fingers along my chin.

Beth rolls her eyes. "Close your eyes and hold out your hands."

"Seriously? What are we, like five or something?"

"Just do it!"

I sigh and dutifully hold out my hands. I can hear Beth rummaging behind my seat, and then feel her place something in my hands. My brows crease. It's light and obviously paper, but definitely not a book. The texture feels rough and thick.

"Can I open my eyes now?" I ask, unable to keep the curiosity out of my voice.

I hear Beth chuckle as she says, "Open sesame."

It looks like a scroll, that's the only thing that I can think of when I see it. The paper, some kind of paper anyway, is rolled up into a tube. I give Beth a questioning glance.

"Go on, unroll it," she urges.

I slowly unroll the paper, and as I do, I can feel a prickly sensation flare up and wrap around my head like tentacles. The paper is stiff, but not old. As it slowly uncurls, I see it's some kind of chart like the ones I've seen at Beth's house so many times. There are strange symbols around a circular form, and under this is a full narrative.

"What is it?" I ask, leaning forward to look at the tiny details in the circle.

"It's your natal chart. My mom and I made it for you.

She's been teaching me all about this stuff. Yours is the first one I've done, well, with her help."

I look at her and smile. "Yeah? Thank you, Beth! So, umm, what does it mean? What are all these symbols?"

She pulls the paper into the center between us, above the gearshift. "All of this has to do with when you were born and planet alignment and such. I know you've been into astronomy lately, so I thought you'd like to know which planet you're ruled by and what it all means."

"Totally! Which planet am I?"

"Uranus." She says this like a twelve-year-old boy.

I glance back at the paper, a look of distaste on my face. "Seriously? My planet is an anus?"

Beth cracks up, laughing so hard it ends in a fit of snorting. "It's not really Uranus. I just had to see your reaction."

I give her a look. "Thanks."

She wipes her eyes and catches her breath. "Oh, that was funny."

"Ha-ha," I say in a snarky voice.

"Okay," Beth says, pulling herself together. "You're actually Neptune in Sagittarius in the ninth house."

"You do realize that is totally confusing, right?"

Beth chuckles. "Yeah, I know. So down here," she points to the narrative at the bottom. "Is a whole explanation of what each part means. Basically, you've got a ton of mystical power. It's pretty cool, actually."

I look over the symbols again, running my fingers

along the rough paper, feeling the indentations. "So, this is kind of like a map of who I am?"

"Pretty much."

Much to my surprise, I'm totally captivated by the figures on the chart. Their circular formation draws my eye over and over, and I find myself feeling lost in it for a few moments. Finally, I pull my attention away and give Beth a brilliant smile. "This is the best gift. Could I come over tomorrow so we can go over it with your mom? I really want to understand what it all means."

"Totally!"

I roll up the paper, careful not to bend the edges, and place it on the back seat, so it doesn't get squished by my legs or backpack. Beth cranks up the radio while we wait for the bell to ring. I let the music wash over me as I close my eyes. However, inside, I still see those strange markings, some seeming to flash in my mind as they mix with images from the episode I experienced this morning. Part of me wonders if it's all connected.

# CHAPTER 2

*Planetary predestination?*

Going to Beth's house the next day is like entering another world, one filled with granola and hanging herbs, while a sitar strums in the background. It's a funky place, but I always feel a sense of ease when I walk through the door. Perhaps it's the incense that's always burning or the feng shui vibe, but I inevitably feel like the weight of my life is lifted as I cross the threshold.

Beth's mom is a wispy thing. Barely topping five-foot-two in heels, she typically wears flowing dresses that are right out of some hippie-love-fest clothing catalog. Her hair, blond and hanging to her hips, is always down but somehow manages to look soft and flowing, whereas my red strands just get tangled and stringy.

She sweeps toward me as Beth closes the door behind us. "Terran! Happy birthday, my dear!" As she pulls me in for a peck on the cheek, I catch a whiff of a scent that is purely hers, flowery but not too sweet.

"Hi, Celeste." She's always insisted I call her by her first name.

"Come into the kitchen. I just baked some cookies, a new recipe I'm trying with carob chips and walnuts."

Beth and I follow her into the kitchen, a cheery place of yellow walls and lots of sunlight. One corner of the room is devoted to her herb collection, overflowing from pots or dried and hanging from the hooks that dot the ceiling. I pull out a tall stool and sit at the island, reaching for a cookie. I look at it skeptically, never much of a fan of carob chips as they just can't compare to real chocolate, but I'm used to sampling Celeste's concoctions and take a bite. They aren't terrible, just not a chocolate chip cookie, so I chew gamely and finish it off while Beth makes us some tea.

"Hey, Mom. Terran wants to go over her natal chart."

Celeste's eyes sparkle as I pull it out and unroll it onto the kitchen island. "I'd love to go over it with you. Yours is actually quite unique."

Beth grabs four river rocks from a windowsill and places one on each corner. I lean in as Celeste begins. "Your natal chart is like a roadmap to who you are. It can show you strengths and weaknesses and can help you understand your life path."

"So, it's kind of like fortune-telling?"

"No, not like that. Though I can give you a palm reading later if you'd like." Celeste winks at me. I knew she'd been studying how to do that for the last year because Beth mentioned that she was officially starting to practice. "When you were born, the planets were aligned in a certain way as the Earth orbited the Sun. It is this alignment that shapes your understanding of the world and the direction your life will take. You are ruled by Neptune, in the ninth house, with a ruling sun sign in Sagittarius. Neptune is characterized by creativity and idealism. People in the ninth house often have psychic abilities, especially when combined with Neptune as the ruling planet."

I have to smother a snort as I mentally scoff at the idea that planets and alignment have given me some kind of psychic ability. The only thing remotely psychic about me is knowing I need to leave a ten-minute buffer before entering the bathroom after my dad. Putting on my poker face, I lean in and give Celeste my attention.

The next hour is spent going over each symbol in my chart and its meaning. Beth chimes in often, having been learning alongside her mother as they created my chart. It's a bit overwhelming as they tell me about the pros and cons of each piece of a map, which they claim defines who I am. I know that I will only remember portions of their explanations, and am thankful for the summaries at the bottom of my chart.

As Celeste is wrapping up the last bits of information, she pauses and says, "An unusual aspect of your chart is the path you will take in your life. You have strong intuition and a deep connection to the earth, which I am not at all surprised to see, but there is uncertainty here. Without a conscious effort on your part to see and embrace truth, you could get lost in your dreamy optimism."

I'm taken aback by that comment, as I've always thought of myself as a doer. "Do you mean that I'm kind of a flake and won't see things through?"

Celeste laughs, a tinkling sound totally in tune with her persona. "Not at all. What I mean is that you can't let your ideology keep you from acting. Sometimes, reality is hard to face, and it may be up to you to be a voice of reason and a person of action."

It's an interesting assessment of my character, and I don't totally buy into it. However, I can't argue that most of what my chart says is spot on. I carefully roll it up and put it with my purse, so I won't accidentally leave it behind. When offered, I eat another cookie, smothering a giggle when Beth wags her eyebrows at me as I try to resist a grimace over the utter lack of real chocolate.

Celeste drifts out of the room, heading to her little greenhouse in the backyard. Beth sits next to me, pouring me another cup of chai tea laced with lots of honey.

Setting her mug on the counter, she asks, "What time do you want to hike on Saturday?"

Being one of those people who relish sleep, I have no desire to wake up at the crack of dawn to get started. "I'm thinking that we could leave at ten and grab breakfast on the way to the trailhead."

"Cool. Want to go to The Broken Yolk and pick up some bagel sandwiches and cocoa?"

I smile at the thought. "Oh my God, yes!"

I pull out a trail map and go over the loop I'd like to hike. It should take us to some beautiful viewpoints, and I plan on snapping lots of photos to mark the day. As we chat, thoughts of my natal chart flit through my brain. According to what Celeste said, I have a strong bond with nature on an almost mystical level. This makes sense, and she mentioned that she's not surprised by it. I've always felt more at home in the woods than walking the concrete streets of my town, and it's kind of cool to think that this affinity is predestined or something.

I wonder if my birth parents were like me. I've always known I was adopted, my mom having been unable to get pregnant after years of trying. My parents even bought me a book all about being adopted when I was five. But there's always been a piece of who I really am that's missing from my life. Of my birth family, I know nothing. I was surrendered at the hospital, and whoever gave me away didn't give anyone any information. Sometimes, I catch myself staring at people who look like me and wonder if we're related. Does my birth mom ever think of me? Does she wonder where I ended up? Does she even care? I give myself a mental shake. These thoughts always ramp up around my birthday, and I know better than to dwell on them.

Beth and I chat about the weekend while pulling up the most recent weather forecast. It looks like it'll be a nice day, which just adds to my excitement. While I'm game to hike in just about any weather, Beth has a strong preference for the dry and sunny versus rain-slicked trails of mud. We wrap up our plans, and I'm about to leave when Celeste comes back inside. "Terran, how about that palm reading before you go?"

"Sure!"

We head into the cozy living room, and she pats the spot next to her on a sofa covered in a crazy pattern of colorful afghan throws. I sit down and hold out my left hand, palm up.

Celeste strokes her hands over my palm and smiles at me. "I'm new to chiromancy, so bear with me."

"Chiromancy?"

"Oh, that's the name for palmistry. It's been around for thousands of years, since the ancient Hindus. You'll have to forgive me if I fumble with this." She smiles at me and then leans over my open palm, smoothing out the creases and looking at each line etched in my skin.

I watch silently as Celeste looks me over with great care. Beth sits across from us, and I know that she's probably been dabbling in this art along with her mother. Those two are so alike. Celeste reaches for my right hand and places them side-by-side, palms up. I can see her brow wrinkle as she looks closely at a couple of the creases.

"What is it?" I ask, feeling a strange anxiety wash over me.

"I'm not sure. It's strange. First off, you're a fire hand."

I look hard at my hands. "Is that bad?"

"No, it just means that you are a leader with a clear vision."

I can't help laughing. "I am definitely not the leader-type!"

Celeste looks up at me. "Sometimes we don't choose our roles, Terran. Many leaders in history didn't start out as such."

"Uh-huh. So, what do you see in my future?"

Her eyebrows rise as she considers my question. "Your future seems to be tied to a fate you have no control over. You will have a long life, but your immediate future appears uncertain. See the faint breaks here?" she asks, and I lean forward to get a better look. "The majority of people have a continuous line, but yours has points of fracturing, never a full disconnect, but as though you may not have a precise path."

"Should I be worried?" Honestly, after what happened yesterday morning, I'm getting kind of freaked out by what she's saying. Maybe I should tell her about that whole incident.

"No, you have nothing to worry about. After all, I'm a total newbie and could be reading this all wrong!"

Beth laughs as her mom shakes her head and folds my hands closed. But I don't join in the revelry. This whole experience, from what happened yesterday to my birth chart and the palm reading, has got me spooked.

My voice shakes as I decide to talk about the strange vision I had. "Celeste?"

She looks at me, smiling. "Yes?"

"Um. Have you ever had, like, visions, or anything?"

"Visions?"

I look at Beth, who's watching me with a perplexed expression. "Um. Yeah, like have you ever been one place one moment and another the next?"

"I can't say that I have, though I've experienced déjà vu many times. Can you tell me more about what you mean?"

Licking my lips and clenching my hands, I begin telling them what happened. "I got up yesterday and felt really dizzy. I mean, so dizzy that I actually lost my balance and ended up on the floor. But the weirdest thing was that one second I was on the floor and the next I'm kneeling on some grass that feels all sharp and crisp, and there's a terrible smell all around me."

I stop and look at the two of them, hoping to glean whether they think I've totally lost my mind. But their expressions show no judgment, only curious worry. With a sigh of relief, I continue. "And I heard a voice."

"What did it say?" Beth asks.

"See." They are quiet after I say this. I wait, hoping that they don't look at me like I've turned into a freak.

"And did you see something?" Celeste asks. When I nod my head, she continues. "What exactly?"

"Death. Everywhere there was death. It was awful. The smell and smoke overpowered everything. All around me were these lumps of...of...Well, I don't know what they once were, but they had been living things at some point. It felt like I was trapped in a nightmare landscape, yet there was something familiar about it, as if I had been there before. Just as quickly as it came, it was gone. I was back in my room as though nothing had changed."

After a few seconds of silence, Celeste speaks up. "I wonder if you have some type of psychic connection to something. This would align with your natal chart. You are deeply in sync with the mystical, Terran."

Beth gets up and sits next to me. She takes my hand and gives it a squeeze. "Are you okay?"

I lean my head on her shoulder. "Yeah, it was just bizarre. Nothing like that has ever happened before. With all of the stuff we've talked about, though, I wondered if it was connected."

"I think you should keep a journal," Celeste says as she gets up and heads to the secretary in the corner of the room. Opening it, she rifles through a cubby and pulls out a beautiful book.

I look down at the cover when she hands it to me. It's covered in intricate designs that remind me a little of the symbols on my birth chart. I open it and see that it's filled with blank pages, thicker than regular paper, and soft to the touch. "Are you sure you want me to have this? It looks really special."

Celeste nods. "I think it would be a good idea to keep a record. If you have another vision, put it in the journal, and we can analyze it together. Perhaps it will help us understand what you're experiencing."

As strange as it is, I feel better having this, though I hope to never have another episode. "Thank you. For everything, I mean. Today has been perfect."

Celeste leans forward and kisses my cheeks. "You're very welcome, sweetie."

Beth wraps an arm around my shoulders, giving me a half-hug. It feels good to be here, to have shared that strange experience. Eventually, the conversation drifts to simpler things, and I embrace the feeling of normalcy.

# CHAPTER 3

*And then things got really weird*

On Saturday morning, I wake up at nine and lie in bed, relishing the ability to lounge around in the morning. The sun is shining, a noteworthy event in Oregon, and it'll be a perfect day for a hike. After wasting about twenty minutes, I get up and get ready for the day with a quick shower. I put on my favorite pair of cargo pants, wool sweater, and thick socks to protect me from the chilly December breeze, and head downstairs to fill a water bottle before Beth arrives. My mom is sitting in the living room, sipping a cup of coffee and reading a book, typical mom behavior, while my dad is still sound asleep.

"Hey, Mom." She looks up as I open the cupboard and grab my Kermit the Frog water bottle. It's childish and corny, but anyone who doesn't like Kermit has some kind of mental defect, in my opinion.

"Is Beth picking you up soon?"

"Yeah, she should be here in a few minutes."

My mom begins to get up. "Aren't you going to eat some breakfast? I could make you oatmeal."

"No need. Sit back down with your book. We're heading to The Broken Yolk on the way to the coast."

She smiles. "Sounds like a good plan."

I put some ice in the bottle and am filling it with water when I hear Beth's car horn give a quick beep. "Oh, gotta go!"

I hug her and head out. "Bye, Mom!"

"Have fun!" She calls out while the front door closes.

The air is crisp as I jog down the steps to Beth's car. Opening the door, I hear the crooning sound of Eddie Vedder's voice as he belts out Daughter. Beth's soprano mixes with his, and I join in as soon as the door closes. She turns to me, singing at full volume as I lean in to match her word for word. We laugh, and she turns down the volume.

"Ready to hike?"

"Hell, yes."

We stop for breakfast to go and make the 30-minute drive to the Cape Falcon Trailhead, sipping our cocoa the whole way so we can finish it before the hike. It's about a two-and-a-half-mile walk with incredible viewpoints. Parking the car in the tiny lot, we hop out and grab a small pack Beth keeps in the car, stuffing the bag of food into it to enjoy later. The sun is peeking in and out of the clouds, promising a rain-free day.

As we walk into the forest, a sense of peace steals over me. My shoulders relax, and I take deep breaths of the fresh air. It is insanely green, with rocks and trees covered in a mossy carpet, amid a profusion of ferns. Being a temperate rainforest, the ground is always moist and lush. I look at Beth and grin.

She nudges my shoulder. "You know, you're just as granola as my mom, going gaga for the outdoors as you do."

I stick my tongue out at her. "I may be a forest geek, but I draw the line at carob chips instead of chocolate. So, your mom clearly outranks me in the hippie factor."

Beth cocks an eyebrow. "Can't argue that."

The ground beneath our feet is slightly depressed with each step, muffling our passage through the trees. As we head deeper into the forest, it becomes quiet, giving me time to connect with everything around me. It is as I'm focusing on the birdsong that I trip on a root and land on my knees.

*"See."*

"What?" I say as I turn to Beth, who is a few steps behind.

"I said, are you okay?"

I pause, hands pressed to the damp ground covered in layers of pine needles. It wasn't Beth's voice that I heard. Am I going crazy? Was it the same thing I heard on the morning of my birthday? I listen closely, waiting to hear it again. But it is silent.

Beth reaches down and pats my back. "Hey, are you all right?"

"Yeah, just a little wet. I'm such a klutz." I get up slowly, brushing the dirt from my pants as I shake my head. "You can't take me anywhere."

"I know. But I do anyway." She tilts her head in thought. "What does that say about *me*?"

I chuckle. "Probably that you're a little crazy."

"Maybe you're the crazy one, and I'm just using you for a clinical study."

"Ha-ha!"

"Come on, psycho, let's get going," she says as she pulls me along until we are walking side by side on the narrow path.

As our stride eats up the ground, I want to tell her about the voice I heard, but I'm strangely reluctant. It must be my imagination, not some odd mystical connection as Celeste implied. Or maybe I'm developing early schizophrenia, in which case it's better not to say anything until I'm so far gone that I need to be medicated or put in a padded room. I decide to keep quiet and wait. Maybe it won't happen again.

The view from Falcon Point is breathtaking. Beth and I

sit down close to the edge of the peninsula and pull out our breakfast. It's still lukewarm, having been kept in a thermal bag inside her backpack. I unhook my water bottle from my belt and take a few sips before sinking my teeth into the most delicious egg and cheese on a poppy bagel.

The sun stuck with us, and we are rewarded with a panorama of an ocean that seems to go on forever. From up here, we can see points of land jutting into the waves, some of which have trees that hang over the thrashing water. A little farther out are huge rocks that stand sentry in the ocean, towering above waves that slowly carve away at their base. With the sunlight, the water looks so blue today, topped with foam as currents travel in their rhythm. As I chew, I look over at Beth and give her a huge smile.

She rolls her eyes. "Yeah, I know. You're totally blissed out right now."

I nod vigorously. Being out here is like coming home.

The wind picks up after a bit, biting at us through our layers until it finally drives us to get up and head back to the car. December is not the best time to hike along the coast, but I felt I needed to be here, like the sea was calling to me. We pack up our wrappers, and I take a swig of my water before hooking it onto my belt. Wiping off the seat of my pants, I walk to the precipice for the last look. My gaze travels across the blue expanses, and my lungs fill with the salty air. I close my eyes to savor the moment, and when I open them, everything has changed.

*"See."*

The gently rocking waves are gone, replaced by an ocean of roiling water. An acrid stench of rotted fish fills my nose as raging wind plasters my sweater against my body. There is a vague sense of pain in the soles of my feet, a dull throbbing that niggles in the back of my mind as I watch the bodies of seals bubble to the surface of the water, their skin a mass of blisters as though they have been boiled alive.

Tears sting my eyes as I take in the vastness of the raging sea, now a poisonous body of water. Everything is dead or dying. The haunting sound of a whale's scream seems to travel from the depths into my mind, as I vainly cover my ears to block the noise. It is then that I look down and see my bare feet, hiking boots gone, rooted on the smoldering remains of seagrass. Swinging around, I look for Beth, but she's gone. I am alone.

On some level, I know it's a hallucination, but it's so real. I can feel the heat of the ground, smell the burn, and the stink of death. As I look on, eyes welling with tears, I notice a thick layer of oil covers the sea's surface. Atop it, a flock of gulls flounder, flapping their wings in a desperate attempt to free themselves of the sludge that is trying to pull them under, before they sink beneath the muck, feathers coated in black oil, weighing them down.

The shoreline is littered with the dead, dozens of

dolphins, seals, fish, birds, and other marine life, some of whose bodies are unrecognizable. In horror, I watch as a leatherback sea turtle slowly drags its enormous body from the suffocating water. Its shell is a grotesque mass of black ooze. It lies exhausted, just beyond the lapping black waves, its mouth opening and closing as though gasping for air that it cannot find until it finally shudders and lies still.

All around me is death and decay, a world on fire, swollen with waste so thick that every living thing beneath the surface is in the final throes of agony. I can feel it. In my heart, pummeling my brain, every gasp, and convulsion, each spark of life that withers under this unbearable onslaught. And it doesn't stop. The inhuman screams bubble up from the earth until they pound at my skull. I grab at my head, desperate to get free of it, but it is as though it's coming from inside of me, and there is no escape.

I must have been screaming. My throat feels raw when the scene shifts again, and I feel Beth shaking me. I collapse onto the ground, curling into a ball, covering my eyes so that I don't see anymore. It takes me a few moments to realize the smell of decay is gone, and the wind has died. The ground I lie upon is no longer a burning mass.

Beth's shaking is so forceful that my teeth clack together painfully. I hear the panic in her voice. "Terran! Terran, wake up!"

I open my eyes and look at her through a blur of tears. "Oh, Beth."

Beth wraps her arms around me. "What was that? You just started screaming. What's happening to you?"

I swallow hard. "I had a vision. Everything was dead or dying. It was so awful. They were screaming, all of those creatures were screaming in pain and terror." Hoarse sobs burst from my mouth, cutting off my words. I can feel Beth stroking my back in rhythmic circles. I concentrate on the sensation of her hands. I don't know what's happening to me. Am I going crazy? This vision was so real. I could see, smell, and feel everything. My heart still aches from the horror of watching so many lives violently snuffed out.

"Terran, talk to my mom about it. I think she can help you."

"Okay," I mumble into the crook of my arm. "Will you help me up?"

Beth stands up and then reaches down to slide her arms under me. I make it to my knees and pull myself up with her help. My legs wobble as I stand. Once I feel stable, I take a few deep breaths to center myself and then let go of Beth. I look into the horizon, now beautiful in the light of day, just a blue expanse of sea. It calms me to see it.

I can hear the worry in her voice when she asks, "Are you ready to head back?"

Nodding, I take a deep breath. "Yeah. Let's go talk to your mom."

"Shouldn't I take you home first? I mean, maybe you need to go to the doctor or something."

The thought of telling my parents about any of this sends ice through my veins. "No. I can't talk to them about this. Not yet." I can see Beth's indecision. "Please, Beth. Let's just keep this between your mom and us. Okay?"

Beth agrees, wrapping her arm around my shoulder. "Yeah. Okay."

The hike to the trailhead is quiet. I can't talk about what I saw, not yet. As we pass under the canopy of green, I put all of my energy into being present. This is real. This is the world I live in. By the time we reach the car, I'm feeling more normal, sort of. I know I'll be ready to share my experience with Celeste. Being so connected with the mystical, I hope she can help me understand.

# CHAPTER 4

*Well, that's not the answer I was hoping for*

Celeste is in the kitchen using her mortar and pestle when we walk in. Beth calls out to her, and she joins us in the living room. I park myself on the sofa, leaning into the softness, letting the stress leak into the cushions. Beth settles next to me, grasping my hand as Celeste enters the room.

"Hey, you two," she starts and then stops to look at me. "Terran, what's wrong? Are you okay?"

Beth speaks up before I muster the energy to open my mouth. "She had a vision when we were on the edge of the Cape Falcon Trail. It was like she was somewhere else, and she came out of it screaming."

Celeste reaches over and strokes her hand across my face. "Oh, sweetie. Can you tell me about it?"

I slowly open my eyes and tilt my head toward her. "I can talk about it." I pause, taking a moment to collect my thoughts. "I was looking out at the view. It was such a perfect day that I closed my eyes to savor the moment. And then I heard it again."

"The voice?" Celeste asks.

"Yes," I say, and describe what I saw. I pause, looking at them. "It was so horrible. I could feel it."

No one says anything when I stop talking. I know that Celeste is thinking about what my vision could mean. It's a relief to have shared it. I almost feel like I am sharing the burden by telling both of them.

Finally, Celeste breaks the silence. "Don't you think we should tell your parents about the things you've been seeing and hearing?"

"No! You can't tell them!"

Celeste shifts away from the outrage in my voice. "Terran, they should know what's going on with their daughter."

I shake my head while clenching my hands. "No. No one is telling them, not until I figure this out. Please, Celeste. I just...I can't talk to them about this stuff."

She considers what I've said. "All right, but I really think they should know."

"I'll say something when I'm ready. For now, can't we figure this out together?"

Celeste is reluctant but capitulates. "Okay. If this isn't a strange side effect from a medical condition," she says, giving me a look that implies this is something I should consider. "I think we need to analyze each aspect of these experiences. It is clear that the voice you've heard and the visions are connected." She nods as she says this, as though confirming her statement. "The question is why you're suddenly experiencing these things and what it could mean. Do you have any sense of the voice?"

I'm not sure what she's asking. "What do you mean?"

"I mean, does it seem to be malevolent or something dark?"

I consider that. "No. I don't get any sense that it's evil or anything. The voice is just there, almost as though it's pleading with me, but what I see is horrifying. So, maybe it's an evil thing. I don't know."

"Hm. I wonder if whatever is reaching out to you is trying to help you in some way. You know, Terran, I am a firm believer in the idea that we share this world with beings human history has deemed legend or myth."

My eyes bug a little. It just sounds a bit hokey. "You mean like faeries or trolls or something?"

She laughs lightly. "Well, I suppose. Yes, it could be something humans have categorized as that, creating stories to explain the unexplainable. Just take a moment to consider all of the things we, as a species, didn't know five hundred years ago, two hundred years ago, or even fifty years ago. All I'm saying is there could be a great deal that has fallen into the realm of myth simply because we don't realize it has always been there, living among us, but apart."

Part of me wants to completely dismiss what Celeste is saying, but the other part, that piece of who I am that has always secretly believed in unicorns, reaches toward the implausible. "Could one of these beings be trying to connect with me? Is that what you're saying?"

"I think it's a possibility. And if they are, if they are the ones giving you these strange visions, perhaps they are warning you of something. Or maybe they need your help in some way."

I find that last part hard to believe. "I wouldn't be any kind of help. I'm not that impressive of a person."

Celeste reaches over and strokes my cheek. "I think you are. And I know Beth does too."

Beth wraps an arm around my shoulder, giving me a comforting squeeze. "You're much more than you give yourself credit for, Terran."

I still find all of this too strange for words. Maybe I should've just gone to the ER and gotten a CAT scan. "Fairies?"

They both laugh at my expression. "Who knows?" Beth says. "Whatever is going on, it hasn't hurt you. It's just caused you to experience some awful stuff. But I agree that the voice and the visions are a sign of something reaching out to you. Maybe you need to listen closely and answer."

That's a frightening idea. What if this thing, whatever it is, really does mean me harm? What if it is some evil spirit trying to torment me? I sigh. But what if it isn't? Could Celeste and Beth be right? Could something be asking for my help in this weird way?

I accept that there are things in this world that we have yet to discover or fully understand. I also recognize that I will probably continue to experience oddities. With that in mind, I need to consider how I will face them. "Okay. If, or rather when, I hear or see anything else, I will try to respond, and we'll see where that leads me. Is that what you're suggesting?"

Celeste pats my hand. "Yes. I think you need to look at this as a way to connect on a different plane of existence. You know, people have believed in beings of the unseen world for thousands of years. In fact, those beliefs have even been revitalized since the seventies. Maybe you should do a little research and learn about some of their ideas and experiences. You should also write all of this down in your journal when you get home so you can keep a record. Maybe there is a pattern here or something we will see if we look at the details."

"I'll do that when I get home," I agree while thinking over what she's suggesting about the source of all of this. "I guess if all it is are fairies trying to talk to me, then I shouldn't be too concerned about it."

I watch as Celeste cocks her head. "Not all fairies are good, you know. There are many dark legends and folklore that warn people of the malice of these beings. If you are truly going to try to make a connection, I suggest you read up on the lore so that you know what it is you could be dealing with."

It kind of creeps me out to consider that there could be evil faeries out there trying to hurt me. "Maybe we should just consider that I'm losing my marbles. I think that makes far more sense than some kind of little people with wings."

Beth rolls her eyes at me. "You're not crazy, Terran."

"How do you know that? I mean, this is like the definition of crazy. Plus, if I am a complete nutcase, then at least I could get some magic pill that would make the voice and visions disappear!"

Celeste stands up. "Let's leave this alone for now. You should take time to think about it over the next few days. I also want you to think about what I said regarding your parents. In the meantime, I think a nice cup of lavender tea would do us all some good."

I can't argue with that, so Beth and I follow her into the kitchen and let our conversation drift to ordinary things. Celeste puts out a plate of hard biscuits for dipping into the tea. They're sweetened with honey and, despite being completely organic and gluten-free, they're pretty good. I crunch on one, content to just sit and listen to the two of them discuss what movie to watch.

It's between a romantic comedy and a historical

drama when Beth asks, "Do you want to have a sleepover? You know, get your mind off everything and chill out?"

I jump at the idea. "Definitely."

Avoiding my parents is foremost in my mind. I'm not ready to tell them about any of this. They wouldn't understand. The closest they've ever come to any crazy-mystical stuff was back when I believed in the Easter Bunny and leprechauns. If I told them I'm hearing voices and seeing visions, they'd haul me to a psychiatrist, and that's the last thing I want. If I were to open up to a shrink, I'd be locked away.

My morbid thoughts are interrupted when Beth says, "If Terran is staying over, she should have a vote too. So, *My Big Fat Greek Wedding* or *Elizabeth*?"

"Oh, that's a tough choice. I think I'm more in the mood for some comedy, though."

Beth hops up and down, clapping. "Yay! That was my vote too."

"I'm happy with either, girls. How about we make some popcorn and smoothies?"

"Can we use butter this time, Mom? I don't like the olive oil version," Beth says, wrinkling her nose.

Celeste gives us an exasperated look. "You girls are such junk food addicts."

Beth and I gasp, mouths gaping, before devolving into giggles. "We're teenagers, Mom. It's a prerequisite."

Within seconds, we're all laughing, and the stress of

the day ebbs. I find myself enjoying the moment. But the ideas that have been planted never leave my mind. Instead, they take root and begin to grow.

# CHAPTER 5

*I wish I spoke raven*

If what Celeste suggested is true, I'm in a hell of a fix. The faerie legends that seem the least ridiculous are rooted in Irish folklore, and there are so many stories to sift through. At the heart are tales of the Tuatha Dé Danann, a race of beings with extraordinary power and beauty. I can feel myself going down the mythical rabbit hole as I search the internet for any reference to these beings. Part of me feels foolish at even considering that a race of faeries could be real, but the other, young and fanciful part, bubbles with curiosity steeped in a want to believe in the unbelievable.

After spending over an hour on Sunday afternoon in Google searches, I put my head in my hands. "What are you doing, Terran? Faeries? Really? I'm losing my mind. What has Celeste been filling my mind with?"

I roughly shut off the computer and slam my chair into my desk. Maybe I need to see a psychiatrist because to seriously consider this stuff is beyond nuts. I stomp out of my room, grabbing my hoodie on the way, and head outside for a brisk walk to clear my head. As usual, there is a fine mist when I leave the driveway and head to the Skook Illahee Preserve a few blocks away. I've walked the trails so many times that I know them by heart.

It feels good to be in the chill air. I slow my pace after a block, my irritation at this whole situation slowly leaving me with each step. By the time I get to the preserve entrance, tucked between a couple of old Victorian homes, I can leave all of the crazy ideas behind and simply be in the moment. I pass under a towering canopy of spruce and into the park. Though I know it's silly, it feels like I cross some imaginary border when I pass into the shade of the trees, as though I enter a parallel world that masks itself as it sits within this place of man. My spirits lift with each stride along a path littered with moss and roots.

Half a mile in, off-trail in a hidden clearing, is my favorite spot. There's really nothing remarkable about it, other than a large boulder that juts from the earth forming the perfect bench. I make my way to it, climbing up the side, hands grasping the rough edges as I haul myself up. Once I reach the flat top, I scoot backward until I am sitting in an oval depression in the center of the rock. I fold my legs until I'm sitting crisscross, and rest my arms limply on my knees. The soft trilling of a Bohemian waxwing fills the air. I close my eyes and listen to the song. With each gentle peeping, I feel more in tune with myself. Soon, all thoughts are of the life moving in cracks and crevices all around me. Inside, I sense the pulse of the forest.

It has always been this way. I go to the natural places to replenish my soul and leave the manic worry of my life behind. Beth understands this part of me, but she doesn't realize how deep it runs. I've kept this piece hidden, not because I'm afraid that she wouldn't understand, but because it's always been a private thing that's just for me.

Time passes, and soon an hour has gone by. My butt is starting to feel a little numb from being too still, and the coldness of the rock is seeping into the seat of my jeans. I stand up, stretching my muscles. The sharp caw of a raven interrupts the quiet of the forest. I scan the trees looking for this common resident and find him a few yards away on the branch of a fir tree about twenty feet up.

Cupping my hands around my mouth, I mimic his caw and smile when he swoops to a closer tree and responds.

He cocks his head in that way that only birds can, looking at me from his left eye.

I take a step closer. "Hey there."

The raven hops to the edge of the branch, leaning toward me. *Caw, caw, caw*

"I wish I knew what you were saying, Mr. Raven."

The bird stands motionless after I speak. It's strange to see a raven so still. "What is it? Want some food?" I ask, feeling ridiculously foolish to be talking to a bird and even more so when I realize I don't even have any food to offer. "I'm crazy, by the way. Just thought you should know. I hear voices and experience really messed-up hallucinations."

*Caw!*

"Yeah, I bet you agree that I'm certifiable in that bird-talk of yours." I hop off the rock, landing on the wet ground with a thud. "I'm gonna head home now. Good talking to you, Mr. Raven."

I begin to make my way back up the trail. As I walk, I feel a prickly sensation chase up my spine, as though I'm being watched. I stop and look around, but all I see is that odd raven, standing perfectly still atop a branch, just watching me.

My hoodie is covered in a film of moisture when I get to my front door. As I close it, I'm taken aback by the sight of the raven standing on the path to the house. "Did you follow me home?" I ask, not really expecting an answer. "Go back to the forest, bird," I tell it, shooing him away with my hand, but he just stands there. "Okay. Well, I'm going inside now. So, bye." I close the door, shaking my head in disbelief. Is the whole world going crazy, or is it just me?

My mom's car is sitting in the driveway, but the house is empty. They must still be off on their trip to our local big-box store. I don't know why they insist on shopping there. As a family of three, there's no reason why we need two pounds of cheese or a giant bag of rice that'll expire before we even come close to using it all.

I run upstairs to get out of my damp clothes and then head to the living room, flopping onto the couch, remote in hand. I flip through my favorite streaming app, looking for something that'll suck me in for a good two hours. I decide on a drama and soon find myself captivated.

When the vision comes, I'm completely unprepared. One minute, I'm watching an emotional scene in which the main character has finally let down his guard and opened up, and then the entire scene shifts.

*"See."*

I'm not sitting on the sofa anymore. There is no TV in front of me showing Matt Damon and Robin Williams. Instead, the world is on fire.

My house is gone, a pile of ash and warped metal glowing with orange heat. The homes next to me, and all around, are nothing more than gutted shells of billowing smoke. I watch in horror as a bird screams, wings burning with flames it can't put out, no matter how hard it flaps. It falls from the sky, landing a few feet from me, awkwardly hopping and beating its mangled body on the ground in some desperate attempt to escape the flames. I lurch forward, hands extended to grab the poor, broken creature. It squawks a broken cry and falls to its side in a small heap. I can't tell what kind of bird it was. All the feathers are coated in ash.

I cover my eyes and yell, "Stop!" It takes a great effort to remove my hands and open them. When I do, everything is back to normal. The movie is still playing. My house is whole and untouched by fire. I sigh in relief.

Clearing my throat, I stand up and talk into the emptiness. "What do you want? Why do you keep showing me these terrible things?"

I wait for a reply, feeling utterly stupid for essentially talking to myself, not that I don't do that regularly, but when I do, I know I'm the only one who'll be answering. Five minutes pass, and all I hear is the thud of my heart and the sound of my breath.

Frustrated and angry, I shout, "Who are you? Are you trying to make me crazy?" When there is no reply, I growl and grab the remote, shutting off the TV. "Fine. Don't talk to me."

I hear it when I angrily turn my back to leave the room.
*"You must see."*

I gulp as a chill runs down my spine. "Uh...um...who are you?"

*"You must see."*

"See what?"

*"What they are doing to me."*

What the hell? "Who? What who's doing?" I wait, seconds turning into minutes. "Hello? Are you there?" But there is no more.

Beyond the window, I can hear the raven cawing.

# CHAPTER 6

*Sometimes freaking out is the only logical reaction*

The drive to Beth's house is short, mostly because I decide to use the speed limit signage as suggestions rather than restrictions. The car jerks to a halt against the curb, and I jump out, racing up the slick steps to her front door. I lean on the bell and rap my knuckles against the wood, giving whoever is inside no time to actually get to the door following the first ring. Beth yanks open the door, a look of surprise on her face when she takes in what can only be described as an utterly manic teenager pushing her way into the house.

"Terran? Are you okay?" she asks as I brush past her. "Does your mom know you borrowed her car?"

I brush away her questions. "Is your mom home? Celeste, are you here?" I shout.

Beth grabs my arm as I head into the kitchen. "Mom is out. Hey, what's going on?"

I turn toward her. "I spoke to it or them or whatever it is. I'm freaking out right now, and I don't know what's going on."

I let Beth pull me into the living room and push me onto the sofa. "Okay. Start from the beginning."

I take a deep breath. "I went on a walk in the woods, like I always do, and there was this raven. It's not weird or anything to see a raven, but this one just acted too strange. I don't know, maybe I'm reading into it, and there was nothing odd. It just seems like it wasn't normal when I look back on it."

"So, the raven spoke to you?" It's not the words, but the look Beth gives me that amplifies how completely off this sounds.

"Well, yeah, but just cawing." Beth raises an eyebrow. "Look, I'm not crazy. Well, maybe I am, but that's not the point. It was the voice I keep hearing that spoke to me."

"When you were in the woods?" Beth asks, patient as ever as I spin the most nonsensical story ever.

"No, no. I was at home watching a movie when that happened. I saw the raven in the woods, and maybe it was acting weirdly or maybe not. But that's not important, I guess. The weirdness really happened when I was sitting there watching the movie, and then suddenly, I was in the middle of the ruins of my entire neighborhood. It was so awful. So, I got pissed, you know? And I shouted to whoever or whatever is making me see and hear all this crap."

Beth sits back, puzzling over what I've said. "And, whatever it is, spoke to you?"

"Yeah."

She leans forward. "What did it say?"

"It said I need to see and that 'they' are destroying 'me'." I thought it would feel good to get it out, but after I tell her, I just feel like I have totally lost my grip on reality. I sound like a lunatic. "I sound nuts, don't I?"

"A little, but that doesn't mean you didn't hear something."

"Somehow, that doesn't make me feel any better." I let out a dramatic sigh.

Beth pats my leg. "My mom and I believe you've been chosen for something."

I have to keep myself from rolling my eyes. "Beth, that sounds almost as crazy as me hearing voices." I slump over onto the arm of the sofa, banging my head softly.

"Yeah, I guess it does. But I really think what you're hearing is real, and these visions are a way of communicating something important."

I groan into my arm. "If I've been chosen for something, then I want to be un-chosen."

"I don't think it's that easy."

"Maybe I should see a psychiatrist and get on some serious meds."

Beth clears her throat. "Well, my mom and I actually think you should see a medium."

I sit up and look at her. "A medium? You mean a fortuneteller? Jesus, Beth, fairies and fortunetellers are not exactly helping."

"Don't knock it just because you think it's weird." She stares me down for a few moments before continuing, "Mediums are kind of like psychics, but they have a stronger connection to the unseen world."

I can't help the eye-rolling when I hear this. "Beth, are you saying that I should see a psychic?"

"Yeah. I think they could help you tap into what's going on."

"Going to a psychic just makes all of this sound even more idiotic. I don't really believe in all of that, you know?"

She gives me a look. "Just because you don't believe in something doesn't mean it's not true."

"I guess," I reply with little enthusiasm. "But I seriously don't see how going to some con artist who says they can communicate with fairies is going to help me."

"Don't be such a naysayer. I've been reading up on stuff, and you might be surprised by what these people can do. I really think it'll help. Just have an open mind."

I let out a long breath. "Okay. I promise to be more open-minded."

"Have you considered what my mom said about ancient folklore?"

"Yeah, I was doing some research before I went on the walk." She looks at me expectantly, so I continue. "To be honest, there's so much that I had a hard time narrowing down to a particular set of stories. Most of what I found is set in Irish legends about a race of faeries called the Tuatha Dé Danann. But it was all silly and contradictory. I mean, some sites said that they were an actual race of people, and others that they were more like some fantasy race, like Tinkerbell or something. I don't know. I got frustrated and decided to go walking to clear my head."

"Hm," she says.

"What?"

"Well, you said that after researching, you left to clear your head."

"And?"

Beth straightens, as though physically preparing to tell me something important. "It just seems interesting that you cleared your mind, and that's when the voice and vision came to you."

I shake my head. "No. It happened when I was back at home, watching a movie."

She scrunches her eyes. "Huh."

"When is your mom getting home?" I interrupt.

"I'll text her and find out." She pulls out her phone, fingers flashing as she types and sends a message.

I lean back into the sofa and wait. What if Beth and

Celeste are right? What if I *have* been chosen for something? It seems so strange to even consider. I'm nothing
special, kind of a freak, actually. But perhaps that's what
makes me a great candidate for losing my mind or being
contacted by Tinkerbell. Ugh.

"She's on her way home. Let's get a snack while we
wait, okay? It'll make you feel better to eat something."

I let her pull me up. She slings her arm around my
shoulders, and we make our way to the kitchen. Sitting on
a stool at the island, I watch while she rifles through the
pantry, looking for something that doesn't contain
seaweed or carob chips. Beth returns with a box of multi-
seed crackers and some hummus from the fridge. We eat
in silence for a few minutes, and after a while, I admit that
I do feel better.

We both turn toward the sound of Celeste pulling into
the driveway. The car door slams, and I can hear the patter
of her feet as she races into the house. Beth must've told
her I was seriously losing my mind. The door flies open,
and she sails in, swathed in a hand-knit sweater and
flowing multi-colored skirt.

Celeste gives Beth a quick peck on the cheek before
enfolding me in her arms in a tight hug. "I don't want you
to worry, Terran. We're going to figure all of this out, and
everything is going to be all right."

"Okay," I manage to squeeze out before she releases
me. "Thanks for coming back so quickly. I hope I didn't
interrupt something important."

She waves her hand at me. "Don't you fret. I was just restocking some of my essential oils when Beth texted. I can do that anytime. Now, tell me everything that happened."

I look into her earnest face and retell the events of the day. When I finish, she nods slowly and meanders to the cupboard, taking out a box of tea and muttering softly. Beth and I look at each other, and she shrugs, unable to interpret anything Celeste is saying.

Once the kettle is on the stove, Celeste leans against the island and asks me an unexpected question. "Did you say you heard the raven again after speaking to the voice?"

"Uh. Yeah. Although, at this point, I can't honestly say if I really heard it or if it was just my imagination."

"Hm. I think you heard it. In fact, I think it was trying to communicate with you. You know, ravens are mystical animals. Stories about the powers of ravens go back to shamanism. They are the most intelligent bird species."

I think back to how it felt when I was in the woods talking to that bird. It really did feel like it was trying to speak to me. If only I could understand what it was saying. Like many species of birds, ravens have eyes that seem to look right through you, as though they can see into your soul. It felt like that when I was standing in the woods, feeling it watch me. Maybe I did hear it outside my house before I came racing over here.

"Terran, have you ever heard of a medium?"

I look at Beth, and she smiles. "Beth mentioned that. She said they are kind of like a psychic or something."

"Yes, that's true. But a medium has a much stronger connection to the unseen world. Many of them can communicate with those who've passed on."

"Oh, please," I blurt out. "That's a bunch of baloney. Those people are just trying to get your money."

Celeste smiles a little. "Well, maybe that's true, but maybe it isn't."

I hold up my hand. "Wait. Are you saying I hear dead people? Are we talking about some crazy M. Night Shyamalan crap now?"

Celeste laughs. "You're so dramatic. No, I'm not saying you're hearing dead people. That's just a big part of a medium's ability. I feel this link could extend to other beings. I think we should visit a medium and see if a stronger connection could be made."

"Wait. I'm not sure I want a stronger connection. I mean, what if that just makes all of this worse?"

Beth reaches over and grasps my hand. "What if it makes it better?"

I let out a long breath and look at them both. "I don't know. It's a gamble, don't you think?"

"It may be a risk you need to take to understand what's going on," Celeste replies with a sincerity that cuts through my hesitation.

She's right. I can't go on like this. These episodes will probably only get worse if I don't do anything. But I am also scared to open myself up to a more direct line of communication. What if, whatever a medium does, ends up amplifying what's happening? What if I get to the point where all I see are these hallucinations and can no longer tell the real world from the one in my visions?

Beth can see my inner struggle. "We'll be with you, Terran. You won't be going through this alone. I promise."

I bite my lip, trying to decide. "If I don't like the experience, can we leave?"

"Absolutely," Beth affirms, giving my hand a light squeeze.

"Okay. Who should I see, and when should we do this?"

The next few minutes are spent discussing options, and it's decided that Celeste will take over the research and make all the arrangements. Beth and I leave her as she opens up her laptop. We spend the next hour hanging out, talking about inconsequential things, before it's time for me to head home. As I leave, Celeste asks if I'd like to see someone after school sometime this week. In my opinion, the sooner, the better.

# CHAPTER 7

*I never thought I'd get to meet Thor in real life*

It's a real struggle to get up the next morning. Being Monday is compounded by the fact that it's also a school day. While there are only three weeks left until the winter break, that stretch of time suddenly feels insurmountable. As I stand at the bathroom sink brushing my teeth, I can see the reflection of my bed in the mirror and have a strong desire to crawl back into it and cover my head in piles of blankets. Maybe if I hide under the covers, the voice and visions won't find me. I lean over and spit into the sink.

"You can do this, Terran," I tell myself. In fact, I seem to be talking to myself a hell of a lot more often than I used to, just another sign that I am unstable. Ugh. Wiping my mouth off on the towel, I finish up and get dressed.

As I make my way downstairs, I can hear my parents murmuring. Up until now, I've been able to hide what I'm going through from them. I just hope I can keep it up. It's not that they're ogres or anything. They just wouldn't be able to wrap their heads around what I'm experiencing if I fessed up. I think they'd fly into a panic, calling doctors and scheduling brain scans and whatever else they could think of to fix me. I love them for that, but this is not something I can share. So I put on a happy face and head into the kitchen.

"Hey, sweetie," my dad says as he sees me come in. "Happy Monday!"

"Oh my God, Dad. Mondays are so not worth celebrating."

He chuckles and picks up his coffee, continuing to thumb through the newspaper spread out on the table. I head to the pantry to grab a box of cereal.

"How'd you sleep, honey?" Mom asks, watching as I pull out an organic kid's cereal that's pretty much a few chunks of wheat mixed with tiny marshmallows and vegetable-based food coloring. I often eat like a five-year-old in the morning.

"Pretty good," I tell her as I pour a pile of sugary goodness into my bowl.

She hands me the carton of milk, and I sit down next to my dad, digging in as soon as the liquid becomes stained with hues of pink and blue. I sit there crunching, happy to have something in my mouth, so I don't have to talk. It's a relief when my parents resume their conversation, and I can eat in peace. I've just finished rinsing my bowl when I hear the soft beep of Beth's horn outside.

"I'll take care of that," my mom says as she reaches for my bowl. "Have a good day, sweetie."

"Thanks! You too." I wave and grab my backpack, heading outside.

The fresh air washes over me as I walk to Beth's car. Clearly, I am completely unobservant because it's not until I am about to pull open the door that I realize Celeste is sitting in the back seat.

Opening the passenger door slowly, I lower myself and turn to Beth. "Uh, what's going on?"

"We're ditching," Beth says with a wink.

"What?"

Celeste leans forward as the car pulls away. "Don't worry, Terran. I already called the school and told them you were sick."

"Oh? You mean you said you were my mom?"

She smiles and gives me a wink. "We're going to a medium in the city. He's supposed to be amazing!" Beth announces with a huge grin splitting her face.

My eyes widen in surprise. "I thought we were going to go after school."

"Mom felt we should see someone sooner, and this

guy had an opening today. Otherwise, we'd be waiting a couple of weeks to get in."

I settle into my seat and let that sink in. Okay. We're going to see someone today. This is a good thing. So, why do I feel nervous? "What's his name?"

"Silas Drow."

I chuckle. "That's a totally made-up name."

Celeste ignores me.

"He's got kind of a cult following. From what my mom read, the local paper tried to interview him, but he refused, something about not wanting to commercialize his craft."

I mouth the name to myself. It does sound pretty badass, in a hokey-psychic kind of way, but that's only because I know what it is that he does. Of course, I have to admit that if he were some kid in my high school, I'd be drooling over his name. It takes forty minutes to get to the city, rush hour sucks, and another fifteen to find the address when Beth makes a wrong turn, sending us back onto the freeway. It's a good thing Celeste made the appointment with a time cushion because we arrived fifteen minutes before the hour. Once we park, the three of us make our way to an unassuming two-story building that looks like all the other homes on the street.

It's not at all what I expected. Celeste looks at the slip of paper she's holding and verifies the address before we head up a short flight of brick steps to the front door. Instead of a standard doorbell, it's got a pull chain, which is both strange and cool. Inside, I can hear the deep peal of a bell echo through the house, followed by the sound of footsteps. I focus on the door, practicing my inner talk as I stay calm. Beth is holding my hand, and it helps. I focus my eyes on the intricate swoops and swirls of the patterns carved into the wood of the wide door. Interspersed in these are oddly shaped pieces of glass in varying colors. As I tilt my head to get a better look, I notice that what appeared to be random designs is actually very precise. All throughout the panels on the door are depictions of eyes. It's a little unnerving to see them all staring at me. One has the unmistakable appearance of a raven's eye —dark, round, and deep. I can't stop staring at it and am utterly fixated when the door swings open to a small man dressed in a snappy vest that hugs his slim frame, standing just inside the threshold.

He looks us over, a welcoming smile on his face. "Good morning, ladies. Please come in," he chirps, stepping aside as we enter.

My first impression is one of warmth, but not only in the temperature. The whole atmosphere feels warm and welcoming. The air is suffused with a delicious scent that I can't place. It's not a food-like smell, but it washes over me, adding to the whole appeal of the place. The hallway we are led down is filled with rich wood and covered in paintings that have no rhyme or reason, though they all fit together in some kind of crazy mosaic. We are taken to a small sitting room where a fire burns cheerfully in a tiny wood stove built into a large fireplace. Filling one wall is a huge stained-glass window depicting a scene that looks like it's straight out of obscure Greek mythology.

"I'm Enzo, Silas' assistant," the delicate man tells us. "He'll be with you shortly. May I get you anything? Coffee? Tea?"

Celeste speaks up first. "Thank you, Enzo. I would love some tea with honey."

He looks at Beth and me. "Anything for the two of you?"

"I'll have the same," I tell him. Beth nods her head and smiles when Enzo glances at her.

He indicates the mismatched sofa and chairs that seem to be from different time periods, but somehow work perfectly in this space. "Make yourselves comfortable, and I'll be back shortly."

I watch him walk out. He's very petite, almost effeminate in appearance, with brown hair and a narrow face. His manicured beard, with swoops and points that accentuate the curvature of his features, is so perfect that I wonder how long he spends grooming. I barely have the patience for eyeliner and a few strokes of my hair bush.

We sit in silence. The only sound is the ticking of a clock on the mantle. I concentrate on the stained glass window, trying to determine if the scene is familiar, but I can't place it. I'm not a mythology buff, and the images in the scene could actually be from something totally different.

Enzo returns after a few minutes bearing a wooden tray with a teapot, three cups and saucers, and a jar of honey. As he sets it down on the coffee table in the center of the room, I notice a plate filled with tiny pastries. It looks delicious and puts me right at ease as Celeste pours me a cup while Enzo fills a little dish and hands it to me.

I smile at him, setting it on my lap. "Thank you."

He looks at me, eyes boring into mine as though he's seeing beyond my flesh and into my soul. You would think I'd feel uneasy, but it doesn't faze me. It's kind of strange, really, but it's almost like he's talking just to me, inside my head, where no one else can hear, and they are words of comfort. The moment doesn't last long, but I feel genuinely moved by it, down to my core. When he breaks his gaze, he says, "You are most welcome, Terran."

I watch his every move as he serves Beth and Celeste and then leaves the room. No one says a word, though I feel the weight of their stares. Finally, I clear my throat. "What?"

Beth cocks an eyebrow. "I don't know. You tell me."

I make a face at her. "He just has a calming effect. It was nice." I glance at Celeste and see her smile knowingly.

"We've come to the right place," she announces before picking up one of the scones and dunking it into her cup of tea.

I do the same. Soon, the three of us are talking about safe things, mostly the décor and our hopes and expectations for this meeting. All the while, I feel increasingly relaxed. If I stopped to reflect on that, I might have realized it was all part of the experience, intentional and effective.

When the clock finishes chiming the hour of nine, a man walks into the room and literally takes my breath away. I hear two small gasps next to me and realize I am not the only one affected by what can only be described as the most gorgeous example of maleness to ever cross my path. He's well over six feet, with wiry muscles and broad shoulders. But it's his face that is genuinely arresting—chiseled with a dark shadow of stubble accentuating his strong jaw. His blond hair is shoulder-length, framing a perfect face with startling green eyes. He looks like Thor, just less massive. When a smile breaks through his lips, I think my mouth actually drops open. I want to reach up to see if I'm drooling, but my arms don't seem to be working. So I sit there gawking at him like a moron. At least I'm not the only idiot in the room, though. I don't hear Beth or Celeste uttering a word.

His powerful legs bring him over in a few quick strides, and then he's standing in front of me with his hand extended. "Terran. I'm Silas Drow."

I look at his hand as though I've never seen one before. Beth nudges me, and that serves to juggle my brain enough to reach out. His long fingers curl around mine in a way that feels almost sensual, though how I would know what sensual feels like is beyond me because I haven't even been kissed. As my hand is engulfed in his, I marvel at the smoothness of his skin. He gently squeezes my fingers, and I swear I can feel a thrum of electricity sink into my bones at the contact. It's not an unpleasant feeling.

It's physically painful to let go as he pulls away, greeting Beth and Celeste. "Beth. Celeste. Welcome to my home."

Celeste is the only one to have regained her voice, though I notice a slight crack as she replies. "Thank you, Silas. Enzo has been very hospitable. Your home is beautiful."

Silas' smile is truly breathtaking. It takes me a few moments to realize he's asked me a question. "Excuse me?" I should feel like an idiot, but I'm just too enamored to bother.

"Would you like to come to my office so we can get to know each other?"

"Oh," I look at Beth and Celeste, not sure if I should leave them.

Beth looks at Silas and then back at me before saying, "Go ahead, Terran. We'll wait here. Unless you would rather I join you?" She sounds a bit hopeful, and I can't help noticing her eyes flash to Silas as she drinks him in.

For some reason, actually totally unrelated to his Demigod-like appearance, I want to go on my own. "That's okay. You both wait here." I stand up, my legs feeling a little wobbly. Silas grasps my elbow to steady me, and I feel that current again. It's so strange and so pleasant at the same time.

He leads me through a few twists and turns. The house is much larger than it looks from the outside. I'm led up a short flight of stairs and find myself outside a door that looks like it's from a medieval castle. The wood is heavily engraved with beautiful men and women, barely clothed, as they seem to dance through a forest filled with unicorns and birds. Silas opens the door, and I walk into a room lined with books and paintings. There is a small octagonal table in the middle of a Persian carpet with two upholstered chairs sitting adjacent to one another. It's a cozy room.

Silas indicates one of the chairs, and I sit down, sinking into unexpected comfort. I look at him as he sits next to me, forcing myself to maintain control and not get distracted by his beauty. His hand reaches out and touches the tips of my fingers, holding that contact but going no further.

As I focus on the sensations coursing through me, he says, "I've been waiting a very long time to meet you."

# CHAPTER 8

*Perhaps I should've thought this through more carefully*

Time ceases to exist as I look into his eyes. It's so bizarre, but it feels like I am looking far beyond the dark pupils, as though I'm seeing glimpses of worlds I never knew existed. How long have I been sitting here just staring at him? No clue. And, frankly, I'd be perfectly content to continue. But Silas blinks slowly, somehow breaking that connection and setting me free.

I lean away slightly, feeling flustered. "Sorry. Did you ask me something?"

He smiles gently. "I asked how long you've been hearing her?"

"Oh." I give myself a mental shake and am about to tell

him about the morning of my seventeenth birthday when I realize what he said. "Her? Did Celeste tell you I've heard things?"

Silas tilts his head before answering. "No, Celeste told me nothing. But I can see *her* mark on you. It has been there since birth, conception actually. Was it only recently that you began to hear her?"

Her? While I never gave the voice a gender, being female seems to fit, though the voice itself has no lilting sound or feminine inflection. I clear my throat. "Um, yeah. It started on my birthday actually. It's pretty recent. So... uh...I'm not crazy?"

He laughs. It's masculine but so rich in tenor that I swear I can feel it everywhere, like a living thing. "Well, I can't vouch for your sanity, but I can tell you that what you are hearing is quite real. You see, Terran, you've been chosen. Or, perhaps, that's not the best term. You are fated."

"I don't understand."

"No, I don't suppose you do. Celeste has filled your mind with many fanciful ideas, has she not?"

My eyebrows knit together as he asks this. How could he know what Celeste had told me unless she spoke to him about it whenever she arranged for this encounter? "I'm not sure I understand what you mean. What did Celeste tell you?"

He shakes his head. "She spoke to Enzo on the phone,

though I instructed him to arrange our meeting immediately."

"Why?"

"As I told you, I've been waiting for many years to
meet you."

The room suddenly feels like it's caving in on me. This
is too strange. How would a complete stranger know
about me? What on earth does he mean when he says he's
been waiting? Part of me wants to get up and leave, but
my curiosity is piqued, so I sit back and wait for him to
explain.

"I think this will be easier to understand if I help you
to see."

"Wait...what? Help me *see*?"

"Yes. But I don't mean with your eyes. You need to
open your mind. This will strengthen the connection. It
will allow you to hear Gaia more clearly."

"Who?"

"Gaia, our great mother. She is the one calling to you."

I can't help scoping out the nearest exit as Silas talks.
Without realizing it, my body shifts forward, preparing to
leave what is becoming an increasingly uncomfortable situation. But I am unable to get farther than the edge of the chair. I
watch as Silas reaches out and traces my forehead with the tip
of his index finger, sending pulses of feeling through my skull.

His eyes snag mine, holding me captive. "Everything
around you, from the animals scurrying on the surface to

the rock that forms a great mountain range, is all connected, a living thing. And that is she. Gaia. She feels all. She knows all. We are within her conscious thought, every being a speck of life within her landscape. And you, Terran, are her daughter. It is time for you to open yourself to her completely, to know your true mother."

I feel an urge to get up and march right on out of this room. Silas sounds even kookier than Celeste, and that's saying something with all of her new-age talk. But this is well beyond that. And now Silas wants me to buy into his lunacy and open my mind to more of it? No thanks. I have no desire to make whatever connection I have with this Gaia person—thing—whatever—any stronger than it already is. I am enough of a freak to begin with. The last thing I need is to make my life any weirder.

Shifting my body to get my legs firmly under me, I say, "I don't want to do that."

He flashes one of his heart-stopping grins, stopping me as I begin to rise. "I understand. But I'm afraid that if you don't take this step, Gaia will continue to pummel you with visions that will only become more consuming. It's really better this way. Trust me, Terran."

Trust him? Seriously? I don't even know him. True, he's the most amazingly handsome guy I've ever seen, in real life or the movies, but he's talking about things that scare me, things I'm not sure I'm ready to get into. "Look, you seem like a nice guy, but I don't know what you're trying to tell me or how you think helping me could possibly include exacerbating what I've been going through. I don't know anyone named Gaia, and I just want to understand what the hell is happening to me. I want it to *stop*. Can you make it stop? Maybe do that open-mind-thing in reverse?"

Silas leans forward, reaching out and taking my hands in his. I'm momentarily overwhelmed by the softness of his fingers and the current thrumming through me at the contact. It takes a great effort to rein myself in and focus on what he's saying.

"I'm sorry," his voice entreats, each syllable curling around me, muffling the resistant thoughts peppering my brain. "I'm going about this all wrong. Let me start with a story. Perhaps if you listen and understand my history, then you will see your place in all of this."

He sits back, breaking our physical contact. I want to reach out and grab his hands, feel those feelings his touch elicits, but I restrain myself, clenching my hands into fists and then bunching them in my lap.

"Okay," I mumble, ready to hear the story but unsure if I really wish to listen to the meaning.

Silas laughs softly to himself, the sound snaking through my senses. "My story may sound unbelievable to your ears, but you must understand that there are things in this world you have only glimpsed but never quite seen. There is so much more beyond the life you plod through each day."

"I am from an ancient line. While many consider my

kind to be one of the Tuatha Dé Danann, we are not. Our history is much older than those interlopers, whose stories have saturated Irish lore, giving birth to tales of faeries and little people. We are the true people, the Daoine Fíor in the Irish tongue, but perhaps more commonly known as angels, demons, and sometimes even gods. We are none of those things and all of them. Gaia, our great mother, created our race to watch over her, and we have done so for millennia."

"We look enough like you that we do not stand out, allowing us to blend in. Though I admit, we still have our challenges. You see, we do not age as you do. Our apparent agelessness makes it difficult to stay in one place for too long. We attract unwanted attention, which has led to unfortunate confrontations in the past. However, with all of your plastic surgery innovations, it's actually easier for us to remain for longer periods of time in this century. People just assume we've had work done." He laughs at this inside joke, but all I can manage is a small smile.

"I'm almost two hundred years old," he pauses, looking at my expression, which I am struggling to hide under a poker face. "Having been born just before the Civil War in this country, it was a hard early life. There was so much death and destruction that swept across the continent, bleeding into the earth itself, and my mother often succumbed to bouts of depression because of it. She was also Daoine Fíor. Both of my parents were. I think it was the Sand Creek massacre that pushed my mother over the edge, strangling her spirit. The native tribes were much like us back then, connected to Gaia in ways that mirrored ours, though different in many ways, including bloodlines. To feel them be systematically hunted and cut down was just too much for her, I think." He pauses, looking thoughtful, and I can't help but be moved by what he's telling me. "My father held on for another twenty years or so before he joined her, and I was on my own. But then many of us are rather solitary until we find our mates and give birth to a single offspring to carry on the line. I came to the Pacific Northwest in the early 1900s, drawn to the coastal towns for reasons I've never truly been able to explain. I have been here ever since, waiting these last seventeen years for you to join us."

Silas takes in what must be my dubious expression and continues. "Our role in this world is simple. We are to remain hidden among you, inconspicuous spectators. We wait and watch, as we have always done, for a command to intercede. From time to time, Gaia wakes. She calls to us."

"Gaia commands her progeny to bear witness to the agony she feels thrumming through her heart. We pass judgment on those whose defilement renders them guilty, pulling her energy into us and releasing it in a surge potent enough to pull the wind into a hellish vortex that levels the natural and manmade or fan the flames of fires that swallow everything in their path. But there are times when our power is not strong enough. That is when she rises, unleashing forces that cause the earth to undulate in destruction or pulls the tides into terrible waves that wash away everything in their path. It is a cleansing power. These were once infrequent occurrences, stemming from times in history when mankind's lust for power over the earth went too far. Sadly, since the time of my birth and the years that have followed, that is no longer the case."

"As humans have evolved and multiplied, spreading across the vastness of her domain and into every habitable place in her landscape, she has watched, content to arise when needed before sinking back into the earth. But the last hundred years have seen an ominous shift in the balance, and Gaia has grown resentful. She seeks vengeance. For the first time in our history, she has truly 'awakened,' and our seers tell us that she will raise an army of such might that the face of the planet will be forever altered."

I interrupt, not sure what the point of this tall tale is. "I apologize for interrupting, but what does any of this have to do with *me*?"

His look feels fatherly as he stares at me. It makes me uncomfortable because I have anything but fatherly feelings. "You are one of us."

"Excuse me?"

"You're human, somewhat, but my kind is in your blood. That's what connects you to Gaia and to me. Without it, you would be untouched by the visions and would not hear her calling to you. You are of the Daoine Fíor bloodline."

"Okay. That's my cue." I hop out of the chair and head to the door. "This place is a nuthouse, and you're the biggest loony in it. Coming here was a mistake." I pull hard on the door, attempting to yank it open in a childish display of temper, but the damn thing is so heavy that I nearly end up pulling my arm out of the socket. The soft snort I hear in the background makes me want to grind my teeth.

"You can't run from her, Terran. Don't you realize that?"

His clothing rustles softly as he gets up and moves toward me. "You're crazy," I whisper.

I feel the heat of his body as he stands behind me. His breath stirs the hair on the back of my head. "You can't shut your mind from her. She's calling you. You are one of her soldiers, and it is time to rise up and join her."

My throat feels tight, and internal warnings are going off like some crazy fire alarm, blaring at me to leave this place. "Let me out of here."

Silas sighs. It's a drawn-out sound in the silence. "As you wish. But you'll be back."

"Not likely," I snap, though without much bite.

His hand reaches past me and pulls open the door as though it weighs nothing. I turn my head to glare at him, but his expression stops me. It looks pained, entirely at odds with the surety he conveyed a moment before. Am I making a mistake by leaving? Could this craziness he's been spewing actually be true? I shake my head. Nope. He's a wacko, and I need to go before I get sucked into some cult and become one of his followers, chanting through the streets about the end of the world.

I square my shoulders and walk through the doorway. "Goodbye, Silas." I don't look back at him, and I don't wait for a reply.

Beth and Celeste look startled when I breeze past them, heading for the front door, calling out, "Let's go."

I tap my toe as I stand next to the car door, waiting for them to join me. As the seconds tick by, my mind replays snippets of my strange encounter. Gaia's name circles my thoughts, and, despite my best efforts, I feel a pull inside me, a slight longing to go back inside and lock myself in that oddly cozy room with Silas. Within me, in a place I don't want to acknowledge, is a desire to do exactly as Silas suggested, to open myself fully, to let her in.

Beth's arrival breaks the spell. "Hey, you okay?"

I look at her worried face. "Yeah, I'm fine."

She doesn't look convinced. "You were gone such a short time and looked pretty upset when you stormed out of there. You sure you're all right?"

"Let's just go," I tell her, shooting glances at the windows of the house, expecting to see Silas peering out at me like some creepy peeping Tom. But I don't see his perfect face, and that's almost worse.

Celeste is quiet as we pile into the car and pull away. I

stare out the window, unwilling to talk, and am thankful they are so in tune with me. Aside from a few worried looks, they leave me to my thoughts as the miles go by. The landscape blurs before my eyes until a shape swoops into my line of sight. I watch as the raven dips and glides among the buildings and trees, wings beating as it follows us. For a moment, I can feel the wind rushing beneath its wings.

# CHAPTER 9

*Some kinds of crazy just can't
be shared*

On the way to Beth's house, Celeste stops at a diner. It's one of those funky dives with fifties décor and Elvis tunes pumping out of the speakers. The hostess shows us to a booth. I slide into the shiny aqua bench seat, scooting over enough to let Beth sit next to me. A middle-aged waitress walks over with a tray of water glasses and three menus.

As I begin to look over the selections, my stomach rumbles. I shouldn't be hungry after having a bowl of cereal and a snack of pastries, but my body thinks otherwise, and it looks like I'm not the only one. "Thanks for stopping, Celeste." I glance shyly at her, wondering what I'll see, but she just smiles at me.

"I figured you girls would need some sustenance after drooling over that Greek God." She winks at us and looks back at her menu. I relax a little at her words, thankful that we can wait a bit before jumping into anything serious.

Beth and I glance at each other and giggle. "He was the most gorgeous guy I have ever seen in person," Beth gushes. "I was so jealous when you got to be alone with him. Did you try to kiss him or something, and he turned you down?" she asks as her eyebrows waggle at me.

I laugh and elbow her, relieved that she's not going to press me about what happened. "Nah. He just asked me out on a date, but I told him he wasn't my type." I wink, and we end up in a brief fit of giggles.

When the moment passes, an awkward silence envelops the table. I focus on the plastic menu in my hands, trying to keep my attention on the words that seem to blur under the weight of the strain I feel. Beth reaches over and slings her arm over my shoulders. I take a deep breath. She doesn't need to say anything. The message is there. We'll talk about it when I'm ready. Until then, she'll let her questions go.

"Want to go halves?"

I know exactly what she means. It's something we

often do, being torn between two options and ordering both so we each get half. "Totally. French toast and a cheese omelet?"

She grins. "Yep. With hash browns and a biscuit?"

"Definitely." The mood feels lighter as we set down the menus and give our order to the waitress.

"I think I'll splurge and get Swedish pancakes," Celeste announces. Beth and I raise our eyebrows in surprise.

"Wow! You're sure living on the edge, Mom."

She waves Beth's comment away and focuses on me. "We've got the whole day ahead of us, Terran. What would you like to do?"

"Oh," I say and look over at Beth. "Um, I don't know. Maybe a movie?" I need something that requires no talking on my part.

Beth nods. "There's a romantic comedy out right now. We could do a little shopping and then go to an early afternoon show."

"Perfect," I tell her, and the three of us begin to list some shopping options. We end up choosing the local shopping district that is full of hip stores.

Celeste keeps the conversation light as we plow through our meals, but after our plates are cleared, she folds her arms on the table and poses the question that both of them have been dying to ask. "Can you tell me what you and Silas talked about?"

I bite my lip, debating what I should say. "Silas told me

that I needed to open my mind fully to what I've been experiencing."

I look at Beth and Celeste to gauge their reactions. Beth has a rather dubious expression, while Celeste seems to be in agreement with Silas' suggestion. "I told him there's no way I wanted to do that. I mean, if I'm more open to it, then it'll just get worse. He talked about some crazy psychic stuff, too, but it all came back to me, opening this window into my mind to strengthen whatever connection he thinks I have. Silas was nice and all, but he's a total loon. He can't help me."

I deliberately leave out all of the outrageous stuff he said about who, or what, he thinks he is, and the whole Gaia being. It's just embarrassingly odd, and, for some reason, I feel like it would be a reflection on me if I share that part.

Celeste cocks her head. "I think Silas may be right."

"Of course you do," I snap. Heat crawls up my neck as Celeste gives me a look that mothers across the world have perfected. I feel like crawling under the table. Instead, I settle for a sheepish, "I'm sorry."

She nods, pursing her lips before letting my snide remark roll off her shoulders. "If you'll recall, it's what we talked about before I made this appointment. Perhaps you need to be more open to what you're experiencing, Terran. I understand your reluctance to be exposed to more of these visions, but becoming a willing participant could help you through it. Have you really considered that by trying to shut it out, you may actually be making it worse?"

I grimace. It's no surprise that Celeste agrees with the psychic fairy. She sounds like Silas, and that's not what I want to hear right now. "I'm afraid of doing that. What if it starts to happen even more? If I open my mind, I may not be able to close it. It could be like Pandora's box or something."

"True," she admits. "But the alternative might be that your mind is battered until you're forced to accept whatever is being communicated. Did Silas have any insight into what it could be?"

I feel myself squirming inside. For whatever reason, I can't tell either of them the strange story Silas told me. It's almost like my tongue is tied. I settle for a partial truth. "He said there might be some metaphysical connection that I somehow tapped into. Honestly, most of what he told me was how I should be open to it, like creating a portal of some kind."

It's a relief when Celeste nods her head rather than prodding me for specifics, though her advice is still unwelcome. "You should listen to Silas. He knows more about the metaphysical than you or I do, and can view this from a different perspective. Being a medium, he may be able to establish a connection himself and help you in that way."

There's no way I'm going to tell her that, according to

him, he already has a connection, one much stronger than mine. All of this stuff is too much. It's like I'm being thrown into an alternate reality where everyone is completely off their rockers. "Why should I listen to Silas? He's some palm-reading freak who probably cons old ladies out of their retirement! This stuff isn't helping. All this fairy talk and fortunetelling isn't going to make me any better!"

Beth's eyes dart around the restaurant, stopping me in mid-tirade. Crap. Now the whole place probably thinks I'm some wacko. I lower my voice. "I don't know what to do, and I need to do something, but this guy and what he's suggesting...can't we try something else?"

Celeste reaches forward, taking my hand. "I'm sorry if I'm pushing you too hard, Terran. I only want to help. If you're not willing to talk to your parents about this, I want you to talk to someone. There's only so much I can do. I'm simply not experienced enough to guide you. I know that Silas seems pretty out there, but if he can help, isn't it worth pursuing?"

I drop my head and consider it. "I'll think about it, Celeste. But for right now, let's just wait and see how things pan out. If I'm lucky, it won't happen again."

She pats my hand. "Okay, sweetie. But you let me know if you change your mind. I can take you back to see Silas anytime."

Beth gives me a squeeze of support. "Yeah. At the very least, we just go back there to drool at him."

I laugh. "Now, that sounds like a plan I can get behind."

The talk becomes comfortable, and I let myself relax and enjoy this stolen day. But tucked in the recesses of my brain are thoughts of Silas, Gaia, and the Daoine Fíor, along with an intuitive warning that something is coming.

# CHAPTER 10

*I should've stayed in bed*

I've always thought the memes about Tuesday being Monday's ugly sister are incredibly accurate. Getting out of bed is a feat of pure willpower, followed by lackluster thoughts of what to wear and ending in a pair of jeans and a thin wool sweater ensemble that gives me just enough motivation to leave my room. Even my parents are on the quiet side when I make my way downstairs for a breakfast of cinnamon toast with a side of sliced bananas. I stand by the fact that I'm technically still a kid and should eat like one.

As my crunching fills the room, I listen to my parents

talking about their upcoming weekend trip. Well, it's a business trip for my dad, but my mom plans on tagging along. I think it's the free hotel room with complimentary breakfast and indoor pool and spa that is the biggest draw for her. Or maybe she just likes the idea of getting away from it all. Whatever it is, I'm pretty psyched to have the house to myself. Beth is coming over, of course, and we've planned a total girls weekend with chick flicks and carbs.

After I rinse off my plate and tuck it into the dishwasher, my mom pipes up. "Anything special going on at school today, honey?"

I lean against the counter, wiping my hands on a dishtowel. "Do you mean other than the injustice of making me attend gym class as a junior? Nope, can't think of anything more exciting than being forced to play volleyball with a bunch of kids who'd rather spike the ball at geeks than score a point."

My dad jumps into the conversation at that point. "You mean the coach lets the kids do that?"

"No, Dad. But it's pretty obvious when the only kids getting hit are the ones in the debate club."

"Well, I'm glad *you* don't pick on those kids."

"How do you know I don't?" I smirk as he shoots me a look.

"Ha-ha. Sure wish the coach would step in, though. Doesn't seem right to hear that stuff still goes on." He shakes his head and gets back to his coffee.

"I guess things haven't changed much," Mom adds before heading back upstairs to grab her shoes.

"Apparently not," I reply. Outside, I hear the beep of Beth's car horn. Grabbing my backpack, I peck my dad on the cheek and head out.

From upstairs, my mom yells, "I hope you have a good day, Terran!"

"You too!" I shout before closing the door.

I jog to the car, pulling open the passenger door and slinging my bag onto the backseat. "Happy Tuesday!"

Beth tilts her head to me. "Bite me."

"How hard?" I snap my teeth at her, laughing.

"Geez, Terran. You're way too upbeat for a Tuesday. Did you eat a bowl of sugar or something?"

"Nope. I'm just trying to avoid thinking about the fact that there are four agonizing days until the weekend."

Beth laughs as we meander through the back roads to school. "And this from the girl who ditched yesterday."

"That was a mental health day, like literally. Not that it helped my mental state at all, but at least my ass and my brain weren't going numb listening to Mrs. Egbert drone on about some literary dead guy."

"Seriously," Beth says with a nod.

I lean forward and turn up the volume as Tom Petty and the Heartbreakers come on the radio, pumping through the speakers to fill the car with eighties bliss. Soon, the radio is drowned out by our voices belting out

American Girl. We arrive in the school parking lot as the song is ending, the twang of the guitar still ringing in my ears as I step out. The shell of the high school matches our typical Oregon sky, big and grey, broken up by windows covered with a film of neglect because it's usually too rainy to open them. Agreeing to meet up during our free period, we head inside and split off into different wings of the building. It sucks only having a free period together, but I've been in honors classes that Beth hadn't been able to get into since freshman year, so it's nothing new.

As I walk through the congested halls, which display colorful murals to brighten the dullness, I have to constantly remind myself not to look at my feet. It's a bad habit my mom has been trying to break me of since middle school. Smiling and waving at familiar faces, I make my way to the first period, sliding into the cold seat and pulling out a binder. All around me is a hum of conversation. I look face-to-face, catching snippets of everything from sarcastic quips to talk of an upcoming party. I listen, not part of any clique in this class of smart kids. I guess I'm kind of a floater, on the fringes, friendly to all but not friends with all. It works for me.

Mr. Spinnel walks in two minutes before the start of the period, his shirt stretching over a belly that enters the room before he does. Setting down a coffee mug and a stack of papers, he wipes his sweaty forehead, sweeping his hand over a thinning patch of hair. It looks like the elevator is broken, so Donny had to take the stairs. I chuckle to myself as he begins a lecture on F. D. R.'s New Deal. Let the monotony begin. It's going to be a long fifty minutes.

The morning is painfully slow. By the time my free period finally arrives, I feel like the day should be over. How can it only be ten? My legs feel heavy as I make my way to the library to meet up with Beth. As usual, it's packed with people chatting quietly or cramming to get homework done. I circulate through the tables looking for Beth, greeting a handful of acquaintances as I scan the room. Eventually, I find her sitting at a table with Shane, a senior we've known since kindergarten.

I dump my bag on the floor and pull out a chair. "Hey, Shane, missed you in geometry this morning."

"Yeah, had my 504 meeting." Shane is a classic ADD case, going from space cadet to hyper-focused at any given moment. It drives our math teacher, Ms. Burrows, nuts. I've seen her snap her fingers or wave her hand in front of Shane's face many times, often followed by incoherent muttering.

"Have they suggested meds yet?"

Shane rolls his eyes at me before saying, "Not out loud." Beth and I laugh.

Leaning back in his chair, so it balances on its rear legs, Shane looks at me. "Are you going to tell me where the two of you were yesterday? Beth is keeping awfully quiet about the whole thing. What'd you do? Get into some trouble?"

I look at Beth and receive nothing but a blank stare. I

know it's her way of leaving any disclosures entirely in my court. "Let's see," I begin, tapping my finger dramatically on my chin. "We went to the diner, and after skipping out on the check, we held up a bank and spent the afternoon in a high-speed chase, narrowly escaping down an alley. In fact, I think it made the news or YouTube, at least."

Shane's expression remains unmoved. "Is that the best you could come up with?"

"Hey, you put me on the spot!"

He cocks his left eyebrow, raising it so high it creates a pointed arch. "Are you going to fess up, or do I need to torture you?"

"Torture doesn't sound so bad," I taunt as I fold my arms securely around my waist.

Shane watches me, smirking, and then darts a hand out, finding an open spot between my fingers and digging in. My body spasms uncontrollably as I giggle, trying to swat his hand away. It only takes a minute before I'm breathless and tapping out. "Okay, okay. Stop. I can't take it."

"I'm ready for your confession now," he informs me, pitching his voice low.

"Forgive me, father, for I have sinned. It's been years since my last confession." I look at Shane, and he nods solemnly while making the sign of the cross, taking the whole priest thing to a new level.

"Go on, my child."

I roll my eyes. "It's really not that interesting. Beth and

I spent the morning ogling a hot guy, then ate at a diner – that part was true – and went to a movie after a few hours of shopping for useless crap we want but don't need."

Shane gives me a stern look. "And why wasn't I invited?"

"Because Beth didn't want you to come."

Beth gasps. "Bitch. You weren't supposed to tell him."

"Hilarious, ladies. But fine. Be all exclusive, and don't invite me." Shane leans back, folding his arms across his chest, and pastes a hurt expression on his face.

I've always liked Shane, but he's closer to Beth than me, making me hesitant to say too much. Plus, he's a social butterfly, flitting from group to group, able to blend in like a chameleon. It's not that I think he'd blab about anything I told him in confidence. I just don't feel that connection that Beth and I have. With her, I can say anything, almost anything.

"I'll make Beth invite you next time. I promise."

He smiles. "Good. Now let's talk about this hot guy you were ogling."

It's a safe topic, and I know he'll appreciate it. I spare no details, aside from a name and the whole context of the encounter, as I describe the God-like perfection of Silas. Beth affirms everything I say, and by the time our free period is up, Shane is begging to meet him.

We gather our stuff and plan to reconnect in the lower café for lunch. I wave and head to AP English. Ugh. I'm about to jog up the stairwell to the second-floor classrooms when it happens. My foot misses the step, and I fall to my knees. My hands, having slapped against the surface with a hard smack, are smarting more than my pride as a guy I've never seen before grasps my arm and hauls me to my feet.

"You okay?" he asks, concern etched across his face.

As I look at him, an image of Silas pops into my head, and I'm taken off guard by the striking similarities in their features. "Yeah, thanks. I'm such a klutz."

I watch as he bends down and picks up my backpack that had fallen off my shoulder. He's tall, dwarfing me as he straightens. This boy has a blindingly handsome face, though his hair is so black it makes his skin appear luminescent. My mind flashes to Silas again, as I take in his perfection, a thing so out of place in this realm of pimples and gawkiness. I can't help but make a quick catalog of comparisons. While he doesn't have Silas' musculature - and least not yet - his flawlessly sculpted features and stunningly bright, green eyes are similar enough to cause me to look harder at his entire being. Why have I never seen this guy before? It's not like I could miss someone who looks like him. I doubt anyone could. Is he new? Suspicion blooms as I begin to wonder if perhaps Silas was right. Maybe he is what he claims. Perhaps this beautiful boy in front of me is one of them, too. As I stand there lost in my thoughts, he cocks his head in silent amusement.

"Terran, right?"

There's a protracted pause while I gather my wits in

my suddenly fractured mind. "Yep," I finally reply, each syllable stretched out a bit too long, while I reach for his extended hand.

"I'm Raife."

His hand curls around mine, warm and robust. I look down, mesmerized, as he slowly strokes the space between my thumb and forefinger in lazy circles. His touch sends a familiar current through me. I look up at him, startled by a flash of recognition that races through me. Who *is* this boy?

Raife's eyes bore into mine as though he could read my thoughts. "Can I walk you to class?"

My mouth feels dry as I process what he said. "Um, that's okay. I'm fine." Inside, I cringe a little. I sound like such an idiot.

He flashes a smile and releases me. "You sure? You seem kind of distracted."

It would be hard not to be distracted by Raife. "No, uh, I'm okay." He seems reluctant to leave as I gather my composure and sling my backpack over my shoulder. I look over at him and ask, "Are you new here? I don't remember seeing you around."

Raife indicates the stairs and walks with me, despite my refusal of assistance, but I'm too intrigued to even attempt to brush him off again. As we climb the steps, he fills me in. "Yeah, I just moved here a couple of weeks ago, though I was able to put off starting school until yesterday."

It feels like I'm in a Twilight movie with all of these incredibly hot guys coming out of the woodwork. I force myself to concentrate on walking without mishap as we take the last few stairs before I turn to him. "Where'd you move from?" I'm totally ready for him to tell me he's from Forks, Washington.

"California. San Diego, actually."

I raise my eyebrows in mock disdain. "Oh, you're one of the Cali transplants, huh? Didn't you see the sign on the border welcoming you to visit, but not move here?" It's a longstanding joke in Oregon that we're continually being invaded by Californians.

Raife laughs. "I spray-painted over it."

"Damn, now even more of you are going to cross the border."

"I wouldn't worry about that," he says with a touch of seriousness. "My kind is rather unusual."

And there it is, an odd flutter in my stomach, like a warning. Or is it more like some kind of recognition, maybe on some instinctual level? I give my head a shake. This is crazy. Silas's insanity has infected my brain. "Well, I've gotta get to class before I'm marked as cut. I'm sure I'll see you around."

"You will," he says confidently.

I wave lamely and head down the hall. At the doorway to my classroom, I turn and look back. He's standing there, watching me, in an almost possessive way. If I weren't so enamored with his physical appeal, I might be worried. I give him another short wave and step into the room, finding my seat before Mrs. Egbert's nasally voice pierces my thoughts. As she begins a lecture on the symbolism in the book, The Great Gatsby, I turn my head, peering into the hallway, hoping to catch a glimpse of Raife.

But there's no sign of him. He most likely didn't even have a class in this wing, I mutter. Letting out an irritated breath, I force myself to tune into the lecture on Gatsby's obsession with entering Daisy's world of old money and social standing. Still, my attention only lasts a few minutes, and I find my eyes drifting back to the doorway without conscious thought. It's like a pull that I am unable to resist, my own green light, only I hope mine doesn't end in Gatsby's ruin. What if Raife is some kind of half-breed like me?

Wait. Am I seriously considering Silas' ramblings as plausible? I lean back in my seat and begin to trace patterns swirling through the fake grains of wood on my desk. Silas is an enigma. He seemed so sincere when he explained a history steeped in legend. But crazy people really don't know they're crazy, I remind myself.

What if he's not crazy? What if, as Celeste believes, there really is another part of the world that most of us never see or understand?

No. This is just stupid. It's the twenty-first century. Big Brother is always watching, and there is no part of this world that people haven't explored and potentially exploited. Well, perhaps in some ocean trench a mile deep, there's a new species of giant squid or something, but on the surface, it's all been found and studied, recorded and put on a map, or added to the internet playground. There's no way a species of humans exists unknown to the scientific world. It's utterly laughable. Yeah. It's totally unrealistic.

But what if?

I turn back to the open doorway, peering into the hall. However, it's well into the period, and no one should be wandering the corridors. Regardless of what's sensible, I stare in vain, looking for Raife.

As before, it hits me hard and fast when it comes, like a wave of sickness, consuming my reality. My vision blurs, making everything look like a funhouse version of reality. My stomach clenches in an unwelcome but familiar way. And then I hear it, that voice. Gaia. She utters one word, drilling it into my skull.

*"See."*

The hallway I had been looking into seconds before becomes a mass of molten rock, bubbling and popping, spraying deadly globs of melted metal and brick into the crumbling walls. I can feel heat burrowing into my skin like a living thing. Watching in horror, I see the charred remains of an arm swim past my vision before sinking into the gurgling mass. Spurts of flame shoot up what remains of the walls, devouring murals of pastoral scenes from famous books, scorching everything in their path until it's an unrecognizable mess. In the distance, I can hear screaming, but it's gone quickly, brutally cut off.

My eyes welled with tears, stinging from the heat and smoke. Taking a breath, I choke, coughing violently as my lungs fill with soot and tiny embers that are swirling through the air. I tear my gaze from the scene in front of me, gasping as I try to pull clean air into my mouth and look around in desperation. In all directions is a sea of bodies, classmates who were sitting next to me a moment ago are now covered in skin that is blistered and blackened, mouths slack or frozen mid-scream. Panic fills me as I watch a wave of magma spill into the room, blanketing the floor, consuming the bodies that litter the small space. A scream rips from my throat as one of the corpses next to me, a girl I've talked to a handful of times, bursts open from the intense heat, before being swallowed in flame.

I feel myself backing away from what's coming, but there's no escape. My heart races and my eyes blur. I can't stop it, and I can't get out. I'm trapped. Sobbing, I cover my eyes and wait for the horror to consume me.

Rough shaking wrenches me out of my waking nightmare. "Terran!" Mrs. Egbert's strident voice yells.

I come out of it slowly, afraid to open my eyes. I breathe deeply through my nose, trying to calm my racing heart and bring myself back to reality. When I feel in control, I look into a worried face and glance around, seeing expressions of shock and concern.

"Terran, are you alright? Would you like to see the nurse?" Mrs. Egbert asks, for once, using a voice that is pitched low and calming.

I take a moment to get my bearings. "Uh, no. I'm okay. I guess I fell asleep or something. May I use the restroom?"

She doesn't look convinced but backs away from my desk to give me space to stand up. "Of course. Are you sure you're all right?"

"Yeah. I just had a nightmare, that's all. I stayed up too late last night. I'm sorry, Mrs. Egbert." I get up slowly, my legs feeling a bit wobbly, and leave the room. I can feel the weight of dozens of eyes boring into me. Her hand hovers behind my back as though she's afraid I might fall. I swear, I can feel the heat of it.

I take a shuddering breath as I enter the hallway and head to the bathroom. It's a relief when I walk in and find it empty. You never know who might be holed away in here during class. Walking to one of the open stalls, I see a Juul pod on the dirty floor, carelessly discarded. Needing privacy, I duck into a stall and close the door, leaning against the pea-green wall. Images pummel my brain in an awful movie I can't turn off. Even when I close my eyes, I still see the charred bodies. I still hear the panicked screams. Why is this happening to me? I admit that it's getting worse, the visions becoming more visceral. I worry that soon I may no longer be able to tell what's real from what's not.

Tilting my head back, I let it flop to the side, my eyes

coming to rest on the inside of the stall door. Among the phrases and drawings littering the surface, a message is scrawled under the most recent layer of paint, carved so deeply that each letter is discernible.

**FREE YOURSELVES FROM ALL THIS MADNESS**

I lock onto it, unable to tear myself away. It is madness, all of it. And it can't go on any longer.

# CHAPTER 11

*Some choices are made at the*
*edge of the sea*

After school, I tell Beth about my embarrassing incident in AP English, not that she hadn't already heard numerous variations of it from the gossip mill. As we sit in her car in the parking lot, the story spills out, every ugly piece of it. I don't sugarcoat it for her, needing to somehow explain how appalling the visions are, how entirely real it seems.

"I think it's getting worse," I admit.

She frowns. "Is that why you didn't show up at lunch?"

"Yeah. I just needed to hide out for a bit."

Beth starts up the car. "I know what you need." She pulls out, and we head in a familiar direction, away from home and toward the sea.

I watch the miles go by in a blur as we head out of town. Rather than pushing me to say any more, Beth tunes into our favorite satellite radio station, and I let the hum of the music drown out my thoughts. Soon, Beth is pulling into a small lot with a scenic view of the Pacific. I can feel the pull of the ocean as I open the door and step out into the brisk air. The wind whips through my hair as I breathe in the air mixed with a salty tang.

We walk to a rock wall along the edge of the cliff and sit down, faces to the western horizon. I tilt my head back and close my eyes, letting the smells and sounds wash over me, cleansing my mind. The vastness stretching out before me makes my troubles seem so small. I'm just a blip in this landscape. Minutes pass in silence before Beth pulls me from my musings.

"I think my mom is right. You need to go back to Silas and listen to what he has to say. If the visions are getting worse, you need to find a way to face the source of them."

I sigh. "Yeah, I guess you're right. I'm just scared. I don't want him to rewire my brain or something and have all of this get ramped up."

"I get it, but you can't go on like this, Terran. You haven't told your parents, and you won't see a doctor. Although at this point, I don't think getting on meds would even help."

"I know."

That's all we say for a few minutes. In my head, I go over and over the things Silas told me, stuff he believes to be true but sounds so unreal that the rational part of my brain can't accept it, not entirely. But there is another piece of me that I feel reaches toward it, somehow believing a current of truth lies within the fantastical words he spoke. It's a power struggle, as I wrestle with the world I know and the one Silas claims to exist, unseen and ancient. I don't tell Beth what I'm thinking. There's still something that holds me back, keeping me from saying too much. Inside, I wonder if that is Silas' doing. Did he somehow hypnotize me while I sat in that chair listening to a crazy story about a race that lives in legend but has no place in my world? I admit that it's possible. So many things seem plausible now.

As we sit shoulder to shoulder, the wind rustles through my hair, pulling strands in every direction. It feels like it's washing over me while the waves tumble toward the shore in a relentless current.

My eyes are fixed on the water, mesmerized by the flow, when I hear her voice. It seems to come from deep within the earth, like a living thing, spilling into my consciousness, so that is all I hear. *"Daughter."*

It's hard to keep my body still as she calls to me. She. It must be her. Gaia. An explicit part of me tells me it is. Perhaps this is another side effect of Silas, I try to say to myself, but I don't really believe that. From the corner of my eye, I see Beth sitting motionless, shoulders relaxed as she looks toward the sea. She doesn't hear it, this voice invading my brain.

*"Daughter,"* it calls, pulling me apart inside as I try to fight it while wanting to surrender.

Beth's voice startles me, severing the connection. "Want to climb down and walk on the sand?"

I pull myself together, pasting on a smile. "Sure. Maybe we can do a little shell hunting."

"You okay?" Beth asks.

"Yeah. I'm fine, just a little tired after everything."

She doesn't look convinced, but lets it go. We scoot off the ledge and carefully make our way to the shore, holding onto clumps of seagrass, so we don't slip. The sensation of my feet sinking into the sand feels good. I focus on it, letting the soft depressions distract me from listening to an entity calling to me as though I belong to her.

I turn and smile at Beth. She chuckles and shakes her head. "You are so predictable. Happy, nature girl?"

Grinning, I say, "Yep. You nailed it when you brought me here. I needed this. Seriously."

We take off our shoes and toss them onto the sand, far from the incoming tide. Strolling to the water, I lift my arms and let my anxiety go. *Just be here*, I tell myself. Beth jogs ahead of me, stopping when she gets to a small lump poking out of the sand along the water's edge. Squatting down, she digs her hands into the chilly sediment, pulling out a sand dollar. Beth turns it over, looking for any sign of life, before glancing at me.

"This is perfect! I don't think I've ever seen one still whole before." Walking into the water, she leans down and lets the sea wash away the sand, revealing a perfect specimen of milky white. I reach out, taking it carefully into my hands, turning it this way and that.

"Wow," I say, stroking my fingers along the bottom of the sand dollar, to the mouth where a small creature once lived, scurrying along the ocean floor in some parallel universe.

"I want you to have it," Beth tells me, grinning.

I look at her, mouth open in surprise. "Seriously?"

"Yeah. It's meant for you. I can feel it."

I cock my head. "What do you mean?"

Pursing her lips and scrunching her nose, she thinks it over before replying. "I don't know. I just know it's yours. Like it?"

"Uh, yeah. Thanks, Beth." I gently curl my hands around it, careful not to squeeze too tightly. As my fingers bend along the edges, I swear I can feel a faint thrumming, like a pulse vibrating up my arm. I stare at it in fascination. Is Gaia behind this? Is she sending me a message of some kind?

Beth tugs at me. "Let's walk down to the cave and see if we can get into it. I don't think the tide is too high yet."

I look up and follow her arm as she indicates a place we've visited many times over the years. It's dark and wet, with rocks carved and smoothed by the power of waves. As children, our moms would park themselves on the shore, chatting for hours, while Beth and I played pirates in the cave. I smile at the thought. They were good times. Simple times.

"We haven't been here for years," I tell her, tucking the sand dollar into the large outer pocket of my sweater.

At the edge of the cave is a series of tide pools. We spend a few minutes crouched down, peering into micro-ecosystems teeming with life. It's mesmerizing. The wind picks up a bit, and I feel its bite on my wet feet.

"It's getting pretty cold. Let's get out of the wind and check out the cave."

"Aye, aye, captain," Beth cries, saluting me in some lame imitation of a first mate.

"You're such a dork."

"Takes one to know one," she shouts before hopping from rock to rock, away from me and into the darkness of the cave.

I quickly follow, careful of my footing, as the rocks are slippery. As we enter the cave, the light dims, giving it a secretive air. In the dimness, other worlds and stories were birthed from our vivid imaginations. I sift through my memories, recalling hours of piracy, as we lost ourselves in storylines of treasure hunting and battle. I smile as I remember the tales of Cutthroat Jill and Fearless Kate, our pirate names.

"Do ye be thinking a landlubber stole our booty, Cutthroat Jill?" I ask, waggling my eyebrows.

Beth snorts out a laugh. "I had such a badass name!"

"If my memory is right, you were a pretty ruthless pirate. I do believe you took down the infamous One-Eyed Bart in a serious duel."

"I may have been the fighter, but you were the fearless one, trekking off to uncharted islands in search of treasure. I believe there were quite a few times that we ended up walking the plank thanks to Fearless Kate."

"We sure had a lot of fun, didn't we?"

"Yeah. We did."

I wave my hand forward. "Shall we? I'll let you go first in case One-Eyed Bart is waiting to ambush us."

Beth giggles and steps into the cave, swallowed by the darkness. For a moment, the world stops, and the image freezes, as I am overcome with a feeling of doom, as though the sight of her being consumed in the mouth of the cave is a premonition. I shake off the sensation and follow her in.

It's just the way I remember it, cold, wet, and mysterious. Anything can happen when we're inside, the only limit being our imaginations. I run my hands along the cave walls, feeling the moisture and indentations. If these walls could speak, what would they say? Would they remember when they were rough and jagged before the ocean wore them down? Beth is in the back of the cave, peering at the walls, having pulled out her phone to use the flashlight. She turns to me, her face wreathed in a smile.

"What?"

She waves me over. "Look."

When I get close enough, I peer at the rock she's illuminating, bursting into laughter as I see what she's found. "Are those our 'ancient cave drawings'?"

In the beam of light, I see crude stick figures scrawled across the surface, their forms creating some story that escapes me. I trace my hands over them, trying to recapture the wonder and innocence of the girl who carefully carved them on the rocks with a bit of charred driftwood. But I can't grasp it, that innocent time in my life is lost to me, taken over by too much reality. That pretend world we created, the places and stories that seemed so real, are gone. All that remains are the ghosts of those times.

We talk quietly for a while, poking into the nooks and crannies we used to play in. Eventually, a sound pulls me away, and I look toward the mouth of the cave. It's a strange, flopping noise, too random to be waves lapping at the rocks. I make my way to it, looking in tide pools for the source.

A startled cry rips from my throat when I see what's making that odd sound. Just beyond the edge of the tide pools, a sea turtle flaps its flippers against the rocks. Even from a few feet away, I can see that it's exhausted, mouth gaping open and closed as it continues to try to haul itself onto the rocks. Afraid to scare it and make the situation worse, I bend down, using my hands and knees to get closer in a less threatening posture. As I move slowly toward it, my heart wrenches. Around its neck and snaking along its front slippers, is a matted mess of fishing lines. When I finally reach the poor creature, I can see that the lines have become so tight that they're cruelly digging into the skin on the sea turtle's neck and joints, creating ugly furrows of raw skin. Behind me, I sense Beth's presence.

Pitching my voice low, I say, "Do you still have that pocket knife on your key chain?"

I hear her digging into her pocket and pulling out the keys. The soft clanking doesn't seem to bother the miserable animal whose strength seems to be failing as I watch. Reaching back, I motion for Beth to put the pocketknife in my hand. I open it and move closer to the animal.

"It's okay," I whisper, hoping the sincerity I feel somehow translates into something the turtle can understand.

Its eyes don't seem to register my presence as I reach forward and gently pull a piece of the fishing line away from its left flipper so I can cut through it. It's slow work as I'm forced to pause repeatedly when the animal flaps in a futile attempt to leave the water or get away from me. I've cut away most of the lines on the left side, handing

Beth the pieces as I work, when the flailing movement stops. The sea turtle raises its head, mouth open as rattled breath escapes into the quiet. I watch, helpless, as the gasping becomes more pronounced until it cranes its neck in a desperate attempt to pull air into its exhausted body. Tears are streaming down my face when the turtle gives up the fight and slumps, head landing softly on the rock.

Water laps at my hands as I press them to the rocks. The tide is coming in. Beneath my fingers, a familiar thrumming starts, radiating up my arms. I'm ready to hear her when her voice pierces my skull.

*"Behold, the indifference of mankind."*

I drop my head, hearing her words and understanding them. People did this, tossing garbage into the ocean with blatant disregard for consequences. Gaia, if she does exist, has every right to be angry. In my heart, I understand that. But they can't all be bad, can they? There must be some hope left. I look at the turtle's body. It can be saved, can't it? Hands shaking, I lean forward and gently rest them on the shell of the turtle. There is no movement at my touch.

"Terran, it's gone," Beth whispers.

I shake my head, brushing her away when she tries to pull me from the body. "No," I tell her, focusing my mind on the animal. After a few moments, an odd feeling begins as tremors and grows, flowing from my chest, down my arms, and into my fingers. Sensations rush out of me and into the sea turtle. I feel the moment they sink into its flesh and catch. The animal twitches, then gasps, echoing the sound Beth makes as she watches the impossible become a reality. Somehow, the animal stirs, life filling its body until its head rises, eyes looking straight into me before it turns and makes its slow progress back into the sea.

I get up slowly, wiping grit off my hands and the knife blade, before folding it and handing it back to Beth. My arms are shaking, and I can't tell if it's from physical strain or disbelief or something else.

I hear Beth say, "I thought it was dead. Geez, it's such a relief to see it swim away like that. That was weird, though."

It was dead, wasn't it? I felt it, but it came back somehow. This is beyond the stuff I heard and saw, beyond some voice and crazy visions. This was real, and it simply can't be real. Things don't work like this. People can't truly bring anyone back from the dead. I decided that it must have just passed out, and I woke it up by touching it. That has to be it.

I turn to Beth. "Yeah, I did too."

Standing here on the edge of the sea, looking out at the sea turtle swimming toward the horizon, I make a decision and wonder if I ever really had a choice. "I need to talk to Silas."

"Oh, yeah?" I nod, and Beth pats my arm. "Okay."

We make our way back to the car, steps slow, and my mind is bogged down with what happened and what I've resolved to do. I pull open the passenger door and then reach into my pocket for the sand dollar. It's broken, shards poking from ragged edges as it rests on my palm. I can't help but feel that more than this perfect thing is shattered.

# CHAPTER 12

*A walk in the woods has never sounded so appealing*

Beth and I head to her house, needing to tell Celeste about my decision to see Silas. While I believe it's the right choice, probably the only choice, I feel an urge to pawn off some of the responsibility for taking this step by asking Celeste to make the call and arrange a time to visit him. It gives me some measure of relief to know she'll take the lead. Of course, once I walk into that room and face him, I am on my own.

I park myself on the sofa while Beth finds Celeste and fills her in on my decision, before joining me in the quiet comfort of the living room. After a couple of minutes, Beth and I hear a quiet conversation. I imagine she's talking to Enzo. I doubt Silas would answer the phone himself.

Celeste's voice is soft, but I can make out her side of the exchange. "I see. Does he have an opening this weekend?" There is a brief pause before she continues. "Yes. Saturday will be fine. Ten o'clock? Sure. She'll be there. Thank you, Enzo. Goodbye."

Beth and I glance at each other. She takes my hand, and her grip feels warm, making me wonder if my hands are cold from fear and anxiety. "We'll be with you, Terran."

I give her a small smile. "I know. Just having you both in the next room will be comforting."

"I could stay with you," she says hopefully.

"Thanks, Beth, but I need to do that part on my own. I think it'll be better for whatever Silas is planning if I can fully concentrate."

"You're probably right. Though I'd love any excuse to sit there and look at him." I chuckle as she grimaces before she adds, "I don't know how you could concentrate on anything that man said when you were in the room with him. I think I'd probably just sit there drooling."

A snort escapes as I burst into a fit of giggles at the image her statement conjures. "Thank you, Beth. I needed that."

She laughs. "That's what I'm here for, to entertain you."

Celeste moseys in carrying a tray filled with an entire

tea service, complete with little sandwiches and cookies. "I thought you girls needed something to munch on after today's events," she announces, setting the tray on the coffee table.

"Wow," I exclaim. "Thanks, Celeste. I actually really needed this. Lunch didn't work out too well for me today, and I'm starving."

I grab a cucumber sandwich and begin munching as Celeste gives us a rundown on her phone call. "I asked Enzo if Silas had an opening this week. I actually told him any day and time would work. I hope you don't mind, Terran. I thought this was too important to wait."

"I don't mind at all. I'd rather see him sooner than later, to be honest."

She pats my hand. "That's how I thought you might feel. Well, unfortunately, Silas is out of town until Friday. So I made you an appointment for Saturday at ten. Maybe you could spend the night, and we'll head there after a good breakfast?"

"That sounds perfect. Thanks, Celeste. I really appreciate you and Beth helping me through this."

"You know you're like a daughter to me, Terran."

I nod. "Yeah, I know."

We spent the next hour eating tiny sandwiches and talking about other things. Before long, it's after eight, and I need to head home. Beth drives me, and I wish her goodnight before going inside. My parents are watching their favorite show when I walk in, some crime-solving series that I could never get into.

"Hi, sweetie," Dad calls out as I shut the front door.

"Hey, Dad. Hi, Mom," I shout before dumping my backpack on the floor and walking over to give them a hug.

My mom strokes my hair, smiling. "Did you have a good day?"

"Pretty good."

"How's Celeste these days? Did you have fun at Beth's house?"

Dad is watching our exchange, though I see his eyes dart to the television, trying to catch what's happening on the screen. "She's good. We ate some food and just chatted for a while. It was fun."

"What's the latest new-age stuff she's into?" Mom asks. She's always been sort of ambivalent about Celeste's quirky interests, but curious at the same time.

"Well, I guess the latest thing would be the natal charts. She made me one for my birthday."

"Oh? I'd love to see it after the show," she says, swinging her hand toward the TV.

I look at my watch, considering the homework I need to get done and the level of exhaustion I'm feeling. "Could I show you another day? I've got some work I need to get done, and I'm already feeling beat."

"Sure, honey. I hope you don't have too much to do. I

don't want you up late," she says before adding. "You're looking tired these days."

I give them each a peck on the cheek. "Yeah, I'm exhausted. It shouldn't take me too long to get it done. Maybe an hour, and then it's lights out."

The minute I leave the room, their attention is back on their show, which suits me fine. I don't want either of my parents to start digging around too much. I grab my backpack and head upstairs, resigning myself to the drudgery of homework before I can sink into bed.

---

When Beth and I pull into the school parking lot the next day, I'm surprised to see Raife waiting just outside the student section. He's clearly looking for me as he scans the kids because his eyes fix on me as soon as I step out of the car, and he waves.

"Who is *that*?" Beth asks, jabbing me in the side.

"Ow! Geez, Beth, you don't need to stab me with your vampire nails."

"Who is he?" She says, giving me an exasperated look.

I roll my eyes. "His name is Raife. He's a new kid from California. I met him yesterday."

She shakes her head at me. "I cannot believe you didn't tell me about that gorgeous creature yesterday!"

"Uh. I kind of had other things on my mind, you lech."

"I don't know how you could forget a guy who looks like that. I mean, he may be even hotter than Silas!"

I look over at her, wondering if she somehow senses that Silas isn't all he seems to be, but she's just ogling Raife, wholly absorbed in his perfection. "Yeah. Raife is hot. Want me to introduce you?"

"Hell yes," she says as her fingers sift through her hair to arrange it just so.

I grab her arm, hauling her across the lot until we're only a few feet away. "Hey, Raife. How's it going?"

A smile lights up his perfect face as he walks toward us. How on earth does he manage to get even better-looking just by smiling? "Hey, Terran."

I take his outstretched hand, feeling a little awkward at the formality of a handshake. The moment our fingers touch, I feel it, that strange current, at once pleasurable and alarming. I pull my hand away quickly before I get lost in the sensation and pat Beth's shoulder. "This is Beth. Beth, this is Raife. He's a Cali transplant."

I observe as Beth takes his hand in a quick shake, but she doesn't seem to feel anything unusual. I guess it's just me. Her head tilts upward as she gazes at him before finally managing to blurt out a timid, "Hi."

"Good morning, Beth," Raife replies before his gaze switches back to me.

"Can I walk you to class?" He asks, his voice curling around me like a blanket until I feel momentarily disconnected from myself.

"Um. Sure."

Beth gives me a look that says she knows she's been blown off. "See you at lunch, Terran."

"See ya," I call out as she jogs toward Shane, who just pulled into the lot.

Raife and I fall into pace and head inside. I feel so drawn to him while we walk and have to smother an urge to move just a few inches closer so our arms can brush against each other. What is it about him? Well, aside from his astonishingly good looks. There's something else. Something indefinable, and while I want to explore it, I'm also reticent to look too deeply, afraid of what I might find and what it might mean.

Raife breaks the silence after what seems like a long stretch, but was really only a couple of minutes. "So, where do people hang out in this town?"

I'm not the right person to ask and wince a little. "I guess the mall." Oh, God. I probably sound like a nerd.

"You guess? You mean you don't hang there?"

I look up at him to take in his expression, hoping I don't see a look of distaste. But his face is open and judgment-free. I can't help the sigh of relief that escapes me. "Well...I'm not really into a lot of the popular stuff."

"What are you into?"

"Um. Hiking?" I look at my feet, feeling self-conscious.

Surprisingly, he sounds genuinely interested when he replies, "Oh yeah? Where are the best trails around here?"

I look at him, smiling. "I'm rather partial to the coastal

trails. There are a few that take you to some really amazing vistas."

"Will you show me sometime?"

"Seriously?" I'm so shocked that my face must look absolutely incredulous because he laughs.

"Yeah. I'm more of an outdoorsy type. Honestly, it's nice to meet a girl who isn't obsessed with selfies and social media. It's good to disconnect."

I think I just fell in love. Could he be any more perfect? It's like Raife was made for me. "I hear ya. I feel like myself when I'm deep in the woods. It's weird, I know."

"It's refreshing," Raife counters, slowing his steps so that I'm forced to stop and really look at him. "Don't be afraid of who you are, Terran."

"I'm not. Being who I am is much easier than trying to play the part of an average teenager. It's just not that often that I meet someone who shares my interests. Beth has been the only one, and that's been going on since we were kids. None of the other girls here seems interested in trekking through the forest on the weekends."

He flashes a smile. "I guess it's lucky for me that the guys you know don't either."

My face feels hot as his implication sinks in. "You think?"

"I know. Care to join me for a short hike after school?"

I look out the window at the end of the hallway. As usual, it's overcast and drizzly, not that the weather would faze me at all, but he's from a perpetually sunny state. "Sure, if you don't mind the rain."

He shakes his head. "If it doesn't bother you, then it won't bother me."

"Cool. Should I meet you in the lot after school?" I ask before adding, "Do you have a car?"

Raife nods, "Didn't you know all us Californians have cars?"

I laugh, "Oh yeah, I did hear something like that. I'll see you after school then."

We swap a brief goodbye and head into our respective classes. I take a seat but am unable to focus. My head is still swimming with my encounter with Raife and the prospect of spending time with him in the only place I feel like I can be myself. Beth is going to flip when I tell her at lunch. I look at the clock. It's a nonsensical action, as I know class hasn't even started, but I can't help it. It's going to be a very long day.

# CHAPTER 13

*What happened to the world I thought I knew?*

I meet up with Raife in the student lot at the end of the day. Of course, I had to beg Beth not to follow me so she could ogle him. She settled into a spot overlooking the lot and brought Shane with her. Those two were utterly incapable of not gushing over Raife when we met up at lunch. From the corner of my eye, I can see Beth and Shane watching, talking to each other as they observe my progress. I can only imagine what they're saying and want to roll my eyes.

Jogging the last few feet to Raife, I reach him, feeling a little breathless in anticipation of being alone in the woods together. I toss my head toward a cloudy sky that's on the verge of rain and ask, "Still up for hiking?"

He cocks an eyebrow. "Are you implying that Californians can't handle a little rain?"

"You saw rain in Southern California? And here I thought you'd probably stood in shock at the first Oregon drops that hit your head."

Raife laughs and reaches for my backpack, which I gracelessly sling off my shoulder and hand to him. Wow. Gentlemanly. Don't see many of his type around. "Well," he says gamely. "I did take some video when we moved here just to prove to my friends back home that it really does exist."

"So, you're a myth-buster too, then? Good to know."

He leads me to his car, some kind of electric hybrid I've never heard of. I have to keep my mouth from dropping open when he opens my door for me. How can this guy even be real? The boys I know wouldn't recognize chivalry if it bit them in the ass.

"Thanks," I tell him as I slide into the passenger seat. From my side-view mirror, I watch him walk to the trunk of the car. He's got a fine form, I admit, enjoying his loose-hipped walk in the low-slung black jeans he's wearing. My face flames as he shuts the trunk, and his eyes catch mine in the mirror. Crap. Now he knows I was checking him out. I'm such a dork. Being inconspicuous is obviously not in my skill set.

I'm too embarrassed to look at his face when he hops

in, so I fix my sight on the parking lot exit and point in the direction we'll be heading, "Make a left out of the lot, and we'll head west."

Raife is kind enough not to say anything about my gawking and pulls onto the main road. The engine's electric purr soothes my nerves, and as the minutes pass, I feel myself relax. It starts to rain, I knew it would, but it's only a light drizzle, typical Oregon. I give him a few directions and sit back, enjoying the novelty of heading for a hike with a guy I could seriously fall for.

We make small talk as the miles go by. About twenty minutes in, Beth texts me, begging for details. I send her a quick emoji and then text my mom to let her know I'm going out. I'm about to press send when it occurs to me that Raife is my only ride. This is one of the times when I wish my parents could afford to help me buy a car.

"Do you mind dropping me off at home after we hike?"

He glances at me with a grin. "I had planned on making you walk home, but I guess I could give you a lift."

I roll my eyes. "Such a gentleman." Still shaking my head and smiling, I send the text to my mom and put my phone in my pocket. "So, did you do a lot of hiking in San Diego?" I've never been that far south and imagine it to be a beach resort-like paradise.

"Honestly," Raife tells me. "There aren't a lot of open spaces anymore. I went inland a few times, but the heat gets to me, so it wasn't all that fun. It's kind of a desert down there, you know?"

"Really? I always thought it looked so beachy."

"A lot of people think that, but it's really only right along the coast that you've got the sand and palm trees, and most of those aren't even native to the area. A lot of the state is desert-like. Not cactus crazy or anything, just lots of drought-resistant shrubs and trees and stuff. It's pretty in its own way, but I prefer it here. I feel like I can breathe in this moss-infested paradise."

We both laugh. "How did you end up here? It seems like a big change from Cali."

"My dad got relocated for work, some big promotion. It was a little strange to move after the school year started, but I think it's going to be good."

I try not to analyze that statement, but I can't help my lips curving up at the thought that I might have something to do with that. "I'm glad you're here," I tell him before I can stop myself.

"Me too."

Eventually, we pull into the lot at the end of one of my favorite trailheads. The rain is just a mist now, perfect for hiking. I don't bother pulling up the hood of my jacket. The forest canopy will block anything anyway. Raife grabs a couple of water bottles from the trunk, and we head into the woods. The forest is quiet, our muffled footsteps and birdsong are the only sounds.

"It's insanely green here," Raife notes, his voice pitched low to match the solitude.

"Yeah. It's beautiful, isn't it?" It feels good to have

someone aside from Beth, whom I often have to drag along, see this place as I do.

"Breathtaking. Thanks for bringing me here, Terran."

I flash him a huge smile. "Anytime."

We walk side by side where the trail allows us and switch to single file when needed, with me taking the lead. Under the overhanging branches, we make small talk, sharing little details about our interests, trying to get to know each other. I'm happy to discover that we enjoy many of the same things, from Mexican food to 80s music.

When we reach a specific spot on the trail, I stop and sweep my arm forward, pointing out my favorite view-point. I want to see his face when he looks out at the ocean. I need to know if he loves it as much as I do. As Raife comes out of the line of trees, I'm not disappointed.

"Wow. This is amazing."

I feel a little thrill as he says it. It's like all of these small pieces are coming together so perfectly. "I come here a lot. It's kind of my special place."

"I can see why."

He walks to the edge of the cliff, taking in the beauty of the Pacific, and sits. I join him, sitting on the damp ground hip to hip. We don't say anything for a bit, content to enjoy the view. I feel a familiar peacefulness that always washes over me when I'm out here. Stress and anxiety leave my muscles, and I relish the sensation of a weight being lifted. It's in this moment of relaxation that a voice I both dread and long for reaches into me, eclipsing all thought in its powerful tenor.

*"You are mine. My chosen."*

I'm afraid to open my eyes. I don't want to see terrible things, not here. Not with him. I clench my lids shut, willing Gaia to leave me in peace, begging her, reaching toward her for the first time, in desperation.

I almost scream when I feel Raife's hand stroking my face. I can't look at him, though, too fearful of what visions might mask reality. I take deep breaths, talking to her. Pleading with her. I almost don't hear Raife when he makes a shocking confession.

"I hear her, too, Terran."

My eyes snap open. There's no horrible vision of a desiccated world, only Raife looking at me with a knowledge that is almost as frightening as the visions themselves. "W...What?"

"I hear her. Gaia. She speaks to me, and I hear her speaking to you."

I jump up, unable to contain myself. "Wait. What are you saying?"

He gets up, brushing off his jeans, and takes a deep breath before responding. "I mean, you're not the only one."

I start to pace in circles, trying to wrap my head around what he's saying. If he can hear her, then I can't pretend this is all some crazy stuff Silas concocted. And if it's true, then I'm in serious trouble. Anxiety begins to build. Okay, Terran. You were ready to meet with Silas and accept all of this before. Raife's comments don't really change anything. But I can't fully convince myself of that. This is too real now.

"Terran, it's okay. I freaked out when it started, too." I don't respond, and he makes a strangled noise in his throat. "Damn, I shouldn't have sprung it on you like that. I'm sorry. I just heard her and saw your face. I wanted to let you know you're not alone in this. Can you stop for a moment and look at me?"

He grasps my arms, anchoring me to the ground, and then uses his index finger to slowly lift my chin until my eyes meet his. "It's okay. I'm still the same guy you were talking to five minutes ago."

"I've fought this...this connection. There've been terrible visions, awful things she's shown me. I didn't know what they were at first, and then when I met with someone last weekend, he told me this unbelievable story and I..." I shake my head, not sure how to continue.

"You felt the truth of it but didn't want to accept it."

Catching my bottom lip between my teeth, I look at him, this beautiful boy who is suddenly so much more than I could have imagined. "That's exactly how I felt."

Raife runs his thumb along my lower lip. "I went that way too."

"How did you face it? I mean. Who told you?" After I ask, I begin to wonder if he's heard the stories Silas told me about the Daoine Fíor, and their connection to Gaia.

"It started about a year ago for me. I thought I was going crazy," he says, shaking his head at the memories. "Finally, I met this guy who said he knew of someone who could help. I admit that I was a total skeptic, but after a couple of sessions, it all became clear."

Suspicion blooms as he talks. Could this person possibly be Silas or someone like him? I can't stop myself from asking. "What was his name? This guy who helped you."

"Silas."

It feels like I'm about to have a total panic attack. "Silas?" I demand, my voice rising in panic. Raife nods. "But Silas lives here. I mean, I met him last weekend, and he lives here, has for years, according to the story he spun when we met. How could you have met him?"

What the hell is going on? How would Raife have talked to Silas when he just moved here? Unless Silas travels or something, finding people like us. Wait. Didn't Celeste say that Silas was out of town this week? Oh, my God. How many of us are there?

I sit down with a thump, not caring if I plant myself in a patch of mud or whatever. I stretch my legs out, too overwhelmed to care about anything but what's spinning through my head. This is insane. What kind of world do I live in?

"Terran?" Raife calls softly. "Hey, I know it's a lot to take in, but we're meant to be together. You're why I'm here."

"Excuse me?"

"I moved here for you. Silas told me I needed to come."

My face freezes in shock. What? He moved here for *me?* "But, you said your dad got a promotion, and that's why you moved. Did you lie to me?"

"No," he assures me, squatting in front of me so he can look me in the eye. "My dad did get a promotion, and his company moved us up here. Honestly, though, I've wondered if Silas didn't have something to do with it. It was shortly after Silas told me about you that my dad got the job news. I've always thought it's too much of a coincidence."

"Okay. This is a lot to take in right now." I rub my hands on my jeans while my brain ping-pongs from revelation to revelation. Raife sits quietly, giving me some time and space to work this out in my head.

I sift through my memories of everything Silas told me, all that crazy stuff about who he is and what he thinks I am. If that's true, then Raife is part of his mystical story too. "Are you adopted?"

"Huh?"

"Are you adopted?"

He gives me an odd look before answering. "Yeah. Why?"

"So am I. I think...all that stuff Silas told me, things too crazy to be considered by any sane person, is true. We're not really human, are we?"

"No. I think we're something more. I feel kind of

stupid for not connecting the whole adoption thing, but it makes sense. I wonder how that even worked, you know?"

"I bet it wasn't so hard. People give up babies all the time, and my adoption was a simple abandonment, not a drawn-out thing with birth parents and all." I stare off into the horizon for a bit, just watching the waves roll in. "You said you heard her, right?"

"Yeah."

Looking at his face, I ask, "Do you talk to her too?"

Raife dips his head before looking back at me. "Sometimes. Do you?"

I shrug. "Does she talk back?"

"No."

It's strange to feel relief at his answer, but it calms me a bit. If he had some open line of communication with what amounts to a goddess, then I don't know if I could really go through with opening my mind. But if all it would do is make her voice clearer in my head, and I wouldn't be stuck looking like I'm some kind of psycho having conversations with myself, then I think I can do this. Of course, that still leaves the visions. "Did you ever see visions, like terrible things?"

Raife fiddles with a small rock while he considers my question. "When it started, I'd be anywhere, home or at a store or whatever, and suddenly the world, as I saw it, would just change and become something horrible. It was so real. I could feel it and smell it. I thought I was going crazy. There was no one I could tell, though. My parents would've had me committed, and my friends were never really close enough to be people I would share something like that with. I didn't have a Beth."

I couldn't imagine having no one to talk to. I'd be so lost, maybe even on some serious meds by now. "That must have been awful."

He bites his lip. "Yeah. The day Enzo found me, I had had enough." My mind sparks for a moment at the mention of Enzo's name, but it makes sense if he met Silas, and I don't have time to dwell on it, too startled by what Raife says next. "You know, that guy talked me off a ledge, literally. I owe him, and Silas, a lot."

It's horrifying to think of Raife having been driven to such an extreme that he'd actually considered killing himself. I wonder if I would've ended up like that without Beth. Probably would have, I'm just not that strong of a person. "That must have been awful for you. I doubt I would've been any better off without Beth. She and her mom are the people who have kept me sane in all of this. But...I haven't told them everything."

Raife's eyebrow shoots up. "Oh? What didn't you tell them?"

I fold my hands in my lap. It's hard to explain. They are such good people, and I trust Beth completely. "I didn't tell them about what Silas thinks he is, about what he thinks I am, well, we are."

His head tilts as he considers that. "Why not?"

"I don't know," I mutter. "It's not like they wouldn't

believe me or understand. Celeste would buy into it completely. Beth would take some convincing, but she'd come around. I guess I just couldn't tell them."

"You mean you wanted to keep it to yourself or something?"

"No. I couldn't tell. It's like there is some force or uncontrollable compulsion that keeps me from it." I look at his expression. He probably thinks I'm nuts. "I sound like I've got a few screws loose, right?"

Raife laughs. "Only a couple, but I can handle it."

I reach out to punch him in the shoulder, and his arms snake out, wrapping around me and not letting me go. "You're not alone in this, Terran. And, finally, neither am I."

I nod against his chest and let my body relax into his grip. "I wish you could see Silas with me."

Raife pulls away. "I'll take you. When did you want to go?"

I laugh at his enthusiasm. "Actually, it would be kind of weird if you went with me. Celeste made the appointment for this Saturday, and the three of us are driving over. I need the support, and just having them in the next room will help me go through with it."

"Go through with what?"

"Silas wants me to open my mind to her, to Gaia. I wasn't ready for that when I saw him the first time, but now? I can't go on like this, with her pummeling my brain with awful things." I give him a shaky smile. "Plus, if you did it and you're okay, then that gives me hope."

He surprises me when he says, "You know, you're pretty lucky."

"How so?"

"Aside from the whole confidant and support system thing you've got going on, at least Silas gave you a choice."

I'm taken aback by what he's implying. "You mean Silas forced you?"

Raife shakes his head. "Nothing so dramatic. He just didn't specifically ask me if I wanted him to, shall we say, clear an open pathway to an angry entity. But I can't really blame him. I wasn't in the best mental shape when I saw him."

I mull that over. I suppose it would've seemed like the right thing to do if I were in Silas's shoes. But it still feels rather heartless. "Did it get better after that? I mean, the visions and stuff?"

"It wasn't a magical portal that suddenly changed my life or anything, but things did change. It's hard to explain. After that meeting with Silas, the world just didn't look the same anymore."

I'm a little nervous about delving into what he's saying, but I need to know. "What do you mean?"

He pauses for a moment. "You know how you feel when you're out here? That connection or rightness?" I nod, and he continues. "It's kind of like that. Wherever I am, I see things and feel things differently."

"I don't understand."

Raife takes a deep breath, and I wonder if he's choosing his words carefully, not wanting to scare me off or anything. "When I'm in a place with a lot of people, I see and feel a sickness, *her* sickness. It's like my connection to Gaia somehow makes me feel what she's feeling. With that awareness, or whatever you want to call it, I see the world around me differently, almost like there's this dirty filter over all of it. I can see the waste and feel the indifference. But when I come to a place like this," he says, casting his eyes to the horizon. "I feel clean and at peace."

What he said doesn't scare me. I feel the same way, actually. Being in crowds or in the city has always made me feel out of place, almost claustrophobic. It's a relief to hear him say that things didn't go nuts when his connection deepened. I was so afraid that everything would escalate, and I'd be having crazy hallucinations all the time. "I think I understand what you mean. Thank you for telling me. It makes me feel a little better about taking this step."

Raife traces a finger along my hairline. "I don't know where any of this is going to lead us, but I'm glad I found you."

"Me too."

# CHAPTER 14

*She waits for me*

Raife's integration into our small social circle is rather seamless. Beth is positively glowing, which I can detect even over the phone when I call her after Raife and I go hiking. I keep my comments in the safe zone, though. Raife and I don't talk about the earth-shattering stuff with anyone. It's just us, and Silas, I guess. Shane feigns a pout when it becomes clear that Raife is into me, but I see his sly smile and wink of approval as we sit in the cafeteria the next day. So, aside from the whole 'not quite human' thing, the remainder of the week flies by, and then Friday evening is staring me in the face.

Raife offers to drive me home from school, since Beth is needed for an errand with Celeste. I don't put up any protest, more than happy to be alone with him. Instead of heading straight to my house, I show Raife the way to the Skook Illahee Preserve in my neighborhood. I want to share my special place with him and take him to where the raven was perched when all of this really began.

"Pull in right there," I tell him, indicating a part of a curb at the head of the residential trailhead.

Raife parks, and we hop out. It's not rainy for a change, though the air still feels heavy with the promise of it. "Want your jacket?" He asks, holding it up.

"Nah. I'm good with my hoodie."

He closes the car door, and we enter the trail side by side. As always, I feel it when I cross the border and head into the forest. It's an odd sensation, but I've grown so used to it that it's become comforting. Very little light filters through the trees today, making it seem later than it is, as we trek among the undergrowth.

"I bet you come here a lot," I hear him say.

"Yeah. It's nice to have this place so close to home. I've walked these trails a thousand times, but every time I come here, I see something new. This place changes, from season to season and minute to minute. I guess that's one thing I really love about it. The unpredictability."

"Thanks for bringing me here."

Smiling at Raife, I take his hand, anticipating the familiar thrum as our fingers touch. "Do you feel that?"

He looks at our interwoven hands. "I felt it the first time I touched you. I feel it now." His grip squeezes mine, slightly amplifying the sensations.

Looking down at the source of these oddly pleasant feelings, I ask, "I wonder what it means."

"That we're meant to be together."

"I like the sound of that," I reply, giving Raife my most winning smile.

The forest envelops us as I lead him to my favorite spot. Raife chuckles when he sees it. "Well, that's convenient. A rock bench for two."

I drag him over, and we scoot onto the flat-topped boulder. I burrow into his side for warmth, and he rewards me by slinging his arm around my shoulders and pulling me close. Sitting in silence, we listen to the sounds of a world brimming with life, both seen and unseen.

After a few minutes, his voice breaks the stillness. "I can see why you like it here. If I had had a spot like this back home, I would've come every day, just to get away from everything."

I smile and decide to share something I don't talk about with anyone. "This is going to sound really weird, but, then again, I think we're living a life of weirdness right now. When I walk into the woods here, I feel like I pass through some kind of border, as if there's this boundary that I walk over when my feet cross an invisible line at the start of the trail."

"I felt it too."

"Really?" I'm surprised and overjoyed that I haven't imagined it all these years.

"Just after we got out of the car and stepped into the line of trees, right? Where is that wooden post with the 'leave only footprints' sign on it?"

I nod. "I suppose this means I'm not crazy. I've sensed it for years, but anytime Beth joined me on a walk, she never showed any indication that she sensed something."

"Well, I'm not going to make such a bold statement and say that you're not crazy. For all I know, you're completely insane. But, I will admit to feeling it."

"Ass," I tell him, shoving my body into his while he laughs at my pathetic effort to knock him off the rock.

"Of course, I'm not sure what it says about my own sanity to be willingly hanging out with you." Raife laughs at the face I make and adds, "I'd clearly rather be stuck in the woods with a loony."

"Well, you know what they say about birds of a feather," I reply, giving him my best impersonation of a Cheshire cat's grin.

The moments of levity feel good. Things have been so bizarre lately, and I long for some normalcy. But considering where I'm going and whom I see tomorrow, that's not a likely outcome any time soon.

"You know, the last time I came here, I saw a raven. I could've sworn he was watching me. I even think he was trying to talk to me. He sat on that branch over there," I tell him, indicating the tree where the raven had perched.

Raife looks at the spot I'm pointing to and asks an odd question. "Was that the only time you saw it?"

"Um, actually, no. I think it was following me when I left Silas. Why? Have you seen a raven too?"

"Back home, I used to see one which was odd in itself since they're not that common in urban areas where I lived." Raife's eyes scan the woods as if hoping to catch a glimpse of my strange, feathered friend. "I would rarely see it for more than a few moments, though, which often made me think I imagined it. There were a lot of crazy things I saw in the early days, but part of me knew it was there somewhere. I don't see it anymore, though. Not since I met with Silas and made a connection."

I think about what that could mean. After talking to Celeste last weekend, I read that ravens are somehow bringers of prophecy and insight, death as well, actually, but I choose not to dwell on the latter connotation. If Gaia is real, could she be watching through a raven? Could the bird be here right now, hidden among the trees, listening to every word and carrying that information to her? It's foolishness, for sure, but I can't help but wonder.

Raife interrupts my thoughts. "What do you plan on doing tomorrow when you meet with Silas?"

I sigh, unhappy with the options I face and reluctant to give in to the only one that seems to make sense in a world that has suddenly become a stranger. "I guess I let him tap into my mind and open it, though I have to tell you that I'm really nervous about doing that. What if everything gets worse?"

He nods. "I hear you; I had the same thoughts. But when Silas did it, I felt like I suddenly *saw* for the first time."

*See*. Those are the words that have pounded through my head as visions tore into my skull. To hear Raife say that he finally *saw* should put me at ease, but it has the opposite effect. There are things I don't want to see. Things that have been forced into my brain like a violation, and I can't pull them out and forget. It terrifies me to imagine being unable to stop an increased assault on my senses, to bridge this chasm between me and a being I have yet to fully accept. Is she truly good? How would I even know? How could anyone know? Even Silas.

"Did things get worse? I mean, the visions," I ask.

He considers that for a moment. "Not worse, just clearer, more visceral. But I also had more control over how I reacted to it. It was like I shut it off rather than being completely overrun by hallucinations."

This makes me feel better, like I've made the right choice. I close my eyes and try to listen, straining to hear her if she's there.

*Gaia*. I think, honing my thought like an arrow. I imagine it piercing the earth and into her, pulling at her awareness. Keeping my body still, I wait. Seconds pass. I hear the rustling of the leaves and Raife's soft breathing, but of Gaia? Nothing.

"I don't hear her when I call," I say, turning toward Raife.

He gives me a look of understanding. "You will. Once Silas makes the connection, you can speak to her, and she will listen. You'll feel her read your thoughts. It's hard to explain, but I know she hears me, understands."

"What does she say back?"

"Honestly, she doesn't respond, not in words anyway."

I bunch my lips. What's the point of talking to her, of opening this portal, if she's just going to ignore me? "It sounds rather one-sided."

Raife laughs. "She is Earth, Terran. Gaia is all things. It would be a bit arrogant to assume she would respond to every thought we send her."

"I guess. I just...I don't know. This is all so unbelievable, I mean, being here is surreal. I can't even wrap my head around the fact that I'm having this conversation with you or even considering some idiotic plan to talk to a deity. It's absurd, Raife."

"Trust me when I say you need to do this. She is calling to you, and you cannot keep her will at bay for much longer."

"You sound like Silas," I mutter. "I know you're right. Celeste has been saying the same thing, too. I'm stubborn, that's all."

"You're you, and I wouldn't have it any other way."

He pulls me into his chest, and I let out a long breath, feeling the tension ease out of me. I can do this, and once I have, perhaps Raife and I will become closer as well. All life is around us. I feel it as I always have. Somewhere, deep within the bowels of the earth, she waits for me. Tomorrow, I will come to her.

---

I borrowed my mom's car and drove to Beth's house in the morning. The sun is peeking through the clouds, trying to illuminate the perpetually overcast sky. I take it as a good sign. Parking on the street, I hop out and jog to Beth's front door, trying to put some pep in my step, though I feel more apprehension than anything else.

Beth is waiting for me and opens the door before I have a chance to knock. "Hey, Terran. Come on in. Mom made some cocoa to give you strength."

"I could use a dose of sugar right about now," I tell her, closing the door behind me and heading to the kitchen.

Celeste greets me warmly, handing me a warm mug while giving me a peck on the cheek. "Hi, sweetie."

"Hey, Celeste. Thanks for the cocoa. I needed this," I tell her. It smells like real chocolate as I bring it to my lips. I cock an eyebrow at Beth as she watches me take a sip. "*Real* chocolate?"

Beth laughs and looks at her mom. "Told ya she'd appreciate the good stuff."

Celeste just shakes her head. "You girls are processed food junkies."

"All that stuff is good for us, Mom. The chemicals are really preserving us rather than the food, you know. We're going to live forever."

"Very funny, Beth," Celeste replies, giving her daughter a light swat. She turns her attention to me. "Terran, would you like to drive, or would you prefer me taking you?"

I think it over. My mom doesn't need her car today, and my original plan was to drive all of us. Now that I think about what I'm going to be doing, I wonder if I should be in charge of what equates to a killing machine. "If you don't mind driving, I think it would be best if you took me."

"I don't mind at all. Finish your cocoa, and we'll head out in about ten minutes, okay?"

"Thanks, Celeste," I tell her, watching as she sweeps out of the room, giving Beth and I some privacy.

We sit in silence for a few moments, just enjoying the infusion of refined sugar and processed chocolate. I was up late thinking about my conversation with Raife and the decision I made to go through with this. There are so many unknowns, so many unbelievable pieces to this enigma I find myself wrapped up in. I feel anxiety begin to build. Beth must sense it because she reaches over and squeezes my hand. I take a deep breath. It's comforting to have her here, though I wish Raife were with us too.

"You don't have to do this if you're having doubts," Beth tells me.

"I know. But I need to, and I want to. Raife and I talked about it yesterday, and while I'm still nervous, I think Silas and your mom are right. Maybe this will help."

I can see the concern, and something else, in Beth's face when she asks, "You told Raife?"

"Um. Yeah," I say, though it feels awkward to admit that I'm sharing things with some guy I hardly know. It is weird, but that's my new normal. "He's easy to talk to," I finish lamely.

Beth frowns a little. "Okay. Well, I'm glad he's a good listener." She gives me a quick side hug. "And I think it will help to talk to Silas. Besides, you can always look at it this way: you get to be in the same room as the most gorgeous man we've ever seen."

"Good point. I can't argue with that logic." We laugh for a few moments, and the action removes the last of my reservations.

Celeste comes down as we finish our hot chocolate. "Ready?"

Taking a deep breath, I turn to her with a big smile and say, "As I'll ever be."

The three of us pile into the car and head into the unknown.

# CHAPTER 15

*I am a daughter once again*

Enzo greets us at the door when we arrive. His impeccably groomed face and form sweep aside, inviting us into the same waiting room as before. Celeste sinks into the upholstered sofa, crossing her ankles and leaning back into the luxuriant softness, as Beth and I take the two chairs opposite her. Having expected us, Enzo returns to the room after getting us situated, bearing a tray filled with pastries and a full tea service.

Beth and I lean forward, barely able to keep from licking our lips as we eye a small plate of gourmet mini-donuts.

"Thank you, Enzo," Celeste offers on behalf of all of us.

"You are very welcome, ladies. Terran," he says, looking my way. "Silas will be with you in a few minutes. Please enjoy your repast and let me know if you need anything."

I smile shyly. "Thank you."

Luckily, there are two of each type of donut, leaving Beth and me free from having to fight over the delicious concoctions. I take a bite into a red velvet creation that is so good I have to stifle a moan of pleasure. I look over at Beth and see the same blissful expression. When Celeste snatches one of the chocolate-covered donuts right out of Beth's hand, I have to cover my mouth, so I don't spray my food all over her in a burst of laughter.

"Mom!" Beth yells, trying to grab her mom's hand before she can stuff the last bite in her mouth.

"What?" Celeste replies. "I'm just saving you from eating too much processed sugar."

I finally manage to swallow and double over in laughter. Beth looks at me in outrage before the giggles set in. Soon, my stomach hurts, and my eyes water. Beth's face has turned red, and that just makes it more comical. Even Celeste has joined in, having been caught up in the contagion of the moment.

That's how Silas finds me, doubled over, holding my sides in an uncontrollable fit of giggles. I don't know how long he stands in the doorway before we finally notice him, but when my attention shifts to his still figure, I almost gasp in appreciation of his perfection. It hits me like a wave, though I know I should've been more prepared. It's not like he would've gotten plainer in the time it's been since I saw him last. But to my eyes, he looks even more handsome, truly fantasy-worthy. I can't help the image of Chris Hemsworth drifting through my mind. There are just too many similarities to my favorite superhero. I can practically see electricity crackling from his fingertips.

While it seems impossible, the smile that splits his face literally takes my breath away. How can any living thing be this incredibly good-looking? As I sit there like an infatuated preteen, it finally registers that the room has gone silent. I can't pull my eyes away from Silas, but I imagine that Beth and Celeste are just as awestruck.

I can't help leaning over, whispering to Beth, "He looks like Thor."

She turns her head just a bit and replies, "I'd like to see him wield his hammer."

I go beet red in less than two seconds and have to suck in the guffaw that croaks up my throat and end up pretending to cough. Beth snickers softly.

Matching the perfection of his face comes a voice that curls around me, making my insides feel hot. "Good morning, ladies. I apologize for keeping you waiting."

Beth and I are obviously tongue-tied and sit there gawking at him. Celeste saves us from embarrassment.

"We only arrived a few minutes ago and have enjoyed your wonderful hospitality."

"Excellent," he replies, taking in our plates littered with crumbs and cups of tea. "Terran, would you like to get started?"

I swallow hard, my mouth having gone a bit dry as I'm reminded of why we're here. I stand up, irritated at the slight tremor in my legs, and straighten, putting on a brave face. "Yes. I'm ready."

I glance back at Beth, who gives me a questioning look, one that asks if I would like her to join me. I offer a small shake of my head and follow Silas out of the room.

As we walk through the short maze of hallways, Silas turns to me. "I'm glad to see you again, Terran."

"Thank you," I say lamely, not sure how to reply.

He gives me a small smile. All too soon, we come to that amazing door that leads to a room in which I will face a future I'm not sure I'm ready to accept. I breathe deeply as I walk across the threshold and head to a chair. Behind me, I can hear the soft click of the door. I try not to imagine that it sounds foreboding, but the thought is there. I focus on the textures of the luxurious fabric I sit on, working to calm my nerves.

Silas sits down and reaches over, taking my cold hand. I feel that current again, a strange vibration that begins at my fingertips before making its way up my arm. It feels like that when Raife touches me too. It is when that thought passes through my head that everything seems to click into place.

"I met someone who knows you," I tell him, looking closely to gauge his reaction.

"Yes, I know." Silas' eyes crinkle. "Did Raife help you make up your mind?"

I nod. "He told me about how you found him and helped him deal with all of this. He said that after he met with you, things were different, better."

"I'm glad. Raife was a lost soul when I found him, plagued by the same visions you have experienced."

"Yeah. He mentioned that. He also told me that he was meant to find me. Is that true?"

Silas leans back, breaking our connection. "Yes. Each of us has a mate, one we are destined to find to make us whole and continue our line with a single offspring. Raife is yours. He needed to find you, and I just simply pointed the way."

I take a few moments to let that sink in. Someone who is predestined to be with me is an odd concept, to say the least. But then, all of this is so far into the realm of weird that I shouldn't balk at this new development. Plus, I have to admit that when Raife and I are together, I feel whole. "I'm glad you found him."

"I'm sure he's just as happy," Silas chuckles. "Did Raife tell you about his own experience?"

"A little. He said it's hard to explain how things

changed for him, but that he felt different and more connected. He said he speaks to her, and she listens."

"Raife is right. Gaia listens to her children, and though she may not respond, she takes in your thoughts and emotions, and they become part of her, just as she is part of you. That is a piece of the connection I want you to have."

I wonder what he means by this being only a part of the connection. "What's the other piece?"

"Do you recall me telling you about our histories?"

"Yes."

"As the Daoine Fíor, we are imbued with her essence, and during times throughout mankind's history, we have taken in Gaia's power to bring back balance. You and Raife, while not pureblood, are her children. You are among the chosen and will have that power too."

I consider what he means, and as I think it over, the image of the sea turtle strangling in an old fishing line, gasping for breath, floats through my brain. I understand Gaia's purpose. If she is the earth, what must she feel as we thoughtlessly abuse it?

"I'm ready."

Silas stands up, and I watch him take a couple of steps toward me, then kneel down until he's on his knees, chest brushing against me, causing that same current to thrum in entirely different places. I watch warily, trying to keep myself from pulling away, as he reaches out and enfolds my head in his hands, thumbs pressed to my temples. My heart is racing at the contact and the knowledge that what I am about to do could have unfathomable consequences. I feel the pads of Silas' thumbs begin to press on my temples, tapping into pressure points that I can feel across my scalp. He closes his eyes and lowers his head. I watch, mesmerized as he begins to murmur under his breath, words with a cadence and meaning that I cannot interpret. The movement of his lips and the sound of his voice mesmerize me. The words seep into my mind like tentacles. I imagine my brain flashing in recognition of something elemental.

As the seconds pass, my mind grows fuzzy. My sight starts to dim as though my eyes are closing, though they are still fixed on Silas' perfect face. It is like a shadow passes before me, eclipsing my vision. And then I see it, a tiny flicker of light behind my eyelids. When did I close my eyes? I want to shake my head, but I can't move, can't open the heavy lids. A flare of warning bubbles up, but it goes just as quickly as it came. The pinpoint of light grows, splitting into two distinct forms. As I sit, immobile, I realize that the glowing forms are not light, though they illuminate the darkness. Rather, they are eyes, her eyes, looking into me, glowing with ancient knowledge and awareness. I can feel my mind open, an eerie sensation like strange wakefulness flooding my senses until all thought it utterly eclipsed by Gaia. Golden orbs see into me, pouring over every thought and feeling, pulling them out and taking them in, before a wave of consciousness crashes over me.

I feel my body gasp, but it's almost like a separate entity, as though I am somehow outside of myself. A new awareness slowly builds, an intangible thing at first. It is not she, exactly, and yet it is. She is everything, but she is separate. Within my mind, I can feel the thrum of the earth, a strange heartbeat moving through my veins. It is a part of me now. I sense it. Beyond that sensation is sickness, like a muddy haze. I feel it in my gut. It's nauseating, coating my mind and mouth with a strange infection. I can feel saliva building up as my stomach roils. I'm going to vomit.

My eyes pop open, and I hunch over to purge myself into a basin that is suddenly resting in my lap. The heaving of my stomach seems to go on forever, muscles clenching to rid myself of something noxious. My throat burns with acid, jaw locked open as wave after wave chokes out of me. By the time it passes, my face is coated in sweat, and my whole body is shaking. I feel Silas wipe a damp cloth slowly over my forehead and cheeks. The coolness feels good.

I take a few shuddering breaths, focusing on my body as I gauge whether or not another round of sickness is going to come pouring out of me. My insides feel hot. I manage to lean back in the chair, letting my shoulders slump. I feel Silas taking the basin away. I don't want to see it, so I close my eyes and focus on calming my racing heart and queasy stomach. Beyond my closed lids, I hear Silas opening and closing the door and assume he's taking care of my mess. It occurs to me that I should feel embarrassed, but I can't hold onto that thought for more than a moment. Before long, he returns, the rustle of his clothing and creak of the chair indicating that he's sitting down.

When my body finally settles, I feel a fluttering in my head, and then I hear her. *"Daughter. You are mine."* And I am. I am hers now.

# CHAPTER 16

*There are more questions*
*than answers*

"Open your eyes, Terran," I hear Silas tell me. With some reluctance, I stop squeezing them shut and glance at him. He looks different. It's subtle, but I notice a soft glow around him, like some inner light, is pouring through his skin to create a hazy luminance. I open my mouth, swallowing around a film of bile before I remark on it. "You're glowing."

Silas laughs softly. "Yes, that can be one of the side effects of your connection to Gaia, a beneficial tool actually. All of the true people, and those like you, will appear this way. You see it so clearly because her energy is newly infused with your body. Over time, the appearance will dim, still there but more imperceptible. It makes it easier to find each other."

I mull that over as I look at him. The soft radiance that surrounds his form isn't distracting. It's too faint to overpower anything. I wonder if Raife will look this way at me now. In fact, do I look that way?

"When you look at me, do I have it?"

Silas smiles. "Yes. Though yours is a softer hue than one of my kind, more of an understated pink."

"Hm. And Raife?"

"He has it too, much like yours, and when you look at him, you'll see it, just as he has always seen it when he looks at you."

Interesting. So, even though I hadn't opened myself to Gaia, he could see that I was different, that I was like him. I wonder if there's some reason for that, on a purely animalistic level. Looking down at my body, this thing that now feels strange and different, I recall what Raife said about speaking to her, to Gaia. I decide to test it out and send her a message, a silent communication through my mind.

*'Mother'*

I feel it when she hears me, like a pull or a sponge, as though she soaks it in. There is no response, at least not directly, but there is an impression of intense feelings that swarm over me with warmth. That must be what Raife spoke of when he tried to explain that she heard him but didn't respond. My eyes must be glowing as I look at Silas. His expression as he stares back at me is so fatherly, so proud. I have entered the fold, a lost lamb found and brought to the light.

"She hears me," I tell Silas with awe.

"Yes, and she feels your emotions just as you feel hers."

And I do. I can sense a motherly love that wasn't there before. As I soak it in, I begin to feel something else, something darker, angry. I chase the feeling to its source and find a burning resentment, like a molten core in Gaia's heart. There is such rage that I shy away from it, afraid of the power that I sense within those emotions that swirl like a menacing mass.

Silas watches me, and I get the impression that he can read my thoughts. This suspicion intensifies when he says, "You feel her anger, don't you?"

"Yes."

"She has much to be angry about. Man is destroying his mother, and she has awakened. Through you, and others like you, she will restore balance."

"I don't understand. What would I even be able to do? People won't listen to me. Adults completely disregard teenagers. They listen to us with amusement but never sincerity."

"Gaia doesn't want you to speak for her with words, Terran."

"I don't understand. How will I be able to bring any kind of balance, to convince people to see the changes they must make before everything is destroyed?"

Silas leans forward. "Think about what you felt when you were overcome with sickness. What did you sense that brought it on?"

"I thought that was her," I say softly.

"It was, but not in the way you're thinking. What did you feel?"

I don't want to remember what I felt before I vomited. I still sense it, though it's not overwhelming as it was before. Instead, it's on the periphery, fluttering on the edge of my senses, and if I focus on it, it'll consume me.

"I don't want to think about that," I gulp, swallowing down the gorge that is threatening to surface.

Silas seems amused by my reaction. "I don't blame you. But now you understand some of what she feels. That is part of your connection. You feel the earth's sickness because you are part of her."

I grimace. Great. Feeling queasy is just awesome. "Are you saying that I'm going to want to puke my guts out all the time?"

He shakes his head. "No. You'll learn how to cope with that, and soon it'll only be a mild unease that comes over you from time to time. You have to understand that your connection to Gaia means many things. One of those is that you can feel and smell the earth's sickness. It is this ability that will aid you when you are called upon. At times, it may overwhelm you, bringing about waves of nausea, but that is not a typical experience. Just know that you are tied to the earth. She is your mother, and she has fallen ill under an onslaught of indifference and callousness."

Making a face, I turn away and stare at a small painting I never noticed before. As I look at it, I hone in on one of the figures in the foreground. Unable to stop myself, I stand up to get a better look. I'll be damned. That's Silas. Only this piece of art looks too old to be some relic of the past with his image. I turn toward him and raise an eyebrow in question.

"That's my father, though I do admit the resemblance is striking. I told you we age more slowly than humans," he informs me, rising from the chair to stand next to me. "That was done in Ireland in the early sixteenth century."

My mouth drops open. Is he serious? What kind of crazy world do I live in? "Are you saying that your kind is immortal?"

"No, but we can live for hundreds of years."

I look back at the painting. The textures are rich. I can see where the brush swept paint onto the canvas in elaborate swirls and sweeps, capturing that moment in time. "Am I going to be like that? Living so long?"

Silas takes my hand and leads me back to the chair, gently pushing me down and sitting across from me again. "Once the chosen have opened themselves to Gaia, their very being changes, on a genetic level. Of course, your genetics have always been different, but this acceptance of her brings about a greater shift, accelerating those traits that have been lying dormant. While you will not live the span of hundreds of human lives, you will live well beyond your expected lifetime. Many, like you, have lived well into their late hundreds."

Wow. I have a hard time wrapping my head around that little tidbit. "What's the point of living so long?"

"I don't believe there's any specific purpose to it. It's just a side effect. Of course, the longer you live, the more you can do in her name. So, perhaps this is the point."

Living to the ripe, old age of one hundred fifty sounds crazy. That would mean that I would outlive all of my friends. And what if I ever had kids? Would they automatically be like me, or would they be human? Would I outlive them, too? It is too much to take in, so I shut away those thoughts and focus on what this new connection means in the present.

"What is it that Gaia wants from me? Is she going to show me more awful visions?" I want to physically shudder as images from the mental assault I had at school fill my mind.

Silas leans into his chair, lifting his right leg and resting his ankle on his knee. "I cannot say whether or not she will 'show' you things as she has done before. Each one of us has an individual relationship with Gaia, and none of our experiences is precisely the same. I know that for Raife, the visions tapered off and stopped. But for others? I can't say."

It's not the answer I want to hear, but I guess there's nothing I can do about it. "So, what does she want from me?"

I watch Silas considering what to say. After a few moments, he looks into me with a seriousness I haven't seen before. "You felt the sickness of the earth when you opened yourself to her. What is the root of that affliction?"

It's obvious what, or who, is at fault. Ever since I was a young girl, I've looked at the world around me with different eyes. I've seen the indifference and waste. On some level, I have always felt the imbalance. Now I wonder if it was *this* part of me all along. I think it must be. But it's hard to speak the words that condemn a species I am still part of. Silas waits, watching my inner struggle, until I slowly close my eyes, take a deep breath, and open them to him.

"Humans." It is that simple and that awful. Here is a species that has corrupted every facet of the world, forever altering the natural order. And for what? Because we were too busy to consider our actions? Because it was easier to pretend we didn't have any real impact? Or is it that we are too selfish to acknowledge the responsibility we have to every living thing and work to protect it? There are no easy answers. Sadly, some consequences are all too easy to see.

"Mankind has turned its back on its mother, Terran. It is time to restore balance."

Part of me doesn't want to ask, but I'm unable to stop myself. "How?"

Silas leans forward, fixing his gaze on me so that I am immobile. "Gaia has been calling on her children to prepare to fight for this world. Through her power, we will harness nature and unleash her wrath. We will show humanity the face of their true mother."

It's a frightening picture that he paints, though I can only wonder what it really means. My mind conjures memories of storms that I've seen plastered all over the news from time to time. Would it look like that? Would people continue to be blithely ignorant of the power that's behind it? Yes. Of course, they would. There is no way to tell a vast population some crazy story about a being so powerful it can bring forth storms and earthquakes, fires and tsunamis. No one would believe it, and I wouldn't blame them.

"Could people be killed?" I ask, recalling the aftermath of natural disasters.

"Well, that may be inevitable. The balance has tipped too far, and it is not sustainable," Silas says matter-of-factly.

"I can't kill people, Silas. That's just wrong," I tell him, as images of war spin through my mind. "Besides, I don't have powers like you."

He gives me a sly grin. "Not yet." Incredulity must be

stamped across my face because he barks out a laugh. "It is a latent power, Terran. I will teach you how to harness it, and when you are ready, to release it, showing humanity that Gaia can and will fight back if things do not change. Don't worry. You will not be some chaotic force slaughtering innocents."

This mollifies me somewhat. Just thinking about killing anyone is so far beyond anything I can imagine that it feels unreal. He can't honestly think I'm some weapon against humanity. I'm just a kid, a weird one, but still a kid. I'm all for making the world better, but not everyone is terrible. There are plenty of good people fighting to save the planet. Heck, I'm one of them! If I could somehow show people what they're doing is destroying them, then wouldn't they change?

My brain skips to the last thing he said, that bit about using powers I somehow have inside of me and controlling them rather than becoming something monstrous. I admit that this does sound pretty cool. Visions of X-Men parade through my thoughts, and I can't help a small grin. Maybe I could be like Storm, controlling the power of lightning or something equally awesome. Silas chuckles, making me think he can read my mind. My face is so easy to read.

But that moment of levity is brief. I can't help facing the realization of what all of this means, of what he admitted is a possible outcome. People could get hurt. People could die. Humanity doesn't always heed the lessons that it's faced with. If that happens, will this war that Silas is talking about encompass the entire world? How will it end?

My head is swimming, and I decide that I need time to think about everything that has been said and done. I love the world I live in, but I do feel so much anger at what people have done to taint it. It seems like most people are just too busy to care. So much of what we see and do revolves around our own tiny lives. Perhaps we need to be awakened ourselves. Maybe we deserve to be shown the consequences of our actions. But could I really be a part of that? I sigh, not sure where I stand, but appreciating both sides.

I stand up. "I need time to think all of this over, okay?"

Silas rises and holds out his hand, wrapping mine in a warm embrace. That odd current is still there, but it's different now, more potent. "How about we meet again next week?"

"Sounds good," I tell him, reluctantly pulling my hand away. I feel the absence the moment our physical connection is lost. I wonder how it will feel when Raife and I touch and kiss. A warmth spreads through my belly as I consider it. Turning slowly, I walk to the door. Before I turn the handle, I stop and look back at him.

"Silas?" He looks at me. "Raife and I are adopted." I see him nod. "Do you know who our parents are? Do they ever wonder about us?"

"Both of your mothers are Daoine Fíor, while your

fathers are human. As such, they could not raise you. Only pure Daoine Fíor can be raised with their parents. Half-breeds, like the two of you, are sent into the world, nurtured in obscurity."

"I see." But I don't. There are just more questions now. And I don't want to hear any more answers.

# CHAPTER 17

*It seems I've found a kindred spirit*

It's hard to keep secrets from Beth. Since we were young, we have always shared everything. Not being able to tell her the full truth of what happened behind Silas' door eats at me. But I have to let it. There are some things she can't know, some things that I can't say. The Daoine Fíor are a secret that has been kept for centuries, living among us but apart. Being connected to their strange society, no matter how distant the association, necessitates secrecy. It is not up to me to lift a veil from what she thought she knew, to what she could never have imagined. Instead, I accept that I must keep this secret. It's safer for her this way.

When we leave Silas', I turn Beth's attention to the things I can say, embellishing when possible to keep her from wondering if I'm hiding anything. I guess I do a good job because, by the time Celeste pulls into her driveway, they are both smiling. That hurts a little, but I don't focus on it. I don't like being cast as a deceiver, but it's the part I play.

I hop out after a round of thanks, hugs, and kisses and head to my mom's car that I left parked outside Beth's house. My shoulders slump as soon as I shut the door. The drive home is a bit of a blur as questions burst through my head like popcorn. Where is this all going to lead? What does Silas mean by me somehow creating storms and letting them loose on people? Would I really be strong enough to control that and keep from hurting anyone? I plop down on the front step and bury my head in my arms. This is too much for a seventeen-year-old kid to have to deal with. Maybe I'm just reading more into this than I need to and getting worked up for nothing. After all, he said, I'm some kind of half-breed, not a magical being that's been walking the earth for two hundred years. He can't seriously think I have crazy powers straight out of a science fiction movie.

Cawing rips through the quiet, and I see the raven perched in a tree across the street. I watch it swoop down and settle on a branch in my front yard, cocking its head as it looks me over. "Hey, Mr. Raven," I mumble. "Here to check on the loony?" He just stares at me. The wind picks up, and I stand, ready to go inside.

"See you later," I call out, trudging into the house. I feel him watching me long after I shut the door.

———

Raife and I decided to meet on Sunday afternoon. I'm both eager and nervous to be with him, to touch his skin and feel the connection. My hope is to talk about everything and, if I'm lucky, to get a better sense of how we move forward and what to expect. He's becoming the only person I can be candid with, the only one who also knows the secret.

The bluff overlooking the ocean is one I went to years ago. Since there are no hiking trails, I haven't been back until today. As I pull my mom's car into the small lot, I see Raife leaning against the hood of his car. He turns toward me as I park, and a smile lights up his face. It's infectious, and I return the look with a huge grin.

I walk over to him and tuck myself into his open arms. The moment our bodies touch, I feel it, a surge of energy that pulls at my core. "Wow. That's different." I mumble with my face pressed to his chest. I feel and hear his deep chuckle.

"I had a feeling it would be different after you saw Silas, but this is beyond what I imagined. You were meant to be here, in my arms."

Peace settles over me as his words sink in. Yes. Two pieces of a puzzle have slid into place, locking together. "I feel it too."

He rubs my back, resting his chin on top of my head. After a few minutes, I pull away but keep my arms at his waist. I'm not ready to break our connection. Raife looks into me, really looks, and I feel like he sees *her* reflected. That somehow, I am branded as one of Gaia's chosen. My suspicion is confirmed when he says, "I can feel her in you now. It's almost like she's looking back at me when I look into your eyes. It's kind of weird, actually. Is it like that for you?"

I gaze into him, willing myself to see beyond the surface. He waits patiently, holding my stare with complete openness. I want to see her within him, but I don't. I feel such a bond as we touch, and I know that things have changed since I opened myself to Gaia, but it's not there. *She's* not there.

In an attempt to brush it off, I tell him, "Maybe I'm too much of a newbie." His eyes widen a bit, and he looks unsure of himself. I press my palm flat to his chest. "I'm sure it's me. I mean, everything just happened yesterday, and I don't even understand what it all means. Silas asked me to come back next weekend, and I know I'll figure all of this out over time. You've had months to accept it and let it become part of who you are. For me, I still have so many questions."

Raife's shoulders relax. "Perhaps you're right. Now

that you mention it, I did meet with Silas a lot afterward. For all I know, I wouldn't have been able to sense anything in you if I were just starting out with all of this crazy shit."

I laugh, the sound laced with relief. While what I have told him seems reasonable, inside, I know that I'm lying. I won't see her reflected in him. A part of Gaia is there; otherwise, I wouldn't feel the way I do when I touch him, but whatever is in me is different. Even among freaks, I'm a bigger one.

Raife takes my arms and hauls me onto the hood of the car. I set my feet on the bumper and rest my head against his shoulder, keeping my eyes forward to gaze at the grayness of the ocean under a cloudy sky. He waits quietly as I sift through my thoughts, pulling up the questions that are foremost in my mind. At the heart of my struggle in all of this is how to feel about an imminent attack on humanity. I am pulled in both directions, seeing the issue from both sides and unable to clearly stand on either side. Being of two worlds means I have a stake in both sides. I am stuck somewhere in the middle and need a sounding board to help me through the uncertainty.

Raife's voice rumbles against me when he says, "I assume Silas explained things to you."

"Sort of," I mutter.

"What do you mean?"

Sighing, I tell him, "Well, he explained things a bit, but there are still a lot of questions, you know? I mean, what exactly could happen if Gaia shows people her true self. Silas was kind of callous about it all."

"How so?"

I look ahead, trying to find the right words. "I get the whole imbalance thing. It's undeniable, and I know that we're heading to the point of no return if things don't change. I feel it so strongly now. But when I asked if people could get killed, he was pretty unfeeling about that. He didn't outright say that people will die, but he sure didn't say they wouldn't."

Raife is quiet for a few moments. "I hear what you're saying, and I understand the struggle you're feeling. I went through it myself, but I also know that there's a cost for doing what's right. Think about all the things in history that brought good changes in really awful times. Someone always paid the price for that. When Silas had 'the talk' with me," he says with air quotes. "It was hard because I'm part of the problem, you know? I'm human too."

A gush of relief falls from me when I hear this. They say misery loves company, and while I don't want Raife to struggle, it's good to know he's coming from the same place. "That's exactly how I feel. I see both sides, and I have a hard time choosing which one to stand on. For me, it doesn't matter which side I choose. I'll lose something either way."

"I know."

"How did you do it, Raife? What gave you that push?"

He leans back on the hood of the car, resting his head on the windshield. I scoot back and relax onto his chest, listening to the beat of his heart and feeling that connection that I'm unable to pull myself away from. "I struggled for a while, even after meeting with Silas a couple of times. He had to go out of town before I'd really committed to anything. Looking back, I wonder if he was searching for others. Whatever it was, I had this chunk of time when I couldn't talk to anyone about what I was feeling or thinking. I didn't have a Beth in my life."

It's hard to look at him and imagine this incredibly attractive boy feeling isolated. In my social sphere, the good-looking ones are always snatched up by some clique and seem to effortlessly blend into the high school landscape. I do sometimes wonder what it's like to be popular, one of those people everyone wants in their circle of friends.

"That must have been hard," I tell him, though I can't really conceptualize it because I've never been alone. Beth has always been there. Thinking of her makes me, once again, feel a stab of guilt at keeping her separate from all of this.

"I wasn't some social pariah or anything, Terran. It's just that my group was made up of what I would call 'counterfeit friends,' people who were only there on the surface. So, I couldn't tell them about anything. It was isolating. But then something happened that changed everything."

I wait silently for him to explain.

"I'm sure you felt something when Silas did his whole Jedi mind-trick thing to open your mind." I nod, and he continues. "Well, that connection allows you to feel what she's feeling, and it can be pretty jarring, or so I found out. I was taking a walk, something I did a lot then, to clear my head and try to pull myself out of some pretty morose thoughts. A few blocks from my house was this open area, not like a park or anything. It was too wild for that. It was just this pocket of wilderness, California style, complete with scraggly shrubs and trees like oaks and ash. I think it must've been part of someone's property because developers never swallowed it up, at least, not until that day."

"It started in my gut, this churning that felt like acid bubbling in my stomach. I can remember stopping and leaning over, sure I was going to puke all over the sidewalk. It seemed to pass, so I kept walking. I was a few hundred feet away when it hit again, but this was unlike anything I had felt before. It was like a wave of...I don't know how to describe it. I felt like I could taste terror, pain, and death. The sensations brought me to my knees."

I hold his hand tightly, not quite sure when I grabbed it. "What was it?"

Raife takes a deep breath as though he can still feel that day. "They were destroying that wild place, huge bulldozers tearing through the earth, ripping trees from the ground, grinding any living thing unable to escape into the soil in a bloody mass. It was terrible, and I could feel it all." He looks at me, seeing my horror, recognizing that I, too, have felt pieces of it. "That was it. That day was the turning point. I am with *her*. Gaia is everything, and she is dying from what man has done. It has to stop, or there will be nothing left. We have to show humanity what it's doing before it's too late."

Listening to Raife, I can clearly see the event that pushed him to decide. It brings me back to that poor sea turtle and how I felt as it almost died in front of me. I still can't believe that it may have actually died, and I somehow brought it back. Things like that don't happen in real life.

I can only imagine how much stronger his feelings are now, especially when I think about how violently ill I felt when Silas performed his little magic trick on my brain. Feeling that kind of agony and fear must have been over-whelming to Raife. In his shoes, the decision to be part of something that could have catastrophic consequences was an easier choice to make. But I am not Raife. From everything he's told me about his life in California, it's like he was always apart from people, somehow never really connected to anyone. I don't feel that way, and it's this bond I have with people like Beth and Shane that makes it so much harder.

Perhaps I can remain somewhat in the middle, maybe be a voice for both sides? If what Silas implied is true and I just need to show people the error of their ways, then perhaps all of this is the best option. I feel like, if I really do have these powers, that I could make a demonstration, some display to show Gaia's anger, her pain. Something in the middle of a desert, or an ocean, far away from anywhere. Make sure nobody was hurt, but that everybody sees. Yes, I could do that. But would they listen? What if they didn't? What if people are sure to die? Can I be part of that for the greater good? I don't know. It's too soon and too much to handle right now. I need to let it go and just live in the moment. Gaia is within me now, and I need to try to understand who she is and why I was chosen. I need to know the role she expects me to play.

After a couple of minutes, I share my thoughts. "Thank you for telling me, Raife. I can picture what you went through, and it makes sense that when you saw and felt all that, you made your choice. It's what I would have done in your shoes."

"Are you saying that you think you're going to make a different choice?"

"I'm not sure." Raife's brows crease as he looks at me. "I'm not going to hurt people, Raife. That's not who I am, and I feel torn."

He gives me a small smile of understanding. "Yeah. I imagine you do, but can you really stand aside and let this go on until everything you know and love is destroyed? Things are going to happen, Terran, whether you are there or not."

His indifference to the idea of people getting hurt or

killed bothers me. It's so much like Silas. "I don't know how you can be so cold about hurting people," I snap.

He huffs. "I'm not."

"Yes, you are! You're saying that because things would get better, the cost doesn't really matter."

"What I'm saying is that if we don't do something, then there will be no future for any of us. She's dying, Terran. How can we ignore that? How can we turn our back on her?" He looks at me, and there is so much emotion there. "I don't want people to get hurt, truly I don't. But I can't live in a world that is killing itself and not fight to stop it. No one said you have to kill anyone. You just need to show them what they're doing, make them understand. You can do that, right?"

I look away, fuming a bit inside. He makes it sound so easy. Maybe I'm overthinking this. Am I getting all worked up over something that is going to end up being little more than a few storms scattered across the planet? And Raife is right. Something has to change, and I could be the catalyst.

"I don't know," I finally tell him.

I can sense that Raife has more to say, maybe even arguments to try to convince me. It's a relief when I sense him let those go, feeling his body relax as he settles in next to me. I shut my mind off, refusing to give this indecision any more thought. We spend an hour just talking softly and listening to the waves roll onto the shore.

# CHAPTER 18

*Bookstores are supposed to be*
*safe places*

The whispers start as I enter the school. Covert glances and muffled voices. My meltdown is making the rounds in the school gossip mill. Ugh. Raife squeezes my hand gently as we part, heading to our respective classes. It gets suspiciously quiet when I walk into English class. Great. Let the awkwardness begin.

I shuffle over to an open desk, keeping my eyes glued to the floor. I don't want to look up after setting my bag down and grabbing my binder, but I need to face it sooner or later. It may as well be now. Lifting my gaze, I scan the student body. Most of the kids are polite enough not to stare, and the majority of the ones who make eye contact show concern more than anything else. Of course, there are a couple who snicker and whisper. Jerk alert, I think, shaking my head before resuming my perusal of the room. One girl, I think her name is Janet, actually gets up, grabs all of her stuff, and sits next to me.

"Hey, Terran," she offers, brown, soulful eyes looking me over.

"Hi," I reply, though I'm too afraid to say her name in case I'm wrong.

I'm thankful when she saves me from embarrassment. "I'm Janet. I know we haven't talked much this year, but I just wanted to say I hope you're okay. I heard about what happened. Well, obviously, I heard."

She waits expectantly, and I look deeply into her, trying to sense any intent beyond simple care and curiosity. I feel nothing other than openness. "Thanks. I'm okay. I just wasn't feeling well last week, and I guess it kind of came over me in a rush. I don't even remember what I said or did." That's mostly true. The entire time that I watched the school and kids burn, I felt myself screaming, but I had no idea if I verbalized any of it. When the visions come, they are so real that it's like nothing else exists.

Janet gives me an encouraging smile and says, "I've had times like that, too."

I pause and look at her, really look. A thought pops into my head. Is she like me? I try to reach out with my senses, searching for that connection I feel with Raife and

Silas, but it's not there. Could she be one of us? I look at her and notice nothing unusual. I decide to probe a little and see if she tells me anything that would help. "Oh, yeah? What kinds of things have you gone through? Anything as embarrassing as my experience?"

She laughs. "Well, nothing quite like that, at least not yet. I've just been in situations that are so humiliating that I have a hard time getting over it. So, I know how you feel. It's not easy facing the crowd after something like that."

Janet doesn't offer any details, and I sense that she won't if I press, so I let it be. "It's nice to hear that someone understands." I'm about to say more when a substitute teacher walks in, calling the class to order before launching into a lecture about how she's not some spring chicken who's going to let a bunch of teenagers trick her into thinking they can slack off all period. I roll my eyes.

"Who let the crypt keeper out?" I whisper to Janet.

She barks out a laugh, earning a glare from the sub, before she covers her mouth, her body still shaking from contained laughter. I bite my lips to keep from smiling and get out a pencil.

It's a relief to make it to lunch without any incidents. Sure, there are more stares and whispers, but there have also been a few like Janet, caring people who just want to know if I'm okay. It's these people who get me through what could've been a grueling morning.

Beth waves me over to a table after I pick up a salad

and a cup of soup. "Hey, girl. How'd it go today? Was anyone a douche?"

"What do you think?"

She shakes her head. "There is one in every crowd is what I think. But, you'll be happy to know that the only people who asked me about you were just doing it because they care."

While that should make me feel good, it bothers me. It's like the car accident you can't help staring at as you drive by it. You've got to look. People have got to ask. They just can't let it be and move on. Not that I'm any different, far from it. I've just never had to be on the receiving end before. I don't like the feeling.

"That's nice that they want to know, but it totally sucks that everyone is talking about it. I wish I could crawl under a rock until it all blows over and they stop looking at me like I'm going to erupt in a wave of crazy." I stab my fork into the bed of lettuce and chew with an angry grinding of my teeth.

Beth watches me for a moment. "You can't blame them, Terran. Not much happens in this town, and you're front-page news." I roll my eyes before she adds, "It is what it is. Just try to focus on the people who are genuine and screw the rest. They're assholes anyway. Besides, if they really give you a hard time, you could always ask Raife to take them down a notch. I have a feeling he could kick some ass either with words or his fists."

Leave it to Beth to calm the muddy waters of my mind.

I giggle at the thought of Raife taking on the role of a chivalrous knight. "I would pay to see him punch Devon Slater in the face."

She laughs. "Oh, hell, yes. That guy needs an ass-kicking. Did you hear what he said about Marcy?"

I am so thankful for the topic to drift away from me that I jump at the offer to derail the conversation. As Beth fills me in on the rumor Devon started, I can't help feeling like the biggest hypocrite. Here I am listening to gossip about someone else while fuming about what's going around about me. In that moment of clarity, I let go of my anger at those people who had spent the day whispering and staring.

Shane joins us as Beth is talking, swinging an arm around me. "Hey, freak. How is it under the social microscope?"

"Hilarious, Shane."

He kisses me on the top of my head. "Don't worry about them. There'll be a new drama soon enough, and your incident will be old news. Of course, until then, get used to being in the spotlight, baby!"

Beth slaps Shane for me, and I shoot her a big grin. "I've got your back," she says with a wink.

By the time we head into the next period, I feel better equipped to deal with the inevitable looks. I can handle this.

I finally see Raife just before the last period. He wraps his arms around my waist, his touch bringing those feelings that I long for. "I missed you," his voice whispers in my ear, sending shivers down my spine.

"I missed you too," I say, but there's a part of me that feels a little distant from him now. I can't shake his rather callous attitude from yesterday, though I do my best to block it out.

I feel him breathe in my scent as he presses his face to my hair. "Want to hang out after school?"

"I can't."

I feel his shoulders slump at my response. "Why not?"

"Beth and I are going shopping. She wants to head into the city."

"What's in the city that she can't find here?" Raife asks.

I chuckle at the underlying whine in his voice. "Only the largest bookstore in the state. It takes up a whole city block."

He sighs, and I feel his surrender. "Okay. I guess that's an acceptable reason."

"Gee, thanks. I could go out tomorrow afternoon. Maybe we could catch a movie or something?" It sounds so date-ish when I suggest it, and I realize that Raife and I haven't done anything traditional since we started seeing each other. Wait. Are we boyfriend-girlfriend now?

The bell rings, and he gives me a quick peck on the forehead before saying, "It's a date. Call me later, okay?"

"Ok," I tell him, waving as I duck into class. I don't

even think about the looks I get as I take a seat. I'm on a Raife-high and just don't care.

―――――

I met Beth in the parking lot at the end of the day. She's already got the car started and is bopping to a song I know by an artist I can't remember. I'm terrible with names. I hop in, and we head out of town, filling the forty-five-minute drive with idle chatter.

It may be that the car is some kind of buffer between me and the world outside my window because I don't feel anything until I open the door and step out into the dimly lit parking garage. The moment I set my feet on the concrete and take a breath, I fall to my knees, stomach heaving as waves of sickness wash over me. I can feel Beth grabbing onto my shoulder and hear her voice, but it's muffled, as though coming from a tunnel miles away. I can't make out what she's saying. All I hear is a pounding in my head, a noise, unlike anything I've experienced before. Mixed within it are sounds like crying, but different. They come over me not so much as a sound, but rather a feeling. I can taste them on my tongue, a thick coating of misery.

"*Feel me,*" Gaia's voice drills into my mind.

I want to speak, to tell her to stop, but I'm frozen. Beneath my hands and knees, I can feel the cement. There is nothing left of her here. My body is heaving, reaching toward some part of her, but there's nothing, just artifice, and putridity. She is gone from this place, stamped out beneath the footprint of man, buried under layers of asphalt and concrete. The absence hurts, like an ice pick stabbing into my heart. I try to feel beyond it, but it's all-encompassing.

Panic is filling Beth's voice, penetrating the miasma flooding my brain. I latch onto the sound and follow it out of the web of anguish I'm feeling, like a lifeline. The last pull from Gaia's control is the hardest. I center myself and wrench away. It feels like I'm tearing myself apart, and I think I scream in those last moments. Collapsing onto the cold concrete, I take deep breaths and feel Beth stroking my back and repeating my name over and over.

I manage a soft whisper. "I'm okay." Beth lets out a whoosh of air. I feel it puffing the back of my head.

"Terran, what's wrong? What's happening to you?"

There is much worry in her question, a pleading that's never been there before because we have always been able to tell each other everything.

"I...," I start to say, but my voice is suddenly cut off, like the snip of a pair of scissors by an unseen hand. But I sense the being wielding them and know that I won't be able to share secrets that are not mine to voice. There is so much I want to say, and I can't. It's like I'm drowning, and she is just beyond the shore, holding a rope to haul me back in, but I just can't grasp it. It takes a couple of minutes to fully come back to myself. I get to my knees and sit up slowly, Beth supporting me the whole time.

"I'm okay now."

She shakes her head. "No. You're not okay. This is anything but okay."

Sighing, I drop my head. "No, I guess you're right."

"What is it? Can't you talk to me?" Her eyes implore me. There's so much love and care in them. It breaks my heart a little.

I look at her with the turmoil of my emotions on the surface for her to see. "I wish I could." There's a flicker of betrayal in her face when I say this. "I'm so sorry, Beth. I want to tell you. Believe me." Years of friendship pass before me, so many years, peppered with secret conversations and unswerving loyalty. And here I am picking a piece of it apart.

"I thought you could tell me everything."

"I just can't tell you this. Please, Beth. Please understand. I can't."

Beth wrestles with what I'm asking. I clench my hands as the seconds pass. Finally, she looks at me. "Until you feel ready to be honest with me, I'll accept it," she says a little coldly. "But, Terran, I'm here for you. I have always been here for you."

"I know, Beth, and I love you for it. Trust me that I would tell you if I could."

She purses her lips, but I see the moment she truly lets it go. My body relaxes. I still feel the soft pulse of the earth, but it's muffled under layers of concrete, a sickly rhythm that makes me feel slightly nauseated. The horrible pounding and ghostly screams are like white noise now. I take a few moments to reflect on how I got to this point, because I will need to master these feelings. It's one thing to have an episode with only Beth as a witness. Having breakdowns in public, like at school, is not something I can go through repeatedly. At some point, word will get out, and I'll find myself under the scrutiny of some kind of doctor. That can't happen.

I stand up with care, feeling like an old woman. By the time I make it to my feet, I'm confident enough to continue into the bookstore. "Let's go check out some new titles. I need a good fantasy book."

Beth's brows wrinkle with worry. "Are you sure?"

"Yeah. I've got it under control." She looks uneasy but walks by my side as we head into the bookstore. Surprisingly, I find that being inside, amid the smells and sounds of turning pages and quiet conversations, my feelings are more manageable. It takes a good twenty minutes for Beth to stop shooting worried glances my way, but eventually, she does, and we spend the next two hours lost among shelves filled with imagined worlds and characters. By the time we're ready to leave, smiles wreath our faces, and we each have a canvas bag filled with used books.

I'm a little apprehensive as we leave the store, afraid that I will be swallowed in awful sensations again. Beth holds the door open for me, and I step through it with false bravado. Perhaps it's the fact that I've prepared myself in some way because when the aching world hits me, I'm ready for it. Pausing mid-stride, I grit my teeth and embrace what's coming, forcing myself to feel it, to understand what it means, while refusing to let it take over completely.

"You okay?" Beth asks, having stopped and turned toward me.

I shut my eyes for a moment before responding. "Yes. I can control it. I just have to focus and not let it take over." There are so many questions in her face as she looks at me, biting her lip. "I know, Beth. You'll hear the whole story someday."

"Is it that you don't want to tell me or you can't?"

It's a tough question because part of me doesn't want to share all of this with her. I don't like to think about that. But I know that even if I could, I wouldn't be able to. It's like there's this muzzle that keeps me from saying too much. I don't know if it's Gaia or maybe Silas who controls the flow of knowledge, but I don't see a way around it. "I can't."

We leave it at that, an awkward truce in the quest for and resistance to information exchange. The drive home is rather quiet, but there is no animosity in the silent stretches. Beth and I are simply caught up in our own thoughts. It happens from time to time, and we have always been comfortable going through it side by side, no words necessary.

It helps to be back in the car. The outside world is a blur as the miles go by. I feel somewhat insulated within the confines of the vehicle. It gives me time to think about how I felt at the bookstore and the way I need to handle future incidents because I know there will be more, and they will likely hit me just as hard, if not harder. All I can do is hope that I don't completely lose it and embarrass myself in public.

This stronger connection is part of me now, for good or bad, I will be at the whim of the world, and of Gaia. What she feels, I will feel, and within this is the earth itself and every living thing. I guess they are part of me now, though they always were if I really think about it. Until this moment, that connection has been a minor piece of who I am, always somewhere in my thoughts and heart, but separate from my daily life. Gaia has brought them to the forefront. I know that I will not be able to ignore the anguish of millions of silent voices. She will make sure that I hear them, and when she commands it, I show the world the power of her wrath.

# CHAPTER 19

*Who would've thought watching the news would be a catalyst?*

I'm unprepared for the rage I feel as I watch the broadcast of the Keystone pipeline oil spill after school. The day had been long and uneventful, thankfully, I guess. Beth was too busy to hang out, and Raife had something going on with his dad. All of this left me on my own for the afternoon, and while I love to have some 'me time,' I wish I had never sat in front of the TV.

The news anchor is talking about the millions of gallons of oil flooding farmland and rivers. My body twitches as I view the coverage of a disaster entirely of man's making. I can only wonder what I would feel if I were there, standing on the shore of the riverbank, seeing the black tar coating the surface of everything it touches. Grinding my teeth and clenching my fists, I stifle the urge to growl in anger, though no one is home, and I know I could let it loose. I'm just afraid to give in to the wrath I'm feeling.

As images of the habitats and waterways affected by the spill splash across the screen, my mouth fills with a coating of saliva laced with stomach acid. My muscles start to shake, and I can't sit here any longer. I stand up, punching the power button on the remote, and storm out of the house.

I don't realize where I'm going until I'm about to cross into the preserve in my neighborhood. As I stomp through the undergrowth along the path, I mutter to myself, a one-sided conversation that vilifies people in a rant flooded with profanity. It's a good thing no one can hear me because I probably sound like a crazy person.

Just beyond my conscious thought, there is a new sensation. I don't know how long it's there before it finally cuts through the anger, but once I can focus on it, I pause mid-stride. I feel a strange pull to the earth, unlike anything I have felt before. Instead of the sickening sensations I've experienced, this is more like a surge of power that I can feel building within me the closer I get to my destination, that place of peace and connection deep in the forest. Picking up my pace, I head farther into the wilderness.

By the time I reach the rock, my perch under the

canopy, my body is vibrating, teeth rattling with the force of it. I climb onto the rock and stand in the center. Spreading my fingers, I tilt my head back, close my eyes, and open myself to Gaia. She rushes into me with a force that nearly knocks me to my knees. I root my feet to the rock and embrace her power.

The air begins to stir, blowing my hair softly at first and then whipping it into my face. I can hear leaves rustling and branches creaking. When I open my eyes, I am standing in a vortex of my own making, invisible except for the debris spinning within it and around me. I watch this phenomenon that I've somehow conjured with awe, hardly able to wrap my head around the fact that I am controlling it. Testing the limits of my ability to control it, I channel my energy, causing the air to slow and speed, spread and narrow. I want to laugh with glee as the currents of air shift at my command. It's a giddy feeling, and I am lost in it.

After a few minutes pass, I look up, my attention caught by an object swooping between the trees. Just beyond the turbulence of my mini-tornado, perched on a branch, is the raven. Its caw pierces the maelstrom surrounding me. I listen, eyes trained on him through the swirling air. The raven lets out a complex series of calls that churn through my mind in chaos before coalescing in a way that makes meaning. He's talking to me, telling me to use my power.

I lift my arms, keeping my stare fixed on the bird's

black form. As I do, the air shifts with me, drawing itself into the upper canopy of the trees, twisting branches, and tearing old leaves off of twigs. Inside, the power fills me. S*he* fills me with thought and feeling.

*"Daughter."* I hear Gaia call to me.

"I am here, great mother," I shout through the wind spiraling around me. Though I can't see her, I feel her approval.

*"You are of the earth, my child. Avenge me."*

I have no idea if the smile that breaks across my face is stained with vengeance, but I feel it, this need to punish. And it feels good.

Flexing my senses, I reach toward Gaia, drawing more strength. As my connection grows, I begin to sense the wealth of life under and around me, like pinpoints of light that I can hone in on. I concentrate on one of these and feel the thrum of its life force. It is not afraid of me. I let it go and reach toward the raven that I sense is watching. When we connect, I feel myself pulled into its mind as though I'm falling down a rabbit hole. It's frightening at first, but I surrender myself to it. I close my eyes as we connect, recognizing its presence within my mind. Though I can't understand all its strange thoughts, there is meaning that transcends language barriers. He is a conduit to Gaia, a watcher, and a messenger.

My arms lower, and the wind stops spinning around me. I am lost in the raven's eyes, caught in his web of consciousness. He has been watching me for many years, waiting for me, just as *she* has. The moment he lets me go, my body slumps. I feel drained and exhilarated at the same time. The anger that brought me to this point has been sharpened into something I can harness and use. That realization changes everything.

I can see her plans now, understand their purpose in a way that I couldn't before today. Humanity has gone too far in its greed and indifference. I stand on the rock, absorbed in a moment of clarity, and recall Raife's story, the turning point he described as he felt the earth torn apart with violence. The righteous anger and heart-breaking horror that Raife described is how I felt watching the footage of toxins polluting everything in their path, contaminating rivers and land. For what? So that people can continue to use a resource that has been proven time and again to be poisoning the very earth we inhabit? Have we not learned from our mistakes? What about the future? Or the millions of species we share the world with? The dawning realization is that the majority of people must not care. We are a selfish species, willing to take without considering repercussions.

No more. The time for careless apathy is over. Gaia has chosen me to be her voice and her judgment. It is time for us to begin.

I look up at the raven that stands so still, watching me. "I am ready," I say to him, somehow knowing he will understand. The raven caws once before swooping out of the tree, flying above me in a lazy circle, and then up above the treetops and away. A sense of rightness settles into me. I am at peace – a place I thought may never come when this craziness began. I hop off the rock and head home. As I pass from the forest into the realm of man, I smile. Raife will be happy with my decision. In fact, I'm sure he knew I would come to it soon. I look forward to standing by his side as we take our place among the Daoine Fíor.

---

Raife picks up after the second ring. "Hey, Terran. I just got back and was hoping I'd hear from you."

"Hi. Can we meet somewhere? I want to see you," I tell him, practically bouncing off my bed at the thought of sharing my epiphany with him.

"Sure. How about I pick you up in twenty minutes?"

"Perfect. See you soon!"

We hang up, and I grab a hoodie before heading to the kitchen for a quick snack. I need to eat something to keep myself busy. I've got too much energy to sit and wait. I open the pantry and scan the boxes of crackers and granola bars, but nothing looks appealing. I'm not even hungry, honestly. Grabbing a jar of peanuts, I pop a handful in my mouth just to have something to do. Three handfuls later, and I'm totally peanutted out. There are still at least fifteen minutes, so I look around the room for something else to occupy my time. The pile of dishes in the sink catches my eye, and I attack them with more gusto than ever before. My mom would probably start crying with joy if she could see me. Thankfully, the task wastes another ten minutes. Drying my hands, I head to the front door and look out the window.

The moment Raife's car pulls up to the curb, I yank the door open and jog down the path. The entire car rocks as I plop into the passenger seat with the force of a jump.

Raife's eyes go wide. "Are you trying to kill the shocks?"

I stick my tongue out at him. "Shut up."

He laughs. "So, where are we going?"

"How about Overlook Park?" It's not too far from my house and isn't a popular spot because there are no play structures, fields, or anything. It's really just a groomed park overlooking the town with meandering trails and plenty of benches and picnic tables, best for people who want to go on a leisurely walk with their dog or something. I tell Raife how to get there, and we head out, making small talk along the way.

There are three cars in the lot when we pull in, a good sign that we'll have plenty of privacy. I take his hand, smiling blissfully as our skin connects. I pull him along as we head to a bench that is tucked within a cluster of trees off the carefully groomed path.

Raife keeps giving me sideways glances as we walk, curious about my mood but clearly waiting for me to say something first. I smile at him, letting him wonder, formulating what I plan on telling him, and imagining his reaction.

We pass a woman with her dog. Of course, I stop, there's no way I'm going to walk on by without crouching down and petting such an adorably shaggy mutt. I get a lick on the cheek as Raife scratches the dog's head. We thank the woman and continue on. I feel the slobber drying on my face and rub at it with the sleeve of my hoodie. I love dogs, but that doesn't mean I want to wear a coating of slime on me for the rest of the day.

Our destination is absent of anyone else taking advantage of the clear skies. Raife and I step into the copse of trees and sit on the mostly dry bench. I love the feel of his arm across my shoulders as he rests it behind me. I take a few moments to admire the view. We can see the whole town laid out in some crazy quilt of man's making. A mated pair of hawks circles the horizon in lazy swoops as they scan the ground for an unwary meal. I focus on them for a bit, rather than looking at a skyline filled with buildings and roads. There is so little of nature stretched out before us, only pockets of the forest here and there.

I turn to Raife and find him watching me. It's time to tell him why we're here. "I saw something on the news, and it made me feel anger I've never felt before. I couldn't even stand being at home anymore. So I went to my special place, you know, in the woods by my house?" He nods but lets me continue. "I could feel *her* the moment I crossed into the forest, but there was something more to it. It was like energy was filling me up. By the time I reached the rock, it was making me shake, but in a good way. I guess I should have been scared, I mean, it was crazy. Things like that don't just happen, right?"

Raife tilts his head. "Did you see or hear something?"

I straighten up, excitement tingeing my voice. "Yeah, but before that, I made the air move, I mean, really move! It was like a little tornado, and I was controlling it. That energy I felt was pouring into me. It was the most exciting thing I've ever experienced."

I'm expecting Raife to tell me how he did something equally amazing, controlling some element of nature. But he doesn't. "So, you could control the air? You made a tornado from pure will?"

"It wasn't just me," I tell him, a little uncomfortable with the idea that he isn't able to do what I did. "There was this energy, or something, that I felt and focused on. When I did, I could feel Gaia. It was like I was getting stronger through her power. Have you felt that?"

"No, not like that. For me, it was more of a connection to everything around me. I could feel all these creatures that I couldn't even see, and wrapped up in that was a sick sensation, like I was absorbing some illness with each breath I took. I still feel it, actually, but I've learned to control my reaction to it. There's no way I could even function if I hadn't found a way to muffle the sensations. But what you're talking about is far beyond what I have experienced. You're special, Terran. The moment I saw you, I knew you were."

Raife cups my face, his thumb moving in slow circles on my cheek. "She has chosen you for a purpose. Are you ready to join her? To join me?"

The rightness I feel when I look into his eyes is the final piece in all of this. He is my chosen, just as I am Gaia's. I can picture us standing side by side, fighting for this world together. "Yes. I'm ready to stand with you and face what is coming together.

# CHAPTER 20

*She's there, beyond the ruins*
*of the forest*

A few days later, Raife and I decide to see Silas. My hope is that he'll be able to more fully explain our purpose and the parts we will play in whatever is to come. I need to know that this is about showing the world, not annihilating it. I also have a secret wish that Silas will be able to somehow teach Raife to do what I can, controlling some element of nature. I don't tell Raife this. It still makes me feel self-conscious to be able to do something like that when he can't, although I know it doesn't faze him.

It's a little unnerving when Enzo opens the door,

clearly expecting us. "Raife. Terran. Please come in. Silas will be with you in a few minutes."

We look at each other and follow Enzo. Once we're comfortable, talking quietly, Enzo comes in with a tray of refreshments. My stomach rumbles in anticipation of whatever spread I'll find this time. I'm not disappointed. Enzo smiles broadly as I reach for a small pastry and stuff it in my mouth. I grin up at him, chewing with delightful enthusiasm.

Enzo looks over at Raife, chuckling. "I seem to know exactly what Terran likes."

Raife smiles back. "She's pretty easy to please, especially if it's chocolate."

"Duly noted," Enzo remarks. "Is there anything else I can get for you both?"

"Nope, I'm good." I shake my head, my mouth too full of pastry to say anything. Raife laughs at me. "I think she's having an out-of-body experience with that pastry at the moment."

I elbow him, but can't really argue with his determination. If Enzo is the one making these delicious confections, I need to convince him to start supplying me regularly. I have to restrain myself from grabbing another after I finally finish and wash it down with a few sips of lavender tea. Obviously, Raife knows exactly what I'm thinking because he picks up the plate and begins to slowly pass it under my nose while whispering, "Eat me." I snap my teeth at him, pretending to bite his hand, and we both end up in a fit of laughter.

Silas enters the room as we're talking closely a few minutes later. "You've truly found one another, have you not?"

Raife and I look at each other, smiling at the rightness of it. I twine my fingers with his and turn toward Silas. "Yes. We have, and we're ready to begin all of this together."

Sincere pleasure passes across Silas' face. "Come with me. It's time to get started."

I'm taken by surprise as Silas leads us to the garage, a part of the house that is hidden from the street, as it opens to an alley I hadn't noticed before. Raife indicates that I should sit up front. I slide into the car, another electric vehicle I've never heard of. I can't even hear the engine start as he puts it into gear and pulls onto the road. As we drive, the conversation centers on the various experiences I've had and the decision I made as a result. Silas smiles and nods throughout, showing no surprise as I tell him about being able to curl the air into a small vortex.

Raife chimes in as I explain the feelings I had as I pulled Gaia's strength into me and channeled it into the wind. "She's special, isn't she, Silas?"

"Terran has been chosen."

It feels strange to be considered exceptional. It's like receiving praise that makes me feel awkward and unworthy. Within that is a layer of anxiety that Raife may be uncomfortable with my abilities, but as before, he is nothing but supportive. How is this wonderful boy even real? Raife leans forward and wraps his arms around the seat and me.

"She's destined for great things, isn't she?"

Silas darts a glance at us, his face lighting up as he takes in our undeniable bond. "I believe she is."

A half-hour later, we end up parked on the side of a dirt road. I step out and am immediately overcome with waves of anguish. I turn toward the car, grabbing onto the side of it to keep myself from falling to the ground as I'm pummeled by sensations that are so visceral I want to throw up. Outside of my own struggle, I can sense that Raife is faring no better. I lean my head against my arms, taking gulps of air to gain control. I look at Raife. He's standing so still, chin toward his chest. I can hear his slow inhale and exhale. Watching him master the feelings washing over us helps me, and I begin to gain the upper hand. Before too long, I can let go of the car and stand on my own.

Throughout it all, Silas has stood by, watching dispassionately. This must be part of whatever training he is planning to give us. We have to be able to control our reactions. It won't be easy. I swallow slowly, testing my stomach to see if nausea is going to overwhelm me.

When I know I am under control, I ask, "What is this place?"

Silas looks around before his eyes swing back to mine.

"We're standing on a logging road. About half a mile up is where they're doing the cutting. If I brought you both up there, you'd be on the ground by now, writhing in agony."

Raife and I look in the direction Silas indicated. No wonder we're feeling like this. The earth is being torn apart here. I shudder to think of how awful it would be if we were standing at the site of it.

"Why doesn't it affect you?" I say, swallowing my bile.

"It does, but I have learned to control my physical reaction to it. In time, you will be able to do the same."

I hear Raife's deep breathing and take his hand. It steadies me as our fingers connect. Looking at Silas, I wonder how many years it took to get that kind of mastery over this awful sickness I feel. "I hope it doesn't take too long," I mutter.

Silas smiles and sweeps his arm across the landscape. "I brought you here because it is in places like this that you will be able to learn to draw upon the connection you have with Gaia. The sensations you feel give you strength, though I know it must seem strange because you feel over-come with the sickness of this place. But there is power in that. You must learn to take it in and use it."

We nod, but I have trouble seeing how this would help me. I felt so strong in the forest when I pulled energy from the earth. "Won't these feelings be a distraction, though? I felt so much stronger when I was in the preserve. I feel drained being here."

Silas looks at me knowingly. "Your strength comes from Gaia, and that power is more evident in those untainted places, but you will not be in preserves and pristine forests when this war begins. You will be where the earth is bleeding, where man has corrupted it. Both of you must learn to feel beyond that misery, to find Gaia buried under layers of man's making. She is there, though harder to feel. Think of it as static disrupting a signal. The signal itself exists, but the picture you receive or the noises you hear make it impossible to discern. You must learn to cut through it, to reach beyond, and grasp the power that resides within the chaos."

We trek out into the field next to the road. There are old scars here, remnants of ancient life slashed and ripped from the ground years ago. Across the aching landscape are tiny saplings, hidden among tall grasses, reaching for the light. I can feel old anger as I stand among the ruins of the forest.

Silas indicates where Raife and I should stand. We face one another, forming a triangle. "There is great power in number three. It will help you focus by drawing on each other's strength while reaching toward Gaia."

He extends his hands, and we form a triad. The circuit of our bodies closes when our fingers touch, and I feel a jolt run through me. It is the same current I have felt any time my flesh touches Silas or Raife, but more substantial. I close my eyes and focus on it.

"You will draw on the strength you feel to pull Gaia's power into you. Focus on the earth beneath your feet, the life that stirs all around us, the breath of wind on your face. She is in all of these."

I feel the moment Gaia senses my connection, just outside the old misery and anger of this place. It's like she reaches toward me, taking hold, tasting my presence before she curls around me in a motherly embrace. Just beyond these feelings is Raife, paler but there, a spark of life and subtle power. Energy floods my limbs. I let go of my restraint and let it take me. As before, I feel the air stirring, a slight breeze that lifts my hair in many directions. I clench my teeth and pour my energy into the earth, imagining my hands digging into the soil, through rock and sediment. As I continue to concentrate, I can feel grit in my fingernails and dirt coating my palms. I cup it in my hands, shaping it into a small mound. I smile as I swirl the top, making it look like soft-serve ice cream. I must have laughed aloud because I lost concentration as I heard Raife gasp next to me.

My eyes pop open in time to see a collection of soil and rock spinning slowly before my eyes in the shape of a dirty ice cream cone. I pull my hands back in shock, breaking my connection to Silas and Raife. The mass of dirt hovers for a fraction of a second and then falls to the ground with a soft thump. I can feel my mouth hanging open when I look at Raife. He's staring at the pile of dirt at my feet.

Glancing at Silas, I find him looking into me with a wealth of emotion. He holds me in his stare for a few moments before slowly nodding with approval.

Raife's voice pulls me from Silas' scrutiny. "Terran, you're amazing." I give him a tremulous smile. He walks the two steps toward me and wraps me in a tight embrace. "I can't believe you did that! Can you do it again?"

His excitement is contagious. "I don't know. Honestly, I didn't know I could do it, to begin with." I look at both of them. "Maybe it's our combined energy or something."

Raife grins. "Well, I doubt much of that was me, but I can't deny that we're stronger together."

Silas walks over, clapping each of us on the shoulder. "You've made an excellent observation, Raife. Collective strength is always more powerful, though you are right in your assessment of Terran's abilities." He turns to me. "You are truly a wonder. I have never seen this degree of ability beyond my kind."

Raife gives me a huge hug, lifting me off the ground and twirling me in the air a few times. I'm laughing and out of breath when he puts me down. The world spins for a few moments. Just before the earth settles beneath my feet, I sense *her* within it, as though she is somehow looking on us and smiling.

"That is a good start, but there is more work ahead of you," Silas announces, taking our hands and reforming our triangular circuit. "Raife, I want you to reach out and feel the air moving around you. It is the easiest element to control. Focus your energy, feel Gaia's power, and use that to control it."

Raife acknowledges Silas' instruction, and we close our eyes and begin again.

# CHAPTER 21

*Sometimes, you just need*
*a girls' night out*

I have a natural connection, Silas told me, something about my bond with Gaia being present long before all of this began. Apparently, that is why I can pull her power into me and channel it more easily than Raife. Although Raife did finally manage to create violent gusts of wind as we stood in the field, hands clasped, minds focused. He was absolutely thrilled and spent the entire trip back to Silas' talking about how it felt to control the air and bend it to his will, and then our drive back to my house, retelling the whole story. I love his boyish enthusiasm.

We make plans to 'practice' in the preserve by my house. I guess I should call it homework since Silas pretty much assigned it to us until we meet up again on the weekend. It should be noted that it's the only assignment I've ever been enthusiastic about. If only teachers could give us interesting stuff to do.

Beth can sense something has changed when we see each other every morning, but true to her promise, she doesn't ask ,and I don't offer, though I wish I could. Everything is becoming more complicated and secretive. I miss Beth. It's been too long since we hung out. I decide it's time to change that. I can't let this new part of my life eclipse everything else.

I kiss my parents goodbye when I hear Beth's horn honking on Friday morning. Before I head out the door, I call out, "Hey, I may not see you guys until late tonight. I want to hang out with Beth."

My mom responds first. "Have fun, sweetie! Try to be home before midnight, okay?"

"I will!" I shout and skip down the steps to Beth's car.

I sink into the passenger seat and look at Beth. She smiles at me, but it's tinged with sadness. I hate to see it. "Want to hang out tonight? I've missed you."

She brightens immediately. "Hell, yes! I need a girls' night. Movies and lots of carbs at my house?"

"Totally," I say, grinning. "I think we may need to make a store run before we go to your house, though. You know, load up on the good stuff."

Beth agrees, and we make a quick list of necessities. Our excitement fills the time it takes to get to school. I see Raife pulling in as we park. We stop and wait for him, still chatting about which movies to consider.

Raife slings his arm around me. "Good morning," he says with a kiss on my cheek before flashing a smile at Beth.

She rolls her eyes in mock irritation. "Get a room."

"Only if you join us," I taunt, earning a swat on the arm.

"I just might and keep this whole thing rated PG," she says, waving her hand at Raife and me.

We fall into step and head inside. It feels good having Beth and Raife on either side of me. It's like I'm balanced with the two most important people in my life, keeping my world from tipping into insanity. In the hallway, we make plans to meet at lunch just as Shane trots up to us.

"It's Friday, party people!" He announces. "Anyone up to joining me at a little soiree this evening?"

"Beth and I have plans," I tell him. Shane looks momentarily crushed before his face lights up as he looks at Raife.

"How about you?"

Raife shrugs. I know he'd rather be at home than go to a party. All the noise and mayhem is not his style. But he's a good sport. "Well, since my girl has plans, I'm game."

Shane is positively glowing. "Excellent! Walk with me, and I'll give you the address. See ya, ladies." The boys head off, and Beth and I stand there for a moment watching them before chuckling and going to class.

The day passes slowly but uneventfully. Janet sits next to me again in English. We've kind of got a bond after my whole embarrassing episode. She's a genuine person, one of those rare souls who don't put on some sort of front for others. That's why we hit it off, I suppose, kindred spirits and all that. I invite her to join me at lunch, but she's got her own crew to sit with.

I'm surprised to only see Beth at the table when I scan the room with my salad and bag of chips. "Where is everyone else?"

Beth gives me a look and then says one word that explains it all. "Shane."

"Ah," I say, setting down my tray and digging into my food. Most likely, Shane and Raife went off campus for lunch. There's a cool little coffee shop around the corner that serves some pretty damn good sandwiches. They're expensive as hell, which is why Beth and I don't go very often.

"You know a girl named Janet?"

Beth considers that for a moment. "Dark hair? Nose ring?"

"Yeah."

She nods. "Not well, but we had a class together last year. She's pretty cool. Why?"

"She's in my English class and was really nice after my

meltdown. In fact, she mentioned that she'd had a similar experience in terms of embarrassment. I like her."

"I think I heard something about that, but I can't remember the details. I'm glad she's understanding, though. I know you feel kind of awkward about what happened, but it'll blow over, and people will forget."

"I just hope it doesn't happen again," I tell her, grimacing. "People still look at me funny like I'm going to lose it."

Beth reaches over and grips my hand. She doesn't need to say anything out loud; the message is there without words. True friends are precious things. "Enough about me and the insanity that is my life. Anything interesting going on with you? Any tidbits you've left unsaid?"

She laughs. "Nope, you've got the market cornered in the realm of weird and interesting."

"Very funny," I say, nudging her in the side before we head to class.

I'm practically giddy with excitement when the bell rings. Beth and I meet in the parking lot and hop into the car. Our first stop is the grocery store. We've got twenty bucks between us, plenty to pick up some much-needed snacks. A full basket later, we head to Beth's house.

Celeste isn't home, so we unload the food and lay it out on the kitchen island to make it easier to decide what to start with. After deliberating for a couple of minutes, we select the tortilla chips and salsa. I figure it's got tomatoes, so it's somewhat healthy. We'll save the really yummy stuff for after dinner – mac and cheese, my favorite.

Beth spreads a blanket on the living room floor, and I toss a couple of pillows down. We make our own little picnic and simply enjoy the crunchy goodness, slathered in organic salsa, for a few minutes.

Eventually, I break the silence. "I'm sorry I've been kind of distant the last few days."

Beth shrugs. "It's all right. I mean, I don't like it, but I'm here for you no matter what. Just don't leave me behind, okay?"

"I won't. I promise. Things have just been...different. But I'm feeling good now, like I'm getting a better hold on all of it." I know she doesn't understand what I mean, not really. I can see it in her face.

"I'm glad, Terran. I hope someday you can tell me everything."

"Yeah. Me too." After that, I don't bring it up again, and it's better that way. We fall into our old habits and soon find ourselves giggling and filling the quiet with simple things. Celeste comes home to find us sprawled out on the floor, looking through an old photo album.

"Happy Friday!" She calls out. "Are you girls having fun?"

"Hi, Mom," Beth says, hopping up to give Celeste a hug.

"Did you have a great day, honey?"

"It was a school day, nothing exceptional there, Mom."

Celeste sighs and then turns her attention to me. "Terran, it's so good to see you. I've missed your lovely face around here."

I get up, and she opens her arms so I can give her a hug. "Hey, Celeste. I've missed you, too. It's been kind of crazy these days."

She looks at me carefully, tucking a few loose strands of red hair behind my ears. Celeste is one of those rare people who see more than you think they do. I hope she doesn't see too much.

"Do you want to talk about it?" She asks, eyes probing mine. I feel like she can see the secrets lurking there.

"Thank you, but no. I want to just ignore all that today and pig out on real chocolate while watching some chick flicks."

Celeste acquiesces. "Well, you let me know if you need an ear. I'm always here for my girls." She looks at both of us, and we smile. "You two have everything you need? Want me to make you some tea? I've got a new green blend with ginger."

I am not a big fan of ginger unless it's buried in my chicken teriyaki or something. "No, thanks," I tell her, and Beth does the same.

Celeste breezes out of the room, taking the ease of the last hour with her. Beth and I look at each other. All around us, I can sense the questions and longing for answers floating through the air in a thick fog. I know she won't ask, but I feel them, and it bothers me. I close the album we had been looking at and fold my legs, wracking my brain for a neutral topic that will diffuse the disquiet.

"What's this party that Shane is dragging Raife to?"

Beth gives an exasperated look. "Oh, my God. It's Bryce's party. You know, the senior quarterback? Apparently, he got a full ride to some big football school and is throwing a party to celebrate. In other words, lots of cheerleaders and jocks."

I wrinkle my nose. While I'm friendly with pretty much everyone, I've never been the sporty type and don't gel with people who live and breathe football or cheering. It's just not my thing. It's not Raife's thing either. From what he's told about his life in Southern California, there were a lot of plastic people, and that kind of crowd was at the top of the list. I wonder how he'll manage to get through the evening with Shane dragging him from group to group.

"Raife is going to hate it," I remark, making a face to convey the feelings I'm sure he's going to experience. "Poor guy."

Beth laughs. "Yeah. I bet Shane is going to be in full social-butterfly mode, dragging him around. I wonder how long he'll last before he makes up some excuse to bail."

"I'm sure I'll hear all about it tomorrow. Better him than me, I say!" Our laughter finally cuts through the tension, and I feel myself relax again. I wasn't lying when I told Celeste I wanted to let things go and just be here. I really need this, an escape from things that are becoming too real. Beth and I return to our usual selves, comfortable and silly. The evening passes without incident as we watch a couple of comedies, one so raunchy my sides are aching by the time it's over. It's a good night.

# CHAPTER 22

*I didn't think it would be like this*

Silas and Enzo leave town for reasons he doesn't divulge, but Raife and I have our suspicions about the nature of the trip. We can't help but wonder if it's some type of recruitment for people like us. The two of us are left to our own devices with explicit instructions to practice what Silas has been teaching us. I'm eager for my 'homework' and to pore over some maps with Raife to find a perfect spot to get to work. We need somewhere away from it all, out in the woods, where we can really concentrate without the risk of discovery. One of my stipulations is that we go far from any logging or anything like that.

Without Silas with us, I don't want to be too close to something that could completely overwhelm us.

Raife and I chose a primitive trail system in the Cascades. After doing a Google search, we found minimal references to it and feel secure with the knowledge that it's highly unlikely to have any foot traffic aside from us. We pack up some gear: bottles of water, sandwiches, and snacks. Raife drives while I sit back, watching the forest crop up all around us as we go through lazy turns deeper and deeper into the wilderness. The trailhead is hard to find, nearly overgrown with moss and branches from nearby trees. Raife parks in the tiny lot, a spot so small that it can hardly be considered a parking area. We grab our gear and head for the overgrown blue trail.

"It's so quiet," I whisper to Raife. Aside from the soft thump of our feet along the path, there is little noise beyond the songbirds we hear now and then. I breathe deeply, pulling myself to the center of it all, to her. The connection is there, but it's pale today.

"Do you feel her?" Raife asks, breaking into my thoughts.

"Yes, but not as strongly as before. You?"

He pauses, eyes closed in concentration. "A bit. It's almost like she's asleep."

I consider that. "Maybe she is. You know, Silas told me that she has awakened from time to time over the centuries, which would mean that she is dormant or something the rest of the time. I don't think Gaia is ever completely unaware of anything, but maybe she just rests."

"That makes sense," Raife says, looking into the horizon of trees stretched out before us. "I wonder if that'll affect what we can do."

"Huh. I hadn't thought of that. It'll be like a science experiment, then."

He laughs. "If you ask me to take lab notes, we're leaving."

I poke him in the side. He grabs my hand, and we trek into the woods, content to be with each other and the life that surrounds us. A mile in, we stop at a break in the woods. It's a rocky spot where the trees thin, letting weak sunlight filter down. Raife climbs onto a large boulder and pulls me up. Sitting side by side, we eat our lunch in relative silence. I have just put our cloth napkins back into the pack when a movement a few feet away catches my eye. I turn slowly, afraid to move too quickly if it's an animal.

There, standing still under overhanging branches, is the most beautiful buck I have ever seen. His antlers branch out a good foot from his head, arching in perfect formation to create a regal crown. Liquid brown eyes watch me, connecting with mine on a level so deep that I can feel his heartbeat echo my own. We remain utterly still, watching one another. Raife senses my stillness, and I feel him turn to see what has captured my attention. The buck's eyes dart to him for a moment before returning to mine as though drawn by some magnetic pull.

In my head, I tell the animal that I mean no harm. I reach out with something inside me that has always been there but never fully explored. It feels like tentacles of energy and thought weaving out of my body, spanning the distance between the deer and me until these fingerlings of feeling penetrate his form. The moment he recognizes the connection, the buck's muscles quiver. I see his body lock in recognition before slowly relaxing. The animal lets out a huff of breath, dipping his head as though bowing to me.

My eyes widen as the stag takes a step toward me. I remain frozen, watching his slow progression from boulder to boulder. And then he is standing above me, this beautiful animal, like some kind of king of the forest. I hear Raife's sharp intake of breath as I tilt my head back to look at the deep, brown eyes gazing down at me. The buck stretches his face toward mine while I remain perfectly still, eyes locked on his, heart and mind speaking words of friendship.

I smile as his wet nose grazes my cheek, snuffling through my hair. Closing my eyes, I reach out with my senses. It's like he knows me. Somehow this creature of Gaia sees who I am, feels what I am. It's incredible. Slowly, so slowly, I lift my arm, testing the limits of whatever boundaries this beautiful animal has set. It is with

surprise and humble gratitude that he seems to understand the movements of my hand and dips his head into
my palm, letting me caress the smooth texture of his face.
I don't know how many minutes have passed. Time ceases
to exist for me as I revel in the moment. Eventually, the
buck straightens, giving Raife a silent look, before turning
and leaping into the forest, swallowed by the beauty of the
underbrush as though he had never been.

Raife and I kept our eyes fixed on that spot for many
minutes. I can still feel the connection in my mind, though
it is growing dimmer. I look down at my hands, rubbing
my fingers in circles, exploring the remnants of dirt and
hair from that magnificent animal. I come back to myself
in slow degrees, but the memory of this will live with me
forever.

"That was amazing, Terran," Raife says softly.
"Watching it, I felt like you were communicating on some
level."

I nod. "We were. I don't know how to describe it, but it
was like I could speak to him, straight into his heart and
mind. He seemed to know who, or what, I was. The
connection I felt was amazing, Raife." I'm positively
glowing as I look at him.

He shares the moment, his face mirroring my own
excitement. "You are incredible."

I fall into his arms, happy beyond belief. Raife strokes
my back, telling me how special I am, how he's so glad to
have found me. He talks about how lost he was before and

the way he feels now, like he's home. I echo his sentiments. We are meant to be together.

We spend another half hour perched on the rock before deciding it's time to continue. Raife pulls out a trail map, and we decide on about a mile from here. From what we can see and from a few online blogs about this trail system, it'll be a perfect place to practice what Silas has taught us. Our hike is pretty strenuous, impacting my ability to carry on much of a conversation. Eventually, we see a break in the trees, and I know we are almost there. My legs are rather tired, and I know I'll feel it tomorrow. Raife grabs my hand, sensing that I need a little motivation, and we step into a large, open meadow.

I look around, somewhat fearful that I'll feel waves of sickness wash over me from deep-seated anger and anguish within the earth. But the farther we walk into the openness, the clearer it becomes that this is not a scarred section of forest, decimated by man.

Raife heads to a large fallen tree and waves me over. "It looks like there was a lightning strike at some point. See how the tree is split here?"

I lean over to get a better look. "Oh, I see what you mean. Well, I have to say that I'm relieved it's some natural thing that made this place rather than the other option."

Raife agrees, and we fan out, looking for a place to get started. We choose an area that is somewhat free of fallen trees and branches, and Raife sets down the pack. While we can't form a triad as we did with Silas, there is still strength in our connection. We stand face to face and grasp each other's hands. I close my eyes and concentrate, feeling Raife do the same.

It's a wonderfully strange sensation as we connect on a deep level. In my mind, I imagine strands of energy reaching toward him, mingling with his own until they become knotted and woven, like a complex web. I can't help the smile that breaks across my face as I feel a wealth of love within our joining. I send out my own and feel the moment that he latches onto it.

Taking on the role of Silas, I ask Raife to concentrate on one element. I've decided to try to join our strengths and work in unison. "Focus on the earth itself. Feel the texture of the soil and the rock. Imagine burying your hands in it, digging it up, shaping it."

I put all of my energy into communicating with Raife and feeling the thrum of the earth. It takes some time for Raife to manipulate the soil beneath our feet. In my mind, I have been thumbing through it, feeling textures and living things. When I sense the dirt move outside of my making, I follow it and reach out toward Raife, linking with him on a level I never had before. Together, we pull the soil into the air. I send out an image of a vortex and feel Raife take that in. Working in conjunction, we create a spinning mass of dirt and rock between our linked arms. I open my eyes and marvel at what we have been able to do together. Amid the debris, I see Raife looking back at me, mirroring my joy.

The moment the shot rings out, my heart wrenches, my mind screaming in anguish. The mass of soil swirling a moment ago falls with soft thumps to the ground. I grip my head, gasping as I feel overcome by terror and pain. There is a whimpering sound coming from somewhere near me, but I can't focus on it. My heart feels like it's struggling.

Help. It hurts.

The sounds of distress are getting louder, and I realize they are coming from me. I let out a scream of pain. "Help me!"

Raife has his arms around me. "Terran! I'm here. What is it? What's wrong?"

"It hurts! Help me!" I scream, overwhelmed by a fear I have never experienced before. Sobs rip from my chest, the pain of it hammering at my heart. Suddenly, my body seizes, jaw locked, eyes bugging. I can't breathe. I'm dying. Oh, God. I can't breathe. My heart thuds in a terrible rhythm, erratic and straining to pump blood through a body that is slipping away. I claw at my throat, desperate to drag air into lungs that have stopped working.

I'm going to die. Oh, God. It hurts.

Raife's voice is becoming faint, barely perceptible. And then I let go. The moment I do, breath rattles out of me, and I slump to the ground.

Raife is shaking me, anguish in his voice. "Terran! Terran, wake up!"

I want to reach toward him, but my arms are leaden, anchored to the ground. My mind is going fuzzy, and I can't open my eyes. There is just darkness. I welcome it. It's safe there.

I don't know how long I remain still. In some cognizant part of my mind, I can sense Raife. He is panicking as I am slowly pulled from the soothing black-ness that enveloped me only moments before. His hands are on my neck, feeling for my pulse. Gently, he turns my body, positioning me onto my back to give me CPR. I want to tell him it's okay, but I can't move my limbs or lips. He tilts my head back, thumb pulling my chin down to open my mouth. I try to open my eyes as his lips press to mine.

Suddenly, my lungs spark to life, filled with his breath. I gasp, taking in a rush of air as my heart begins pumping, filling my body with strength. I lie there, coming back to myself by slow degrees. And then it washes over me, grief like nothing I have felt before. A spark of life is gone, a connection violently severed. I sob into Raife's chest as he rocks me back and forth, telling me how scared he was, asking if I'm okay.

No more than a few minutes pass when I feel a new emotion surge through me. Anger. A rage so powerful it eclipses everything. I stand up, sparking a worried protest from Raife, but I brush off his arms and turn to the west.

"Terran?" Raife asks, trying to pull me back to him. "What is it? Where are you going?"

The rage is building, and I grab hold of it, stroking it until it feels like a living thing. Power rushes through me, energy so intense that my limbs vibrate, and each step I take causes the air and soil to move about me. I walk into the woods, pulled in a direction I can't articulate but must go. Raife follows me. He has stopped talking, seeming to understand that I am caught in something bigger than his fears.

I grit my teeth as we get closer. It hurts to feel the lingering fear and pain, but I press onward, brutal determination in every step. The moment I see his still form, my steps falter, and I stumble. Raife is there to catch me. His gasp echoes mine as we look at our fallen friend, that beautiful buck. His open eyes stare at nothing, and his body is still, chest splattered in blood around a small bullet hole. I sob, staggering toward him, and fall to my knees.

My hands tremble as I lay them on his motionless body. I can still feel the remains of his anguish as I make contact, like some ghostly presence. I bow my head, tears streaming down my face with a grief so deep that it muffles my anger. Raife kneels next to me, hands resting beside mine. This regal creature is just a shell now, his life snuffed out by pitiless hands.

I can hear them before we see any movement in the trees. Their loud voices cut through the stillness, boasting of their kill, laughing at the ease of taking down such a large trophy. My anger rekindles. I lift my hands from the cooling body of the deer and press them into the earth, burrowing my mind through the dirt and into the heart of Gaia. I call to her, letting her feel my rage and retribution. She stirs, reaching toward me.

As we connect, power snakes into my limbs. I lock my jaw, clenching my teeth as I draw more and more of it into me. Trembling with raw energy, I slowly rise and turn toward the caustic laughter and careless noise of the two hunters. Raife remains on the ground at my feet, watching this play out.

I focus on the sound of their feet crashing through the undergrowth. My eyes squint in concentration as I hone in on the path they are taking to the murder scene. I can taste their pride and pleasure. It adds fuel to the rage. My body begins to shake the closer they come. I wait, biding my time until I can finally make out their shapes in the dimness.

I close my eyes, focusing on the rocks buried in and on the forest floor. Subtly, they begin to tremble, a slight vibration under my feet. I reach out with my mind, feeling the forest floor as it extends to where the men are coming through the mass of trees and shrubs. I sense their foot-falls and pour all of my strength into the earth, deep into the very ground their feet press into. With a scream of rage, I extend my arms, pulling up rocks the size of base-balls. I let them hover for a moment before their shocked faces, taking pleasure in the sudden burst of fear, before I let loose, hurling the rocks at them. I can hear the impact, the pounding of flesh, the grunts of pain.

Their frightened thoughts flicker for a moment and then are gone, as each man falls into unconsciousness. Part of me wishes I had done more, that they would never awaken. I shove the thought away. I push it deep into my body and let it wither as I come back to myself.

# CHAPTER 23

*Who wants two eyes when you could have three?*

We bury the buck while the hunters lie prone in painful slumber. They'll wake up at some point, heads aching, and I can only hope that what happened today convinces them to put the guns away for good.

Patting the mound of dirt covering the magnificent animal, I let my anguish go in powerful sobs that wrack my body. I am burying more than this beautiful creature. A part of myself now rests alongside it. While it hurts to let that piece of me go, I cannot regret its passing. What happened today changed me in ways I can't conceptualize. I have become an instrument of Gaia. Part of me wonders just how far this will go.

Raife pulls me gently to my feet, wrapping an arm around me, giving me a gentle squeeze. There are no words that can capture what we are feeling, but we both understand the turning point. I take comfort knowing that Raife will be with me as I walk a new path.

When my body begins to shake with exhaustion and cold, Raife announces, "It's time to go."

I agree, resting my head on his shoulder for a moment before I straighten and indicate that I'm ready. "Okay."

We make our way back to the car in silence, hand in hand. The contact is reassuring and gives me strength. Despite my protests, Raife insists that we stop and eat along the way home. He pulls into a small diner, and we get a table in the back, tucked away from harsh lights and boisterous conversations. Sitting across from each other, we link our hands on the tabletop. The waitress smiles and gives us glasses of water and menus.

"No straws, please," I tell her after she sets a couple down. She gives me an odd look before scooping them back up and into her apron.

Raife smiles and slowly pulls away, severing our physical contact. I'm feeling more like myself when he hands me a menu. "I think you should get something that'll warm you up. How about soup? Maybe a sandwich too?"

"That sounds good. I'll get the broccoli cheddar and a

grilled cheese sandwich." There is no such thing as too much cheese in my world.

"Me too," he says and waves the waitress over to give her our order. When she leaves, he reaches for my hand again. "How are you feeling?"

I think for a moment. "Hollowed out."

"I feel that, too," he tells me. "But I'm glad you did what you did."

My head snaps up. I was kind of nervous about that. I don't know how I should feel about hurting people, and I was afraid he would look at me like I was some kind of monster. "You are?"

"They deserved it. Honestly, you could've done more, and they would've had it coming."

I bite my lip. "I wanted to. Part of me wasn't satisfied with simply knocking them out. I was so angry, Raife. I just wanted them to suffer, to feel what that poor animal felt. I don't even know if it was my anger, though. Maybe it was *her*."

"Why *didn't* you kill them?"

His question is bold and uncomfortable. Kill. It's such a strong word, such a violent act. Am I capable of that? On the one hand, I now know I can do it, but is that truly what I am becoming? Have I abandoned showing mankind the harm they are doing and instead agreed to kill for Gaia? I search my feelings, pulling up awful memories from today. They are interspersed with moments of joy and awe, I felt when that living creature communed with me. Anger stirs as I reflect on it. It's hard to rein it in.

"I wanted to hurt them," I begin, fumbling with how to phrase the thoughts and feelings that ran through me in the act of vengeance. "They deserved it."

Raife agrees, squeezing my hand in support. "They did."

"Part of me," I start to say, taking a gulp before continuing. "Part of me wanted them dead. I could've done it so easily, just shifted the path of the rocks or increased their speed, so they shattered bone. But I couldn't. I'm not a killer, even though a piece of me wanted to be. I will fight for her. In fact, I am eager. But I can't kill for her."

"You have to do what feels right. But," his voice fades away for a moment, "you must realize there may come a point where there will be little choice. We might end up in some situation where you have to take that next step, no matter how hard it is. If that happens, you know I'll be with you, right? I'm here for you in all things, Terran. We are meant to be together. I think we're stronger when we are."

"Thank you, Raife," I tell him. It feels as though a weight has been lifted to hear him say he'll stand with me. It's different to listen to the words. "I'm glad we found each other. I don't know what's in store for us, but I get the feeling that things are just getting started. Do you feel it too?"

He nods and pulls away as the waitress brings our order. "Anything else I can get for you two?" She asks.

Raife looks at me, and I shake my head. "Nope. We're good for now."

"Enjoy," she says, before bustling to another table.

We dig in. As the soup coats my mouth, my stomach lets out a loud snarl. I glance at Raife, who cocks an eyebrow. "Hungry? Want my bowl too?"

"I'll let you know when I finish this one."

He laughs softly and shifts his attention back to the soup. I'm famished. Clearly, the events of the day are catching up with me. I alternate between dipping my grilled cheese in the soup and scarfing it with my spoon. All too soon, it's gone, and I look over at him. "I'm ready for your bowl now."

Raife grins, popping a finger in his mouth before dipping it in his soup. "It's got my spit in it, so it's mine."

"You think that's going to stop me?" I ask, slowly reaching for the bowl.

He inches it away and asks, "How about dessert?"

I purse my lips, giving it its due consideration. "Deal."

After a large brownie sundae, I lean back against the booth and give a sigh of contentment. "I guess I needed that."

Raife scrapes his spoon along the bottom of the dish, scooping up the last puddle of ice cream. "I did too. Feeling better?"

"Yeah."

Heading home is a reflective time. The events of the day spiral through my head, and I pluck out parts of them to analyze. I focus on the power I felt coursing through me in that act of anger. It felt good. I felt justified. That scares me a little because I know that kind of power could easily get out of control. I've seen enough movies with characters that have superpowers to accept the adage that power equates to responsibility. I can only hope I'm up to it.

---

She calls to me in my sleep that night, a voice rich and melodious, so unlike what I have heard before. But it is her, Gaia. I waken by slow degrees, drawn to the words spinning in my head.

*"Come to me."* I hear her say over and over, in a litany of commands.

I roll to my side, looking at the clock. It's three in the morning. Ugh. I don't want to get up at this ungodly hour. I'll never get back to sleep if I do. But the words continue, and I know it will not stop until I do her bidding.

"Okay. Okay," I mutter into the stillness of my room. "I don't know where you want me to go at three in the morning. My parents are going to kill me if they find out I left the house, and it'll be all your fault."

Of course, I realize the futility of arguing with Mother Earth, but I just can't help myself. Sleep is a sacred thing, and I cherish every minute of it. Being wrenched out of my bed before the dreaded alarm clock goes off is irksome. I throw on a pair of fleece pants, warm socks, and a hoodie before tiptoeing out of my room and downstairs. I can hear my dad snoring loud enough to wake the dead as I pass by my parents' room. How in the hell does my mom sleep through that? At least the sound of a human chainsaw hides the creaks and cracks of the floorboards as I move through the house. I open the front door inch by inch, begging it not to squeal like it so often does. Once I step outside and shut it, I let out a huge sigh of relief. But it's short-lived because I know sneaking back in will be even riskier.

"This better be worth it," I mumble into the darkness. As I take a step toward the walkway, I nearly scream as a black shadow swoops in front of me before landing less than a yard away.

"Are you trying to scare the crap out of me?" I accuse the raven in a harsh whisper. He's staring at me, eyes eerily reflecting the light of the moon. I watch as he opens his mouth to let out a caw. "Sh. Just be quiet. I don't need you making a racket." I rub my hands down my face. "I can't believe I'm out here talking to a frigging raven. There's something so wrong with this."

The raven glides forward, landing a few inches from my feet. I look down at him, imagining I can feel his censure. "Okay. I'm sorry." He tilts his head in that odd bird way, looking at me askance with one eye. "So, where are we headed?"

I shouldn't be surprised when he hops a few feet away and then stops to look at me, clearly letting me know I should follow. I pull my hood up before tucking my hands in my pockets. It's pretty chilly out, and I didn't bring a coat, something I am already regretting. I follow the raven as he intermittently hops, walks, and swoops his way toward the preserve.

I pull out my phone and switch it to flashlight mode before entering the darkness of the forest. This isn't the first time I've come here at night, though it's never been quite this late. Walking to the outcropping of rock takes longer than usual as I'm forced to pick my way past exposed roots and loose rock in the dark. The raven, obviously too impatient to wait, flies ahead of me, and I'm left to make my way alone. I shine my light on his sleek body when I finally arrive.

"Some friend you are, ditching me in the woods."

*Caw!*

"Yeah, yeah. Well, it's harder to get from place to place when you don't have wings to take you there," I tell him, sitting on the rock. It's strange to be so close a wild thing that shows no fear. I'm reminded of that beautiful stag. My heart squeezes painfully at the thought. Forcing my mind away from those events, I look around me. The landscape is different at night, cloaked in shadows and secrets.

I'm not sure how long we sit there, Mr. Raven and I, but eventually, I notice a disturbance in the dimness to my left. I look at it, trying to make out what I'm seeing, but it's too dark to discern. I reach into the pocket of my hoodie to grab my phone and shine a light on it, and am taken aback when the raven pecks my hand. "Ouch! What was that for?" I snap at him. He just looks at me, then points his incredibly sharp beak into the darkness. I huff and let go of the phone.

It starts as an odd shimmering just above the ground. Faintly, I can see the movement of dirt and small stones. The particles begin to rise in a spinning mass, so much like what Raife and I created as we stood facing each other. I watch the particles spin and grow. It's easier to see now with whatever light-colored fragments are mixing in. The vortex expands and begins to take on a shape. I squint my eyes, hoping to pierce the shadows and get a better sense of what I'm seeing, but it's too indistinct for details. And then the soil and rock begin to change, gathering in what can only be called limbs. Within a matter of minutes, I am looking at a humanoid figure about my height. I think my jaw became permanently unhooked from my mouth as I sit there, unable to move or speak, watching as nothing more than the elements of the forest floor becomes a woman.

She walks toward me. As much as something made of nonliving particles can walk. As her figure comes closer, the light of the moon breaks through an opening in the forest canopy. The shape is definitively female with rounded curves and large breasts. It moves forward with slow lifts and drops of its legs, while its arms remain immobile at its sides. The face. How can I describe the face? It is too alien to be beautiful, but it captivates me, and I cannot look away from eyes that seem to glow as pieces of mica reflect the light cast by the moon. I sit motionless as it makes its slow progress, finally stopping a few inches from the tips of my shoes that poke out beyond my rocky outcropping.

The head tilts downward until those crazy eyes meet mine. I wonder if she can see anything. She stands there for a few protracted moments. My heart is racing, and I feel frozen, caught within her inhuman gaze. My eyes dart to the side as I watch her left arm reach forward, toward my face. Rough, phantom fingers caress my cheek. It feels like sandpaper gently stroking my skin.

Within my mind, I hear her. *"Daughter."* I give this strange apparition a small nod but can't make a sound, my voice seemingly gone. *"You are my chosen."*

My throat feels tight and dry, I cough to clear it, and finally manage to croak out a small, "Why me?"

The alien mouth splits into a smile. There are no teeth, only an open maw filled with rock and dirt. *"I have given you great power, my child. More than you know. You will stand beside my progeny in the war to come. When my will has been carried out, you and your mate will birth a new generation with others of your kind. There will be balance again."*

Of course, the one thing I fixate on is the thought of Raife and me coming together and actually making a baby. The darkness is my friend as my cheeks burn at the thought. There's no way in hell that I'm ready for anything even remotely close to that. It's another bit of crazy in this long list of insanity that has become my life. "Um," I start to say before my thoughts come to a stuttering halt. How can I explain to the mother of all things that I'm not ready to be a mother? I decide to skip trying and focus on a different part of what she said. "What do you mean by war?"

Her form seems to fall apart by slow degrees before reforming as I await her reply. *"My progeny will rise and take vengeance for the corruption of man."*

I still don't understand precisely what she's implying, but I'll feel like I've got rocks for brains if I ask her again. Wait, doesn't she have rocks for brains? OMG. I can't believe I just thought that.

I refocus and try to imagine this battle to come. Will there be massive storms and earthquakes? Will innocent people get hurt? Or will they be more focused attacks on the truly corrupt, those individuals or groups whose decisions have plagued the earth? Somehow, I sense that I can't ask these questions. Gaia speaks in such generalities that I wonder whether the specifics are beyond her perception or if she's just not interested. I will have to ask Silas about all of this. From what I recall, he has been through it before.

I fidget a little under her alien gaze when a new thought pops into my head. "Why did you call me here?" It's a reasonable question because she could've just used her weird mental communication thing to tell me this stuff.

I watch her arm lift again, extending a finger. I go a little cross-eyed as the appendage reaches toward my forehead. The first impression of contact feels rough, like before, gritty texture on my skin. But this paltry sensation is suddenly eclipsed by a jolt of feeling that blooms within my head. It feels like blood floods my brain, creating an odd pressure in my skull. It's not painful, but it encompasses every thought until all I am is feeling. The sensations continue to build and spread, traveling down my neck and filling my limbs with heat. I sit rooted to the rock, as waves of power seem to fill every vessel in my body, every pore of my skin. The feelings leave in a rush, and I collapse.

The world around me is quiet, yet I can feel the very heart of it, beating to the rhythm of my own, in a strange symbiotic relationship. Earth. Gaia. Mother. They are one. I am part of her, as she is part of me. A pocket of my mind pulls Celeste's image to the forefront. I can almost hear her telling me about opening my third eye. Kooky new-age talk. But now I feel as though it is open.

*I see.*

# CHAPTER 24

*It's hard to prepare when you don't know
what's coming*

I don't know how long I lie on my back in a heap, simply marveling at the sight which Gaia's touch imparted. This must be how Lestat felt as he looked upon the world with his newborn vampire eyes. But nothing actually *looks* different. It's just that I feel changed, and this perception taints everything, painting it in colors rife with feeling. Most prominent in those feelings is heartache. Sickness. And Rage.

Slowly, I sit up and look around. Gaia's form is little more than wispy swirls of soil and rock, so thin that I can see the dark shadows of trees behind it. I stare at her slowly undulating limbs, transfixed as they coalesce once again, only to lose their shape after a few moments. *"Prepare,"* her voice whispers through my brain before all semblance of her is gone, falling to the forest floor in an inanimate pile of dirt.

All around me is stillness, as though every living creature feels her absence. I sense movement before I see it, a soft fluttering in my thoughts. The raven glides toward me, and somehow, there is meaning in its thoughts that reaches out to me. I raise my arm, and he lands, talons poking into my skin without breaking it. I reach out with my free hand and stroke his chest, feeling the rapid beat of his heart beneath my fingers. Tilting his head in an invitation, I rub the feathers behind his eyes and under his beak, spreading the quills to reach the skin beneath.

I'm not sure of the exact moment the connection is made, but I am suddenly aware that I can hear him, though the raven makes no sound. "What?" I ask, my voice filled with awe.

A name, unlike anything I have heard before, sinks into my mind. *"Scilti."*

"Is that your name? Scilti?" I'm totally beyond feeling like a complete idiot for talking to a bird. There is so much in this world that has been kept hidden behind a veil, and I know I'm just beginning to see beyond it. I watch his beak tap my hand once, as though answering my question with perfect clarity. "Are you like a messenger or something?"

He taps my hand again, as the embodiment of Gaia fills my head. So, he's Gaia's messenger. I wonder what that means. Does he keep tabs on me and report back or what? Is this some kind of bird Gestapo? I shake my head. Now I sound paranoid, and that's the last thing I need added to my list of crazy shit. Gaia isn't some monstrous entity. She is the mother of all things. Mothers nurture their young. They raise them in the warmth of their bosom and keep them safe. Sadly, mankind has defiled its mother, and this is where anger took root, sinking into the heart of her over hundreds of years, maybe even thousands, like some infection that is undetected until it spreads into every living tissue, destroying its host. Not a pretty picture.

"Scilti, do you follow Raife around too?"

The raven taps twice, which I assume is a no. I once read that ravens are incredibly smart, as intelligent as chimpanzees. It's no wonder that ravens have been a feature in mythology. Maybe that's why he's some kind of familiar, or whatever. But why only me?

"Are you *my* bird? I mean, you only come to me?"

Scilti paces along my arm, bobbing his head. Well, I guess that answers that, sort of. "Does Raife have his own raven?"

Scilti just looks at me, cocking his head. Hm. I'm going to assume that he doesn't know. My arm begins to ache. He's not heavy, but holding my arm up is taking its toll. Geez, I need to work out if holding a four-pound bird is too taxing. I lower my arm slowly. Scilti looks down, watching the movement, and scrambles toward my shoulder. 'Okay. This is weird,' I think as he makes himself comfortable and begins to preen his feathers. I stand there, letting him groom, growing accustomed to his weight and proximity. It's not that I've never held a bird before. I've been to an avian rescue shelter a couple of times, back when I was obsessed with the rainforest and wanted to learn more about the animals that live there, and I held a few species of parrots. But this is different. Scilti isn't some rescue animal. He's wild and, apparently, he's mine.

The chill in the air seeps into my bones as I stand and marvel at the fact that I have a pet raven. Actually, I guess he's not really a pet, more like a partner of sorts. Goosebumps pebble my arms, and I begin to tremble with cold. Scilti is totally unaffected but seems to notice my discomfort. I decide to try something out and focus my thoughts on him. Turning my head so that we are eye to eye, I send out an idea. 'I'm cold, and it's late. I need to go home.'

Scilti leans forward, and it's all I can do to remain still as his giant beak fills my vision. He reaches up and preens the hair along my forehead, then leaps from my shoulder, gliding effortlessly onto a nearby branch. Wow.

My legs feel stiff as I begin the hike back to my house. Scilti follows, flitting from tree to tree or hopping along the ground in front of me. It's nice to have some company in the darkness. There is so much to think about as I make the climb. I can still feel dull warmth at the spot where Gaia touched me. Aside from my deep connection with Scilti, I know there is much more I am now open to, and that scares me. That anger I felt, seething all around me, festering like a putrid sore in the heart of the forest, is sure to spill over into my life, and I don't know what that will mean.

It doesn't take long to find out the full effects of this encounter. As I step through that invisible border I've always felt but never seen at the edge of the woods, I'm overcome by a wave of sickness that drops me to my knees. I fall hard, retching violently the moment my hands slap upon the ground. The remnants of dinner flood out of my body in a terrible surge, and I continue to retch, neck locked, and stomach heaving. Tears pour from my eyes as sweat beads on my forehead. Wave after wave washes over me, and I begin to wonder if I'm going to pass out. There's nothing left in my gut, but the dry heaving lasts so long that it feels like blood vessels in my head are bursting.

I sob as the sickness begins to ebb, and I slowly crawl away from the yuck, grabbing onto the rotted trunk of a felled tree. I dig my fingers through the soft bark and fibers, grounding myself in the feel of it as I work to take control of my body. I breathe in the scent of moss and detritus, letting nature's smells fill my lungs and wash away the last of the sickness. The sweat covering my face begins to cool. It feels good, cleansing. I focus on that and stifle the other sensations that are working their way into my mind and heart. The earth is awash in sickness, layered in toxic indifference. I feel Gaia's intent buried beneath all of it. Suck the poison out. Heal what has been diseased and injured. Gaia told me to prepare. Somehow, I must be ready for what is to come, but I have to admit the rage I feel within her is frightening. What if her wishes go from request to command? How far am I willing to go?

---

When my alarm clock goes off, it takes a supreme effort to reach over and slam my hand on the off switch. My body protests, stomach muscles bruised and aching. Inside, I feel hollowed out. There's no way in hell that I'm going to make it through a day of school. I flip through the school year and catalog the number of sick days I've taken, cognizant of the fact that when you begin to approach ten days, the letters start showing up warning you of truancy. Thankfully, I've only taken four this year. I sink back into the mattress and close my eyes, coming back to awareness when my worried mother comes in.

"Terran? Are you sick, sweetie?" I crack my eyes open and watch her come toward me, concern etched across her face.

My voice croaks, "Yeah. I feel awful." There's no need to embellish as she leans over, pressing her inner wrist to my forehead. I can only imagine the dark circles that must be shadowing my eyes.

"Well," she says, pulling her arm away. "You don't feel hot, but you look terrible. Go back to sleep, and I'll call the school. I'll call Celeste too, so she can let Beth know not to pick you up."

I nod slightly, already falling back into the arms of Morpheus. I hear her leave my room, closing the door softly and calling out to my dad, who shows up a short time later to give me a gentle kiss on the cheek. Then there is nothing for a while, just the warmth of the bed and healing sleep.

My dream is so real, a recreation of the night's events. I can hear the sounds of the forest, feel the chill of the air. But the similarities don't last. Soon, the dream becomes a nightmare. The earth shakes beneath my feet, trees swaying as loud snaps break the stillness. My arms swing outward for balance. The forest floor heaves, undulating in a rolling mass of dirt and rock, before splitting violently, opening a deep fissure in the ground. I topple to the side as the crack opens further, belching out plumes of gas and melted rock. I watch, transfixed, when molten ooze bubbles to the surface before popping, sending globs of magma in all directions. Horrified, I try to scramble away, wrenching my body to the side. A small blob lands on my shoulder, burning through my nightie and sinking into my skin. I scream in pain. It burrows through muscle like acid. Panic fills me as the heat penetrates every fiber of my being. It's going to burn right through my heart! All around me, trees are engulfed in flame. I am burning.

I awaken all at once, slapping at my arms, still feeling singed hair and smelling smoke. My heart races, my breath shallow. I look around my room, trying to orient myself. It was so real. I reach up and swipe my hand across my forehead, trying to clear my mind. My fingers come away feeling gritty. I look down at them and see a fine layer of soot covering each digit. What the hell? Throwing back the covers, I hop out of bed. The sheets are caked with ash smears. Grabbing my nightie, I tear it off and look for the spot where I felt the nugget of molten rock sink into me. It's there, a singed ring. I poke my finger through it, watching as flecks of burned fabric break off onto the floor.

Breath whooshes out of me in a rush as I sink down, legs folding in an odd pretzel. It feels like my room is spinning, or maybe it's just me. I look at my feet, charred black from a forest fire I dreamt of. What's going on? With a shaking hand, I reach behind my back, fingers stretching to touch the spot where heat burned through me in my nightmare. The skin around it feels blistered. A whimper turns into a scream when the tip of my finger sinks into a hole that shouldn't be there. I rip my hand away and look down at my chest. There, dug into my left breast, is a hollow, straight through my heart.

My mind fractures, sucking me into a miasma of scattered thought and feeling. When the blackness begins its slow invasion, I welcome it. Aware only of the way it seeps into me, eclipsing everything until I feel nothing. I am nothing.

Awareness comes slowly, stealing over me even as I try to escape it. But it will not be eluded. With a sense of trep-idation, I open my eyes and look around, slowly peeling back the covers of the bed. All I see are white sheets. No remains of ash. I run my hands along my body, but feel only my nightgown. I am whole and not singed. I think I'm losing my mind.

Rolling onto my side, I look at my clock on the night-stand. It's just after two in the afternoon. I really zonked out, but I still feel weighed down with exhaustion. That dream. Or, rather, that nightmare within a nightmare within a dream still lingers, circling my brain. It was so real. I wonder if it was a premonition. Are we doomed? Will I be too late to save anything that I love? Is Gaia's wrath so great that she will swallow the world in a ball of flame? I shudder at the thought. Inside, I know this is an irrational idea. Her aim is simple. I felt it, heard it. But I still feel the cinders peppering my body and the grit caking my hands. I still feel the hole in my heart.

The text tone on my phone pulls me out of my morbid musings. I reach over and grab it, fluffing my pillow just so before I read the message. Apparently, Raife has been texting on and off all day. I scroll through his series of texts, all of them some form of worry over my absence from school. I send a quick reply to let him know I just woke up, then type out a longer text. My thumb hovers over the display as I decide what to write. I don't want to scare him into ditching class to come see me, but I also want to talk to him. There is a compelling need to see him and share the night's craziness. I settle for a simple request to see him after school. It takes me only a couple of seconds to see those three wonderful dots as he replies. I short laugh escapes when he writes, be there in twenty minutes. I send a quick okay and hop out of bed.

As soon as my feet hit the floor, dizziness washes over me, and I take a moment to breathe deeply while assessing whether or not I'm going to either puke my guts out again or fall to the floor. Thankfully, neither happens, and the sensations pass. I make my way to the bathroom and take the fastest shower of my life, racing against time to get ready before Raife arrives. I've just thrown on a pair of sweats and a hoodie when the doorbell rings. I thump down the stairs and swing open the door. Raife swoops in, capturing me in a giant hug.

"Are you okay?" He asks, his voice sending chills down my spine as he speaks into the crease of my neck.

"Yeah. No. I don't know," I say before pulling away and inviting him in.

We head to the kitchen, my stomach rumbling, having finally realized that it's been empty since my episode in the woods. I take out a box of crackers and sliced cheese. Raife watches as I scarf down some of the food before the questions begin.

"Something happened, didn't it?"

I nod, still chewing, and get myself a glass of water, chugging down half of it before wiping my mouth with my hand. "You could say that," I begin, but stop as I realize what a terrible host I am. "Want something to drink?"

Raife chuckles and shakes his head. "Nope."

I sit next to him at the island and rub my hands on my legs, gearing up for a telling that has utterly wrung me out. "I was pulled out of a deep sleep last night by her voice," I start, looking at him. "When I sneaked out of the house, not a fun thing to do, I might add, I found that raven I told you about waiting outside. He asked me to follow, not with words, but there was no other way to interpret his actions. So, I followed him and ended up in my forest. She came to me, like in a physical form."

Raife's eyebrows shoot up. "Seriously? What did she look like?"

I make a face because I know this is going to sound like something straight out of the Sci-Fi network. "Well, that's kind of hard to describe. Basically, she infused herself into the soil and rock that took on a human form. It was a little creepy because her eyes seemed to glow from the light of the moon, reflecting off some chips of mica or something."

"Did she talk to you? I mean, through the dirt," he clarifies. "Wait. That sounds stupid. But you know what I mean, right? Was there an actual voice coming out of it?"

"No," I tell him as he settles into the stool, leaning back a little with a look of awe plastered across his face. At least he's not looking at me like I'm a total freak. I was worried about that, though I realize now that it was stupid to even think it. "Her voice still came through my mind, like before. But she moved. It was so weird seeing her body make its way toward me."

Raife tilts his head as though imagining the scenario I'm describing. "Why did she call you there?"

I look straight at him, needing to see his expression when I tell him what Gaia did. "She touched me, placed her finger against the center of my forehead, and did something to me."

His mouth purses a little, but there's no squeamishness in it, just wonderment at what I'm saying. "What did she do?"

"I don't know how to explain it," I tell him, thinking back on the sensations that raced through me at the contact. "It was like I was flooded with energy or something. Everything around me was different, yet the same. And I could feel so much more powerful feelings, frightening things. It was as though she gave me a part of herself. I still feel it, swimming under the surface of my skin."

Raife reaches over and strokes my face, caressing his fingers in a gentle curve that ends at the base of my neck. "You are so special, Terran. She's chosen you for a purpose. That's what Silas believes, and I know he's right."

I duck my head, feeling self-conscious at the praise. I'm not used to being anything special. Clearly, I'm not some ordinary girl, no matter how I prefer to perceive myself. There's something different inside. I accept this. There's little point in trying to deny it. Gaia sees it too, and she's counting on it in the fight to come.

I take a breath and launch into the rest of the story, trying to speed through the most embarrassing part. "Gaia has plans for me, for us, actually, all of us. She says her progeny will give birth to a generation that will bring balance, which I assume will take a long time, since she can't possibly mean wiping out humanity or something. Gaia wants me to be ready, and somehow, I have no idea how, I'll stand beside her."

The smile that began to spread across his face when I started talking is now a full-blown grin worthy of a Cheshire cat. I feel my face flame because I know exactly what he's going to want to talk more about. "So, she wants us to have kids?"

I cover my face with my hands. "I knew you were going to hone in on that."

Raife laughs. "And you didn't?" I giggle when he pokes me to draw me out. "Huh? You didn't think anything of it? Are you ready to get started?"

That did it. I rear up, mouth open in protest. "Hell, no! I'm not having any kids, so don't get any ideas."

He feigns a mortal wound, and I watch him fall into a fit of laughter at my expense before joining him in the absurdity of this whole situation. Here we are, sitting in my kitchen, talking about spawning a new generation. You can't even make this stuff up!

The levity dies down after a few minutes, and I tell him about Scilti. Raife listens intently but shows no sign that he has an animal buddy of his own. I'm a bit disappointed but not surprised. Yup, I'm an anomaly in a world of anomalies. Rather than make him and me feel queasy, I gloss over the whole puking my guts out part of the night and launch straight into the dream within a dream.

When I finish the entire tale, he says, "I don't know what it all means, Terran. But I feel like it's connected, all part of whatever Gaia has in store for you. Maybe the nightmares were just from the whole stress of everything. Whatever is coming, I'll be there with you. I promise."

I wrap my arms around him and let his words sink in. It feels right to have him here. It's meant to be.

# CHAPTER 25

*There is so much power in anger*

I'm nervous as I walk through the halls at school. Raife and I parted ways as he went off to his class, and Beth is on the opposite side of the building. In this sea of people, I feel alone, awash in worry. I feel something stirring inside of me, caressing my body under my skin, like ghostly fingers of awareness. It's hard to say if it's *her* or just whatever connection was strengthened after she reached inside of me and flipped a switch I never knew existed. My body tingles in anticipation, along with a sick sense of dread balled up in the pit of my stomach. But staying home again wasn't an option, so here I am, raw nerves firing warnings, portents of things to come.

Sliding into a desk at the back of the room, I keep my head down and simply try to keep myself together. My heart is beating too fast. What the hell is coming? I can't sort out my fragmented thoughts enough to decide if these feelings are some kind of panic attack or forewarning. I sense a body sit in the desk next to mine, but I keep my eyes down.

"Hey, Terran. Are you okay?" Janet's familiar voice asks.

I let out a soft sigh and turn to her. "Yeah. I'm just having an off day."

She nods her head in understanding. "I didn't want to get out of bed today, but I've got like five absences, and my mom will flip out if I get one of those stupid truancy warning letters."

I've always resented the idea of that letter of warning. Sure, I get the reasoning and all, but give me a break. Everyone gets sick, and we all need mental health days now and then. "I got that letter my freshman year," I tell Janet. "I had gotten the flu and then a couple months later ended up with strep. My mom flipped out when it came and called the school, all worried that I was going to end up with some note in my file about it. It's such a joke, you know? Like, somehow it's my fault my immune system couldn't cut it in high school."

"There are some teachers who should get that letter," Janet mumbles as a sub walks in the door. We laugh quietly as we watch what looks like a recent college grad fumble through papers, turning beet red when he can't find whatever he's looking for.

This is the third substitute we've had in this class in the last couple of weeks, and, from the looks of it, the sub-pool is getting pretty thin. The guy looks like he must have rolled out of bed, barely taking the time to brush his hair, a blond mess with a cowlick causing a lump of strands to poke out from the side of his head like some bad eighties hairdo. I try to feel some empathy as he stutters slightly, trying to get the class to stop talking so he can take attendance, but it's just not my day to be sympathetic. It doesn't help that his name is Mr. Shartez, but once he writes it on the board, there's no going back. There's also clearly no way the class is going to recover when Ben Miller makes a comment about shitting your pants. It's going to be that kind of morning.

Janet and I settle into our seats as the man tries to gain some semblance of control. Poor Mr. Shartez. It makes me wonder if he too wishes he'd just ignored the call from the school and stayed in bed. It's painfully obvious that Mr. Shartez just wants to run from this school and never come back.

Janet settles into her phone as the class devolves into rounds of toilet humor at the poor sub's expense. I watch his panicked looks toward the classroom door and glances at the clock for a few minutes before my attention drifts from this scene of mortifying embarrassment, and I fix my gaze out the window. That's where I want to be. I feel the pull.

As I'm looking at the scene beyond this prison, a flash illuminates the sky just above a tree line, followed by a thunderous bang that shakes the earth. My face wrinkles as I try to make sense of it. When a ball of smoke billows upward, I gasp in horror. What's going on? I stand up, unable to keep my body from remaining still, and head to the line of windows. A black shape swoops by. Scilti. He caws before landing on a tree. I can sense panic in his trembling form.

I hear Janet call my name, but I can't respond. All around me, kids are jumping up, looking out the window, and shouting. I can hear the conversation, but none of it penetrates my mind. Inside, I am in turmoil. My hands grip the windowsill as waves of nausea come over me. No, no, no. Not here, I tell myself, gritting my teeth to keep the sickness at bay. Beyond the glass, clouds of gray and black fill the sky, drifting slowly toward the school. Is this real or another vision?

As the wind blows, specks of ash brush against the panes, sticking to the grooves or falling to the ground in some twisted illusion of snow. Something awful has happened, something is scorching the earth, and she is writhing in agony. My skin is in flames, blistering on the inside while my stomach churns in protest, threatening to disgorge everything I've eaten.

"*It burns!*" Gaia rages.

A nail breaks as my grip tightens. I can feel a trickle of blood among the flashes of pain. Gaia is squirming under an onslaught of some explosion beyond the border of town. What's out there, the lumber mill? I reach toward her to understand what's happening, but there is only anger. The smattering of thoughts that come to me are laced with blame for men whose actions have somehow caused this. Her will crashes into me, and I let it take over, unable to keep her at bay.

Heat begins to build in my muscles. Energy from the heart of the earth flows through me, snaking through the brick and mortar of the building, punching through the soles of my shoes, and into me. My body begins to thrum, pulsing with Gaia's strength and purpose. I press my hands to the windowpanes, tilting my head downward and gritting my teeth as I take in her wrath and vengeance.

I let it fill me, a willing vessel, as smoke fills the sky. Beyond the glass are fear and panic, pain and death, hundreds of voices screaming in agony. From the trees to the grass, from the burrowing animals to the birds, I feel it all. Channeling the power, I pour my energy outward, sensing it sink into the ground and take root. I use it as an anchor and lift my hands upward. The earth shudders, then begins to undulate in slow waves. I lift my palms toward the source of whatever disaster humanity has wreaked and send the wave of earth toward it.

I can feel people panic as they become aware that the

ground is shifting beneath their feet and their cars. In my mind, I latch on to blistering earth, the source of whatever explosion has rocked the town. It feels like my hands are burning as waves of dirt and rock tumble forward beneath the surface in an unrelenting rhythm. I hold out as long as I can, then thrust my will forward in a final push. The ground opens, swallowing the remains of fiery buildings; the origin of the blistering pain Gaia feels, before settling. Sweat is pouring down my face as my arms drop to my sides. It takes me a few moments to realize that I am alone in the room. The fire alarm is blaring across the campus as students run for safety or take shelter in small pockets of the building. I let my body sink to the floor.

Gaia grieves. Her sadness fills my soul. Beneath her sorrow is anger, and mixed within that fury is me. I am her hand of vengeance. My muscles ache as I slowly get up. The classroom is in total disarray, desks shoved this way and that, bags and other belongings strewn across the floor. I grab my things and head into the hallway. It looks like a stampede came through. As I walk toward an exit, I can hear sirens. Some are far away, while others sound like they are getting closer.

A few stragglers run by me, bumping me in their flight for safety. I watch them, feeling detached from it all. My mind is filled with Gaia. Her thoughts and feelings crash over me, clouding my thoughts. It's as though I am watching myself pick my way through a minefield of backpacks and other belongings, unaffected by any of it. Perhaps I'm in shock or something.

The entire school is on the front lawn or in the parking lot. The hum of conversation is overwhelming as students yell, hug, or just sit in disbelief. Within it all are phones buzzing, ringing, and dinging all around me. I feel my own begin to vibrate in my pocket and head over to a less crowded area before I pull it out and pick up.

I hold it to my ear, covering the other side of my head so I can hear my mom. "Hi, Mom. I'm okay."

Her voice is panicked. "Terran! Oh, thank God. You're okay? Are you sure?"

"I'm fine, Mom, just a little shook up but not hurt or anything. There was an explosion. I could see the smoke from here. Are you and Dad all right?"

"We're both just fine. I don't want you to worry about us. Dad is on his way to the school now to pick you up. Something happened at the mill, and then an earthquake! I don't understand it. Oh, honey, I was so scared. The streets are in terrible shape, and people are so panicked."

"Yeah, it's like that here too."

"Keep an eye out for your father. I have to go. Your uncle is calling, and I don't want him to worry. I'll see you soon. I love you, sweetie."

"I love you too, Mom."

I hang up and scan the road, but there's a tree down on one side, and the other is quickly becoming congested with cars pouring out of the lot or trying to get in. It'll be a while before my dad can get through. Scanning the grounds, my eyes skip from one person to another. I don't see Raife or Beth, but there are so many clusters of people that it's hard to make out individuals. The rush of adrenaline recedes, leaving my muscles trembling. I make my way to a large oak tree before I fall down and collapse against the trunk. Digging my hands into the grass grounds me. I press my back against the bark of the tree and reach toward its heart, feeling the life that stirs within. Closing my eyes, I release a long breath and let my mind empty of everything but the ground and the tree. Peace settles over me. In the branches above, Scilti sits, watching.

Beth finds me first. "Terran! Oh, my God. Are you okay? Did you get hurt?"

I open my eyes slowly and take in her worried expression. I wonder what she would do if I told her I caused it. "I'm okay. Are you?"

"Now that my heart has stopped pounding out of my chest, yeah," she tells me, sitting down. "Can you believe we had an earthquake? I mean, I thought that was a California thing. I wonder if anyone got hurt."

At that moment, an ambulance and a fire truck came barreling down the road, before swinging into the lot. Paramedics bustle out, taking the gurney from the back and heading toward the front entrance, following a small group of firefighters. I can see a couple of teachers and a custodian holding open the doors to usher them inside.

Raife comes running up as the doors close. He falls to his knees and hauls me into a bear hug. "I'm so glad you're okay."

"I'm fine, just shaken up a bit. Are you all right?" I look him over. Aside from the fading concern in his face, he looks perfect.

"Yeah, no need to worry about me."

I look back at the school, a sinking feeling settling in my stomach. "Did someone get hurt?"

Raife strokes my hand. "I heard a custodian say something about a substitute teacher getting pinned under a bookshelf."

The three of us sit in silence for a few minutes, keeping our eyes on the front of the school. Eventually, the doors open as paramedics wheel out a gurney. I hope Mr. Shartez is okay. Shane joins us as the ambulance sirens turn on, and the vehicle pulls away.

"Hey!" Shane calls out. "Happy to see you all didn't get hurt or anything. This was some crazy shit, right?"

We give him a chorus of agreement. Shane settles down next to Beth, and the two of them launch into accounts of what they did when the quake hit. Raife and I say nothing. He knows. I focus on the feel of his fingers, stroking my skin. We'll talk when we're away from all of this chaos.

# CHAPTER 26

*Are you kidding me?*

T he explosion was caused by dust at the lumber mill, a couple of miles outside of town. That's what Raife and I found out as the evening news flooded television and radio waves that night. While no one was killed in the blast, several people were injured, and many more were hurt in the earthquake that followed, an unprecedented 5.9 on the Richter scale. I'm weighed down by guilt at the latter. It's hard to explain what came over me when the explosion occurred. I only know that I was overcome by anger that arose from deep within me, leaving nothing but thoughts of retaliation.

"I don't know why I did it or how," I tell Raife. We are

sitting in his car outside my house with the radio turned down low. I was able to slip out without any notice. I know my parents are inside, still glued to the television as newscasts after newscasts air stories about the event. I just can't sit and watch any more. "When the explosion happened," I continue. "It was like I just sort of reacted, you know?"

Raife looks at me with a measure of understanding in his eyes, but there's something else there, too. "What you did wasn't wrong, Terran."

"No? It feels wrong, like I lost control. People could've been killed by the quake I caused, people I know."

He nods. "I understand, but this is bigger than us. What you felt, whatever connection you have that gave you the power and will to move the earth, that was *her*. Gaia is working through you. In a way, you're like a messenger. It's not up to you to determine the message. You just have to deliver it. People need to wake up. That explosion wouldn't have happened if the people in this town weren't ripping trees from the earth and processing them in such large numbers that the mill itself became a potential death trap. You've seen the ruin of the forest up on those logging roads. You know what they're doing. You've felt it, and so have I. That accident is just the result of this greed humans have in some crazed attempt to consume everything."

"I know, but what I did just made everything worse!" I shout. "I should've been able to rein myself in instead of causing something that was even more damaging than what happened at the mill. At least that explosion didn't rip through the town, not like I did."

"Terran, you can't blame yourself for reacting as you did. People need to be made to understand that what they're doing is destroying their mother. If you don't help them see, then how is that all going to end?"

"You make it sound so easy, like I should just shrug my shoulders and say, 'oops, my bad,' but I can't do that. You weren't the one who opened up a frigging crack in the earth that swallowed an entire lumber mill!"

He sits quietly while I fume, finally speaking when my heart is pounding, and anger isn't coursing through my veins. "You're right. You could have controlled it, but would that really have been better?" My mouth drops open, but he touches his finger to my lips before I can talk. "Just hear me out. If you hadn't reacted the way that you did, that mill would've been rebuilt in a matter of months, right?"

"I don't know," I reply.

"From what I saw on the news, the blast took out the main building but left a bunch of the outbuildings and most of the lumber processing equipment. So, doesn't it seem logical that they would've started up again in a short time?" I nod. "And more forests would be ripped from the earth, and more animals would be displaced or killed, and it would go on and on until there is no more forest left." He pauses, looking closely at the emotions washing over my face. "If this kind of thing goes unchecked across the world, how will it all end?"

Raife's words put things in a harsh perspective. "People will destroy the earth."

"Exactly," he says, rubbing my back to ease the tension that's sitting there in tangled knots. "If we stand by and do nothing, there won't be anything left. I wonder if it would destroy Gaia herself. What if that's what this really needs to be about? If the heart of the earth is murdered by a species gone mad, how could the planet even survive? It would be like a light being snuffed out."

The image his words paint fills my mind, and I follow them into the depths of my body. I can feel her in me, writhing, and within this connection is a sickness rooted so deep within her that there's no way to dig it out. And it's spreading, a disease with no cure. "You're right. I know you're right. But...but what if I kill someone?" Inside, I wonder how Raife would look at me if I did.

Raife curls his hands around my head, framing my face before pulling me gently forward for a soft kiss. My lips tingle as warmth spreads through me, flooding my cells with awareness and feeling. The sensations last long after he pulls away, a smile pulling up the corners of his perfect mouth. "There's nothing you could do that would make me love you less."

My heart stutters as he says this. "You love me?"

He chuckles. "Desperately."

School is canceled for the remainder of the week until the building can be assessed for any structural damage. The rest of the town is in various states of repair. Quite a few trees fell, which hurts my heart a little, as well as lots of utility poles and signage. Most of the damage is rather minor, though. According to seismology experts, the earthquake was unusual in that it shook huge portions of our town and split the ground under the mill, but then sealed itself up like a cauterized wound. Where the lumber mill once stood is just a sea of overturned earth, the entire plant swallowed by the quake.

It's frightening to acknowledge that I did all of that. But a part of me is relieved as well. Somehow, I was able to focus my rage so that the greatest damage centered on the root of what started it all. It could've been so much worse. Inside, I know I could've leveled the entire town. I also recognize that if the majority of the workforce hadn't been at an offsite operation that day, people would've died. I would be a killer. The few foremen who were working there at the time of the explosion and subsequent quake said as much when they were interviewed from the hospital by the local news. It's terrifying to think that things could've gone so wrong.

With no school in session, Raife and I are free to visit Silas. I'm feeling cabin fever setting in, and I know I need to get out of the house. Plus, I need to talk to him and gain some perspective. My parents are so distracted that they agree to let me go out with Raife after only a few half-hearted protests.

"Are you sure you want to go out with this boy today after everything that happened?" Mom asks, anxiety splashed across her features. "What if another earthquake hits and you're stuck in his car somewhere?"

Of course, I can't tell her that unless I summon another quake, there won't be one. It's a bit frustrating, but there's no way I would ever clue them into what's really going on. Ignorance is truly blissful. "Don't worry, Mom. All of those earthquake specialists on the news said it was a freak event. It'll be fine. Plus, I want you to meet Raife, and I need to get out of the house. Sitting around here is going to drive me crazy."

She looks over at Dad, who's been silently listening to the exchange. "Let her go, Eleanor. She needs some fresh air. Besides, I'd like to meet this young man she keeps telling us about." He stands and adjusts the waistband of his pants while puffing his chest as he says this.

I roll my eyes. "Really, Dad?"

He smirks at me and cocks an eyebrow. "As your father, I need to make sure this boy is up to snuff. I also need to make it clear that he better treat my little girl right."

Shaking my head, I sigh and say, "Okay, tough guy. But you need to be nice to him. He's important to me."

I walk out of the room as my parents talk about the

first boy I'm bringing home. I guess it freaks them out a bit, and I can understand that. I text Raife and let him know to come on over. I also prepare him for what's to come. He replies with a few humorous emojis, and I head upstairs to put on a clean hoodie and brush my hair.

The introductions themselves are rather easy. Mom looks Raife over with a small smile after shaking his hand and inviting him inside, asking only a few get-to-know-you questions. Dad is all bluster in the end, and welcomes Raife into the living room for a chat before Raife and I head out. I try to eavesdrop on their conversation as Mom and I stand in the kitchen to give them space, but my dad has lowered his voice so all I can hear is a low rumble interspersed with soft replies from Raife. I grind my teeth and mutter, imagining the worst. Mom laughs at my grumbling and says, "He's behaving, trust me. I told your father there'd be hell to pay if he embarrassed you."

"Thanks, Mom."

She winks at me and sweeps out of the room to let Raife off the hook and scoot us out of the house. As I'm closing the front door, she reaches out and pulls it away from me. "He seems like a really nice young man, Terran."

I give her a big smile. "He is."

"I'm happy for you, honey. You two have fun."

"Thanks, Mom," I say, giving her a quick peck on the cheek.

I hop down the steps and slide into the passenger seat as Raife holds the door open for me. I can see the curtains in the front window of the house moving slightly and know my dad is watching. I'm sure Raife has scored a few points in the gentleman department. I smile and wave, letting him know I see him spying. Rather than pretend otherwise, he waves back, and the curtain falls.

I watch Raife get into the car, all grace and sinewy muscles. God, he's fit. "Can we go straight to Silas' or did you want to stop anywhere on the way?"

He starts the car up, and we head out. "Let's go straight there. I know you're eager to talk to him. Maybe we can make a stop on the way back and hang out for a bit."

I don't know how he does it, but Enzo seems to have been waiting for us. He swings open the door before Raife can even finish knocking.

"Terran," he says, swinging the door aside. "Raife. It's good to see you both."

We swap greetings as he ushers us inside.

"Silas is expecting you."

I glance at Raife, who shrugs, and we follow Enzo into the sitting room. We sink into the loveseat, fingers twining, as we wait for Enzo to return with his customary tray of goodies. He doesn't disappoint, and we find ourselves with an assortment of petit fours and lavender tea. I'm sure it's completely intentional timing, but we find ourselves with just enough time to enjoy a cup of tea and more little cakes than anyone should eat at one sitting.

It takes me by surprise when Silas swoops into the

room and sits across from us. In the past, he's led me to his glorious study. "It's good to see you both," he tells Raife and me. "I assume you're here because of what happened."

I grip Raife's hand a little tighter. He squeezes back, passing along his strength in the movement. "Yes. I wanted to talk to you about that. I need to understand how it happened and what it means."

Silas leans forward, staring intensely into me. "Before we discuss that event, I sense there was something that occurred before. I can feel a difference in you."

It really should come as no surprise that he somehow sees Gaia's mark on me, but I'm a little taken aback by the realization that it's evident from an outside perspective. "She came to me," I tell him. "Taking form from the earth itself, and touched me, right here." I press my finger to the center of my forehead. I swear I can still feel the remnants of her on that very spot.

"And when she touched you, what happened?"

"I don't know. I can't put it into words."

Silas smiles slightly. "I understand. Some things that are so profound they cannot be explained in a way that fully captures them. But I believe that Gaia passed along a piece of herself at that contact. You may have felt her inside you. You may feel her still, on a level much deeper than before. She has singled you out for a purpose, Terran. I believe we have seen a part of that in the events in your town."

"I thought we were all the same kind of people...er, beings...whatever. Isn't that true?"

Silas purses his lips slightly as he thinks about my questions. "From a certain viewpoint, it's true that you are like others of your kind. But Gaia does not present herself to all of her children. And she absolutely doesn't imbue them with gifts that rival or surpass my own."

"Wait. I can do things that you can't?" What the hell? I'm some weird half-breed or something, and he's telling me that I'm more powerful than he is.

"Yes, you can." He pauses for a moment, reading the shock in my face before continuing. "Most of us can harness the power of the air and water. If fire is present, we can bend it to our will and inflame it to greater intensity. But moving the earth itself has always been a power only Gaia possesses. Now, she has passed it to you."

"But why? Why would she want me to have a strength equal to hers?"

Silas chuckles. "I wouldn't call it equal to hers, but it certainly goes beyond ours. As for the reason, I can only speculate. There is something within you, Terran. Something that has not been seen before in your kind, and it calls to her."

I think back to that night and remember Gaia telling me I had power I didn't even recognize. She said that before she ever touched me. I wonder now if that point of contact wasn't so much transference of power, but an unleashing of it. Every time I come here, I seem to have more questions. What is it about me that's so different? Why am I not like Raife? Where is all of this going to lead? I know Gaia has a path for me to walk, but I still don't know how dark that road is. Will she ask me to kill to save her? As I'm fuming a little inside, Silas interrupts my thoughts.

"I wonder," he says, his voice tapering off a bit.

"Huh?"

"If Gaia didn't actually bestow power on you, then perhaps there is something more going on here. There's a legend among the Daoine Fíor about the one who will come when the earth is under siege. Perhaps you are the one the legend spoke of."

"Seriously?" I ask him, trying to keep the bulk of my sarcasm out of my words. I'm entirely unsuccessful, but come on! There's a legend, and he thinks it might be about *me*?

Raife has been quiet throughout but seems keen to delve into this fantasy. "Could you tell us the legend? Maybe if we hear it, some of this will make sense."

I turn to look at him, unable to wipe away my dubious expression. "What?" He asks. "Maybe you are."

"Oh, my God. You can't honestly think that I'm some preordained savior of the planet or something. That's just stupid!"

"Wasn't all of this absurd until you found yourself wrapped up in it?"

I huff. He's got me there. "Okay. You score a point with

that one. But the idea of a legend being told...wait." I turn to Silas. "Silas, how long ago did this story come about?"

"My people have told the tale of Áine's progeny for centuries."

"See? It's some crazy story from a time when people seriously believed the earth was the center of the universe and that drilling a hole in someone's skull would cure headaches." I fold my arms against my chest, indicating the end of this stupidity.

Raife ducks his head and kisses my cheek as I act like a petulant child. "You're so cute when you're angry. But I still want to hear the story."

I grunt softly, dropping my head against the back of the loveseat in exasperation. "Fine. Let's have a story. But don't go drinking the cool-aid just yet, okay?"

"I promise only to drink it if it's my favorite flavor," he replies, nudging my arm until I loosen up.

Sighing, I look at Silas. "Tell us the legend of Áine."

# CHAPTER 27

*There's a reason legends stand the test of time*

It should be noted that Silas is an amazing storyteller. Of course, he is. He's virtually perfect, at least physically. Why wouldn't he also be good at telling a story? Silas begins to spin a tale, and I have mixed feelings about it. If there's any truth to it, then my life is on some predestined path I may not be able to hop off of. And if the legend is all a bunch of baloney? Then I know as little about what's going on as I did before we came here today.

"In Celtic legend, Áine is often referred to as a faery queen or goddess of the earth and nature. It is said that she is a descendant of the Tuatha Dé Danann. In other legends, she has been called a love goddess, her name being twined with the likes of Venus and Aphrodite. But the truth of her nature and her name rests with us."

"Áine was a daughter of Gaia. Her being was infused with so much of our great mother that she could bend the earth to her will. It is said that Áine had the gift to communicate with all life, from the birds in the air to the trees in the forest. In this, the Celtic legends were correct. She truly embodied Gaia. She was a goddess, as terrible in her wrath as she was in her beauty. Vengeful. Powerful. Áine lived within Gaia's landscape for hundreds of lifespans."

"There is a legend of a time when an empire of man began to spread across the land, bringing death and destruction. War erupted in every pocket of the planet; this tide of humanity entered. When the Daoine Fíor rose up to fight, many were lost. The earth ran red with the blood of the Daoine Fíor mixed with the blood of nature. It was a dark time. Gaia, grieving with a sorrow so deep that her voice was silenced, could not awaken to take back what was hers."

"Áine felt this loss as no other could. She nursed the grief, anguish, and terror until it became rage. It is said that entire mountains rained down upon the armies of man in a vengeance so terrible that it slipped into myth and passed through our generations. When her wrath was finally spent, the empire, and many like it, had fallen. Nature slowly crept back across the land, reclaiming a world. It was within that time, this time of rebirth, that Gaia awakened from her grieving, and Áine became a legend."

"The wisest of the Daoine Fíor, the seers, believed this event was a foreshadowing. Mankind would rise up again and wreak havoc across the earth. And when it does, who will protect our great mother if she cannot protect herself? Áine could not live forever. In fact, our histories tell us that following this great upheaval, she began to wander, her mind and body slowly slipping from this world and into the next. Leaving us to wonder who would take her place when humanity, once again, washes over the world in a tide of greed and waste?"

"Our seers reached out to Gaia, the strongest of them conveying the uncertainty of our people. Gaia shared little beyond the knowledge of one, unlike any other before her, who would bring balance when the next dark time blanketed the earth. Seers took this assurance to mean a prophecy. It was foretold that the chosen one would come, born of a mix of human and Daoine Fíor, suffused with such power that she would become Áine."

It takes a few moments to realize that Silas' pause marks the end of the story. I think about the last part of what he said and understand what he's implying. "You think I'm Áine? I mean, the incarnation of her or something?"

"I do," Silas replies with total sincerity. "The earth is overrun by armies of man. Gaia is under siege. She is filled with sorrow and anger. Her heart is broken. I don't know if she is strong enough to rise up on her own. I feel a sickness within her. She has chosen you, Terran, and I believe this is why. I think you are the Áine of the present, and it is time to go to war."

"You've got the wrong girl, Silas. I don't want to go to war. I'm not a warrior-type. I'm the geeky nature girl who walks in the woods talking to the trees and squirrels. Picking a fight with anyone isn't something I've ever done, and I'm certainly not about to change that by picking a fight with all of humanity!"

"Terran, what if all of humanity were lost if you stood aside?" Silas says softly.

It's a punch in the gut when he says this. It's so much like what Raife told me after I went all psycho and caused a frigging earthquake. But that truth aside, this doesn't seem like the path I should be taking. "It's too much, Silas. I'm not ready. I don't even know how I did what I did. That's why I'm here, you know? I came here to get answers and learn how to do these things. And now you're basically telling me that I'm some goddess-savior-type who's supposed to save humanity from itself. I'm a seventeen-year-old kid! What do you expect of me?"

"It is not I who expects something of you," Silas tells me.

When he says this, I sink into the cushions, resignation slowly eclipsing my lingering protests. He's got a point. It is Gaia who works through me or with me, or however this all happens. If that means Silas and others like him need to believe it's because of some legend, then so be it. But that doesn't mean I am the one the myths are talking about. Until today, I was more of an ordinary freak, if such a thing even exists. Yeah, I can do some wild stuff, but I've been coming to terms with all of that. This world has been hiding things for a long time. I can accept that.

But, believing I am somehow transforming into a being from an obscure legend dreamed up by an ancient race? Not likely. Recent events have proven I can deal with the bizarre, but I'm not so far gone that I can get on board with this idea. I look over at Raife. He's rubbing his fingers in slow circles, no doubt trying to digest this newest tidbit from the mind of Silas. I stare at him for a few seconds, needing to see his face. If he looks at me, I can read his thoughts and know if he's just as flabbergasted by Silas as I am or ready to jump into this pool of absurdity with both feet.

When Raife doesn't turn my way, I shift my attention to the window. It's stunning, an octagonal form with light spilling through glass that appears handmade, riddled with lovely imperfections. As I look at it, marveling a little at how the sun seems to bend around the bubbles and dips within the glass, I realize that I may be looking at this situation all wrong. Where do myths come from? They are stories spun from the minds of those who need to explain the world around them, to give direction and hope to the people in their community. Áine could be that, a promise that all is not lost for a people who have seen and felt too much at the hands of a species that has become unconcerned with the fate of the world. Who am I to argue with a legend? Maybe they need me to pretend the story is real. What I know is that things cannot go on as they are. She cannot go on.

Mankind is killing Gaia. In a sense, it is killing itself because if humanity manages to poison her beyond repair, then there will be nothing left of the earth. In my heart, I know it will wither and die. Everything hangs in the balance. I laugh softly to myself. Balance. That's what this is all about. The balance has shifted as people turned their backs on the earth in exchange for the unnatural. There has been little accounting of the cost. Sure, I see groups protesting, rallying, and fundraising in a desperate attempt to gain awareness. My teachers teach us about climate change, global warming, microplastics, and greenhouse gases. But these things are too abstract for most people. They are not tangible and therefore easily ignored and disregarded. Until something crawls across their lawns and stares them in the face with cold reality, nothing will really change.

What is it that Gaia wants of me? Does she know about this legend? Is any part of it true? I decide to ask her myself so that I can try to understand the role she needs me to play. I close my eyes and feel, sinking that secret part of myself through the floorboards, past the foundation, and into the earth. Deep within, I push my

consciousness, searching for her. I sense a flutter of awareness and follow it. The moment I touch her with my mind,
a calm settles over me. I am home.

"*Daughter.*"

"Mother. I am here."

"*See,*" she tells me as she has so many times before.
Only this time, Gaia pulls me into the past, showing me
the legend as it happened. Taking me to the time of Áine.

I find myself standing in the center of what must have
been an old-growth forest before falling beneath an
onslaught of violence. I turn slowly, taking in the ruined
earth and fallen trees, the bodies of deer and rabbit, oak
and fern. All is dead here. It has become a graveyard. I
walk slowly among the remains of this once verdant
valley. The ground beneath my feet is spoiled, littered with
ash and blood. A part of me recognizes that among all of
this death are men, soldiers whose corpses lie in putrid
piles. Their armor is coated in blood and rust, faces
twisted in agony beneath the rocks that pummeled them. I
feel nothing looking at them. It is as though I am apart,
someone else.

In the distance, a lake spans the horizon. My legs take
me to it, as though drawn by its cleansing power.
Reaching the edge, my heart twists, as the bodies of mated
swans and the young they brought into the world lie
mangled along the shoreline, ripped apart by weapons of
steel for no reason other than bloodlust. I pace away from
their tortured remains to a place where the water reflects

nothing but the stillness of the air and sky. Kneeling on the muddy bank, I reach my hands toward the water, breaking the surface in a series of infinite ripples. Cupping handfuls, I bring them to my face, letting the coolness wash away the stink of death. Releasing a breath, I bend my head and look at a reflection I have never seen before. White-blond hair, matted with dirt and debris, frames a face etched with sorrow. Brilliant blue eyes stare back at me. I am Áine.

I gasp, pulling myself away from the vision with sudden force. In my mind, Gaia whispers, *"You have come again."*

Raife shakes me gently as I come to. "Terran? Are you okay?"

I turn to face him. "No, I'm not okay. None of this is okay."

Raife's brow wrinkles. "I don't understand. You blacked out for a moment."

I shake my head. "I didn't black out. I spoke to her. Silas is right. The legend is true."

"Are you sure?" He asks, concern layering each small word.

"Yes. She showed me something from the past, awful things," I cringe a little inside, recalling the bodies strewn across a landscape that was mutilated by the hands of men. "Whether I like it or not, whether I believe it or not, Gaia has made her will clear. I am to be the Áine of our time."

# CHAPTER 28

*So much for being a normal kid*

S ilas looks pleased. That's the only way I can describe his smug expression. I grimace at him, still not sure how I've managed to go from nature-loving-teen to savior-of-the-planet. Life is strange, and mine is stranger than most.

"You look like the cat that got the cream, Silas," I announce.

He snickers, nodding his head. "I suppose I do. You have no idea what this means to my people and me. Honestly, the legend has been sitting in my mind since we met, but I wasn't sure. There are many like you, scattered across the globe, and the state of the world is not so unlike other parts of our history. Until I saw the change in you today, I hadn't seriously considered that the time of Áine's rebirth is now. It's quite an honor to be the one to find you."

I look at him and wonder why he didn't tell me this story when we first met. "I feel like you've been holding out on me. How could you not have told me this story before? Didn't you say Gaia wanted me to help her fight a war?"

"There is always war, Terran. Since the dawn of man, there has been war. I admit that the current onslaught eclipses events of the past, but we have faced similar times and seen the balance slowly tip toward sustainability, only to fall back again. Look back on your histories, and you will see our hands. We have shaped tornadoes and fires that have ripped through parts of the world on massive scales. There have been earthquakes and volcanic eruptions brought about by Gaia as her wrath bubbled to the surface. And yet, mankind has persisted, making little progress but never truly seeing the error of its ways. We have done all of this without the rebirth of Áine."

"Why now, then?" I ask.

"I do not know. Perhaps there is more that is occurring than I can sense."

It's not a substantial answer, but I can see I'm not going to get any further clarification. This must be what having faith is like. You just have to believe it. "So, I guess what you're saying is that I don't have a choice in this, right?"

Silas cocks his head. "There is a choice, but you were born for this. It has always been within you, and now Gaia has set it free."

---

Silas agrees to meet with Raife and me the next afternoon to tap into this newfound power and hone it into something I can fully control. It makes me a bit nervous to consider what this means. I don't want to cause another crack in the earth to open up under someone's house or a retirement neighborhood or something. The thought of the damage I am capable of is daunting. But I have to admit that it is also exhilarating. To be able to essentially shape the earth, to mold rock and water by my will, is a bit intoxicating.

"Did I ever tell you about the natal chart Beth's mom made for me?" I ask Raife as we head home from our visit with Silas.

"No. What's a natal chart?"

"You'd have to ask Celeste, that's Beth's mom, for a really thorough explanation, but it's kind of like a celestial roadmap of who someone is that is based on the day of their birth."

Raife considers the idea and asks, "So, did yours tell

you that you'd be communing with the goddess of the earth or something?"

I punch him in the arm, and he snickers. "No, it didn't say anything like that, you ass. It told me that I've got a lot of mystical power, though. I've been thinking about it since things started to get really crazy, and I'm starting to believe that it's right. Maybe this is how I was born, and there was never any avoiding it."

Raife nods. "Silas would agree with you. What did Beth's mom say about it? I mean, did she explain what the whole mystical part meant, or did she just give the chart to you?"

"She explained it, going over all the planetary alignment stuff and what it all means. It's really out there, to be honest, but now that so much has happened, it's not some far-fetched fantasy anymore. One thing she said that keeps coming to mind has to do with me being able to face things and take action, rather than kind of sitting on the sidelines and hoping things will get better."

I watch his face change to one of surprise. "Really? That's pretty freakin' cool. Silas said basically the same thing, you know."

"Yeah. He did. That's why I feel like what's coming is something I must have been born to do. It was in the stars. At least it was from Celeste's perspective."

"Listen to you, getting all new-age-hippie. I like this side of you. Exactly how much of a free spirit are you turning into, huh?" he asks while leaning over, waggling his eyebrows at me.

"Don't go thinking I'm going to turn into some kind of hippie-love-fest-chick. Just concentrate on driving, Romeo."

"Yes, ma'am. Want to stop anywhere on the way? Maybe swing by the beach for a bit?"

I consider the idea and find it incredibly appealing. "Actually, that would be fantastic. I could use a bit of nature watching right about now."

Raife begins to head west while I look out the window, watching the world go by and thinking about how everything is the same, but it's all so different, at least from my perspective. As the outside blurs by, I catch a glimpse of a black shape swooping in and out in dips parallel to the car. I crane my neck to get a better look, and, sure enough, Scilti is following us. I smile at him, knowing he probably can't see my expression, but wanting to communicate it all the same. I have a feeling he'll be hanging around as we walk along the shore.

A short time later, Raife pulls into an empty lot. The wind is blowing, making my hair fly into my eyes as we exit the car. From the trunk, Raife pulls out a couple of fleece blankets, wrapping one around me before we walk among the seagrass to the beach. It's a beautiful day, the sky a deep gray, almost purple, with the promise of rain. The waves roll in at a lazy pace, curling just a bit in a foamy crest before tumbling to the shore. Raife spreads his blanket on the sand, and we sit, using mine to trap our warmth as we huddle. On an outcropping of rock a few yards away, Scilti perches, sifting through his feathers and darting glances my way.

"Do you think you could control the ocean?"

Raife's question jars me out of a rather peaceful state of catatonia. "What?"

"I'm just wondering if you could control it, the waves and all. It would be really cool to see."

I'm a little surprised by his line of thinking. "I guess I could, but it's not something I should be playing around with, you know? I could hurt someone accidentally."

"There's no one in the water today, too cold. How about you just try and see what happens?" He's looking out into the waves as he says it.

I follow his gaze, scanning the horizon for any swimmers, human or otherwise, but he's right. Still, there could be something out there that I can't see from the safety of the shore. "Silas is going to help me with that tomorrow," I remark, trying to dissuade him. "It makes me a little scared to dabble after what I did before. What if I can't control it?"

Raife strokes my arm. "You're not going to cause a tsunami just by making a few waves."

I laugh, but my heart's not in it. Looking at the waves, I can feel their power. It is like a living thing, a rhythm that is tied to huge swaths of the earth, and beneath it, there is a multitude of life. Stretching out my senses, I can feel beings of all sorts under the current. They are like tiny pinpricks of light, dotting the landscape of my mind. Recognizing each of them, I can feel that my power could keep them safe as I pull the waves into greater crests. I center my thoughts, analyzing the movement of the water, taking in the pull of the tides, and imagining how I could affect the flow, making it swirl and churn, drawing it up into a wall of water.

"Wow. Just wow."

Raife's voice penetrates my mind, severing all thoughts tied to the sea. My eyes snap open. I hadn't realized that I had closed them for a few minutes, so deep into my mind, my consciousness had traveled.

In front of us is a wall of water, easily ten feet above the shoreline, curling in and over itself in a circular motion that reaches from the crest to the base of the wave, but it never encroaches beyond some invisible barrier keeping it at bay. My mouth drops open. Within the churning wave, there and gone in the movement, is a face. It is one I have seen before, both beautiful and alien.

The mouth pulls into a smile as her voice drifts into me. *"Daughter. I feel your power."*

"Mother. I am frightened of it," my mind calls to her.

There is no movement of her facial façade. All that she says sinks into my head as though no barrier could keep it out. *"No fear. You are my chosen. Embrace your gift."*

"What do I do?"

*"Let it go."*

I have no will. It has been snuffed out, smothered by a strength sinking its teeth into me. Fighting it is pointless, so I release myself to it, feeling a flow of energy pouring out of me and into the ocean, where it is caught in netting too strong to resist, before tumbling back inside of me, filling my muscles with heat. I feel Gaia take it in like the last breath of a drowning man. Sensations rush through me the moment she lets me go, my mind snaps the tether, and my body jolts backward.

"Are you okay?" Raife asks, reaching over to cup my cheek.

"I think so. That was weird. It was like Gaia absorbed some of my strength before letting me go."

"She absorbed *your* strength? Don't you mean it was the other way around?"

I don't reply and turn to look at the giant wave, seeing her face, her eyes alien, glowing, a strange illusion from the sun and sand churning in the water. There is no menace in the look, but somehow I feel that things have been set in motion, things I have never dreamed. Gradually, Gaia's visage sinks into the wave as it slowly recedes, until it is nothing more than one of the many currents slowly cresting toward the shore.

"Is she gone?"

"Yeah." But inside, I knew that she wasn't. Not really. She is still there, sunk into the waves, gorging on the convergence of our power.

# CHAPTER 29

*Monstrous things lie buried within the earth*
*and mind*

S ilas calls me at eight in the morning. It's strange to
get a phone call from him. I kind of put him in this
category of mythical beings that would never use
something as mundane as a cell phone.

"Good morning, Terran," his voice rumbles deliciously.
"I hope I didn't wake you."

I blink my eyes slowly. He didn't wake me, but I'm still
in bed, curled under the covers, reading one of my favorite
dystopian novels. I'm a classic re-reader. "Uh, no, I'm
awake, just not up and about yet. What's up?"

"Raife is unable to join us this afternoon, and I wonder if I can pick you up early."

"Oh," I reply, surprised that he would've heard from Raife before I did. "Actually, I was going to grab breakfast with my friend, but we could meet up after that."

"Hm," he says. "Could you reschedule your breakfast?"

"Um, I don't know." My conscience rears its head at the thought of calling off hanging out with Beth.

"It's important."

I sigh. Beth isn't going to be happy that I'm bailing on her. "Okay. What time were you thinking? I could be ready in a half-hour or so."

"I'll pick you up at 9:00. That should give you enough time to eat something before we get started." There is an underlying excitement in his voice that makes me curious about what he has planned.

"Sounds good, but could you let me know what you've got on the agenda today?"

He chuckles, and despite the sound coming merely through my phone, it makes my stomach tie into rather pleasant knots. "I'd like to surprise you."

"Hm. Alright," I say before giving him my address and hanging up.

I text Raife and find out that his dad has requisitioned him for some major basement project resulting from a leak his mom discovered early this morning. I grimace, imagining the mess and amount of work Raife will be stuck with. I wish him luck and tell him I'll try to call later. Next is a call to Beth.

She picks up after the first ring. "Hey, Terran! Ready for a breakfast burrito? I can pick you up in a few."

God, she sounds so bubbly. Guilt is circling my mind like a murder of crows. "Hi, um, I'm sorry, Beth, but I've got to cancel. Silas wants to try some new therapy with me, and he's picking me up soon."

There is a long pause before she says, "Oh. That's cool. How about this afternoon?"

"Could I call you? I don't know when I'll be back."

"Sure. Talk to you later, I guess." She sounds so down, and it makes my stomach sink.

"Thanks, Beth. I'll call you."

"Bye."

I pull a pillow over my head. I'm a terrible friend. After a few minutes spent chastising myself, I throw back the covers and get up. Unclear as to what we're doing today, I decide on comfortable clothes that don't make me look too homely. I don't analyze why I care how I look. Looking shabby next to his perfection simply isn't what I'd like to go for. I check my clock and note that he's given me over an hour to get ready. Suddenly, that seems like an eternity. I putz around in the shower, shaving my legs unnecessarily, and then follow that up by actually blow-drying my hair, a thing I rarely do, since the air does a fine job no matter the weather. By the time I make it downstairs, I've managed to waste thirty minutes.

I pass my dad, who's snoring on the sofa with the TV humming in the background. He must've fallen asleep watching a movie again. I don't know why my mom bothers trying to watch anything with him. It always ends with her smacking him upside the head when his nasal chainsaw kicks in. My mom is sitting in the sunroom, cradling a cup of coffee laced with lots of cream and sugar, while reading her latest Scottish romance.

I poke my head in. "Morning, Mom."

She turns to me, a little dreamy-eyed from whatever scene I just wrenched her out of. "Hi, sweetie. Want me to make you some breakfast?"

While I know she'd leave her book and get up to make me something, the highlands are calling her, and I can already see her eyes drifting back to the pages. "No, thanks. I'm having some cereal. A friend is picking me up at nine."

"Beth?"

I feel remorse at the mention of Beth. "No, not Beth, but I may see her tonight at The Last Drop, though. I'm going out with Raife."

The lie comes easily and is immediately swallowed, as I watch my mom smile and nod before drifting back into her book, content to know I'll be enjoying myself today. I've never told either of my parents about Silas, and don't plan on starting now. That would open up a can of worms that I couldn't possibly explain.

Heading into the kitchen, I pour a bowl of my favorite

cereal, making sure the marshmallow-to-cereal ratio is acceptable, and sit down at the table to eat. I shake my head when dad's snores reach truly obscene decibels and do my best to overpower the sound with some serious crunching.

There's a newspaper from yesterday lying on the table. I grab it and scan the headlines, my pulse starting to pound in my temples as one snags my attention: *Thousands of Geese Die in Toxic Lake*. While migrating, the geese landed in a manmade lake, exhausted from a long journey, and drank water poisoned by the defunct open-pit mining operation. The images splashed across the page are tragic, masses of bodies floating on the surface of red-tinged water. Tears fill my eyes as I read about the physical effects the birds experienced after landing in acidic wastewater from a century of mining, a haunting reminder of the cost of negligence and greed. It hurts my heart.

As usual, environmental groups are up in arms, pointing fingers of blame and offering ideas to prevent future tragedies. But it's too little, too late, I think to myself. There are simply too many people who shut down such efforts, the cost of cleaning up mankind's mess being too high or too overwhelming. Those in charge don't truly hear the cries for action, or if they do, they don't really care. People seem to be in a cycle of indifference in which the problems around us are so great and so many that, as a species, we don't know how to start and simply decide not to. It's such a shortsighted view of the world with no thought given to the future that will inherit this mess.

I feel torn, wanting to do something but afraid of the power I have. Gaia tells me that I need to let it go, and I know she means let it loose, this anger and sadness. Most people aren't affected by news stories like this one, at least those in charge certainly aren't. Instead of working to protect what remains on a large scale, the powerful are stripping away those protections, leaving the natural spaces and species at the mercy of a body of people whose greed far exceeds their responsibility. Perhaps I was meant to see this today, to see another reminder of what is at stake, to reinforce what Gaia has pounded through my brain over and over.

A beep pulls me out of my musings, and I hop up, putting my bowl in the sink. Silas' car is exactly what I should've imagined if I had bothered to think about it. It's an all-electric ride in a deep blue that reflects the anemic sunlight in a glittering swath. Music I have never heard pours softly through the speakers as I open the door and slide into the passenger seat.

Silas flashes a brilliant smile. "Good morning, Terran."

"Hey, thanks for picking me up," I reply. "Where are we off to?"

He shakes his head. "You'll find out soon enough. It's not far."

I make a face, and he chuckles. "Why all the secrecy? Are we going to do something illegal?"

"Not exactly."

That response takes me by surprise, and I feel my eyebrows shoot up, and my heart skips a beat. I'm not a rebel. I've never even stolen a pack of gum, though I was tempted to at the age of five when having a pack of gum to dole out automatically put you on everyone's friend list. "Um, could you clarify what you mean by not exactly?"

Silas pulls onto the main road as we head toward the center of town. "Let's just say that we're visiting a spot where the public isn't necessarily welcome."

I look out the window, biting the inside of my cheek. While I trust that Silas would never put me in harm's way, I worry about what he's up to. Outside the window, keeping pace with the car is Scilti, wings beating as he flies parallel to us. It eases my anxiety to see him there, not that he could save me from myself, or anything. As we continue, I see piles of debris lining the streets, along with yellow caution tape blocking off areas deemed unsafe. I clench my hands as I take it in. I have avoided coming anywhere near the parts of town that took the brunt of my powerful outburst during the lumber mill incident. Construction crews are busy repairing street and sidewalk damage, though it looks like the bulk of the major work has already been completed.

Silas continues on, leaving me to my thoughts as we head out of town. I now know where he's taking me and feel a wave of unease as he eventually pulls off the road and into what used to be the large lot of the lumber mill before it became the wreckage that it is now. I stare out the window, unable to take my eyes away from the scene before me. The ground looks like it imploded, only to be sucked back in on itself, folded into mounds of dirt and rock. There is nothing left of the mill. Nothing. What had once stood here has been wiped away from the surface as though it never was. Here and there, I see bits of green. Nature has already begun to take over, further erasing what once stood here.

I hear Silas get out of the car, but feel anchored to my seat. He pulls my door open and takes my hand. I feel a current go through me at the contact. It pulls my mind toward him like a magnet. "Why did you bring me here?" I whisper.

"You asked me to help you understand the power that lies within you."

"I don't want to be here," I tell him, my eyes drifting to a deep crease in the center of the landscape.

His fingers caress mine, somehow tempering the unease I feel. "There is nothing to fear in this place."

From the corner of my eye, I see Scilti perched on a tall mound of dirt, preening himself. His apparent disinterest helps a little. I grip Silas' fingers and let him pull me toward that sealed wound in the center of what used to be a hive of human activity and production. The dirt is soft under my feet, and I feel myself sink slightly into it with each step. I look behind me and see the deep imprints of my shoes. The phrase, leave only footprints, floats through my mind. I have left so much more than footprints here, though I can't help noticing bits of green breaking through the surface. Gaia is already reclaiming this place. Before I'm ready, we are standing on the rim of the deepest fold of the earth. It is here that the buildings and equipment were pulled into the ground as the earth gaped open its hungry maw. I wonder how far down it all went. Is it poisoning Gaia as it sinks into her being?

Without warning, I lower myself to my knees and lay my hands flat upon the ground. Closing my eyes, I burrow my conscious mind into the layers of sediment, trying to get a sense of what is there and what lies beneath, in the heart of it. I reach for her, and within moments, she reaches back.

*"Mother,"* I call to her.

*"Daughter. It is time."*

I open my mind further, letting her in so entirely that I feel her writhing throughout my body. I shy away, suddenly afraid of this invasion, but she will not be so easily brushed aside. Her power and will are too great. As though outside of myself, I feel Silas' hand upon my back and sense him kneeling next to me. Through the contact, a surge of power passes through my skin, joining with my own before it travels to Gaia. She takes it in. I feel her pull on it like a straw. And then images flood my brain, in a barrage, pelting me with visions of a world gone mad.

Poisoned oceans churning around an island of trash that spans miles, carcasses whose bloated stomachs are filled with plastic, left to rot. Entire forests are destroyed for cattle or fields of palms. Emaciated polar bears are staggering through landfills in desperation, while oil-slicked birds flap useless wings before being sucked into rivers of tar. And through it all, a species that stands idly by, going about their days in a frenzy of reckless consumption, as the planet slowly withers.

Silas' voice penetrates the images swirling through my brain. "Your power can show them the way, Terran. You can be the voice of those without one, and they will have to listen."

I feel Gaia's life force filling me with purpose. In my mind, I see the article I read today, and I visualize the photos of white wings spread upon a lake of death in a morbid distortion of art. Beneath my fingers, I feel the residue of power I left in this place, like a stain. Things start to fit together in a puzzle, each piece needing the other so that I can understand the bigger picture. The ground beneath my palms begins to shift slowly. I curl my fingers, digging into it until I feel the shapes of the buildings buried beneath, entombed under rock and soil. The earth churns as I bend it to my will, centering it on those manmade structures, crushing them until none are whole. With grim determination, I grind them to dust between rocks, finally opening my eyes when there is nothing left. The ground is flat now. That awful, puckering wound is smoothed over.

"You must be Áine."

"I don't know how to do that," I plead, hands still pressed to the earth.

Silas stands behind me and places his hands on either side of my head. "Listen to Gaia, not her words, but her will."

I feel the press of his fingers on my temples and beneath them, my erratic pulse. My mind tries to pull away at first, self-preservation rearing its head again. But I push it down inside and listen with a part of me that is beyond any sense of hearing. She's there, coaxing me to greater understanding.

At first, it is a jumble of images, much like those horrible flashes I saw before, but these are not of wasted earth and tortured flesh. This is something different, something grotesque in its power and purpose. I latch onto one such thought emanating from Gaia's memory or intention. She feels me pulling at the thought, and I sense her approval though she communicates nothing. I open my eyes and stand, Silas, releasing me at my movement.

I say nothing as I stretch my hands outward, feeling the breeze sift through my fingers. I look at the expanse of land before me, now a barren lot of dirt. I reach toward it with my whole being and begin to shape something horrifying in its appearance and magnificent in its design.

Rock and dirt shift, rising slowly above the surface as though being pulled by an unseen force. I move my hands in arcs and sweeps, shaping it, forcing the sediment up and up, until it reaches a height that towers a few feet above me. Tilting my head back, I look upon my creation, pulling limbs from nothing, until it stands, this animate giant from insentient earth. I shape a face where there is none, drilling eye sockets into a head that bears a frightening resemblance to monstrous things I have seen in movies. The slash of a mouth follows, and I watch it open with a grinding sound that makes my jaw clench. Silas is silent next to me, observing what he must have known I could do.

As my creation looks down at me with eyes that cannot see, I marvel at what I have done. There is a part of my mind that recognizes that I should be exhausted at the effort of molding something from nothing, but I feel no fatigue, only power, mine and hers, thrumming through me. It is intoxicating.

With grim intent, I command it to move, watching in awe as legs formed of dirt and rock bend and straighten in a mockery of human motion. The ground trembles beneath each footfall as this thing begins a slow march toward the heart of my town.

# CHAPTER 30

*A global network of power makes the impossible possible*

Silas tugs my arm, bringing me back to myself. I look at him, and the being making its lumbering progress stops mid-stride. I glance at it and back at Silas. He shakes his head, further bringing me out of this haze that I seem to be trapped in.

"Not yet, Terran," he tells me, stroking my cheek with the pads of his fingers. "You have done well, but we must wait."

I look back at the fantastically horrific thing I created and frown. "Wait," I call out. "Where is it going?"

I hadn't meant to send it toward my town, toward people I know, and places I visit. I command it to return, feeling a resistance that sends my heart racing. I watch in horror as it continues its slow, unstoppable progress. Sweat pops out across my forehead as I focus all of my will at the being. Breath whooshes out of me as I sense the command catch and watch all eight feet of it shift slowly until it faces me once again, giant steps leading it closer to where I stand. When it's about a dozen feet away, I release it, watching as all semblance of a human form collapses in a pile of dirt.

Silas nods to himself as he stares at the lifeless heap. "Well done, Terran."

I hear him, but my thoughts are a jumbled mess. I can't believe what I did. It's right out of a sci-fi movie, but this is real. "Is this what she wants? This power to shape something from nothing?" My eyes wander back to the mass of dirt and rock, still, now that I've let it go.

"It is not nothing. Within everything is a piece of her life force. You can harness it in a way that I cannot, and it is this gift that draws Gaia to you. In the coming days, you will fuse your strength with hers, and it will truly begin."

I crouch on the ground, staring at the mound in front of us, and wonder what I could've have willed it to do. Inside, I sense that I have barely tapped the scope of how large and powerful it could be. Closing my eyes, I can easily envision something so massive that it could demolish entire buildings with the sweep of an arm. Images pass through my head of places I long to wipe off the face of the earth, structures and operations that poison the ground, water, and air. With this power, I could destroy it all.

I hear Silas talking to me and turn toward him. "Gaia is calling all of her children. If you concentrate, you will be able to feel their presence. We are mobilizing across the globe." My brows crease as I wonder how he communicates with others. "Shut yourself away from this place and reach out with your mind."

Looking at Silas, I watch him tilt his head back, closing his eyes and parting his lips just a little. He inhales deeply, as though taking in so much more than air. I copy his movements and try to reach out toward beings I have no sense of, beyond Silas and Raife. I feel nothing for so long that I nearly give up, and then, I feel it, a tiny pull, almost like a thread tugging at a part of my mind. I follow the feeling, and suddenly there is Scilti, and beyond him is another tug and another. Soon, there is a network of connections, all pulling from different directions like a spider's web, the tremor of each strand sending a small vibration toward me. I gasp as I realize how many links are parts of this maze encircling my brain. There are hundreds, spread across distances great and small. We are all connected, and within each is Gaia, drawing us to her.

I open my eyes and look at Silas, marveling that I can still feel them, all of them, as though we are part of each other now. He smiles knowingly. "When it is time, you will feel it, and together we will bring balance. For now, let's begin again."

The next two hours are spent shaping the earth into many forms. With each attempt, Silas adds a different element, every figure becoming more sophisticated, able to do more with a fluidity that begins to feel like a natural extension of myself. I pull the earth to my will, shaping mythical creatures that cause Silas to laugh as they stroll across the expanse of this empty space, owning it. By the time exhaustion finally washes over me, I have created dozens of creatures, each imbued with more strength than the last.

My stomach suddenly snarls, and I watch Silas' face as the noise registers with him. "It sounds like you've earned a meal. How about I take you to a new place?"

I rub my belly. "That sounds perfect. I'm starving after all of this."

We head to the car and hop in. Pulling away, I look at the many heaps of dirt scattered across the landscape and smile. Part of me wants to jump right back out and do it all again, but I recognize the need for restraint and know I wouldn't be up for another round anyway. I can't wait to tell Raife about it. He's going to be so disappointed that he wasn't here to witness. I wish I could tell Beth.

Instead of heading toward town, Silas goes north, jumping onto the freeway. The landscape blurs as the car hums along the asphalt. I assume we're heading to the city. I don't go there much. It makes me feel kind of claustrophobic, especially since I had that little episode in the bookstore. We eventually pull off and head to a funky part of town with a total hippie vibe. Silas drives to a Thai restaurant, and my hunger spikes as I imagine digging into pad Thai and curry dishes.

Lunch is a rather quiet affair. Frankly, I'm too busy shoving food in my mouth to want to talk, but my mind is going a mile a minute. In my head, I keep replaying moments from earlier, becoming more energized the longer I think about what it all means. "Do you think she'll make things like I did today? You know, when the time comes?"

Silas swallows a bite of food. "Perhaps," he says. "I imagine we will see a great many things, and you will be part of that. I don't think you fully understand how unique you are, or how important. There is no one else who can do what you have done today, not at this time. Only Gaia can shape the earth to her will. Gaia and her chosen."

"Like Áine?"

"Yes," he says, setting his fork down on the side of his plate. "She was an instrumental force in that time, just as you will be."

"Do you think I'm ready?"

"I don't believe there is such a thing as being ready for what is to come. In a way, yes, you are, but when it begins, you will be infused with such power that any latent ability will be pulled to the surface, and you will truly be a force to be reckoned with." Silas leans forward before continuing. "I trained you today so that you can tap into your strength and fashion it in a way that it becomes an instrument of precision. But I also wanted you to feel things that can share your power. It is this collective pool of strength that you will draw from when it is time. Those creatures you fashioned today will be insignificant compared to what you will create when you tap into the energy of my people and meld it with your own."

"I can do that?"

"Not yet, but we will see what you are capable of this afternoon."

I dig into my lunch with greater enthusiasm, eager to do more, see more. When we finish our lunch, instead of strolling through this funky part of the city, Silas takes me into its underbelly, into places I have never known existed. The car snakes through narrow streets, darkened by towering apartment buildings with metal-mesh-covered windows. The sidewalks are littered with all manner of trash, things heaped in piles so tall that debris has tumbled into the street. I look out my window nervously, not wanting Silas to slow too much and praying that we don't hit any red lights and end up trapped.

"Why did you take me here?" I ask, my voice hardly above a whisper, though there's no sense in keeping it low when we're in the car.

"You need to be shown what has been hidden from you in your small pocket of the world. You must understand what these teeming masses experience. She feels it all, the desperation of so many mixed with virulent greed that crosses all lines of socio-economics. There is more toxicity in our world than the factories spewing poison into the air and water. So much more. Look around you, Terran. What do you see?"

As he slows, I watch the slow progress of an elderly woman pushing a shopping cart with one wheel spinning out of control. It's filled with bags of all sorts, perhaps every item she owns, and sways precariously as she ambles along the gutter. In her hand is a length of twine, a handmade leash for the dog that limps along beside her. His coat is mottled with brown and gray, but it would look white if only he had a bath. The dog looks at me as I watch his painful progress, eyes boring into mine through the glass, and I feel his despair like a tangible thing.

"I see misery," I finally respond, while looking into an expanse of darkness between two buildings that are dotted with ragged tents and tarps, making the entire area into some makeshift shantytown.

If I rolled down the window, I could probably feel and smell the wretchedness of this place. My muscles begin to quiver as the privation surrounding us sinks its teeth into me. It feels like a festering wound being here, an infection boring into the earth, going so deep that everything it touches resonates with suffering. Without thinking, I let go, allowing a wave of feeling to pass through the metal box we sit in and into the ground. I watch the old woman jolt to the side, knocked off her footing by a subtle shift of the ground beneath her. The dog's hackles rise, and he looks at me again, this time in accusation. It's that look that snaps me out of wherever I had gone.

Silas is watching me, a knowing look in his eyes, as he grips the steering wheel. "This is but one spot among millions, one tiny fragment of the bigger picture. Imagine a world that is nothing but what you see and feel here. That is the world Gaia fears and the one that is coming if you don't stop it."

To my relief, Silas leaves this decrepit part of the city, heading out of the concrete jungle and into the surrounding hills. I breathe a sigh of relief as greenery fills the view outside. Despite the cold, I roll down my window, letting the chill, moisture-filled breeze wash away the noxious layer of misery that sits on my skin. I close my eyes and reach toward the growth that surrounds me as we head farther up. I sigh in contentment when Silas pulls into an outlet overlooking the city. Old-growth forest lines the tiny lot, and I walk toward a towering Douglas fir, sensing its ancient being in a subtle throb of energy. Pressing my hands to the bark, I make a connection, feeling a flicker of response.

"It can sense me," I say in wonder.

"Yes," Silas replies, moving next to me to put his hands flat upon the trunk. "There has always been a kind of conscience, though you perhaps haven't truly been able to feel it before now. You can speak to the trees, you know, control them like you did the rock and soil."

I look at him in surprise. "Really?"

He smiles, nodding his head. "Try it."

It feels different from the sensations I experienced when I molded rock and dirt into something new. This tree has its own life force, a thriving thing with a long memory. As I push my mind into it more fully, I detect an ache within the woody fibers, like a rotten tooth, filled with resentment and rage. I reach toward it, pressing my forehead against the rough surface to get closer, deeper, looking for the source. It feels as though it shies away from my invasion for a moment until I coax it with soft strokes of my mind and fingers. The moment it lets down its guard, my knees buckle spastically, taking me to the damp ground with a hard thump, as my brain is filled with hundreds of years of history, the last of which is filled with toxicity that begins in the earth itself before being pulled into roots desperate for something clean. I feel Silas reach for my arm, and I make an inarticulate sound in protest as I continue to be pummeled by the wrenching anger of a living thing that should know nothing of the waste and degradation of the world. He pulls away and watches me roil under the onslaught, not nervous, just an observer of things he may have predicted.

I have to rip myself away when the sensations begin to consume me. Rubbing my face to clear my head, I look up at Silas. "It is filled with rage."

"It has a right to be. Use that anger, Terran, command it. You will find that it is a willing participant, just as it would be if Gaia were to infuse her power into every piece of this forest. Reach out further, and you should feel an entire network of consciousness. It is yours to command. They will stand with you when it is time."

I sit back on my heels and look at the tree, this ordinary thing in a forest filled with them. "It feels like it left a residue inside my head," I tell him as I swirl some spit through my mouth to wash away the film of bile that is coating my tongue.

"It is communion. You cannot command it without also taking in a piece of its being. Just as Gaia is part of all things, you must also be to infuse them with your will. Try again, only this time reach beyond this one tree and tap into them all."

I shake my head slowly, reluctant to open myself to an entire network of raw anger. What if it overwhelms me completely? Would I even be able to come back to myself? "I don't think I can do that, Silas. There is so much rage, and I'm afraid it will take over my thoughts completely. What if I can't pull myself out of it?"

"You underestimate your abilities, and you forget that you are part of a much larger picture. If you wish, you could pull from my energy and fuse it with yours. In fact, you could draw it out of every one of my kind, taking it into yourself, not to deplete us, but to bind our power into something that will give you strength beyond all imagining."

"Is that what Áine did? She drew her power from your kind? I thought she was born with it or something." My voice tapers off as I look at the base of the tree I am still kneeling in front of. Here I thought this goddess was so powerful that she could do incredible things with her own will. Now, he's telling me that she borrowed the will of others and added it to her own. Does it diminish who she was and what she could do? I suppose not, but it makes me feel more vulnerable and uncertain for some reason.

Silas squats down next to me, rocking back on his heels, as only men seem to be able to do. "Our legends, born thousands of years before your own historical records, tell us that she had immense strength, more than any Daoine Fíor. But in her time, men had waged such a war on each other that they swallowed the earth in their quest for power, overwhelming Gaia until she could not rise up on her own, bringing to the forefront the need for Áine. As for Áine herself, she could move mountains, shape the sea, and bring the wrath of the wind like no other, but the wars waged across the globe were too much for one to fight alone. So, yes, my people lent her their strength, small though it was compared to her own, and together they restored a fragile balance, a measure of peace. We are one, you see, with Gaia and each other. Now, we will stand with *you* and begin again."

He moves my hands until they press upon the ground, resting above knotted roots and carpet of moss. "Now, try again. Only this time, go beyond this one life force and feel them all, tree, shrub, squirrel, and bird. Reach for all of it, pull the energy into you, and then find us within the mosaic of this world. We are ready to join you."

My heart accelerates as he talks to me. I feel the soft vibrations of his being pass through my skin, where the pads of his fingers still rest on the backs of my hands. Clenching my fingers a little, I dig them into the moist soil, through the moss, and onto a nub of a root. I close my eyes, take a deep breath, and push my will forward in a powerful surge. The ancient fir seems to tremble beneath the onslaught but not in pain, rather in some strange welcoming, opening itself until I touch every thread traveling up its trunk, each needle and pine cone, from the root to the uppermost point, and then back again, into the soil until I connect with another. I am the earth, the soil, and rock, the roots burrowing so deep that their anchors are immovable. My energy spreads across the mountainside, tentacles of power reaching out to everything it touches. And then it stops abruptly, a sick feeling washing over my mind as something foreign and ghastly sits just beyond the root of a conifer. I have reached the edge of this ancient forest. I pull away from what lies beneath the surface, some manmade thing sunk into the ground, and draw myself around the natural life I am buried within.

A slow pulse of life begins to move through my body, a cadence that draws my muscles into a familiar rhythm, making me sway as I kneel on the ground. Before my eyelids are patterns of color, hues of every shade in swirls of movement, each one a reflection of the living force behind it. I let myself join this dance of pigmentation, both drawing and infusing strength. Focusing my thoughts on one command, I push my will into this dance of color and feel it take hold. Branches begin to creak as roots, buried hundreds of feet in every direction, slowly undulate. The entire forest moves to my thoughts in waves that bend supple trunks and sturdy limbs. I marvel at the exchange of energy coursing through me.

"Reach beyond now, Terran, find us," Silas' voice whispers in my ear.

It's a little frightening at first, like letting go and falling, not knowing if anyone will be there to catch you before your head strikes the pavement. But I manage to push my resistance aside, sending out a signal of sorts while looking for the same. For a few minutes, I sense nothing, just the breath of life all around me, above and below. But then my mind is caught, pulled by a wispy beacon, a faint light glowing dully in the distance. I fixate on it for a moment, defining its shape and origin, before scanning for others. It is impossible to gauge any distance. They are all faint, giving no impression of location, but they begin to tug on me like tethers, only I am unable to determine who is pulling whom. It is an equal partnership, each drawing from the other until it feels like a cyclical churning of power. By the time my clothes become damp and cold against my skin from the constant moisture in the air, I have found hundreds of Silas' people, and I feel more powerful than I could ever have imagined.

Silas breathes strange words into my ear. "Táimid ar cheann," his voice rumbles, penetrating the beautiful chaos of the multitude of life within and around me.

I release my hold on everything, feeling the break in a snap of invisible threads of connection. My shoulders slump, and I experience intense exhaustion, unlike anything I have felt before. It feels as though my heart should be hammering with effort, but it's calm, a steady beat within my chest, as feeling floods my body and brings me into the present.

"What did you say?" I ask softly, unwilling to speak too loudly and break the perfect stillness.

"Táimid ar cheann. We are one."

# CHAPTER 31

*Some people are a balm to the soul*

Heading home, I'm quiet, thinking over everything that happened today, from the decrepit streets to my communion on the mountain. It all blends together, overlaid by a stirring of power, an ebb and flow beneath the surface of my thoughts. The world outside my window looks different somehow, even more at odds with its mystical underbelly than I had realized before today. There now seems to be a film covering it all, a sickly haze blanketing the throng of life, slowly smothering it.

"How do you feel?" Silas asks.

That's a good question, and it has more than one answer. "Strong. Connected. Angry. Afraid."

He nods, unsurprised by my responses. "I believe you are ready, Terran."

"Yeah? I guess I'm ready, as ready as I'll ever be. I know all of this needs to stop before it's too late."

Silas looks at me with deep understanding. "Yes, it does."

"I realize where it could all lead if I stand by and do nothing," I continue. "I know that you took me to that rundown part of the city for a reason, and I think I understand what that is. But it was being up on that mountain today, sensing the ancient awareness and history, which was so incredible. And awful. There is so much of the earth that's rank with sickness. I felt it in the roots of every tree."

"They are the witnesses of mankind's history," he explains. "The first tree you came upon was nearly two thousand years old. It has felt the spoiling of the land and air, sensed others of its kind fall under the ax, and saw. It is important that you make that connection today, not only to draw from its strength but to appreciate the interconnectedness. We are all part of Gaia."

"How can your people stand it? How do they go on feeling all of this misery all the time?"

"I suppose we are much like the ancient forest, witnesses who intervene when the balance has shifted too far. We were born into this world, as you were, and our lives are not so long that we remember the world as it was before it began to sour. For me, it has always been this way, and I have grown used to it, though I feel the ache at all times. It is there, residing with festering anger."

"I feel pretty lucky then. At least I haven't lived every minute of my life with the weight of the world on my shoulders. That kind of sucks, Silas."

He laughs. "Indeed, it does. But I have had faith in the future, knowing the chosen one was coming."

I look at his profile, smiling crookedly. It's weird to be told that I'm destined to be the savior of the planet. That's just not something I could ever get used to, but I have to face the fact that, according to Silas and others like him, that's exactly what I am. Boy, those are some big shoes to fill. I hope I don't let him down.

I glance at the clock on the dashboard and am surprised to see that it's after four. How long was I up on that mountain? It felt like only minutes. I had hoped to see Raife before possibly meeting up with Beth, but there's no way I'll have time for that. I just want to talk to him and tell him about the day. I need to tell someone. Ugh. I guess I'll have to wait until after school tomorrow, when we can get away for a bit and have some privacy. I settle back into my seat, resting against the headrest, and wait for the miles to go by.

My parents are out when Silas drops me off. I let myself in and head to the kitchen for a bite to eat, suddenly ravenous after the day's events. Opening the fridge, I scan the contents, hoping for some tasty leftovers, but it's looking rather bare. I settle for a peanut butter and honey sandwich, smiling to myself as I drizzle a thick layer of locally sourced honey on the peanut butter. I take my snack to the table, shoving the newspaper I was looking at this morning to the side, so I don't get lost in another disturbing article, and begin to eat as I pull out my phone to text Raife. He doesn't respond as I stare at the screen, waiting to see an indication he's read my text. I grumble to myself and reach out to Beth to see if she can hang out. As expected, I have less than a minute to wait before she replies. I breathe a sigh of relief as I read the upbeat tone of her text. Clearly, I'm forgiven for backing out of our breakfast plans. When I finish eating, I plop down on the sofa and turn on the TV. I settle for a sappy eighties flick to pass the time. It's one I've seen so many times that I don't mind cutting it off a half-hour early so I can meet up with Beth at the coffee shop.

The Last Drop is a local hangout, far removed from the nationwide coffee chains that seem to crop up every few blocks. It's a dark hole in the wall with funky décor and mismatched chairs, plastered in murals from local artists and flyers for everything from farmer's markets to music festivals. You can smell organic baked goods and coffee grounds from the street, as though they pump out of a vent to entice you to come in. It's our favorite spot.

Beth is standing in line to order when I walk in. I sneak up behind her and grab her shoulders when I'm a few inches away, "Boo!"

She squeaks, body jumping under my hands as I crack up. "You know, you're lucky I didn't have a drink in my hand or anything, you dork."

"That would've just made it funnier," I say, grinning. I nudge her shoulder, and she smiles, pushing back, before giving me an odd look. "What?" I ask.

"I don't know. You just look different. New makeup or something?"

Tiny alarms go off in my head. Can she see Gaia's stamp on me? "Uh, no. I did get a full night's sleep, though," I tell her, trying to smother any unwanted expression on my face.

She shrugs. "I guess that's it. I bet I'd look so much better if I actually got more than five hours a night."

"Maybe you should stop binge-watching so many shows." She rolls her eyes and looks at the menu. "What are you getting?" I ask, scanning the daily specials.

"I think the gloomy weather calls for a very large mocha."

"Yum," I say, debating whether I want the same or feel more like going for a classic vanilla chai. I decide on the latter, knowing I can steal a few sips of her drink too.

We sit at a small, round table next to the window. It's covered with intricate knot-work, some kind of Celtic tree. It feels appropriate considering everything that is happening in my life these days. I trace the ridges of paint with my fingers while my tea cools.

Beth silently watches me for a few moments before interrupting the quiet. "I've missed you."

I look up at her. "Yeah, I've missed you too. I'm sorry I've been such a flake lately."

She shrugs. "I don't blame you. If I had a hot guy wanting to spend every minute with me, I'd dump your ass too."

It hurts a little to picture what she says. I can see myself running after Raife, and Beth stuck in a cloud of dust behind me. I suppose the reality isn't so far off from that image. "Raife or no Raife, I've been an absentee friend lately. Any news you care to catch me up on?"

Beth shakes her head. "Sadly, no. My life is just not that interesting."

I laugh. "That's not always a bad thing. Let me tell ya," I remark, slowly stirring my vanilla chai.

"Oh?"

Looking up at her face, I realize she is completely in tune with my underlying message. There's so much I want to tell her about all that's happened. I decide, to hell with it, and open my mouth to spill my guts and tell her everything, but all I get out is a cough, followed by a series of incoherent noises like my coffee went down the wrong tube.

"You okay?" She asks, reaching over to forcefully pat my back.

I nod, catching my breath. "Wrong, pipe," I manage to

croak. "Ugh. Sorry about that. Things are all right, just kind of strange these days, you know?"

"Not really. We haven't really hung out much. Honestly, Terran, I feel like you've been keeping something from me ever since you and Raife started dating. It's like you both have some big secret."

She's looking at me, and there's no way to lie, not to her. Beth has known me for too long, and she can see right through any lame excuse I try to muster. "You're right," I finally manage. "There are some strange things going on in my life, things that I can't really tell you about, and it hurts not to be able to talk to you. It's just that this stuff is bigger than me and I...I wouldn't even know where to begin. I'm sorry, Beth. I really am."

She sips her mocha, watching the play of emotions cross my face. "I won't make you tell me something you're not ready to share, Terran. But I'm here, okay? Whenever you can talk to me, I'm here."

I give her a half-hearted smile. "Thanks, Beth."

After a few awkward minutes, we both enter an unwelcome but necessary realm of acceptance, allowing our conversation to drift to other things, but the unanswered questions remain on the fringes, and I know it won't take long before they crop up again.

So, when Beth asks about Silas, I'm prepared. "Have you gone back to see Silas?"

"Yeah, a couple of times. He's easy to talk to and fun to look at."

"Sheesh, I could stare at him all day. You're lucky to have an excuse to go there. I wonder if I could come up with anything," she muses, tapping her mug with a spoon. "Nope. Nothing comes to mind. I'm just too ordinary," she sighs.

I roll my eyes. "Being a freak isn't so great either. Be thankful that you're normal."

"So, am I allowed to ask you what you talk to him about? Are you having more episodes?"

There is such genuine concern in Beth. I know she loves me and sincerely cares about my well-being. That's what makes keeping things from her so agonizing. "I've had a few," I admit. "But mostly we talk about other stuff. He's helping me understand a part of myself that I need to face. It's hard to explain, and I wish I could tell you more, but there are things about me that you don't know, things I'm trying to wrap my head around."

Beth looks into me with a wealth of emotion. "Are you okay?"

"Yeah, it's just..." How exactly do I tell her without really telling her? "Beth, you know things in the world are kind of messed up, right? I mean, like, environmentally." I can hear how odd my voice sounds as I strain to push the words out.

"Sure. People have poisoned the planet, and any steps that were taken to try to clean up our mess are now being stripped away. It's terrible. What does that have to do with you?"

I let out a long breath, trying to find the right words. "It has a lot to do with me, but I can't explain it." I look away from her and focus on the Celtic tree staring up at me from the tabletop. I shake my head as I battle with myself over what I can say. Beth waits me out. Finally, I look up at her. "If things go on like they are, the world is just going to wither and die. I can't let that happen."

She looks at me in confusion. "How, exactly, are you going to stop it?"

"I don't know, but I can't do nothing." And what I say is true. I don't know how this is all going to play out, but I just know that it will.

"Is there something I can do to help?" Beth asks, leaning forward with enthusiasm. "Some charity I can do a fundraiser for or something?"

"I'll let you know," I say. "For now, let's just do our part in our little pocket of the world. Every bit helps." She knows there is more, so much more, but Beth isn't pushy, so she lets it go, and I love her for it.

"Are you ready to head back to class tomorrow?" I ask to change the subject.

Beth smirks at me, on to my conversation switch. "No, dreading it actually. It'll be day six, which means no free period. Plus, I've got a lab with Mr. Frink. His voice could put me into a coma if I had to listen to it all day."

"All I want to know is, when is he going to retire? He must be pushing seventy."

"I know, right?"

It'll be strange to return to school following the quake. I imagine there will be a lot of nervous kids and parents, and wonder if anyone will stay home, too freaked out to set foot in the building. What must it be like in California when earthquakes regularly roll through? People are probably so used to it that they couldn't care less. "You're not worried about being in the building again after what happened, are you?"

She thinks it over for a moment. "No, I'm not scared, but my mom is a bit nervous. She's been really into this psychic stuff she's learning about. She's convinced that we're heading toward some cataclysmic event or some nonsense. Don't ask, because I can't even begin to explain. This stuff is way beyond anything I'm into. She asks about you, though, wants to know when you can come by the house because she wants to do another kind of reading on you." She shakes her head, "Personally, I think she's off her rocker a bit with some of this, but you've gotta love her for it!"

I laugh it off with her, but inside, my stomach is churning. If I were to let Celeste do another type of reading, what would she see? On one point, she's absolutely right. Something is coming, and I'm at the center of it.

# CHAPTER 32

*Knocking, knocking at my chamber door...*
*I mean window*

Raife picks me up in the morning. It's such a relief to see him, having only had a few minutes to chat before bed last night. He leans over to cup my face and gives me a deep kiss. I feel a bit woozy after, which only makes him laugh.

"It's your fault that I lose my senses when you do that," I tell him.

"I like it when you lose your senses," he says, pressing his lips to my neck. A current rushes through me, and I shiver involuntarily as chills race up my spine. "Sensitive this morning?"

I elbow him playfully. "Drive before we're late."

Raife pulls away, sighing dramatically. "You're such a hardass."

I make a face and tap my wrist where a watch would be if I bothered to wear one. "Tick, tock."

He gives me a salute and puts the car into gear. "So, how was it with Silas yesterday? I'm sorry I couldn't join you."

"It was amazing and terrifying at the same time."

"Tell me about it."

I launch into a recounting of the morning and don't get any farther than describing what Raife quickly refers to as the 'rock-monster.' He seems obsessed with the idea that it could tromp around and lay waste to the high school, and spends the remainder of the drive detailing how awesome it would be while trying to come up with a good nickname for it.

We plan to meet for lunch and then part ways in the hall. I watch his loose, confident stride for a few moments before heading to the second floor. There is a hum of conversation as I enter the classroom, with people telling their versions of what happened the last time they were in the building and wondering whether it will happen again, and if so, whether they will just cancel school for the rest of the year. I shake my head and take a seat.

The morning drags. I dip into a few conversations here and there. Still, my heart's not in it, and I spend most of the time listening, but not really processing anything that's being said. If any of my teachers gives us a pop quiz tomorrow, I'm utterly failing. The bright spot of my day is seeing Raife at lunch. I offer a genuine smile as I notice him sitting with Beth and Shane. It's good to see them all together, these people who are so important in my life. Raife gives me a smile and a wink as I put my tray down next to him.

Beth grabs my attention when she asks, "Hey, Terran. Want to go to the film festival this weekend? It's a John Hughes movie marathon."

I'm a movie nut, eighties movies, in particular, thanks to mom and dad, and any excuse to see some favorites on the big screen is a little slice of heaven. I was totally born in the wrong era. "Heck, ya. When does it start?"

"The first movie is at one, and it goes until midnight."

I spastically clap my hands, my nerdiness taking over momentarily. "Oh, my God. That's awesome! Could you pick me up? I don't think my mom will want to lend me the car for that long."

"Totally," Beth grins. We spend the rest of the period talking about our favorite John Hughes moments while Shane and Raife listen in.

The remainder of the day passes at its usual tortoise-pace, but eventually, the bell rings, and I head to the parking lot to meet up with Raife. I see Beth in the distance, she's talking to a guy I vaguely remember from one of my classes last year, and I wonder if there's a little romance brewing between the two of them as I watch her lean into him just a little. Raife comes up behind me, curling his arms around me in an embrace before following my gaze toward Beth.

"Who's that?"

"I can't remember his name. Jeff or Jake or something? He was in my algebra class last year."

Raife pulls me along to the car, and I slide into the seat, eyes drifting to Beth again as she and the guy continue talking. If Beth is into him, I hope it works out.

"Where do you want to go?" Raife asks as the engine purrs to life.

"Hm. How about…" My phone ringing cuts me off. I pull it out of my bag, surprised to see my mom's number. "Hey, Mom. What's up?"

"Hi, sweetie. I hope I'm not bothering you during class."

Mom can never keep my schedule straight. "No, school's out. I'm just sitting in the lot with Raife."

"Oh, good. I wouldn't want you getting into trouble with your teachers." I give Raife an 'I'm sorry for the interruption' look as my mom continues. "Could you come home? I need your help with this darn project I'm working on. I can't get this program to work right, and I'm up against a deadline. You're always so good at computer stuff."

I roll my eyes. My mother and technology have been at odds since the birth of the computer. Instead of adapting and learning to use it, she seems to have developed a severe allergy to all things techie. One of these days, she's going go into anaphylactic shock from the computer and need a technology-infused EpiPen. Helping her in situations like this is hardly 'helping' as I always end up just taking over and doing whatever she needs myself rather than trying to explain it. Thankfully, there has been a considerable gap in time since she asked for help, so I feel kind of obligated to pitch in. "Sure, Mom. I'll be home in a few."

"Thank you, honey! I'll make it up to you, I promise. How about I order Chinese takeout?"

I laugh. She knows I'm a sucker for Chinese food, and we get it so rarely because it gives my dad gas, and no one wants to be within a ten-block radius after he's eaten it. "Sounds good, Mom. See ya soon."

I hang up and look at Raife. He's giving me the most pitiful puppy-dog eyes I have ever seen, complete with his bottom lip jutting out. "That's not going to work," I tell him as he begins to whine. "I'm immune to it. Beth has been doing it for years, and I've been inoculated."

He sighs dramatically. "Okay. Fine. Go help your mom then. But we're carving out some time this evening when you're finished."

"I can't."

"Why not?" He asks. The whine is back.

"Clearly, you didn't have Mr. Frink for a lab today because he assigned a lab report that's due tomorrow, and that's in addition to the other homework my awesome teachers decided to pile on in some cruel retribution for the school closing. I'm going to end up working until one in the morning to get all of this crap done."

"Well, that sucks," he says, but I can hear the pout in his voice. "Tomorrow afternoon, then? No excuses."

I lean over and give him a peck on the cheek. "Yes, sir."

He's slightly mollified, and as we head to my house, he picks up where we left off this morning, going on about the rock-monster and the various places and people he wouldn't mind squishing if he could command it. I chime in here and there, but let him do most of the talking as it's just too funny to hear him carrying on. I kiss him goodbye and head inside when he pulls up to my house.

Mom is waiting, and I dive right into the computer problem, listening with only half my attention as she explains the many ways she's tried to figure out why she can't upload what ends up being the wrong file format into her new program. I rename a bunch of stuff and then spend twenty minutes deleting suspicious programs she downloaded. I hate it when she does that, as it slows the computer and could be a virus, but I've told her this too many times, and it just doesn't sink in. When I've cleaned up her desktop, she places an order for delivery and then gets straight to work, worrying over her looming nine o'clock deadline tomorrow morning. I head upstairs to get started on the mountain of homework that is sure to keep me up way too late tonight, coming down to enjoy the food when it arrives before racing back up when my dad stretches out on the couch, a sign that the air will soon be peppered with unique sounds and smells.

I fall asleep at my desk, something I have never done before, and am jolted awake by noise, toppling from my chair with a soft thump. "Ow," I say to the empty room, rubbing my head. I'm about to crawl onto my bed and burrow beneath the covers when I hear it again. It's a tapping sound. I rub my eyes, cock my head, and listen. It's coming from the window, so I make my way over and look out. There is only darkness covering everything, but as I crane my neck to see more, a loud tap right by my face startles me, and I jump back with a squeak. My heart races and then slows as I realize it's Scilti. Shaking my head, I go back to the window and open it, stepping aside so he can swoop into the room. He perches on my chair, looking at me.

"Hey," I say, watching his head tilt to the side so that his right eye is staring up into my face. "Um, what are you doing here, Scilti?" He opens his beak as though to let out a loud caw, and I dart forward, almost touching him. "Ssh, don't be loud, okay?"

His beak closes, and I watch him bob his head in a jerky movement as though indicating the window. It takes a few times watching him do this for it to sink it, must be exhaustion. "You want me to come outside?" I swear he actually nods. I grab my hoodie, thankful that I never got my pajamas on, and shoo him outside before heading downstairs and out the front door.

Scilti is waiting for me as I come down the walkway. The moon is full, casting its light on the stillness, making strange shadows as the trees shift in the calm wind. I'm not surprised as he hops around at my feet and then takes off, heading to the neighborhood preserve. The forest welcomes me as I cross that strange barrier and head down the hill. She's waiting for me when I get to my small clearing, standing next to the outcropping of rock, a specter with ethereal beauty and alien eyes. My steps slow as she slowly turns her body, chips of stone reflecting the moonlight from the sockets that would hold her eyes if she had them. He ghostly hand reaches toward me, and I come within inches of her, feeling the rough touch of her phantom fingers.

*"Daughter. It is time."*

My stomach roils as doubt and anxiety flood my mind. I look into her face that is not a face, only a shell of what she really is. "I don't know if I'm ready," I say aloud.

Her features turn into a smile. *"It is time."*

I watch her arm sweep toward the rock, and I climb atop it, somehow knowing that it what she wants. She stands at its base, and I face her, towering above as she looks up at me. I watch as her limbs anchor themselves to the earth, and her arms open. Her face holds mine in an unbreakable tether, alien eyes boring into me without any true sight. She sees me with different eyes, not this shell that stands before me. I feel a strong wrenching in the center of my chest, forcing me to temporarily lose my balance. I shift my feet and take a deep breath, opening myself to her invasion.

There is no preparation for it when it comes. I had thought I knew power before, thought I had felt the depth of her being in numerous moments, but I was wrong. Gaia fills me, warmth radiates through my muscles, spreading from my chest and into every pore until all I feel is her within me. My arms open on her command, and I am rocked backward, swaying so far I should fall but somehow manage to remain upright. I close my eyes as stars burst within my mind. A spinning sensation funnels through my head, and I feel as though I am falling into the earth, pulled down by gentle but insistent hands until all life on the surface rests above me. I am below, feeling the origins of it all. I have become one with the roots, the trees, the grass, the plants, the animals, the birds, the earth, the sea, the world. Within that is what can only be described as noxious, black ooze that seems to permeate the pureness, seeping into everything it touches as it makes its slow, unrelenting progress. I shy away from it, as it appears to reach for me, this repellent thing. I try to find Gaia within the depths, panicking for a moment when she seems lost to me. I feel her embrace and move toward it, though I do not move at all.

Her voice, thunderous in my head, commands me, *"Find them. Find them all."*

I reach out toward those faint pulses in Earth's land-scape that I felt before. They flicker to awareness as I find each one, two stronger than the others, brighter beacons among the hundreds. A part of my mind recognizes these two are Raife and Silas, but I cannot concentrate on that. I only feel, connect, and infuse. My body throbs with a power I have only tasted. Now I am drunk on it, so full that I can feel it spilling from my fingertips, where Gaia drinks it in, sharing her own with mine in a never-ending exchange. The sickness I sensed within the darkness is there, slowing but not stopped, an unrelenting underground wave of corruption. It has smothered so much of Gaia. I sense it. Feel it. She writhes beneath it but cannot escape. My anger flares at her torment batters me. I feel the energy flowing through me grow as emotions sweep through me until I can't hold onto it any longer. Rage will not be stopped. Wrath spills out of me and into the world.

# CHAPTER 33

*She is there, in the crest*
*of the waves*

Those people whose part of the world is bathed in daylight when it starts are the first to see them, monstrous things ripped out of some nightmarish fairy tale to sow havoc on man's domain. Unimaginable beings shaped of rock and soil rise up from the earth alongside funnels of wind that seem to form a face and limbs within their vortex. The assault is unstoppable, and I watch it all with an omniscient sense that has lain dormant until this moment. Like Gaia, I have awakened. Her thoughts, slipping through my head like an oil slick, tainted with furious anger and withering pain, fuse with mine in greater and greater constructs, until our combined power boils over and into the world. Together, we rise to wreak terrible vengeance.

My strength, paltry before, chases through me, engulfing everything, from the follicles atop my head to the soles of my feet that lie anchored to the rock. I am infused with Gaia, the Daoine Fíor, and the very earth itself. It flows out of me in a torrent that I am unable, and unwilling, to rein in. I feel drunk on it, intoxicated by the will and anger of so many voices, lives, creatures that have suffered under the yoke of man. Within this thriving landscape, beneath the surface, man's poisonous corruption bleeds into Gaia, choking her as it slips along our connection and into my awareness, adding to the rage. I feel that sickness, the plague that dots *her* landscape, this species that spat in the face of their mother, polluting her with callous disregard. I hear the echo of a snarl escape my lips, but the pounding in my head muffles the sound as I fully let go, releasing power in fantastical aberrations onto mankind. Somewhere, at the edge of my consciousness, I hear human screams, pleas for mercy and help. My mind splits as part of me cries out to stop this madness, but it is quashed the instant it bubbles into my awareness by a fresh surge of anger. And then I feel nothing. Nothing but Gaia's fury, her rage.

The first city my will touches, a monolith of man's arrogance, fractures under a crush of arms and legs made of rock that sweep through buildings, pummeling them like battering rams, as lumbering giants carve a path of destruction through every structure. These are the rock-monsters Raife spun crazy scenarios about, vengeful creations that do my bidding with singular intent. They tower over scurrying masses trying to escape the destruction, their faces bearing masks of indifference that sweep the landscape with eyes that cannot see. Bridges collapse under the crush of stone bodies that crash into them. Smoke and debris blacken the sky as fires erupt, blooming out of buildings that are flattened under rocky fists. In minutes, the skyline resembles nothing of its former self as more beings converge, coalescing from the earth to surround the city. All is chaos. Only my protected, for they are mine so long as I am part of *her*, remain unscathed, caught in mysterious bubbles of refuge or sent from the epicenters of destruction to live and fight another day.

The police and military are quick to respond, mobilizing S.W.A.T. teams, helicopters, jets, and troops to fire uselessly at beings that seem unaware of the bullets striking their forms. Missiles do nothing to stop the carnage, merely slowing it, as the entities fall only to reform to greater heights and continue on with single-mindedness, seemingly unaware of the aircraft, men, and tanks that surround them. When only ruin remains, the monstrous beings slip back into the earth, leaving the once-flourishing metropolis a place of silent devastation. Another, and another, quickly follow the first city as the planet comes under an unprecedented onslaught.

As monsters of my creation walk the earth, tornadoes rip through the landscape, brought to life by hundreds of souls scattered across the world who raise their arms and voices in battle cries. The winds blow across the land like freight trains, wiping away entire towns in minutes as they reach categories of strength that are far beyond any previous calculations.

Ancient knowledge, sick with anger, begins to stir. Having witnessed millennia of abuse, trees awaken to terrifying life, reaching toward structures with bends and creaks of their branches to batter homes and businesses, some of them so filled with rage that they sacrifice themselves, roots ripping from the ground to fall onto buildings that rest below their towering trunks. Rivers surge, pouring over embankments and barriers, flooding everything in their path, while lakes rise up in horrifying crests to loom over structures that dot the shoreline before slamming down on them like hammers. Within a few short hours, panic envelops the world.

But I don't stop, cannot stop. I continue my siege, bringing forth true Titans to walk the earth, Gaia curls within herself, expelling toxins that have robbed her of strength for too long. Wrenching free, she reaches toward the sea, her domain, that vast expanse that covers the earth. She channels her power, a mixture of my own and all her children, before flinging it outward in a surge of energy. The ocean waters take hold of it and become an extension of her being. The sea retreats from the land, pulling itself inward to churn in circular motions that build and build, before charging back to the shore in a series of waves that span one hundred feet in height. They crash upon the land, pounding it under wave after wave, carving trenches where there have been none, erasing entire communities until all that is left are mounds of sand. Whole coastal cities are washed away, plucked out of the earth, and scattered into the sea. And through it all, I stand upon a rock, arms extended, body rigid with currents of energy and will that eclipse all thought but one: vengeance.

———————

By the time dawn breaks, the entire planet has felt the wrath of Gaia. I drop to my knees upon the rocky outcropping, taking huge gulps of breath as my body trembles in violent spasms.

The world is calm when I come to full awareness, though my thoughts are a jumbled mess, mixed in some schizophrenic cacophony of noise that seems to swirl all around me. My brain feels hazy, as though I am caught in a sticky web of temporary amnesia. How long have I been in the forest? I look around, noting the sun shining and groan. Crap. Am I late for school? I shake my head. My parents are going to kill me when I get home.

I plop down on my butt and swipe my hand along my face, startled to see a bright trail of blood when I pull it away. "What the hell?" I gasp, grabbing a fistful of my shirt to wipe again. I pinch the bridge of my nose and lean back to lie flat on the rock. This sucks. I roll my head to the side and find Scilti looking at me from the branch of a large cedar.

"Hey," I call to him in a nasal voice. He swoops down, landing next to me. I reach over, and he tilts his head, inviting me to ruffle his feathers with little scratches and rubs. "I feel totally wrung out. That was the worst nightmare of my life. It was so real."

I don't know why I bother asking a raven anything, but my brain seems to be stuttering, hopping from one strange image to the next, making no sense. Gingerly, I sit up, still clasping my nose, and look around. Frightening visions pop into my head, there for a moment, and then are gone. Things that seem familiar but are completely foreign at the same time. I blink slowly, trying to remember what I did last night. Something is tugging at me, but I can't latch onto it. Realizing I can't just sit here in a state of confusion while my parents could potentially be calling the police to report that I'm missing, I stand up, swaying to the side as dizziness engulfs me. It takes a minute to find my balance and clear my head, though I can't make sense of why I feel like this.

I make my way slowly up the trail, muscles straining as though I have run a marathon. Halfway up, my knees give, and I fall hard, hands slapping against the ground. God, I feel awful. Am I coming down with the flu or something? My breath is labored by the time I reach the top. I rest my hands on my knees for a bit before straightening and continuing my slow progress. There are no cars on the road as I make my way home, which I find strange for a weekday. If I had a watch, I could check the time, but I didn't even take my phone with me last night. Ugh. Mom is probably freaking out.

I go through the backyard and try the door off of the deck, sending pleas into the ether that maybe they think I went to school early and haven't been spiraling into a frenzy of worry when I didn't come down this morning. I let out a sigh of relief when the knob turns, and I slowly push the door open, cringing a little when it squeaks. Stepping into the kitchen, I see nothing unusual, but I can hear the drone of the TV. That's odd. My parents don't usually turn it on in the morning. Instead of going into the living room, I duck up the backstairs and sneak into my room, resting against the door when it closes. Grabbing a pair of pajamas, I fling off my clothes and stuff myself into them, hoping I can pull off some lame excuse of oversleeping. It's after eight, and there's no way my mom hasn't come in to check on me.

The creak of the stairs announces my presence before I make it to the living room, but to my surprise, neither of my parents says a word. When I reach the bottom step, I peek out and see them glued to the TV, still in their robes. I look at them for a moment and note that they are as pale as ghosts. Distracted by the relief I feel at not having been caught sneaking out, but soon my eyes drift to the screen, and I nearly fall to the floor.

Mom hops up and comes over to me in a shuffling sort of run. "Oh, sweetie, I'm sorry I didn't wake you! It's just..." she glances back at the TV. "The world has gone mad. Your father and I have been watching the news for hours. I can't make sense of what's happened."

She pulls my arm, and I follow her into the living room, reluctant to get too close to the images on the screen, but they are unavoidable. Then it all pours back to me in a wave of shocking realization. This is what I did last night. Memories stir in my mind, slipping in and out like slick eels. I sink into the chair, grunting a reply when my dad gives me a distracted greeting. My heart begins to race, and I can feel droplets of sweat pop out on my forehead. Oh, God.

Blasted across the TV are images too incredible to put in the same category as reality, but it is real, and my mom was right. The world has gone mad. A news anchor is talking a mile a minute, eyes wide in shock, while he licks his lips with nervous energy while trying to narrate a clip. In the split-screen, videos pop in and out, obviously filmed by witnesses rather than a professional. People's cameras and phones captured everything from rock giants swarming into cities, toppling buildings in plumes of dust and smoke, to tornadoes so massive they swallow entire building complexes.

And then comes footage of a wall of water. The news

anchor is calling it a tsunami, though the multitude of these massive waves sweeping the globe is at odds with the earthquake-induced phenomenon. My parents flip to another channel where scientific experts are debating everything from video hoaxes to the possibility of an F6 tornado. Every channel is consumed by the horror that killed millions. Millions, they are saying. I feel sick.

"What's happening, Mike? Is the world ending?" Mom asks in a quivering voice.

I glance at my parents, watching as my dad turns to her and wraps his arms around my mom's shoulders. She hugs him tightly, burrowing into his neck. "I don't know, Eleanor. I just don't know. At least we're safe. Let's try to focus on that for now." Dad pulls me into his arms for a group hug, squeezing hard enough to stop my breath, but I am too frozen to truly feel it. I stumble a bit when he lets me go and watch as if from outside myself as they talk quietly.

I feel numb as I listen to their quiet conversation. How could I be part of the ruin of the world? How is this what Gaia wanted? So many people are dead. Entire families are gone, washed out to sea, or crushed under piles of broken buildings. This is not how it was supposed to be. I never wanted to hurt anyone. Vaguely, I become aware of a thundering in my chest, a rapid tattoo that creeps into my ears, muffling every other sound. Spots form before my eyes, as anxiety washes over me in a full-blown panic attack. I killed people. Oh, my God. I killed them. A film of sweat coats my face, and my stomach fills with a bubbling sickness. I'm going to throw up. Slapping a hand over my mouth, I take deep breaths through my nose. The sounds I make are so quiet that they are drowned out by the hum of voices on the screen. I watch the footage through a haze of tears as I struggle to keep control of my body.

Unaware that I am falling apart, my parents leave the room to get more coffee and talk out of earshot. With shaking hands, I reach for the remote and flip through a couple of newscasts before stopping to listen. On a British news channel, an anchor is speaking with survivors from India, where the ocean retreated so far that many people walked out onto the exposed seafloor for hundreds of meters, viewing the phenomenon as neither dangerous nor unusual. Those who remained on the shore, safely atop tall buildings, lived to talk about what happened, telling the anchor of the moment when the tide suddenly returned in a series of waves that swept away anyone caught in its path.

According to their first-hand accounts, the initial waves were the shortest, but the ocean seemed to grow stronger and, like an arrow, bent around landmasses in a crazy wraparound effect, heading straight up the Hooghly River in a massive wave over one hundred feet tall. It barreled like a freight train, gaining momentum rather than slowing naturally, swallowing entire villages until it reached the city of Kolkata, a place with a population in the tens of millions. The tsunami, that's what they're calling it, raged on, ripping the largest cable bridge in India from its anchorages, filling the streets, and consuming entire structures, leaving in its wake an unrecognizable mass of destruction. It took just over an hour for it to be over. The waves simply retreated, as though being pulled back by some unseen force, like a magnet. The ocean churned, then quieted. What remains of the affected towns and cities leaves little hope for survivors.

Interviews immediately commence with climate and earthquake scientists, both weighing in on the event and its causes. It is so hard to wrap my head around the scale of destruction. Eventually, mom returns from the kitchen, eyes teary, and knuckles whitening, as she grips her coffee mug. I watch from the corner of my eye, wondering how I could ever try to explain what is happening. How could I ever let her know I was a part of this? She sips her coffee, all attention on the discussion in front of her. I let my eyes drift back to the news, heart aching with guilt and regret.

It is as the channel begins to air amateur video and photo footage of the waves that I see it, barely discernible, but there. And I know what, or who, it is. Within the crest of the waves, staring out at the world with pitiless condemnation is a face, *her* face. The rise of Gaia has only begun.

# CHAPTER 34

*It's hard to face the truth*

The doorbell ringing makes me jump. The sound hangs in the air for a moment, the shrillness echoing, before wrenching me away from the news and into the present. I get up.

"I'll get it," I say to my dad, who has begun to rise. He sinks back down on the sofa, already distracted by another series of videos showing a staggering amount of destruction brought upon by the stuff of nightmares.

I look through the peephole and feel my heart stutter as I see Raife on the stoop. I rub my hands on my pajama pants and open the door. His relief is evident in every line of his face as Raife visibly relaxes as he looks at me. Stepping forward, he pulls me into a hard hug, squeezing me tightly and whispering in my ear, "I felt your presence in me last night, and I knew. I knew it was beginning. Are you okay?"

A sob catches in my throat as I struggle to swallow it. I shake my head in jerky movements, unable to say anything right away. Clearing my throat and pulling myself together, I manage a few nonsensical sentences. "Scilti came and led me to the preserve, and she was there, and I climbed onto the rock and...and...I don't know. I just kind of lost myself, or something, and I woke up and was alone. I didn't know what I'd done...I didn't know."

He grasps my hands and tugs me down the steps and onto the front lawn, where he stops under the shade of a pine tree. "It's okay, Terran. You knew this would be hard. It's okay. I'm here. You're not alone."

"It doesn't feel okay. What I did...all those people...it's wrong. I killed people, Raife. Killed them." The last part came out as little more than a whisper.

"We all played a part, right? I felt it when you touched me with your mind, that moment of recognition, and the pull of energy. I knew it was happening and what it could mean, but it had to happen. Gaia is dying, Terran. If we do nothing, there will be nothing. People will swallow the earth until all that is left is choking air and polluted waters."

I shake my head, unwilling to see things this way, though I knew deep down in my heart that this shift to balance would never really be anything other than brutal; I didn't want to face that truth. I only wanted to show the world, not destroy it. I fooled myself into believing I could avenge the earth with such precision that only the genuinely guilty would suffer. "Have you seen the news, though? Did you watch the videos people took? I did that. I created monsters that tore apart the world. How can that be a good thing?"

Everything decent within me seems to shrivel. I curl into a ball, clutching my chest, trying to keep myself from splintering into a million pieces. I don't know who I am anymore. With this act, I have murdered the part of me that was human, along with a thousand other lives. Raife strokes my back, but I can't hear what he's saying through the anguish that rips from my chest. All I hear is the echo screams for help pounding through my head.

Raife tries to pull me up, but I grab fistfuls of his shirt, refusing to uncurl my body and break our connection. He manages to wrestle away just far enough to cup my face, tilting my head so that I am forced to look into his eyes. "Did you really think this would be easy? That people could just be told to stop and realize what they're doing and change their ways? They don't care, Terran. They turned their back on Gaia hundreds of years ago. There is no other way but this one." He pauses, reading my expressions. "This is a war being waged to save the planet. You and me, we have to do our part, because if we don't, then we may as well surrender to everything wrong in this world and let it all burn."

It's impossible to even attempt to see what I've done as anything but horribly wrong. "No! This isn't right. I killed people. Killed them! Thousands!" I double over and begin to retch, my body trying to force out something it can never be rid of.

Raife pulls my hair away from my face as my neck arches painfully, and my guts twist. When the waves of sickness are over, I collapse on my side, body shuddering with the force of my sobs.

"Terran," Raife says quietly. I cover my face and shake my head. "Terran, look at me."

"No," I whisper. "You want me to become this thing. I can't. I won't."

"I don't want you to be anyone but who you were meant to be. Terran. Áine. You are one and the same."

I shake my head. "I'm not her. I can never be her."

"The world needs you. Gaia needs you."

"No."

Raife strokes my sweaty cheeks, and I clench my eyes, refusing to open them, to look into him and see things I don't want to face. He waits me out, fingers tracing the tracks of my tears until my body calms and nausea leaves. I feel wrung out and raw.

"You aren't wiping out an entire species," Raife says in a voice pitched low and soothing. "You're only trying to tip that balance to something sustainable. If you don't, then the world is lost. Everyone will suffer. Everyone and everything will just shrivel and die."

"But not everyone is to blame, so how can I just punish them all? That's not fair," I plead. "It's not right. I can't just kill people," I cry, sending me into a new fit of sobbing.

"I want you to do something for me, okay?" I look at him but say nothing, breath hitching in my chest. "Close your eyes and reach out to her."

"What? No! I never want to feel her in me again!" I yell, pulling my hands away.

Raife reaches for me before I get more than a few inches away. "Just listen," he begs as I shake my head. "Reach out to her and just feel what she's feeling. I'm not asking you to dip into your pool of power or anything like that, just speak to her. Just listen."

I squirm away, staggering to my feet to pace in small circles. "I can't do that. She's too strong. She'll make me... no. I won't do it."

"Terran, please. Just listen to her. She deserves that much. She is your mother, the mother of us all. Don't leave her to die in the darkness, alone."

My heart twists as I grimace. "What if I lose control?"

"You won't."

I hear him stride toward me and let him stop my movements. "Just reach out? Nothing more?"

"That's it. I'll be here with you. I won't let things get out of control. I promise."

Wringing my hands, I look up at him, and all I see is a deep love and sincerity. Raife caresses my face, and I close my eyes, releasing myself into the earth. It feels different, as I seem to drift beneath the layers, closer to the heart of Gaia, cleaner somehow, as though the infection that's been festering like a rotten abscess has been lanced, drained to the point of relief but not eradicated. She's there, a tickling sensation that flutters all around me as I make contact.

*"Mother,"* I think to her.

*"Daughter. You have come."*

Gaia embraces me in the only way she can, flooding me with warm awareness, showing me through flashes of imagery and feeling, the relief she feels, the freedom from the weight of a world that has smothered her very essence. I can only translate the sensations passing through me as joy, though she doesn't use that word. It is too mundane, and she is all things. Gaia is feeling and intent, a seeker of balance and fruition, a voice of command, and vengeance. There is a powerful feeling of possession as she twists around me in complicated patterns. I give myself up to it, unable to stop a flow of thought and power that seeps into her without provocation. She takes little sips, spilling herself back into me until my mind is Gaia. I am Gaia, and she is all her children.

Somewhere, just outside of this drunken haze of communion, I feel Raife. I turn my mind toward his presence and see the pulse of his being, blindingly bright just beyond this cocoon in the bowels of the earth. He's saying something, pulling me away from her. I resist for a moment, as Gaia whispers in a parade of sound with no meaning beyond their soothing pull. I listen, taking it in until I feel unanchored, drifting to a place within the sanctuary of her being, into arms that welcome me, promising a new world, new beginnings, new life. From a distance, I feel tugging and hear Raife's voice trying to wake me, to pull me up and out. But Gaia is too strong. Her warmth and love envelop me until she is all I feel. Until within her arms is the only place I long to be.

---

My mom pokes her head into my room as I slowly sit up in bed, having no memory of getting here. I watch her pad softly toward me, a cup of milk and a plate of cookies in her hand, at odds with the worried expression stamped across her face. "Hi, sweet girl," she says, setting the plate and cup on my bedside table. "How are you feeling?"

I look around, confused that I'm here at all. "Okay, I guess. How did I get back to bed? I was outside talking to Raife and then...how long have I been asleep?"

She sits next to me as I scoot over to make room. "You've been out all day. Raife carried you in after you fell asleep outside when you two were talking. I was worried, but your father said it was just you being so overwhelmed by everything." She gulps, eyes drifting toward the door where the sound of the TV is drifting through the open space. "I don't blame you for just wanting to go back to bed. What's happened is too much for any of us to take."

I reach for the milk, gulping it down slowly so that I can think and not be tempted to say things better left unsaid. "Has anything else happened?" I ask, though a big part of me is afraid of the answer.

"No, thank God. There have been scientists from all over the world trying to explain what happened, but I don't think any of them have a clue, and I guess that's the scariest thing. If the experts don't know, what chance do the rest of us have if it happens again? Lots of people are saying it's the end of the world, Judgment Day." I can see that she's just speaking aloud, unmindful of the things she says, as there's no way she'd want me to think the outlook looked that bleak. Seeming to snap out of it, she tells me, "Beth called a few times. She's worried about you and asked that you call her back."

"I will. I'm going to hop in the shower first and just try to wake up a bit more."

Mom gets up, gives me a quick hug, and leaves the room, shutting the door with more care than needed. I sit on my bed, thinking, trying to recall the moment I must have passed out outside when I was with Raife. But there's nothing there, no memory niggling in my head. I grab my phone and see that I've got over sixty unread texts. It seems like a lot of people have been reaching out. I scroll through and note that many of them are from group threads. I look at the first few, then switch to Raife's feed, texting him that I'm up, going to shower, and will call him later. Then I reach out to Beth and tell her the same before I put my phone down and make my way to the bathroom.

The warm spray of the water helps to clear my head. I still have little sense of what I did earlier, but recognize that I spoke with Gaia, in a way, while with Raife. Somehow, I know that nothing happened in that union, nothing that caused havoc in the world like what I had done before. I flip through my conversation with Raife, his certainty that what I did was done out of necessity, not some blind need to destroy, but I keep seeing the images from the news, the number of people that have been wiped off the face of the earth is staggering. I understand what Raife is trying to tell me, but I can't swallow it. It just keeps coming back up, a regurgitated mass that bubbles with self-loathing.

The shower is the right place to cry, and I let myself embrace my misery, curling into a ball on the shower floor, wishing the water could wash away what I've done but knowing it never will. I lie there until the temperature turns cool, and my skin begins to pebble, quivering along with the racking of my sobs. By the time my teeth start to chatter, I feel a bit better, like some of the poison is gone, taken in the flow of water and down the drain. I turn off the shower and hobble out, grabbing a towel and burrowing my face in it.

"You don't have to be a monster, Terran," I mutter into the thick cotton. "You aren't a killer." But I am. I am.

I dry off and throw on a pair of pajamas; there's no way I'm leaving the house today. The world is safer if I just stay here. I decide to call Beth, needing to hear her voice. She answers after the first ring. "Terran! Oh, my God. Have you watched the news? Did you see those things walking around and smashing entire buildings? I can't believe this is happening. I mean, what is going on? This stuff is right out of a science fiction horror movie or something! And my mom is totally freaking out, not just with the monsters running around the planet, but with other stuff too, like she can feel stuff happening or something. She keeps asking to see you. It's been so crazy, and I've been really worried about you. Are you okay?"

"Wow, Beth. That was a lot of stuff you just said," I say slowly, overwhelmed by the barrage of words that she blasted through my phone.

"Sorry. I'm just really freaked out right now."

"I am too," I tell her. "To answer your questions, yes, I did see the stuff on the news, and it's insane, and, yes, I'm okay, but apparently fell into a semi-coma for the day after Raife came over. I think all of this was a mental overload or something."

Beth lets out a sigh. "What's happening, Terran? What are those things? They look like something from the mind of Tolkien."

She has a point there. The rock-monsters, as I now

have to refer to them after Raife's obsession, are the stuff of horror-filled fantasy. I want to tell Beth that I know exactly how they came into being, to spill my guts and let her look at the evidence of my collusion in this global assault, but I don't say anything, nothing of substance anyway, and it hurts to keep it secret, especially now. "It looked like they came right out of the earth from what I could see on the news."

"Yeah, they sure did, all made of rock or something. And it seemed like those things didn't even feel it when the army tried bombing them, they just got right back up and kept on going. How do you stop something like that?"

"You don't," I blurt, wishing I could take it back the moment it comes out. I don't want her to feel as though the world is doomed, because it's not. Things will get better now. I'm not going to be part of it anymore. "At least you can't destroy them with weapons that don't make a dent. Maybe something else would work, though."

"Yeah. I guess," she says.

I try to shift the subject. "You said your mom is going crazy. Is she alright?"

"She's gone nuts, talking to her hippie friends on and off all day while consulting everything from tarot cards to astral charts."

As Beth talks, I wonder if Celeste knows more about the unseen world I've been thrust into than what she led me to believe. "Why is she doing that?"

"Beats me. Maybe it's her way of coping."

I feel a bit let down hearing that. I had hoped that maybe I could talk to Celeste. It would be nice to have another mind helping me find a way to end this nightmare, possibly by severing my connection to Gaia. Then again, she would probably be even more horrified by what I've done than I am. It's a depressing thought. "Well, if your mom finds any answers in the cards or stars, let me know, okay?" And if she doesn't? If there is no way to keep Gaia out of my mind, no way to stop myself from becoming something so monstrous that I consume the world? The options are few, and all make me shy away, appalled to even consider them.

"Of course, but don't count on it," Beth says, bringing me back to the conversation. "And she keeps asking for you, wanting you to come over, but she won't tell me why. She's being so weird." There is a long pause before Beth adds, "Do you think they'll come back?"

I swallow hard, wanting to say no but reluctant to give her false hope. "I don't know."

"I hope they don't come here," she whispers. In the background, I can hear Celeste calling her. I'm ashamed at the twinge of relief I feel at needing to get off the phone. "Listen, I've gotta go," Beth tells me. "School's canceled tomorrow, so I'll call you around noon or so."

"Sounds good. Bye, Beth. Be safe."

I hang up and fall back onto my bed, looking at the swirls of paint plastering the ceiling. I imagine that I can see Gaia's form looking down on me, in sweeps of texture.

It is, at once, both disturbing and comforting. Is this the beginning, or has this one global event tipped the balance in such a way that it has ended at the start? I can't say, though, when I touched Gaia's being with my mind today, she felt untainted, pure. I hope that it's enough. I don't want to lose myself in the carnage only to slowly disappear into nothing, as Áine did. I bury my face in my pillow and cry, "All those people, all those people."

# CHAPTER 35

*There's a reason it's called*
*Skook Illahee*

Raife tells me that Silas wants us to meet with him tomorrow. I'm not sure how I feel about it, torn between adamant refusal and reluctant agreement. If I see him, then I can tell him it's over for me. I want out. But the reality of seeing Silas, being under his sway, makes me unwilling. When Raife gives me the alternative of sitting at home with my parents glued to the TV rather than finding some purpose and direction, the choice becomes obvious. I can end this now, and I must.

Later on, I accept the fact that sleep will not be forthcoming, the result of napping most of the day, combined with nervous energy. So, I am up as dawn fills the sky with hues of pink, red, and orange. It's breathtaking and somehow more beautiful than any sunset I've ever seen. As light spills across the horizon, slowly bleaching out the vibrant colors, I can't help feeling like it's a reflection of what I have become a part of, erasing the ugliness that has splattered Gaia's landscape, flooding it, killing it with singular intent, until the world born of that vengeance is as new as the dawn.

It seems so simple when I remove feeling and look at the bigger picture, one of survival and balance for future generations, but this is not simple. I cannot wash away the death of millions with a swipe of a painter's brush and call myself innocent of wrongdoing. I am tainted with each action, just as Gaia is corrupted with eons of exploitation. I don't know how to walk away from what I've started, and some part of myself doesn't wish to. I sigh into the emptiness, tired in a way that goes beyond the need for sleep. I peel back the covers, shivering when the chill air of my room touches my skin, and sit up. Where do I begin now? I shake my head. Outside, I hear Scilti cawing, feel the tug of his awareness, but I refuse to respond. I shut him away and look around my room, hoping my eyes fall on something to distract me.

I glance at the clock. Ugh. It will be hours before Raife picks me up, so I decide to take a bath, convinced that a good two-hour soak with bubbles and a sappy romance will be just the thing to distract me from the realities of my life. I turn the light to dim, setting the mood to relax, and fill the tub with hot water, watching the bubbles rise in a perfect layer that covers the entire expanse of the tub. The scent of lavender fills the room as the foam rises, and I close my eyes, breathing it in before climbing into the bath.

Resting my book on the edge, I sink into the warmth, focusing on nothing but the feel of the water and bubbles tickling my skin, and close my eyes. I seem to drift, bobbing on the surface, arms weightless, breaking through the uppermost layers that film the top of the water. It takes a few minutes for me to realize the sounds around me are not those of the dripping faucet or the hum of cars passing by my house. These are louder, deeper, rolling over me in currents. I am no longer resting in the safety of my bathroom, tucked within a body of warmth. This is the sea, and I am in the arms of Gaia.

My first reaction is to return her embrace, taking in the flow of energy her very presence exudes. Then I remember and fear floods my mind, internal warnings that flare behind my eyes, reminders of what that power means when I unleash it. I pull myself away, from the inside, putting up invisible barriers. I sense her feeling them out with probing touches, looking for cracks in my resolve, and finding them. The penetration of her will is painless and not wholly unwelcome. I am her daughter, bound to her by more than blood, and there is no denial, no escape, no real will to resist. Sensing my capitulation, Gaia plunges into me, to my core, consuming every part of me until I am awash in her being. The moment I am hers entirely, every nerve ending comes to life in a riot of sensations that make me twitch and writhe before spilling into my muscles in pulsing spasms until I am suffused in incredible power, seeing with ancient eyes through spirals of time and into the future, a place where life abounds untainted and unthreatened. It is beautiful.

When my eyes open, the harsh reality of the world, as I know it, twists my heart in painful knots with hurt so deep that it sinks into my bones like cancer. I clench my fists, tears spilling from my eyes as sobs break from my chest, ripping through the quiet of the room. The water has grown cold, and my teeth chatter, keeping rhythm with my anguish. Gaia is not healed by this one event. The wound still festers, and she is dying. The true war is to come. If ever I am to feel whole again, if she is to be restored, I must rise again in greater vengeance for her.

Images of carnage flash through my mind, fracturing it. At that moment, I recognize what all of this means. "No! Get out of my head!" I shriek at her, pummeling her being with the force of my refusal. "I won't kill for you!"

She cringes away for a brief moment before throwing herself into me in a massive swarm, smothering every thought, every instinct, until I lose myself, body convulsing under the force of her will. Determination courses through me, obliterating protest, swallowing guilt, before snuffing out the last piece of resistance.

Slowly, so slowly that time seems to spin in a sluggish pace, I pull myself from the mire, pack away my misgivings, and get ready. It must be today. There is no point in waiting, in allowing the world to think it is over, to get comfortable again in their arrogance.

*"Arise with me, my daughter,"* Gaia's voice whispers in my head.

"Yes. I am ready," I say aloud. Beneath my skin, I feel her presence, a living thing that surges through my blood, giving me purpose.

I grab clothing at random, too wrapped up in the haze of her possession to care what I look like, and leave my room, creeping down the stairs. The low buzz of the television drifts to my ears, but I ignore it, the murmur of voices too abstract to penetrate my thoughts. Leaving the house, I feel a sense of relief, the falling away of the shackles of my humanity. A sigh curls around my mind, blanketing me in warmth that makes my thoughts fuzzy and indistinct while keeping their purpose. From without myself, I see Scilti swoop down, landing at my feet before launching back into the sky, dipping in lazy patterns, leading me despite there being no need. I know where I am going and need no guide. She beckons me, a beacon I am unable to resist, pulling at my soul. I know I will feel no relief until we are one, in the heart of the forest.

The houses I pass are meaningless, ugly structures that sit upon her aspect in defiance of her reign over this world, reflections of an arrogant race that has gone unchecked for too long. My lip curls with distaste, and I feel her feeding my anger. I lap it up with gluttonous intent.

Passing into the forest, I feel the trees welcome me. I am with them, one of them, as we all are, brought together through Gaia's being, which nurtures all life, even those whose actions revile it. Midway down the trail, I stop and look up at a giant cypress, branches spanning tens of feet as it towers over everything in mute dominion. I walk toward it, pulled somehow by its energy, and press my hands to the bark. The pads of my fingers tingle at the contact, sending a feeling up my arms and into my chest. I close my eyes, pressing my cheek to the tree as I would press my face to someone's chest to listen to their heartbeat. The life force coursing through the fibers of its trunk welcomes me, not with word or thought, but with a slow release of energy through my skin until I feel the roots buried beneath the soil, snaking through rock and dirt into depths cloaked in the deepest darkness, twining with others as they span the ground for miles. I am not myself, not entirely. There is an air of detachment as I speak with the trees in a language that transcends words, imbuing them with subtle power, feeling it catch within their fibers, causing them to bend in acknowledgment and promise. All around me is the slow creak of limbs and trunks as the message is passed across the landscape. Slowly, I pull away, leaving traces of my will, her intention, behind so they are ready, so they can continue to pass along the knowledge that it has begun, that it must also end.

By the time I reach the outcropping of rock on the forest floor, I am committed in a way I have never been before this moment; all doubt is gone, all anguish and regret, drowned out along with the lives of thousands who perished under the waves of retribution. I climb upon the rock and sit, hands pressed to the rough surface, and reach out. She is waiting, just under my skin, under the layer of rock and minerals beneath my fingertips.

"Mother, I am ready."

"*Yes, daughter. Let us begin. Reach for them. Reach for them all.*"

The moment her thoughts take root, I clench my teeth, rocking back at the force of her power until my head strikes the hard surface. I am nothing, only spinning in weightlessness, caught between this world and hers, taken into her heart where it is darkness and warmth, purity and disease. Oily thoughts slither all around me, the leavings of man whose corruption seeps into the earth, contaminating everything it touches, coating the purity of Gaia in a smothering residue. I arch away from it, burrowing deeper into her being where it cannot find me, but it remains, speckling her landscape with poison darts that stain my thoughts and pierce my being in painful barbs. How can she survive this? It is all around me, inescapable pollution. No matter how I writhe, I cannot escape it.

I scream out to her. "Mother. It hurts."

*"Awaken my children. Call them to you, daughter. Avenge me."*

It feels like my skin is being ripped from my body in tiny tears as I wrench myself away from the sickening contamination that surrounds me. When I am finally free of it, I reach out from a deep reservoir of strength, nurtured by Gaia, fed by her anger, and release it, sending out entreaties to all of the Daoine Fíor. I feel small tugs as each of them responds, mixing their awareness and power with mine, pulling in and pushing out in a never-ending exchange until I am filled to overflowing, currents race through my body, spilling onto the rock beneath me and sinking into the forest floor to mix with the roots of the trees. A small part of my mind senses Raife and Silas, their beings burning brightest. Raife reaches toward me, and I feel him tapping at my mind and respond, conveying my feelings and location, pulling him toward me like a signal. He answers, and I breathe a sigh of contentment, knowing he is coming to me, to stand beside me as we bring it all down.

# CHAPTER 36

*It is war*

The moment his feet cross into the forest, I feel it, a flare of consciousness, spreading through me. I call harder, bringing him to this place where my strength is anchored, rooted in a site of power, sunk into the earth, into Gaia. I feel his footfalls along the trail, each impact sending shivers of anticipation up my spine as my skin pebbles. The trees announce his arrival, bending their branches in welcome, forming an archway of greenery that leads him to me.

The first contact is the sweetest, a balm that slowly brings me to the present as his hand traces the contours of my face, his voice whispering in the stillness.

"Terran."

My lips part noiselessly. "Raife."

"I'm here. I felt you calling to me," he tells me, fingers lacing through mine as I lie prone on the rock. "Are you okay? Can you sit up?"

My eyelids feel so heavy, weighed down by unseen forces. It takes so much effort to open them, to look upon his face. When I succeed, I turn my head slightly, letting it roll to the side where he is perched on the boulder next to me.

Raife gasps when our eyes meet. "Oh, my God. Your eyes...they look...timeless."

My mouth curves minutely as I take in his face, processing his words. I am not alone in my mind. "She is with me," I whisper, my throat feeling scratchy, lips parched.

He nods, cupping my cheek before leaning in to press his soft lips to mine. "I see her in you."

My thoughts dart from one thing to another. taking in so much that I must force my brain to quiet, focus. Gaia's strength is a hum in my heart, her will and purpose, a calling. She has such plans for me, a new generation born of a union between Raife and me, and others, so many others, spread across the world. It must end before it can begin.

I do not balk at her plans. There is no will to do more than embrace her, to be her weapon, and her future. Opening my mouth, I speak words that do not come from me. I am a conduit. "Stand with me, and we will end this and begin again."

Raife leans over, caressing my face in feathery touches, kissing me whenever his fingers stroke, before reaching for my hands and pulling me upward to stand next to him. Lacing our fingers together, we root our bodies, side by side, bridged by a connection far beyond our skin. I close my eyes once again, going into myself where Gaia lies buried in my blood and bones. The surge of power, brought to new heights through Raife's physical connection, rushes out of me, sinking into the rock. I mold it, feeling it rise around my feet, forcing it to bend with deep groans of shifting sediment until it has encased our limbs to our ankles, a stabilizing mass for what is to come.

Raife huffs with surprise as I loose myself, flooding the minds of Gaia's children with her vision, pouring my energy, her energy, our energy into a current that moves in communal spirals, to feed and be fed in a never-ending cycle. Gaia infuses the world's waters while I rip through the land, my will erupting across the globe in deep chasms and monstrous entities. Within our clasped hands, I feel Raife's strength adding to my own while the wind stirs around us, slowly at first before becoming a frenzy.

Gaia explodes from the oceans and the skies, towering over coastal cities in unimaginable heights, her visage painted in the waves and clouds that tumble over the water in violent thunderstorms. She races inland, swallowing everything in her path, erasing the blight on her landscape. Panic fills my mind for brief moments, those millions of flickering lives that scream in terror at a force they should never have turned their back on. I shut them out, ruthlessly, blocking them from entering my thoughts with pitiless judgment.

Tidal waves sweep across the world, crashing through barriers and buildings. Bridges collapse under the onslaught, tearing from their moorings as though made of paper, to be washed into the sea. Mountains of sand spread across the landscape, erasing the taint of man, coating every surface until it is clean, new. Just beyond the waves await a new terror, hungry mouths waiting to feed until there is nothing left of those who entered the ocean, never to rise again. And still, the water rises, floods, and wrenches all within its path from the sodden ground.

Torrential rains pummel the earth as lightning streaks across the sky in blinding flashes, revealing glimpses of her merciless face gazing down on humanity. Flash floods rip through mountain passages and down hillsides, pulling softened earth like wet clay to mix with thunderous water deluges, muddy masses that obliterate everything in their inescapable path.

Lakes bubble, coming to frothy life before horrified onlookers whose mindless panic is drowned under their watery mass. There is no joy in the destruction, only rage, wrath so intense it eclipses every other emotion. Gaia spills into rivers, obliterating levees, blindly consuming all within her path. All of this I see with a sight I cannot explain before I turn my mind to my own action.

The protected, those children whose voices rise to call the air and flame, sing to me. Their songs echo the anguish plaguing Gaia, and their call to arms rings in her name. They are part of me now, this exchange of power and energy, which builds a collective strength within her heart, the core of everything. It is a seedling germinating in awesome speed and proportion until it erupts, spewing out arms of intent that wind through the mantle like worms, until they find one of us, bursting forth and into Gaia's progeny. I feel hundreds of these tendrils slithering beneath my feet, under rock and sediment, searching, searching until they find us. I await them, sensing their blind probing, feeling the moment they lock onto me and drive forward, through the rocky outcrop and into my anchored limbs. A scream erupts from my lungs, not of terror but of fury, emotions stained red, eclipsing everything but my will to unleash it.

I lift my arms, strength gushing from my fingers in torrents, and raise an army like no other. Across the planet, mountains erupt from the ground, standing hundreds of feet above the paltry dwellings that fall under their forceful, empty eyes. Their numbers eclipse the first event as though that's what practice for this moment is, a test of my power. This is the war beyond human history. This is true power.

Lumbering, stone giants shake the earth in a relentless

tide, knocking through buildings and borders as though they are nothing. Arms made of granite and quartz swing massive fists across the landscape, smashing everything into unrecognizable lumps that are quickly erased by massive fires and windstorms that seem to rise from nowhere. Weaponry rains down on the beasts, the only targets in this unrelenting onslaught, but their bullets and bombs strike, shattering rock that only reforms and rises again.

I grit my teeth and sink into the earth, feeling along fault lines, sensing each tectonic plate. While my vengeance walks the earth, I begin to move the land, opening cracks that swallow entire cities before grinding them to nothing in massive compressions. The entire planet is at war, waging a battle that will change the face of the world forever, leaving the chosen to rule, those whose blood is tied to Gaia in intricate webs of connectivity, binding them to her like no other being on earth.

My hair violently whips around my face, pulled in every direction by the wind Raife unleashed. As though outside myself, I hear a sound like a freight train, something massive bearing down, ripping through structures before lifting huge chunks of cement and wood and flinging them in every direction. I smile faintly at Raife's strength, feeling a deep connection to him, so much greater than anything we have shared before. It is purity and purpose. He speaks to me of an untainted future, of new generations, guardians of Gaia. I take it in, letting my mind fixate for a moment on the visions he shares, relishing this new world his mind conjures. I reach for the idea, embracing it, using it as though it were a source of strength, before funneling it across the earth.

I don't know how long I heard it before that moment, when her voice penetrates the storms swirling in my mind, but when I hear, truly hear it, the sound pierces my thoughts, and I open my eyes. She is on the ground, crawling toward me. Twigs and dirt plaster her body so that she is almost unrecognizable. Her mouth is twisted in pain and effort, and I notice a large gash across her brow, leaving dark trails of blood that have matted her hair. My thoughts are fractured things, tortured by her presence, writhing as they battle with hundreds of voices and wills that share my being, one more powerful than all of them combined. It feels like daggers stabbing into my brain as I try to wrench myself away from the chaos and focus on what is before me.

"Terran!" Beth screams, her voice ripping through the forest, tortured and hoarse, but strong. Like a barbed arrow, her presence penetrates every part of me, fastening me to her with a bond that has grown since babyhood.

My eyes, though they are not only mine, as behind and within them Gaia stares out with me, and into Beth's face. I cannot speak, cannot move, held fast to the rock by more than a physical connection. As I look at Beth, whose face is turned up to me as she claws her way closer, I feel a sick twisting of pity, love, anger, and fear, all mixed together in a confusing mass until I can't separate my will from Gaia's, my thoughts from hers. We are one. There is no me.

Beth staggers forward in a huge lunge, grabbing hold of the lip of the rock. "Terran! Stop!"

I want to say something, but my voice is gone, too tangled and not my own. Instead, I look down at Beth, my body trembling with a need to reach for her, but unable to force my muscles to obey my command to move. I fight an internal battle to free myself, only able to look upon Beth's face with dispassion.

I watch as though I am outside myself, while she attempts to get her feet under her and rise up to get to me. Her face is a mirror of pain and anguish. It hurts my heart to see it, but that pain is transitory, muffled by the intertwining of Gaia and all of the Daoine Fíor who seem to sense my struggle.

Beth's broken sob tortures me. "Terran, please."

The moment Raife looks upon Beth, I can sense it, that awareness traveling through our fingers that remain laced together. Though I do not turn to face him, it is as though I see Beth through his eyes, an interloper in this place of power, a threat to our war to restore balance. I know his intent before he channels it, but I can only stand aside, unable to fight my way out of Gaia's grasp.

"You should not have come here," Raife shouts, the deep resonance booming across the forest floor.

Flares of alarm light up my mind as I watch Raife call to the wind, creating a vortex that erupts from the sky, funneling to the earth in pointed pursuit of Beth. Some-how, I manage to crane my neck to look at him, horror eclipsing my thoughts as I hear his command to the wind deep within my body.

*"No!"* my mind screams at him, but he brushes it aside, staring down at Beth with singular intent.

Curling inside myself for a moment, I call to Gaia. *"Mother!"*

She hears more than my voice, but I can sense her inhuman thoughts before she speaks to me. *"That one is not my child."*

I feel my heart racing as violent, twisting air shoots toward the earth, aimed at Beth. She looks up at me and says something, but her voice is lost in the deafening wind that has touched the ground a few feet from where she kneels. Debris spins in vicious spirals, twigs, small rocks, and dirt, mixing together with deadly intensity, coming toward Beth in an unstoppable force. Tears streak across Beth's face, cutting tracks through dirt and blood. I see the moment Beth gives up. I feel it. And so does Raife.

His passive face watches Beth's shoulders slump in defeat as he brings the storm of wind straight at her back. I watch it lift her up, ripping her fingers from the rock, twisting her body in unnatural contortions before flinging her like a rag-doll across the open space. Though I cannot hear it, I sense the break as her arm slams into a rock, body crumpling around it to cradle the injury. Raife's mind directs itself to the air, infusing it with greater strength as it barrels toward Beth to finish the job.

The moment I tear myself away from Gaia, I feel my heart twist painfully, torn in a way that seems to shred every aspect of it. Her voice rages at me, *"Daughter!"* It brings me to my knees, and I use that momentum to rip my hand from Raife, severing the strength of our connection but not the roots that hold us together.

The twister disintegrates in a pile of debris and soft breaths of wind as our separation floods Raife's mind. "Terran! What are you doing? She is not one of us."

My hands press against the rock as I take gulps of air, each helping me focus and remove the barriers that have forced me to be an audience to what has happened before my eyes. My mouth feels coated in a film of dry spit. I swallow a few times to clear it and finally find my voice. "No," I croak, shaking my head as tendrils of alarm from hundreds of voices rock through me. "She is not one of us. But she is my friend."

"She's human!" Raife rages at me. I feel his anger like a palpable thing battering my brain. "It is her kind that has poisoned our mother, and they do not deserve this planet! Look what they've done!! They're killing her!"

"Not Beth," I whisper, as my body slowly gains physical strength. I pour it into the rock, peeling back what has anchored our feet throughout this devastation, and slowly stand, legs shaking with effort. "I can't do this, Raife."

"Then I will," he snarls, hopping off the rock and striding toward Beth, who still lies curled on her side.

"No!" I scream, legs trembling as I try to jump to the ground. I fall the moment my feet touch the dirt, too weak to take the force of the impact. I get to my knees and reach toward Raife. "Stop! Raife, don't do this!"

He looks back at me, and I see understanding there, but it is a frail thing compared to the black purpose behind it. "I'm sorry, Terran. I knew this would be hard for you when I saw the friendship you both shared, but there is no other way."

"Please," I yell, anguish twisting through the word. *Don't make me do this* I cry inside, watching his relentless approach toward Beth. "Raife, please!" I scream until my voice is nothing but a scratchy thing.

I watch him pick up a rock, testing its weight, before looking back at me with regret tainted by a decision that will not restrain his hand as he swings it upward to bludgeon Beth.

"No!" I scream, my energy pouring into every facet of the earth around me. Rock, molded into a spear, shoots from the ground, exploding from the soil in a fall of dirt as it rips its way into the air, not stopping its ascent until it tears through bone and blood, muscle and tendon, lung and heart. Raife yelps in shock before slumping over the point that has pierced his body. His mouth goes slack, blood and spit spilling onto the tip coated with gore. My

name ripples through his mind in the last moment before
his thoughts are silenced forever.

# CHAPTER 37

*I'm no savior*

Heartache, unlike anything I have experienced before, consumes me. Uncontrollable sobs burst from my chest, shaking my entire body, as I kneel on the ground, looking at the grisly scene in front of me. Gaia's anguish, mixed with those of the Daoine Fíor, batter my mind, adding depth to the grief that threatens to pull me under and bury me under its weight. I clutch at my chest, feeling like it's going to rip apart. The war across the world has grown ominously silent. Wind and rain clear in moments, waves recede as though they never were, great chasms close in puckering wounds while monsters fall apart in piles of rock.

Beth's voice pierces the turmoil of my anguish. "Terran?"

I look up and watch her roll onto her knees, holding her broken arm close to her ribcage. She glances at the morbid scene, shuddering and squeezing her eyes closed for a few moments before she opens them to shuffle forward. I try to focus on her movements, but my brain feels battered. Drowning under the weight of what I have wrought, not just here, but everywhere. How could I lose myself to this rage and do what I've done? How could I condemn an entire species? My head falls forward as shame so powerful that it takes my breath away, over-shadows everything.

*"Daughter! You have forsaken me!"*

A cry falls from my lips as I respond, "I'm sorry, Mother."

"Terran?" Beth calls out, having made her slow, painful way to me.

She reaches out a shaking hand, touching my shoulder. I can feel her fear of me, and it hurts to accept that it is well deserved. I look at her, this friend who is more of a sister than anything, and take in the shock just below the surface of her expression. That is for me, for what I have become. There is no escaping my actions. No one made me do anything.

Beth's gaze locks onto Raife's contorted body. "He's

dead. Raife is dead. Oh, my God. Terran, what's happening?"

I force myself to look at Raife, his limp form dangling in a grotesque mockery of a doll. "I killed him."

"W...what?"

"I killed him," I say quietly, but with conviction. "I had to. He was going to kill you, and I couldn't...I couldn't let that happen."

Suddenly, Gaia's voice blasts through me. I fall backward, hardly hearing Beth's yelp of surprise. *"You killed my son!"* She rages.

I feel the agony she feels. It is rebounded in every one of her progeny, adding to the sensations overpowering me. I buckle under their collective grief and rage, my chest squeezing as though an unseen hand is compressing it. Spots begin to form in front of my eyes. I blink rapidly, dragging air into my lungs, and lunge at Gaia with my mind. I feel her flinch, curling in a protective ball for a moment before she unfurls, aiming her fury at me. It hits me so hard that my mind goes blank, bleeding light, swamping my vision utterly. My mouth opens and closes silently, robbed of sound for a few protracted moments until air suddenly rushes into me, and I gasp.

*"You killed my son!"* Gaia roars in a voice rife with pain.

"I had to!" I cry, intense remorse hammering every word.

*"He was mine! My son!"*

"I couldn't let him hurt her. I couldn't."

Beth shakes me as I lie prone on the ground, panic infusing her voice. "Terran? Who are you talking to? We need to get out of here. I want to go home."

I feel Gaia's hungry gaze fall on Beth. *"She is not my child. She is not my chosen."*

I understand the anger she feels, the need for justice, the longing for vengeance. It is deserved. But when Gaia's will churns, aiming itself at Beth, my mind goes black with rage. Power that I thought I had depleted rushes into me at that moment, with such force that I feel it thrumming through my muscles and blood, singing through me with heat that seeps from my pores in rivers, ready for my command.

"I know, Mother," I scream, biting every word as I channel my strength. "But she is mine!" I assail Gaia with every ounce of my power, pummeling her being as she pummeled mine. Overpowering. Battering. Flooding her awareness with a thousand memories of Beth and me. They wash over her in unrelenting waves. Gaia writhes under my assault, trying to block the barrage of images but unable to escape them. She grows small under my assault, pulling away from me, from this place, from the very surface of the earth, sinking into its heart, her heart, Gaia's source of power. My heart begins to race with the effort of sustaining my attack, thundering in my chest until it becomes erratic, out of control. My thoughts stumble. *I think I'm dying.* I accept it and fight on, giving this small battle the last of me.

Beth is shaking my shoulder roughly, I feel her panic all around, and hear her screaming my name over and over, but I can't reply. My heart feels like it's going to burst, thrumming like a hummingbird's.

Suddenly, Beth's voice slashes through my head, stopping the flow of energy I aim at Gaia. "Stop!" She screams into the void. "Take me, not Terran. Take me!" Her voice breaks at the end, and she stops shaking me. "Take me. If we're all doomed, let it be me. Not her. Not Terran."

*No!* I rail inside, too weak to move, to speak, to fight. Gaia's will stirs. I sense her rise from the depths and coalesce into a tangible form, pulling soft dirt and small chunks of rock into an otherworldly shape of a woman. She reaches for Beth, enveloping her, tasting her sincerity and sacrifice.

"Please," Beth sighs, trembling under the touch of Gaia's inhuman hands.

Gaia looks upon this human, this frail thing, crouched in the dirt at my side. I feel her every thought. There is confusion mixed with awe, rage, twined with hope, conviction laden by realization.

Gaia's voice, a true sound pulled from the swirling mass of wind and dirt that shapes her form, scratches out of her alien mass, making sound into words. "You would give yourself for my own, my chosen?"

I let my head roll to the side, looking at Beth, whose face is a mask of terror and acceptance as she gazes on an ancient entity. She looks down at me before turning back to Gaia. "Yes."

Beth's assurance washes over Gaia in calm waves, taking with it the residual wrath that had lingered until this moment. Gaia is the mother of all life, even those she has cast aside for their blind arrogance and toxic indifference. I feel her acknowledge this aspect as she looks on Beth, a paltry being whose blood does not course with her life force and sense the exact moment that Gaia embraces Beth's sacrifice.

Tears escape my eyes as I look at the two of them, knowing that Beth cannot take back what she has offered, and grief-stricken at what it means to lose her, my truest friend, my sister. I open my mouth to speak, but my voice is gone, torn away from me, along with the strength I have exhausted.

Beth glances at me, a sad smile curving her mouth. "It's okay, Terran," she says softly before turning back to the being hovering before her.

Gaia reaches out a ghostly hand, tracing Beth's face with a rough finger. "I accept your offer, my child," she says in a voice that comes from the elements, more sound mashed together than true speech, before leaning forward and placing a kiss on Beth's brow. Beth seems to crumple, becoming a boneless mass on the ground in the next moment. Small sobs with no sound shake my body as Gaia looks on her prone form before gazing back at me with sightless eyes. *She is mine now,* her voice echoes through my mind, no longer filling the space around us with actual sound.

I look back at Beth with a quick dart of my eyes and see the slow rise and fall of her chest. She isn't dead, only sleeping, overcome by whatever Gaia passed through at their contact. *"What does this mean?"* I ask, hope flaring in every word.

*"You are my daughters. All that remain are mine, daughters and sons. If one can be shown the way, all can. All will be my protected. My chosen."* Gaia's metallic gaze falls on Beth. *"There is hope in this world now. Let them inherit it and bring balance."*

Her form slowly breaks apart, falling to the ground in hushed piles until all that remains is dirt and rock, while two large shards of mica sparkle in the sunlight that breaks through the forest canopy. It's over, I think to myself. Gaia sinks into the earth, down, down into its heart, cocooned in safety and warmth, the rank poisons that have coated every aspect of her being slowly shatter, releasing their stranglehold, though remnants will always remain, as the dawning of a new world breaks across the planet.

# CHAPTER 38

*Picking up the pieces*

T he sirens must have been going off for hours by the time they finally penetrated my mind. My body aches, stiff and cold from lying on the hard ground. I groan as I slowly roll to my side, face pressed to the earth. I reach into it, searching for Gaia, but she is quiet, asleep, and no more aware of me than any being scurrying across her vast expanse. Ragged breath shudders from my mouth. It is truly over.

I sit up slowly, pushing past the deep ache in my mind and muscles, and clench my teeth as a wave of dizziness turns my brain into a whirlpool of chaos, then clutch my head and focus. Blinking a few times slowly to clear my mind, I take in the scene around me, seeing Beth on her side, her swollen arm resting at an awkward angle. Her breathing is soft from whatever deep sleep Gaia's touch put her in. It takes a moment to realize that Beth and I are not alone.

Twisting my body to look behind me, I find Silas perched on the rocky outcrop, arms draped over his knees. His eyes bore into me, staring out of his perfect face, not with the expected accusation, but with understanding.

"Terran," he calls to me. I close my eyes and let the feelings embedded in his words reach into me, calming my racing heart.

As the beats in my chest slow to a regular rhythm, realization dawns, obliterating every thought but what I have done, here in this place, and across the planet. I seem to wither inside, awash in regret so powerful that it smothers me. "What have I done?" I cry, hoarse sobs punctuating each word.

Silas looks down on me, dispassionate but not cruel. "You have done what you were born to do. It is not an easy burden, but you were born into this world to right it, to cleanse the earth, so that others can live."

"I'm a monster," I scream, though it comes out sounding so small. "I've killed thousands. Millions." My eyes shift to Raife, but his body is gone. Somehow, I know that Gaia took him with her, burying him in the earth to become life to new things. All that remains is a massive spear of rock caked in blood that has blackened in the cold air. "I killed him. I...I stabbed him with a rock." I look back at Silas, pleading. "Is this what she wanted? A murderer?"

I watch as Silas' body slowly unfolds. He looks like a god standing there, like Zeus on Mount Olympus. He hops down and comes toward me as I sit on the ground, a ball of human misery. Well, not human, not really. I close my eyes as his fingers brush away hair that has become matted against my cheek. That strange current is still there, pulsing through me in waves with every touch. But I don't embrace it. I let it pass over me until it is gone.

"Gaia is all things, Terran," Silas says. "Though mankind turned its back on its mother, in a way, Beth showed her that humanity is not beyond redemption. It's fascinating to me that one small human could sway the forces raging across the world." He laughs quietly, looking at Beth, who remains unconscious. "I suppose *she* is the savior of humanity. The one person who stood face to face with Gaia's wrath, accepting that humanity may be doomed, but her friend need not be, and was willing to lay down her life for yours. Gaia's chosen. Gaia's Áine." Silas sighs, gathering his thoughts for a few moments while I try to digest what he's saying.

"Men are fickle beings," he continues. "I have lived lifetimes alongside them and seen them in their greatness and their ruin. They are intent on their pursuit of power and pleasure, deaf to the screams of the voiceless and the hurt done in the name of progress. Now, mankind has seen the earth fight back, and your friend has shown our great mother that there are some who can be shown the way. People will have another chance. All is not lost. Millions have survived and will remember these days as events when the earth rose up in vengeance, and they will understand the cause. Mankind will tell new generations, and each will understand the earth as no ancestor has before." He pauses and looks at me, deep into my eyes and mind. "No. All is not lost. This is only the beginning, a new dawn."

I look around, my gaze drawn to the bloody rock then to Beth. "I don't know how to go on after this. I don't know how I can live with what I've done."

Silas leans forward, gathering me in his arms. My body freezes for a few protracted moments before emotions burst forth in wrenching sobs as I return his embrace, burrowing in the comfort of his chest. Through the contact, I feel his emotions take hold of me, not romantic, but unbreakable and filled with love. "You will go on, Terran. A new world awaits you, one that needs your voice of reason and your power to show it the way."

I shake my head, refusing to even consider unleashing what I did today in the future. "Yes," he says firmly. "Your power will only grow, not diminish with age, and the Daoine Fíor will stand beside you, answering your call when you need us."

"I'm not worthy of that power, Silas. Look what I did," I cry, swinging my arm to the jut of rock before sweeping it in a wide arc to include everything around us.

"I'm sorry it came to that, Terran. Raife..." he starts to say but stops to find the right words. "Raife was meant to help you, to bring you into the fold, so to speak, but he was consumed by his power in the end, unable to see beyond its intoxicating grasp. He loved you, but that was not enough. Raife couldn't see the repercussions of the choice he forced you to make. It should not have come to this, but we are all fallible, no matter how much we think we are not."

"How do you know what he was even thinking? You weren't even here! You didn't see him pick up the rock. You didn't see the look on his face. It was like I was betraying him," tears fall down my cheeks in a steady stream. "And I did. I betrayed him."

"Do you think we did not feel his thoughts in those moments, or yours? Our connection goes beyond distance and into the very essence of who we are. I could hear his mind, and I saw his intent. We all did."

I suppose I should feel some measure of peace, but I don't. How do you pick up the pieces of a life you've ripped apart? "Will she ever call to me again?"

Silas sighs. "I cannot say. For now, she sleeps, and her rest is deep and healing. The war you waged in her name has forever altered the planet. In your lifetime, you will see new growth spring up across the world, taking over the fresh landscape with multitudes of species. It will be remarkable. I do not see humanity falling into old habits as long as you walk the earth, but when you're gone, there may come a time when a new Áine will rise up to right wrongs and bring balance, but not now. Your work is done, Terran. You can rest easy."

Rest easy. It sounds so appealing as I sit here, away from the reality of what is beyond the boundaries of this forest. The sound of Beth stirring jolts me. What will she think when she looks at me? Will she see a killer? Have I lost my truest friend? As her arms and legs begin to shift in wakefulness, I look at Silas with anguish.

He reads my thoughts and understands my fears. "Do you want her to forget? To never know what happened in this clearing?"

I look from Silas to the bloody rock and back to Beth, images and knowledge spinning through my mind in horrible clarity. "Yes."

"Are you sure? It can never be undone. She will have no memory of what went on here, of her contact with Gaia."

It's not really a tough decision. No one should have to live with what happened here. I wish I could wipe it away, but it is my burden to carry. "I'm sure."

Silas nods. "Press your hands to either side of her head."

I reach over and cup her face, looking into a visage that I love. Silas's hands overlap mine, and I hear him mutter words in the tongue of his people. Currents pass through our skin and into Beth as his voice drones on, each word imbued with power. When it is done, his hands fall from mine, and he sits back on his heels.

"We should move her from this place, maybe to the edge of the trail."

I agree and watch as he bends over and picks her up, cradling Beth in his hands with care. We make our way to the foot of the path, but I turn before we begin our ascent and press my hands to the ground, sending energy into the earth until it finds the rock jutting from the surface and pulls it back, blood and mineral sinking into the ground. When it is done, I stand, and we leave the forest. As we climb the trail, I realize that I may never come here again. It's too painful.

At the top of the trail, Silas gently lowers Beth, whose eyes have yet to open, though awareness is slowly creeping across her face. "She will have no memory of what occurred in this place, only the recollection that she was desperate to find you when everything happened."

I nod, crouching down at Beth's side. "I understand."

"I will leave you now, but I am always with you, Terran. You need only call, and I will come to you." He presses a kiss atop my head and walks away, the sound of his steps fading into the distance.

It takes about ten minutes for Beth to open her eyes, but when she does, a look of profound relief crosses her face. "I found you. Oh, my God, Terran. I was so scared. No one knew where you were, and I came looking for you."

"It's okay, Beth. I'm here." I look at her, aching to say so much, but knowing I never will. "I think a branch may have fallen on you or something. Your arm looks broken."

She looks down at it as it sits across her chest, a swollen mass of purple and black bruises. "Yeah, I guess it is. My head feels fuzzy, too, like I might have been hit with something. I don't know, I feel like...like something is missing, like I forgot something."

She looks around in confusion as though hoping to see something that will unlock some memory, but I know she'll find nothing. "Don't worry, Beth. Let's go home, okay? I bet our parents are going crazy worrying about us."

She looks at me. "Okay. Can you help me up?"

"Of course," I tell her as I tuck my arms under her shoulders and pull her up. "Can you stand on your own?"

"Um, I think so. My legs feel kind of wobbly, though, so let's take it slow."

I swing my arm around her waist, and we make our way slowly along the street to her car parked a short distance away. The windshield is smashed on one side, and the entire passenger door is caved in.

"The world's gone mad again, Terran," she tells me, looking at the damage. "That's why I came to find you. A tornado came through the middle of town and tore up everything. It just came from out of nowhere, like it was pulled from the sky right above this place. Did you see it?"

I shake my head. "No, I had gone for a walk and must've been hit by a branch or something because I totally blacked out. I didn't even know you were lying up here until I came out of the forest and saw you."

Beth looks at me strangely, uncertainty washing

across her features for a moment before she shakes it off and says, "It was so scary. Your mom had called me looking for you. She was all panicky because she didn't know where you were." She looks at me before going on. "I was at The Last Drop when she called, and I told her I'd bring you home. I knew you'd be here in your special place. But then things were flying everywhere, whole roofs ripped away and windows blown open. I don't even know what hit my car. I just stepped on the gas and tried to outrun it. I needed to find you. And then on the radio, they were going nuts, talking about monsters and earthquakes, floods and tidal waves. I thought it was the end of the world."

"I'm sorry, Beth," I tell her. Inside, I have a deep well of remorse that threatens to bubble up to the surface if I don't keep it under control. I know that Beth only knows a fraction of the events that unfolded across the world, and I dread her finding out the rest of it. To be honest, I dread seeing what damage I have wrought, but I will force myself to watch it, to accept it because I must.

"Let's go home," I tell her, unlocking the car and opening up the rear door since the passenger side is too damaged. She slides into the seat, and I buckle her in, mindful of her broken arm.

I drive to Beth's house, needing to get her home to Celeste so she can go to the hospital. The moment I pull into the driveway, Celeste comes pouring out the front door in streams of pastels, shrieking Beth's name.

"She's okay, Celeste," I call out, opening the car door. "But her arm is broken, and she'll need to go to the hospital."

Celeste gently pulls Beth out of the car, wrapping her in a warm embrace as she sobs with relief. She reaches over to me and pulls me in. I resist at first, feeling undeserving of the affection, but I am unable to hold out and quickly return the hug. "I'm so glad you're safe," she cries, peppering Beth's face with kisses. "I was so scared. I didn't know where you were, Bethy." I haven't heard Celeste use that name for years. "Terran, your mom was worried sick and told me Bethy went to find you, and then neither of you could be reached. Thank the goddess you're safe."

As we walk arm in arm into the house, the place where all of this seemed to start, I know I will face hard truths. Somehow, I will need to accept them. I owe it to Beth. All of humanity owes its very survival to my selfless friend, a girl who's been in my shadow of late, but is now blazing across my sky.

# CHAPTER 39

*The end is the beginning*

It's been hard to move on. Even after all these months, I still struggle, always half-listening for a voice I both long to hear and hope I never do. But Gaia has remained quiet, her power and will lie dormant in peaceful slumber. I wish I could say the same, but memories have a way of sneaking into my dreams, turning them into nightmarish landscapes.

I haven't been able to reconcile what I unleashed across the world. I know Gaia's power and purpose stood beside and within me, but I welcomed it, let it fill me up until all I could see was her rage, her thirst for survival, and balance at any cost. All I could feel in those last

minutes, before Beth broke through my barriers, was
righteousness. That's a hard thing to accept when I hold
that proverbial mirror to my face. I recognize that I did not
come to this place alone. There are many at fault, from the
perpetrators of a dying planet to the entity that embodies
it all, to me.

I've seen pictures and videos of the devastation. In
fact, I've forced myself to watch them through a blur of
tears. But in my heart, deep within a tiny chamber where
it can hide, there remains a shadow of justification, a
ghostly judge and jury that wears Gaia's face. I don't think
I will ever be able to let go of that, despite how hard it is to
watch the footage of it all unfolding and know my part
in it.

I don't talk about Raife. It hurts too much to hear his
name. While I now realize the depth of his manipulation,
it doesn't make it any easier to accept what I did. Beth has
stopped asking about him, and so have my parents. I
pretend he went back to California with his folks, to whatever is left of it, and that helps most of the time, but the
memories are always there, waiting for me when I close
my eyes or standing in the peripheral like a specter. Raife
is one life among countless others that stain my hands.

Over a billion are gone. Billion. It's hard to fathom
such a number, but that one was scrawled across countless newscasts in the months that followed a war that still
has no name. No one seems to know what to call it. Some
say it was the apocalypse, that God punished man for the

evil it had done. Others claim that an alien race invaded Earth, remaining hidden in the water and rock that attacked the planet. A few even think that it was a hoax perpetrated by governments across the world that got together and killed off all those people to stay in power. No one talks about the face in the waves and the thunder-clouds. No one knows about me.

What has become undeniable for the survivors is what we are left with. While entire cities across the world were obliterated and no country was left wholly untouched, the world that remains is different, cleaner, fresher, slowly blossoming with new life. The term Renaissance has been bandied about by some, and with it comes a greater appreciation of what we have left and how we can rebuild. I've taken a hard look at myself, too, and acknowledged that I need to do more because I'm part of the problem, just like everyone else.

Life carries on, different now, but here. There are still billions of people left, and they have Beth to thank for it, though they will never know it. Neither will she. I some-times wonder if I will tell her what happened, if I can come clean with the whole story, all of those things I kept hidden, the stuff I helped to erase. Maybe when we're old, when time has worn creases into our faces, and our hair has gone gray with age. Yeah. Maybe then.

For now, I try to muddle through each day, putting my life back together while knowing it can never be the same. My senior year is about to start. In the aftermath, the school district moved everyone to the next grade, whether or not we had completed the classes. Grades and test scores just don't seem to matter much anymore, a rather nice result of it all. I would like to say I'm excited to begin a new year and to think of the future. College. Career. Marriage. Kids. But that all seems so indistinct now, as though those things are for someone else.

Celeste helps me in my darkest moments. She has become a talisman of sorts when I feel weighed down with regret. She senses it, though she has no idea where it's rooted. She doesn't pry, and I appreciate that.

From outside, I hear the sound of Beth's horn signaling her arrival. Grabbing my purse, I head downstairs, taking each step in slight hops, until I reach the bottom, where my mom is waiting. "Hey, Mom."

"You look tired, sweetie," she croons, leaning forward to kiss my cheek. "Are you sure you're up for an outing with Beth?"

"I'm okay. It'll be good to go out and shop for school. There's a new, used clothing store we want to visit."

She purses her lips, but I know she won't stop me. "Okay, but be home for dinner at six." I give her a salute and smile as she rolls her eyes at me. She grabs her wallet and pulls out a couple of hundred dollars, forcing it into my hand when I try to protest. "I want you to have this and pick out some nice things."

I smile, closing my fist around the bills before shoving them into the zipped pouch of my bag. "Thanks, Mom," I tell her, giving her a quick hug before heading out the door.

Beth sits in her car with music pumping. I can tell by the way she's bopping her head and mouthing the words that it's a rock ballad. I pull open the door to Free Fallin' by Tom Petty blasting through the airwaves. She looks over at me while belting out the chorus in quite possibly the loudest, most obnoxious singing voice to have ever plagued my ears. I hop into the car, shaking my head. She nudges me and pulls forward into the road. Soon, my voice joins hers as we head out.

I roll down my window, letting the breeze blow back my hair, closing my eyes, and breathing in the world around me. Scilti is there, keeping pace as he always does, and always will. Gaia is there too, buried under a mantle below humanity. I will make sure we take better care. My voice will be my greatest asset, hidden until I need it. I hope I never need it.

Beth sings louder, holding her left arm out the window and swooping her hand in wavelike motions. I do the same, smiling at the sensation of air currents flowing over and under. I'm going to be okay. Life persists, finding a way to give birth to new generations. I will go on as well, tied to the past, but looking toward the future.

Mankind deserves this second chance. We all do.

*The End*

# ACKNOWLEDGMENTS

Writing a book doesn't happen in a vacuum. In fact, vacuuming doesn't happen while writing a book either! Or laundry for that matter. Throughout the process, there are people in the background who make the writing itself possible. Without these individuals, I would never be able to get from that little blurb I jotted in my notes on my cell phone to a four hundred page book. My husband and three sons have given me love and support throughout the process of crafting a story, allowing me to spend hours in my writing chair on weekends and in the evening. These four wonderful men are my foundation and I would never have begun my author journey without them.

In addition to family supports are my friends. Vanessa and Christina, you are my core fan club! I'm so grateful for your unconditional support and willingness to listen to me ramble on about a story day after day without cringing when I launch into new ideas. David Taylor, my editor, you understand my vision in a such a way that our collaboration truly deepens and enhances the characters and story. Thank you for your thoughtful recommendations, especially the funny ones that you almost delete!

The beginning of a story comes in dribs and drabs, little thoughts that eventually coalesce into something with depth and purpose. *Rise of Gaia* began with many stops and starts, sometimes veering off in unexpected directions courtesy of my often distracted mind - squirrel! When the story truly took shape, life was breathed into every character and every scene. Interestingly, a lot of myself is reflected in Terran. Her quirkiness and quips are things I do and say which made for a strong connection with her character.

The premise of *Rise of Gaia* grew from my own perspective of the world and our responsibility to it. I wondered what Mother Earth would say if given a conduit through which she could communicate. Would she grieve? Would she rage? How would we react to such messages? Across the globe, people are recognizing the need for positive, environmental change. It is my hope that Rise of Gaia provides a backdrop for productive dialogue about the environment and what each of us can do. A river begins with a drop of water. Change can begin with a single thought or action. We are all a part of the solution.

# About the Author

Kristin Ward is an award-winning young adult author living in Connecticut. A science and math teacher for over twenty years, she infuses her geeky passions into stories that meld realism and fantasy.

A lifelong lover of books and writing, she dreamed of becoming an author for thirty years before publishing her award-winning debut in 2018. Her first novel, **After the Green Withered**, is one of many things you should probably read.

~www.kristinwardauthor.com~